Acclaim for
Jessica Sorensen's Mesmerizing Books

Saving Quinton

"This story pulls at so many emotions and is written so well...I would recommend this to anyone looking for a gut-wrenching yet very realistic book full of hope and second chances."

—DarkFaerieTales.com

"*Saving Quinton* addresses intensely personal issues that will hook right into the reader's heart. As emotions take a toll, this book will have you cheering on its characters."

—UndertheCoversBookBlog.com

Nova and Quinton: No Regrets

"Totally consumed me...heart-wrenching...[Sorensen] is masterful when it comes to dealing with the hard issues life throws your way."

—LiteratiBookReviews.com

"Torn, twisted, and beautiful are the best words I can use to describe this story. Jessica Sorensen has taken her talent on a new level with this one."

—LittleReadRidingHood.com

"[*Nova and Quinton*] just dug into my heart...This book was more than entertainment for me; it was a lesson in life...Five stars and highly recommended!"   —TheBoyfriendBookmark.com

"This series goes down as one of my all-time favorites...It was definitely heartbreaking to read some parts, but oh so worth it...I can't recommend this enough."

—TheBookHookup.com

Breaking Nova

"*Breaking Nova* touches the heart and squeezes the most powerful emotions from your body...one of those books that pushes you to the limits and makes you feel things you never thought you would feel for characters."

—UndertheCoversBookBlog.com

"Four stars! I am committed to this series."

—SweptAwayByRomance.com

"*Breaking Nova* is one of those books that just sticks with you. I was thinking about it when I wasn't reading it, wondering what was going to happen with Nova...an all-consuming, heartbreaking story."   —BooksLiveForever.com

"Heartbreaking, soul-shattering, touching, and unforgettable... Jessica Sorenson is an amazingly talented author."

—ABookishEscape.com

The Destiny of Violet & Luke

"Gripping and heartbreaking...You will be hooked, and you won't be able to not come back."　　—ReviewingRomance.com

"Sorensen's intense and realistic stories never cease to amaze me and entice my interest. She is an incredible writer as she captures the raw imperfections of the beautiful and the damned."
　　　　　　　　　　—TheCelebrityCafe.com

The Redemption of Callie & Kayden

"Extremely emotional and touching...It made me want to cry, and jump for joy."　　　　　　—Blkosiner.blogspot.com

"I couldn't put it down. This was just as dark, beautiful, and compelling as the first [book]...Nothing short of amazing...Never have I read such emotional characters where everything that has happened to them seems so real."　　—OhMyShelves.com

"A love story that will overflow your heart with hope. This series is not to be missed."　　　　—UndertheCoversBookblog.com

The Coincidence of Callie & Kayden

"Another great story of passion, love, hope, and themes of salvation."　　　　　　　—BookishTemptations.com

"Romantic, suspenseful, and well written—this is a story you won't want to put down." —RT Book Reviews

The Temptation of Lila and Ethan

"Sorensen has true talent to capture your attention with each word written. She is creatively talented…Through the mist of demons that consume the characters' souls, she manages to find beauty in their broken lives."

—TheCelebrityCafe.com

"An emotional, romantic, and really great contemporary romance…Lila and Ethan's story is emotionally raw, devastating, and heart wrenching."

—AlwaysYAatHeart.com

The Ever After of Ella and Micha

"This is a perfect conclusion to their story…I think Micha Scott may just be my number one book boyfriend!"

—ReviewingRomance.com

The Forever of Ella and Micha

"Breathtaking, bittersweet, and intense…Fans of *Beautiful Disaster* will love the series."

—CaffeinatedBookReviewer.com

"Powerful, sexy, emotional, and with a great message, this series is one of the best stories I've read so far."

—BookishTemptations.com

The Secret of Ella and Micha

"A beautiful love story...complicated yet gorgeous characters... I am excited to read more of her books."

—SerendipityReviews.co.uk

"A really great love story. There is something epic about it... If you haven't jumped on this new adult bandwagon, then you need to get with the program. I can see every bit of why this story has swept the nation."

—TheSweetBookShelf.com

"Absolutely loved it...This story broke my heart...I can't wait to get my hands on the next installment."

—Maryinhb.blogspot.com

"Wonderful...delightful...a powerful story of love...will make your heart swoon."

—BookswithBite.net

Saving Quinton

Also by Jessica Sorensen

The Secret of Ella and Micha

The Forever of Ella and Micha

The Temptation of Lila and Ethan

The Coincidence of Callie & Kayden

The Redemption of Callie & Kayden

The Destiny of Violet & Luke

Breaking Nova

Delilah: The Making of Red

Nova and Quinton: No Regrets

Tristan: Finding Hope

Saving Quinton

JESSICA SORENSEN

FOREVER

NEW YORK   BOSTON

Copyright © 2014 by Jessica Sorensen

Excerpt from *Nova and Quinton: No Regrets* copyright © 2014 by Jessica Sorensen

Forever
Hachette Book Group
1290 Avenue of the Americas, New York, NY 10104

www.HachetteBookGroup.com

Printed in the United States of America

RRD-C

Originally published as an ebook

First trade paperback edition: February 2015

10 9 8 7 6 5 4 3 2 1

Forever is an imprint of Grand Central Publishing.

The Forever name and logo are trademarks of Hachette Book Group, Inc.

The publisher is not responsible for websites (or their content) that are not owned by the publisher.

The Hachette Speakers Bureau provides a wide range of authors for speaking events. To find out more, go to www.hachettespeakersbureau.com or call (866) 376-6591.

Library of Congress Cataloguing-in-Publication Data has been applied for.

ISBN: 978-1-4555-8273-0

For everyone who struggled and survived

Saving Quinton

Chapter One

Quinton

I wake up every morning feeling content that I'm drowning in darkness. Blissfully, mind numbingly content, without worrying or being haunted by my fucked-up past, because I can't feel a fucking thing—at least after I take my first hit. Once I get the taste of those bitterly sweet, wonderfully toxic, white crystals up my nose, they'll burn out the back of my throat along with all my emotions. Then I'll be good to go for days. The guilt that I carry around in me will briefly die and I'll slowly die right along it. I'm glad because I want to be dead.

And I'm working on getting there, one numbing line at a time.

I can't remember the last time I slept, just like I can't remember the name of the woman lying beside me in my bed, passed out with her top off. I met her last night when she showed up with Dylan and Delilah and somehow we ended up in my room, where we had meaningless sex and then she passed out from whatever she's on. It's become a routine, a painfully long-standing routine that I'm addicted to. Part of me wishes

I wasn't, but the other part knows that I deserve exactly what I have—nothing.

After struggling all night to shut my eyes, seeking sleep but never getting there, I finally climb off the mattress on the floor. I've been going for days, strung out on line after line, my eyes bulging out of my head, my body and mind so tense and worn-out from the energy overload, yet still fighting to stay awake. If I don't get more into my system soon, I'm going to crash.

I grab a pair of jeans from off the chipped linoleum floor and pull them on. My bedroom is about the size of a closet and contains a shitty mattress, a box with stuff that I never look at anymore, a lamp, and a mirror and razor that are always within reach. I pick them both up off the floor and then the empty plastic bag next to it. I must have finished it off last night…although I can barely remember doing it. I can barely remember anything anymore. Days and nights are blurred together in pieces that are quickly fading.

"Shit," I mutter, wiping my finger along the mirror's dry surface, and then I lick my finger clean, sucking every last drop off it. It doesn't do anything for the starving beast stirring inside me, ready to wake up and claw at my skin if I don't feed it. I toss the mirror across the room, watching it shatter against the wall. "Dammit." I snatch a shirt up off the floor and pull it on as I hurry out into the narrow hall, tripping over a few people passed out on the floor, none of whom I know, but they always seem to be around.

When I reach the door at the end of the hall, the room

that belongs to my cousin Tristan, I turn the doorknob but it's locked, so I hammer my fist against it. "Tristan, open up the fucking door...I need to get in there. Now."

There's no response, so I bang on the door harder, slamming my shoulder into the wood. My body starts to shake by the third slam...My mouth is salivating by the fifth...By the seventh I feel like I could fucking kill someone if I don't get my goddamned dose in me.

Finally, the door weakens and starts to cave beneath my violent slams, but it won't give in completely. The need to feed the irrational and unstable monster inside me becomes too much, and I kick the door over and over again as hard as I can. Panic starts to set in as a stream of images of the people I've lost flow through my head: Lexi, Ryder, my mom, whom I never met. They all ram me in the chest, sucking the air out of my lungs. Then, at the end of the images, I see Nova's eyes, which look blue at first unless you look close enough to see the green hidden in them. I don't know why I see her. It's not like I lost her. She's still alive and out there somewhere in the world, hopefully happy. But for some reason I can't stop thinking about her, even though I only spent a couple of months with her last summer during her brief fall into the drug world. Yet I can't seem to get her out of my head, at least until I get my dose of fake bliss. Then all I'll be thinking about is where to channel the burst of energy. If I could get this fucking door down—

With one last kick, the trimming splinters apart and the door opens. I stumble into the room, sweating and shaking like a rabid dog. Tristan's passed out on the mattress with a girl lying beside him and her arm draped over his chest. On the floor beside the mattress are a spoon and a needle, but I don't go for them. It's not my thing, not what I want. No, what I want is in his top dresser drawer.

I rush over to it, kicking his clothes out of the way, the memories of everyone I lost swarming around me, surrounding me, pounding at my skull and making me feel like I'm going to hurl. Lexi dying on the side of the road, soaked in her own blood, and me beside her with her blood on my hands. The life I never had with my mother, the heartbreaking look in Tristan's eyes whenever he mentions his sister, Ryder. Nova in that goddamned pond, where I ultimately left her to cry her eyes out alone because she was going to hand her virginity to a piece of shit like me. Then I see her face at the concert when she saw me dealing and then when she got in her car at the trailer park, ready to drive away and leave me forever—the last time I saw her.

That's how it should be. She should be away from me and this shitty mess that's supposed to be a life, because I'm too much of a pussy to fully give up, die, finally just take that last step and end my life, instead of slowly doing it. Finally dose my body up with so many drugs that my heart will stop beating and for good this time, in the dark, where no one can save me.

I jerk open the dresser drawer and snatch hold of the plastic bag, my hands trembling as I open it. I don't even bother looking for a mirror. I need it now. I dump a thin line out on top of the dresser, grab Tristan's driver's license, and chop up the clumps of crystal with the edge of it. My heart is thrashing deafeningly in my chest and I wish it would shut the hell up, because I don't want it making any noise at all. I want it to be quiet. Silent. Nonexistent.

Dead.

Grabbing a pen and taking it apart, I lean down, put my nose to the tip of the line and suck in, allowing the white powder to fill up my nose and flood the back of my throat. My heart speeds up, but somehow it becomes quieter—everything around me does. As it spills through my veins, body, heart, mind, and soul, it instantly kills all thoughts of Lexi, Ryder, my mom. Nova.

It kills everything.

I walk back to my room, finally able to breathe again, my body and mind reaching this weird place of harmony where nothing matters—not the past, the future, or the present. I sit down on my mattress, pushing the woman aside toward the wall, needing space. Then I pick up my sketchbook and open it to the drawing I've been working on for weeks. It's a picture of Nova, which should make me feel guilty, but it doesn't. It's just lines and shadings, soft movements of my hand pouring out thoughts that I'm not even aware of. It's just art and it means nothing, like everything else inside me. And when I'm finished looking at it, I set it aside and quickly forget it, just like I've done with everything else. Then I lie down on my side, wrap my arms around myself, and let my mind go to wherever it wants to...

"Can you hear me?" Lexi whispers softly in my ear. "Quinton, open your eyes."

I shake my head, smiling to myself, as I keep my eyes shut. "No way. You're going to have to wake me up if you want me to open my eyes."

"You are awake, you goofball," she says, and then I feel her fingers touch my side. "Come on, we're going to be late for the party."

"That's okay with me," I tell her, still keeping my eyes closed. "I didn't want to go anyway."

"Only because you're a party pooper," she says, and then I feel her shift as she swings her leg over me and straddles me on my bed. "Come on, old man. Let's go out and have fun tonight."

My hands find her hips and I hold on to her. She makes me feel so much better simply by being here. My house seems less empty and it's easier to deal with the two to three words my dad says to me every day because Lexi's here and she loves me.

She breathes on my cheek purposefully, trying to get me to open my eyes, and finally I give in to her, lifting my eyelids and smiling when I see her. She's leaning over me, her hair hanging down to the sides, creating a veil around our faces. Her lips are only inches away from mine, her eyes are shining brightly, and she smells like perfume mixed with cigarette smoke, a scent that annoyed me at first but now I love it because it belongs to her.

"Can't we just stay in?" I ask her, tucking a strand of her hair behind her ear.

She pouts out her lip. "We only have a few more weeks left of high school and I want to have some fun tonight. Let loose." She pushes away and I feel a little colder inside. "Plus, I told Ryder we'd go out tonight."

I sigh. "That just means that I'm going to spend the night watching the two of you get drunk while I stay sober and be the dd."

Her lips curve upward into a pleased smile. "That's because you're the only one responsible enough to be the dd."

I frown. "Well, what if I don't want to be tonight? What if I just want to have fun?"

She sits up, still smiling, knowing she's gotten her way even though I'm still arguing. "You know as well as I do that you couldn't get drunk even if you wanted to."

"Only because I worry about you," I say. "You always get so crazy when you're drunk."

"Not crazy, just fun," she argues. "Now, will you please get up and get changed so we can go? Ryder's waiting for us in the living room."

I hesitate and then sigh. "Fine, but I'm only going to keep an eye on you."

She grins, then places a soft kiss on my lips. "Thank you. You take such good care of me."

"That's because I love you," I tell her as she hops off my lap, and I sit up, stretching my arms above my head.

Still grinning, she picks up a pair of my jeans and throws them at me. "If you love me, then hurry up and get dressed." Then she walks out of my room, without saying I love you back.

But I know she loves me just as much as I love her, which is why I get up and get dressed, like she asked. Then I head out, not because I want to but because I love her, more than anything.

She means the world to me. Always will. Until the day I die.

May 10, six days before summer break

Nova

I remember when I was younger and everything felt so simple. Life seemed full of smiles and dancing, candy and costumes, so full of happiness and light. Dark things weren't clear to me yet, not until I was twelve and realized that not everything was sunshine. The memory is as clear to me as the sunny sky.

"I bet you can't beat me to the bottom of the hill," my dad says, laughing as he pedals his bike down the hill.

I smile, pedaling my bike faster. It's brand-new, with purple and silver paint, and has stripes on the pedals that reflect the sunlight. My tires crunch against the dirt as they spin and spin, and I grip the handlebars as

I speed down the hill, trying to win. Really I don't care, though. No matter who wins, I'm still having fun riding bikes with my dad.

He stays a ways ahead of me as we wind down the hill, trees around us, a blue sky above us, and the air smells like dirt and leaves. I honestly won't be surprised if he slows down right before we reach the bottom and lets me win. He usually does stuff like that, pretending that something happened so that it seems completely accidental.

So when he disappears around the corner and then I hear the sound of his tires slowing down, I think: Aha! I pedal faster, hitting bumps, steering my bike around rocks, slowing down slightly when I reach the corner. I'm grinning, filled with the excitement of the race, but when I make it all the way around, my happiness all burns out.

My dad's bike is on its side in the middle of the path, tires still spinning, and he's lying on the ground on his back. For a split second I think he's playing a joke, taking letting me win a little too far. But then I notice that he's clutching at his heart, groaning.

Pressing on the brakes, I slow down, worried he's fallen off his bike and hurt himself. When I reach him, I hop off my bike and drop it to the ground as I rush over to him, then kneel down in the dirt beside him. The first thing I notice is how white his skin is, like the cotton falling off the trees. Then I see the fear in his eyes. Sheer terror that something bad is about to happen.

"Nova…get help…" His voice shakes.

Tears sting at my eyes. "Dad, what's wrong?"

"Just go get someone…" He groans again, clutching at his arm.

The look in his eyes makes me run back to my bike. I get on it and pedal back up the hill. It's a very steep slope and it usually takes forever, but somehow I make my legs stronger than they normally are and move faster than I ever have. When I reach the top, I search the parking lot for someone. There's a family at one of the picnic tables and I run over to them, leaving my bike near the trail.

"My dad," I pant, leaning over, grasping my knees. "He fell back there and he's hurt."

The father of the family gets up from the table, telling his wife to go call an ambulance. Then he tells me to take him back to my dad, and we go on foot, running down the hill. I really think he's going to be okay. I really think because I got help, did everything right, that everything will be okay, but when we reach him, he's not moving. Breathing. The guy checks his pulse and he doesn't have one.

I don't know what to do. I want to cry, but the guy keeps looking at me with pity, like he feels sorry for me, and it makes me not want to cry just to prove to him that he's wrong, that everything will be okay.

I've been remembering my dad's death a lot over the last twenty-four hours, ever since I found out about Quinton and his past. I think part of it's because Lea keeps looking at me like that guy did after he realized my dad didn't have a pulse. Like she pities me, because I want to find Quinton, because I don't know where he's living and I want to help him. She doesn't think that I can help him, but she's wrong—she has to be.

At least that's what I keep telling my camera while I make my recording. "I've been telling myself over and over again there's still hope, that Quinton's still alive, therefore hope still exists," I say to my camera phone screen as the red recording light blinks. "That hope can only be gone when someone's heart stops beating, when they take their last and final breath, when they don't come back." I'm lying on the sofa in my apartment's living room, with my feet propped up on the back and my head over the edge, so my hair's hanging down toward the ground. My phone is angled at my face and it looks like I'm falling. I'm not sure how long I've been in this position, but I can feel the blood pooling in my head.

I started making recordings of myself partly because I was interested in film and partly because it was the only way I could get my thoughts out. There was also a teeny part of me that did it because it made me feel connected to my deceased boyfriend, Landon, because he made a video minutes before he committed suicide.

Because I let him fall from my life, just like I did Quinton.

I blink at the camera, telling myself not to let my mind

go there and to keep positive. "Hope is what keeps me searching for Quinton—what makes me determined to find him and help him. Even when I know that what awaits me in the future is going to be hard, that it'll more than likely bring up painful memories of the things I did in my past. But I know it's something I have to do. Looking back, I realize that Quinton entered my life for a reason. It may not have made sense when I first met him nearly a year ago, but it does now. And all that stuff I went through, the summer of bad choices, can be used for something good because it gives me insight into what he's going through. I've seen the darkness that's probably around Quinton right now, and I know what it feels like to feel like you're drowning in it..." I trail off as the memories start to build up inside me, weighted and unwelcome, but I take a deep breath and free the tension.

"Although I'm sure there's way more to it than what I know. Not just because he's gone deeper into the drug world than I ever did—into crystal meth...From what I've read on the Internet, it's far more addicting than anything I ever did, but then again, there are so many things that could be classified as addiction..." I trail off and shut my eyes. "Addiction is the fucking devil—I swear to God it is. Whether it's drugs or obsessive counting—something I still suffer from occasionally. It can be so comforting, peaceful, serene. It can make you feel so in control, but it's just a mask, plain and simple, and what's behind the mask—what we're trying to hide—is still growing, feeding off the addiction—"

"Nova, get in here," Lea, my best friend and roommate for the last year, calls out from my room, interrupting my video making. "I think I found something."

I open my eyes and stare at my image on the screen, so different from how I appeared last summer when I was addicted to several things, including denial. "I'll pick up on this later," I say to my camera phone, then click it off and flip upright, getting to my feet.

Blood rushes down from my head and vertigo sets in, sending the nearly empty room around me spinning. I brace my hand against the wall and make my way to the bedroom.

"What'd you find?" I ask Lea as I stumble through the doorway.

She's sitting on the floor in the midst of our packing boxes with the computer on her lap, her back against the wall and her legs stretched out in front of her. "An old newspaper article on the Internet that mentions a Quinton Carter involved in a fatal car accident in Seattle."

I briefly stop breathing. "What's it say?" I whisper, fearing the truth. She skims the article on the screen. "It says that he was one of the drivers and that two people in the car he was driving were dead on arrival." She pauses, sucking in a slow breath. "And it says that he died, too, but that the paramedics revived him."

I swallow hard as denial begins to evaporate and I'm forced to admit the truth. All that time I spent with Quinton and I didn't know the dark secrets eating away at him. "Are you sure that's what it says?" I ask her, denial trying to grasp hold one last time. I'm trying to hold on to the idea that Quinton just does drugs because he's bored. Things would be easier if that were the case. Well, not easy, but then I'd just be helping him with addiction instead of what's hidden beneath the addiction. And things are never easy—life never is. Mine isn't. Landon's wasn't. Quinton's isn't. Lea's isn't. So many heartbreaking stories and I wish I could document them all.

Lea glances up from the screen with a look of sympathy on her face. "I'm sorry, Nova."

I take several deep breaths, fighting the urge to count the cracks in the ceiling as I sink down on the mattress, wondering what I'm supposed to do. The plan was to move out of the apartment and head back home for summer break. Spend three months in my hometown, Maple Grove, before I return to Idaho to start my junior year of college. And I'm one for following plans. Otherwise the undetermined future unsettles me. It's one of the things I learned to do to help alleviate my anxiety.

I had plans this summer, to spend time with my mom, play music with Lea when she visits for a few weeks, and work on a documentary, maybe even get some better camera equipment. But as I take in what I've just learned about Quinton, I'm starting to wonder if I should be following a different plan, one that I should have followed nine months ago, only I wasn't in the right state of mind to.

"It also says that he was driving too fast." Lea adjusts the laptop, angling the screen so the light doesn't glare against it. "At least that's what it says in this article."

"Does it say that it was all his fault?" My voice is uneven as I drape my arm across my forehead, catching sight of the leather band on my wrist and the scar and tattoo just below it. I got the tattoo a few months ago when Lea suggested we each get one to mark something important in our lives. I loved the idea and decided to get the words "never forget" to always remind me of my downward spiral. I got them just below the scar on my wrist, the one I put there myself, because I never want to forget just how dark things can get and how I pulled myself out of them.

She leans closer to the screen again, her long black hair falling into her eyes. "No... It says that it was both drivers' fault... that Quinton was driving too fast, but that the car in the other lane was, too, and the other car took the corner way too wide and swerved into the wrong lane... It was a head-on crash and some of them weren't wearing seat belts."

"Does it say anything about the other two people in the car being Quinton's girlfriend or his cousin?" Sadness shoves its way into my heart.

She pauses, reading something over. "It says something about a Lexi Davis and a Ryder Morganson, but not how they knew Quinton."

"Morganson." The painful reality seeps into my skin, and I prop myself up on my elbows. "That's Tristan's last name... Oh my God... Ryder has to be Tristan's sister." The pieces start to connect, but it's like the outside of the puzzle is put together and the middle pieces are still missing, so it's still incomplete and doesn't make sense. "I don't get it...Why would Tristan let Quinton live with him after that?"

"Maybe because he's a forgiving guy," Lea suggests with a shrug, and when I give her a doubtful look, she adds, "Hey, some people are like that. Some people can forgive and forget easily, and when you're high all the time...well, I'm guessing it's really easy to forget, although I have no way to know if this is true or not. I'm just guessing."

"It is," I admit, remembering the few months I spent wandering around in trailer parks and fields, tasting but never fully indulging in the land of drugs and misdirection. "And now that I think about it, there was tension between the two of them...God, I can't believe I didn't know about this...I spent all that time with him and never knew."

She twirls a strand of her black hair around her finger. "Nova, I think you and I both know that you could spend a hundred years with a person and still not know them if they don't want you to know them."

"Yeah, you're right." I knew Landon for years and even though I knew he was sad, I didn't understand why. When he died, I was even more confused—still am. Lea knew her dad for twelve years, and then he took his own life. She told me that he always seemed content, not ecstatic about life or anything, but still she'd never thought he'd do that. A lot of people don't think someone they love will end their life.

Lea reads the screen for a few minutes longer, while I mess around with my long brown hair, braiding it to the side, trying not to think about the many places Quinton could be, how much harm he has to be doing to his body and mind, but it's all I can think about. I can feel myself drifting to that place where I don't have control, just like I didn't with my dad and Landon. Everything is just happening and I'm lying here, unable to know how to stop it.

"Please tell me why you're so sad," I whisper as I watch Landon flip through the pages of his sketchbook, desperately searching for a specific drawing.

He shakes his head as he tilts it to the side, observing a sketch. "I'm not sad, Nova, so stop asking."

I pull my knees to my chest and lean back against the wall. "You look sad, though."

He glances up at me, and the anguish in his eyes makes it hard to breathe. "Nova, seriously. I'm okay. I just need to figure out a few things about . . . with this project I'm working on." He roughly flips another page and then another.

I sigh, then get up from the floor and walk over to him, sitting down on the bed beside him. I can smell the pungent scent of weed, and his eyes are a little red. "You know, you can always talk to me about stuff, if you're, like, having a bad day or something." I want to reach out and touch him, but I'm afraid. Afraid he'll get mad at me. Afraid he'll ask me to go. Afraid he'll break down and cry, tell me what's wrong, and it might be something really bad.

He keeps sifting through his pages and tugging his fingers through his inky black hair. When he finally looks up at me again, his honey-brown eyes are not full of anguish, but irritation. "Would you mind giving me some time alone for a little while?"

"You want me to go?" I ask, hurt.

He nods, and I catch him glancing at the glass bong on his desk. "Just for a little while...I'll call you when I'm ready for you to come back."

I don't want to leave at all, yet I don't want to argue with him either, so I get up and go home, feeling like I've done everything wrong.

Feeling like I shouldn't have walked out on him.

"You know what?" Lea shuts the laptop, then gets to her feet, interrupting my thoughts. She's wearing a torn black T-shirt and cutoffs, and when she rubs her fingers under her eyes to eliminate any smudged eyeliner, I can see the tattoo on her wrist: *Live life with no regrets.* It's the one she got with me and it's pretty much her life motto, at least from what she tells me. "I think you need to go turn in your final project for film class."

I secure my braid with an elastic band I had around my wrist and then sit up on the bed. "Lea, I need to find out where he is...I need to talk to him and see if he's okay." I stand up, tugging on the bottoms of my shorts. "Besides, I don't have a final project to turn in."

She puts her hands on her hips and gives me a firm look.

"That's not true. You have a nice project put together, just not with Quinton's clip in it."

I dither, unsure I want to turn in the video without Quinton's recording on it, the one from last summer when he told me a coded, brief part of his life. It's so raw and emotional, which is what my final project is supposed to be, and the project feels incomplete without it, but my professor won't let me include it without Quinton's signing a permission form. "But...it's..."

"But nothing," She strides up to me and shoos me toward the door. "Go turn what you have in so you don't fail. Then get some coffee, because I know you didn't sleep last night and you look really tired."

"But what about Quinton?" It's been more than nine months since I've seen him. I know it seems absurd to be panicking about waiting a few more hours to find him, but after I found out from Delilah about the accident and that he's been doing crystal meth, it seems really urgent to find him.

"I'll see what else I can find out and see if I can track him down," she says, continuing to usher me out of the room. "And leave that Delilah chick's number. I'll try calling her and see if I can get her to fess up where they're all living. "

"Fine." I trudge out of the room and into the small living room that's attached to the moderate-size kitchen and small dining area. I collect my laptop and bag from the sofa, feeling frustration along with a thousand other emotions: sadness, guilt, pain, hopelessness. Yet I also feel a little hopeful, thanks to Lea, so I turn around and give her a hug. "Thank you for being such a good friend."

"No problem," she says and hugs me back.

We exchange this awkward yet simply real silent moment before we step away from each other and part ways. Tears sting my eyes as I head out the door and into the bright sunlight. I know that Lea will go back to her computer and look for more stuff that will hopefully lead me to Quinton, but it still hurts my heart not knowing where he is.

It's a strange feeling and I've only felt this sort of ache over one person before. Landon. But I'm not comparing Quinton to him. I refuse to do that again. Landon was Landon, the beautiful artist who bore the weight of the world on his shoulders, who suffered in ways I couldn't understand, but wish I could, but probably never will. And Quinton is Quinton, the beautiful artist, who carries guilt on his shoulders, who, even in his darkest times made me smile when no one else could, who showed me a dark world that made me want to see the light again.

And I want to make him see the light, too. I just need to find him.

Chapter Two

Nova

After I turn my project in to the professor, I get a coffee from the stand in the quad yard, then rush back toward the apartment that's only about half a mile away from the university, so that I rarely ever drive my dad's old 1967 Chevy Nova. It's a bright day and warm, the sun beaming down as I hurry up the sidewalk with my bag on my shoulder and my laptop tucked under my arm. I sort of feel like I failed, turning in the documentary without Quinton's clip. But I try to look past it and focus on the fact that at least I won't fail my class. Besides, there's always next year, and hopefully by then I'll have at least talked to Quinton. At least I hope we'll still be talking. I hope I'll have the chance to take many video clips of him that I can add to my Novamentary, as he called it.

It hurts just thinking about it, because it reminds me how much I want to help him, but at the same time, I know from experience that I can't make things happen my way. I can't make Quinton get better, just like I couldn't make Landon tell me what was wrong, just like I couldn't make my dad hold on just a little bit longer.

It's hurting my heart and I need to get my emotions out, so I halt at the final street I have to cross, downing the last of the coffee. Then I set my bag and laptop on the grass along with the empty coffee cup and take my phone from my back pocket. I click it on, then rotate slightly to get the sun in the right position so it's not blinding the screen, then hit record.

The red light blinks on and an image of me pops up on the screen. I look so different from how I looked in all the clips I made last summer. My skin looks healthier, my cheeks fuller, and my brown hair cleaner, braided to the side of my head, wisps framing my face. My blue eyes are bloodshot and full of sadness. Actually, my eyes only appear blue, but if you really observe them, then you can see that they're blue with specks of green. Quinton was one of the few people who noticed this and it was a genuinely sweet thing. I just couldn't see it at the time because I was blinded by Landon's death. But it's not just my outer appearance that's different. It's also what's inside me and radiates through my expression—the light in my eyes that I thought had died but that had only briefly dimmed.

I give the camera a little wave. "Hey, it's me, Nova, again. I'm not sure if you watched my last video or not, which I really doubt you did, since it's pretty much just a bunch of my ramblings about my life. But hey, if you're into that kind of stuff, then you'll get what I'm talking about." I shake my head, sighing at myself, but a smile cracks through. "Anyway, it's been almost exactly a year from when I started my very first video and I'm in a completely different place now. I've let go of my past for the most part, mourned my dad and Landon . . . well, let go of them as much as I can." I brush my bangs out of my face. "So here's the start of a new summer, which seems like it's going to hold a lot of possibilities, but not necessarily in a good way. In fact, I have no idea how summer is going to go."

I click off the camera and then grab my bag and laptop off the ground and cross the street, wondering if Quinton will become someone else I'll have to mourn. It makes me sick to my stomach to think about, but I know firsthand that unless someone wants to quit, and I mean in their very heart and soul wants to stop doing drugs, then they can't. And even then, when they decide they want to quit, there's still the huge battle of dealing with inner demons and finally getting to a place where their mind and body can be empty of drugs and still be at peace...I'm not even sure if *peace* is the right word, because the path of drugs will always exist in my mind and so will Landon and I'll never completely have peace from either. Now that I've tasted the freedom of numbness and forgetfulness, it's impossible to forget that it exists. The possibility that I could have it again always lives inside, and that could be ignited at any moment if a circumstance strikes the match.

I just have to know how to blow it right back out—I have to fight it with every breath I have. And I'm not in the same place anymore, so I know I can do it. I just wish I knew for certain Quinton could. What I need is to find something that will get through to him, something that will make him see past whatever's blinding him to the future. For me it was Landon's video. It helped me realize what I'd become, where I was going, and that I was trying to escape my feelings instead of dealing with them. In a strange way, that video helped me want to heal myself.

I drop my bag and laptop onto the sofa and go back to the bedroom. Lea and her boyfriend, Jaxon, are sitting on the floor, staring at the computer screen. Jaxon is tall and sort of lanky with dark-brown hair that's a little overlong and always hangs in his eyes, and he's behind Lea, massaging her back as she reads an article.

"Did you find anything more?" I ask, startling them both. They jump, wide-eyed, like I just walked in on them having sex.

Jaxon's arms fall away from Lea's shoulders. "Oh, hey, Nova," he says, giving me a small wave. "We didn't hear you come in."

I go over and sit down on the edge of the bed. "I didn't know you were still here. I thought you went home yesterday."

"I was going to," he tells me, discreetly glancing at Lea. "But I thought I'd stick around for an extra day...maybe longer if I need to."

The two of them have been arguing over the fact that Jaxon is going home to Illinois for the summer and Lea is going back home to Wyoming to a town not too far away from Maple Grove. It's not the first time the two of them have spent the summer apart, but I guess it's getting to the point where they're committed enough that one of them should go with the other, or they should just get a place here. Yet for some reason they won't. I asked Lea why and she simply said because they couldn't both agree on where they should go. Therefore she's starting to wonder if they're even on the same page anymore. It makes me sad because they're a cute couple. Jaxon plays the guitar and Lea sings, and when they get up on stage, magic happens, because they show so much emotion toward each other. It makes playing drums in the background enjoyable, although playing is always enjoyable.

"He's headed home tonight," Lea states, returning her attention to the computer. "He just stopped to say good-bye."

"How about I take over trying to track Quinton down and you two go spend some time together?" I suggest.

Lea's gaze travels back and forth between Jaxon and me. "You don't have to do that. I'm fine with staying here and helping you."

Jaxon shakes his head, looking aggravated as he shifts away from her, drawing his hands back and putting them on his lap. It's pretty obvious they're fighting and need a moment, and my saving-Quinton mission is getting in the way. "I can take over for a while. Just tell me what you've found out and I'll go from there."

Lea sighs and then leans back on her hands, while Jaxon stares absentmindedly out the window at the clouds moving in. "Nothing really. The article just talked about the accident some more, but there's no information online about where he'd be now. I did get ahold of that Delilah bitch, but she hung up on me when I started asking her too many questions about where they were living—I think she thought I was the police or something."

I cross my legs out in front of me. "She was probably on something and being paranoid."

Lea exchanges a glance with Jaxon and then looks at me. "I really don't like her at all. She called me a skank and she doesn't even know me."

I sigh, wishing Delilah would stop being…well, Delilah, and just let me know where she is. "She'd probably be nicer to you if you were a guy. She has this thing with clashing with other women."

Lea rolls her eyes and then goes back to the computer, lining her fingers up on the keyboard. "I can totally see that."

I remove the elastic from my hair, undo the braid, and comb my fingers through my hair for no other reason than that I'm fidgety and need something to focus on other than the thing I really want to do—count. "Could we maybe do a search on her phone number and see what address is linked to it?"

Lea shakes her head as she types something. "I already did and it brings up an address in Maple Grove, and we know they're not there anymore, since they moved and that damn bitch won't tell you where." She pauses, musing over something. "But what we could do is call her mother and ask her where she is." Lea moves her legs around, lies down on her stomach, and props herself up on her elbows, putting her feet on Jaxon's lap. He absentmindedly begins massaging her feet.

I shake my head. "I doubt her mother even knows where she is."

"What about her father?" Lea asks, clicking the mouse.

"He's been out of the picture pretty much since she was born," I say. "And she doesn't have any other relatives as far as I know."

"What about Quinton's father?" she wonders. "You could do a search for him in Seattle where Quinton lived…Or did he not live with his father?"

"I don't know…God, I don't even know his father's first name," I tell her guiltily. "But I guess you could do a search on Quinton Carter in Seattle and see if it pulls up an old phone number or his father's name maybe."

"Yeah, but are we even sure his dad would know where he is?" she asks. "Maybe we should just see if we can track Quinton's phone number down."

"As far as I know, he doesn't have one," I reply. "And Quinton Carter is kind of a common name, isn't it?"

Lea opens her mouth to respond, but Jaxon raises his hand like a kid in elementary school waiting for the teacher to call on him so he can speak. Lea rolls her eyes, but laughs.

"Yes, Mr. Collins," she says in a fake baritone voice as she rolls onto her side.

Jaxon lowers his hand onto his lap and grins as he brushes his hair out of his eyes. "As much as I'd love to sit here and listen to you bounce your brilliant ideas off each other all day, I have an idea that might be a lot simpler."

Lea flourishes her hand at him, and the tension between the two of them appears to have been alleviated a little. "Well, then, you have our undivided attention, O brilliant one."

He covers his mouth with his hand, hiding a grin. "Why don't I call this Delilah and see if I can sweet-talk her into giving up their location."

"Because you're so much more charming than the two of us," Lea says, playfully prodding him in the side with her foot. "Why would she give up her address to you, if she wouldn't even give it to Nova, and she knows Nova?"

"Um, because I'm a guy." He points at himself. "And I can be very charming when I want to."

"True," Lea agrees. "I guess it wouldn't hurt to try." She looks at me questioningly. "What do you think, Nova?"

"I think it's worth a try." I slant to the side to get my phone out of the back pocket of my shorts.

"Let me call her from mine, since she's been ignoring your calls," Jaxon says, reaching for his phone in the pocket of his pants.

I tuck my phone back into my pocket. "Good point," I tell him as he swipes his finger across the screen. "And, Jaxon?"

He glances up at me. "Yeah?"

"Thank you," I say, because even though he doesn't know it, what he's doing for me right now means more to me than if he were giving me the shirt off his back.

"You're welcome...Now, what's the number?" he asks, and as I rattle it off, he dials.

"And put it on speakerphone," Lea tells him, sitting up beside him. "I want to hear how this goes down."

Jaxon blows out a breath, then hits the speaker button and

sets the phone down on the floor in front of him. When it starts to ring, he hastily says, "Wait—what am I supposed to say?"

"I have no idea." I trade a look with Lea, who shrugs. "How about—"

"Hello." Delilah's voice on the line forces me to seal my lips.

"Um, hey, beautiful." Jaxon glances at me, then Lea, who hangs her head and shakes it disbelievingly.

"Um, who is this?" Delilah asks, sounding mystified.

"My name's Jaxon," he says cautiously. "I'm a friend of Nova's."

I hold my breath as soon as he says my name, worried she'll hang up on him, since she clearly has been dodging my calls.

"Is she in trouble?" Delilah asks, not seeming upset, just neutral.

"No..." He pauses, then picks up the phone and puts the receiver close to his mouth. "Look, here's the deal, Delilah. Nova really needs to get ahold of this Quinton guy... In fact, it's pretty important, and you seem to be the only person who has a direct connection to him, at least the only person that Nova knows. So what I was wondering is if you could either put him on the phone so she could talk to him or if you could let us know how to get ahold of him. If you could do either one of those things," he says charmingly, "I would greatly, greatly appreciate it."

Delilah pauses, and I can hear banging in the background. "Fine, hold on... I'll go see if he wants to talk to her." It sounds like the phone is dropped on the other end, but then voices flow over the line.

Lea smacks Jaxon on the back of the head. "Really?" she hisses. "You called her 'beautiful.'"

He shrugs, and then covers the receiver with his hand. "It worked, didn't it?"

Lea sighs before she snatches the phone from Jaxon and tosses it to me, and I lean forward to catch it. Then Lea gets to her feet and extends her hand to Jaxon. "Let's give her some privacy."

Jaxon takes her hand and she pulls him to his feet. Then they depart for the door with their fingers intertwined. "I'm just in the next room if you need anything," Lea calls over her shoulder. I nod and they step out and shut the door behind them.

I let a slow exhalation ease out as my pulse slams against my wrist, neck, and chest. I'm actually going to talk to him. What the hell do I say? And what if I say something wrong? I start to panic and crave the solitude of counting, but I refuse to go there.

Never again.

I'm stronger than that.

Deep breaths.

Breathe.

Relax—

"Hello." The sound of his voice stops my thoughts, my heart, my breath, as the feelings I felt during those couple of months slam straight into my heart like a shot of adrenaline. I can't find my voice; I'm broken, soundless. *Speak, dammit. Speak.* "Delilah, who did you say this was?" I hear him say, and it snaps me back to reality.

"It's Nova," I tell him tentatively. There's a pause, and I'd think that he's hung up on me, but I can hear chattering in the background. "Nova Reed, the girl you met a year ago."

"I remember," he says, not sounding happy at all, and it crushes almost all my hope, until he adds in a lighter tone, "Nova, like the car."

"That would be the one." I flop down on the bed on my back, searching my mind for the right words, but knowing that they probably don't exist. That everything I say is probably going to sound awkward and might piss him off, but I'm going to have to just go with it if I'm going to go through with this. "I was just calling to see how you were."

"I'm fine," he replies in a formal tone.

"Umm...I hear you moved from Maple Grove."

"Yeah...things got to be a little too intense there for some people, I guess, but me, I'll live wherever."

"Where are you living?" I wonder, brushing my finger across my tattoo. *Never forget. Remember. Move forward. Do things differently.*

"Delilah didn't tell you?" he asks.

"No. I didn't even ask her." I lie, because I did. A thousand times on her voice mail, but she never would answer or call back.

He gets quiet, and I hear a door shut and the chattering quiets down. "We live in Vegas...her, Dylan, Tristan, and me... It's kind of intense here, too, but I guess it works for everyone."

"Vegas," I say, a little shocked because that's not what I

was expecting. Honestly, I don't know what I was expecting, or if I really expected anything. I think part of me might have believed that I would never talk to him again. "Really?"

"Yeah, really," he replies in a terse tone.

I force my tone to be cheerful, even though his irritation hurts. "Well, what do you do in Vegas?" I ask and then shake my head at myself. "I mean, does anyone work there...at all?" I smack my hand against my head. God, I sound like a rambling idiot.

"Sort of," he replies, being evasive, and I think I know why. Because maybe they're doing the same thing as at the concert—dealing drugs.

My heart starts to fracture as pressure builds in my chest, and all I want to do is hang up and find something to count, but I keep going. "Are you drawing a lot?"

"Sometimes...I've actually drawn you a couple of times," he says, and then the line goes silent. "I'm sorry. I shouldn't have said that."

"Why not? You can draw me if you want to." I think I might mean it, and it feels strange after spending all that time viewing it as cheating on Landon if anyone else ever drew me. *When did I get to a place where I'm okay with it?*

His quietness is maddening, but then he speaks again and his voice is lighter. "So what have you been up to?" he asks, changing the subject.

"Not a whole lot. School. Work. I've been playing the drums again, too."

"Really?" he says, and I hear him flick a lighter. "You know, I never did get to see you play."

"I know." Memories flood me, like water rising... rising... rising. I can hear, smell, feel the concert we were at a little less than a year ago. "But there's still time. I could come visit you or you could come visit me."

"Yeah, I guess," he says, his mood instantly deflating, and I know I've said the wrong thing. "Look, Nova, I got to go. Tristan needs my help with something."

"Hold on a second." I quickly sit up, not ready to stop the conversation. I haven't even accomplished anything yet, talked to him enough, saved him. God dammit, what the hell am I supposed to say? What is the right thing to say? "I've actually been wanting to use that video clip you made for a project I'm working on... the one you made in the tent when we were at the concert. I know it's sort of personal and everything, so I won't use it unless you say it's okay." I'm getting desperate to keep him on the phone, keep hearing his voice.

He pauses, but for only a second or two. "I really don't care if you do, Nova. So much has happened between then and now that I can barely even remember what I said on it."

My chest aches and I ball up my fist and massage my hand over it, seeking relief but not getting any. "Thanks, but I also need you to sign a release. My professor won't let me use the clip unless I have one from each of the people in the video."

"Okay... how do I sign the form?"

"Can I mail it to you?" I ask, reaching for a pen and paper

on the nightstand, feeling like a real asshole for not telling him my ulterior motive for getting his address.

"Sure," he responds. Then he tells me the address and I jot it down. As I set the pen and paper down on the bed, I hear someone say something in the background about getting a move on. "Look, Nova, it's been great talking to you, but I have to go."

I'm afraid to let him go, cut the connection, not know he's okay, but I know that I have to. "Okay, I understand."

I wait for him to hang up, but then he says, "Are you okay?"

I nod, even though he can't see me. "Yeah, I'm fine." I pinch the bridge of my nose and squeeze my eyes shut. *I'm just worried about you and I have no idea how to go about this. I have no idea what I'm doing.*

"Are you sure?" he asks again, and I remember all the times last summer when he asked the same thing.

"Yeah, but it's been really nice talking to you." I open my eyes, trying to think of something epic to say, but I just can't get there. "Would it be okay if I called you again?"

He wavers. "I guess, but I don't have a phone."

"That's okay…I can call Delilah's. Just make sure to mention to her that you want to talk to me the next time I call or else I don't think she'll let me talk to you."

"Okay, I will," he says, but I don't think he means it. "Take care of yourself, Nova."

"I will." I feel like a part of my heart has died the moment he hangs up the phone. The line goes dead, and it reminds me of the sound of a flat line after a heart stops beating, desperate to be revived. And I want to do that for him. Help him. Revive him.

I feel so helpless, just like I did with Landon.

I know I have to do something, but I'm not sure what exactly. What way is the right way or if there even is a right way. This isn't some story or fairy tale where I'll set out on this mission to save someone and after a long, exhausting battle we'll reach our happily ever after. I actually don't believe in happily ever afters. They're sappy in my opinion and super unrealistic.

But what I do believe in is not giving up on something that I feel passionate about. And I feel passionate about helping people. I've been doing it on the phone for months now, at the suicide hotline I work at. I talk with people. I try to help them see that they're not alone. That there are other people in the world who have felt the same way and they've survived.

That things may seem really shitty sometimes—dark, bleak, and hopeless, like being stuck in a dark hole with no light and no hope of ever getting out. But that's never the case. There is hope. There is light. There is a way to get back to a life where you can smile and laugh and feel weightless. No, it's not easy, and the hardest part is actually seeing it from that angle, but it exists. I know this for a fact, because I've been in that dark place where smiling seems so hard and giving up seems so easy, and now I smile every day and it's the lightest feeling.

Maybe it's because I understand this that I do what I do next. Maybe it's because I can smile and see the light—see that hope exists for Quinton. Or maybe it's because I want to save him, like I couldn't save Landon or even my dad. For whatever reason, I march out to the living room where Lea and Jaxon are sitting on the sofa and say four words that change the entire course of my summer.

"I'm going to Vegas," I announce, and my voice quivers and pours out all my nervousness in it. I feel nauseous and like I'm going to pass out, which makes the situation even realer. "Who wants to come with me?" It's a desperate measure, but I'm desperate, and it's the only thing I can think of to do.

Lea glances at Jaxon, who looks completely lost. "Vegas?" he questions. He's got his arm draped around her, but he looks tense. "Really?"

I nod, collecting my bag and laptop off the sofa. "I got his address and he's living in Vegas, so that's where I'm going… As soon as I get the rest of the apartment packed up and my finals turned in, I'm hitting the road."

"Nova…" Lea struggles with something to say as Jaxon moves his arm away from her. "I know you want to help people, but this isn't like working on the suicide hotline. It's more complicated… and maybe even dangerous."

"More complicated than helping Quinton realize life's worth living?" I inquire, hugging my laptop to my chest.

"Yeah, because you're going to be doing it in the crazy world Quinton is now living in," she states with apprehension, scooting forward on the sofa. "And that's not the same as doing it from the safety of a hotline."

"Lea, I'm doing this," I say determinedly. "I need to do this, not just to help Quinton, but for myself…This could be my second chance."

I've talked to Lea enough that she gets what I'm saying. Plus, she knows what it's like to lose someone, so she might even understand the need to save people from themselves.

Lea looks at Jaxon again and then gets to her feet and walks over to me. "Nova, I know you want to save him and everything, but do you really think you can without, you know"—she leans in and lowers her voice—"getting back into drugs yourself?"

I drape the handle of my bag over my shoulder. "Lea, I wouldn't go if I didn't think I could…and when I got better, I made a promise to myself that I would never, ever again live with regrets." I tap my finger against the inside of her wrist, across her tattoo. "No regrets, right?" I don't tell her about the other part—how I want to help him because I wasn't able to save Landon or my dad—because I'm not sure what she'd say.

Her stressed expression softens. "All right, but I'm coming with you to keep an eye on you." She raises her pinkie. "And you have to swear that if I tell you that you're getting in over your head, you'll listen and back off."

"Lea, you don't have to—"

She cuts me off, waving her pinkie at me. "I want to. Besides, I have relatives in Vegas that we can probably stay with."

As much as I don't like her sacrificing anything for me, I know accepting is the right thing to do. I'm going to need help and I do want her to come with me.

"Okay, then." I hook pinkies with her. "I promise, but are you sure you can come with me? What about Wyoming?" I lower my voice, leaning in, worried I'm going to cause a fight between her and Jaxon. "Or *Illinois*."

She sighs, then unhooks her pinkie from mine and turns to Jaxon. "How about we make a compromise and go to Vegas for the summer?"

He frowns, his eyes filling with hurt and annoyance. "Why would we go to Vegas when we couldn't even agree to stay here together?" He lets out a frustrated breath, then gets to his feet. "I can't believe this." He pauses, growing angrier. "You know what, I actually can. This is so like you, when it comes to making any sort of commitment with me."

"What's that supposed to mean?" Lea asks, sounding slightly irritated.

"It means that you'd rather do anything else than commit to me." He storms across the living room. "You've been making excuse after excuse not to be with me this summer, so I'm going to make it really easy for you. I'm done." He holds up his hands as he backs out the front door, then spins around and slams the door behind him. A stack of boxes tips over in the foyer, and I hear the sound of glass breaking.

"He doesn't mean that," Lea tells me as she backs up toward the front door, but she looks a little worried.

"Maybe I should go to Vegas myself," I say. "I don't want to cause problems between you two."

"No, I'm going...Just keep packing while I go talk to

him." She spins and hurries around the tipped-over boxes and after Jaxon, leaving me alone in the apartment.

Reality sinks in and it's heavy and packed with pressure. I grow nervous. About myself, about Quinton, what he'll look like, what he'll act like. I worry about the world I'm walking back into and if I'll do everything right. Will I mess this up?

"No. I can do this," I say with determination, hoping with every single part of me that I'm right. That this time I can do things right.

Chapter Three

May 16, day one of summer break

Quinton

My ceiling has a drip in it. Well, several to be exact. And I'm not even sure where the hell the water is coming from. I live in the desert and it rarely rains. Yet the ceiling is dripping like a fucking leaky showerhead. Maybe it's coming from the apartment above. It could have a leak in the pipes, or maybe the neighbors left the bathtub on and water is flowing out all over the floor and seeping into my bedroom ceiling. I could go upstairs and see, but there's no point. The whole reason for moving to this shithole apartment in the first place was that no one would bother us and in return we wouldn't bother them. Silence. That's the name of the game among the people who live in my apartment complex, because almost everyone is doing something illegal.

There's music playing from an old stereo I found on the sidewalk, because ever since the concert, for some reason, the sound of music calms me just a little. I've been lying flat on my back on the mattress for God knows how long, analyzing the drops of water as they fall from above and land around me, on me, everywhere, and I can almost picture myself falling with them, never to go upward again.

My arms are tucked under my head and I'm motionless on the outside, but on the inside my mind is running a million miles a minute, all thoughts focused on the water, the way it drips, moves, how I want to drink it because I'm thirsty, yet I'm not drinking and I don't want to get up to get a drink. And it's sort of become a project for me—not to think of anything else. Because if I do, I know where my mind is going to go and it can't go there, because then my feelings will go there and I'll be breaking my promise.

But no matter how hard I try, I can't not think about her. Beautiful Nova Reed who shouldn't even know me, yet she does . . . or did. I thought she'd outgrown her time with me and my loser ass, but then she called—after nine months—to chat about that video I made back when there was a ray of light left in my life. Nova was the light and I was stuck in the shadows all the time except for a few moments when she touched me, kissed me, let me touch her, and I couldn't avoid her light, if that makes any sense. Actually, it probably doesn't. My head is in this really weird place, where I'm high but the drips of crystal in the back of my throat are becoming few and far between. I'm fading, crashing toward a rocky bottom, and the sharp rocks are going to hurt if I don't get wings and fly again. I'm going to shatter. Break into a thousand shards of glass and metal. Like a car wreck. Like the fucking wreck that I caused, twisted and broken—unfixable. Like Lexi and Ryder. Unfixable because of me. Shit. I need to stop thinking.

"Dude, you're fucking spacing." Tristan cracks through my thoughts as he enters my room, rapping on the doorway. He has a T-shirt on and a pair of baggy jeans, and his blond hair looks wet for some reason, but I doubt it's from a shower, since ours has been broken for days.

"Why's your hair wet?" I ask over the music, slanting my head to the side, and a drop of water falls into my eye, rehydrating it.

His fingers move for his hair, which gives me a view of his forearm and the small holes and scabs covering his skin, some outlined with shades of blue and purple. "Oh, I washed my hair in the sink. It reeked like vodka for some reason...I think someone might have poured it in my hair last night when I passed out on the living room floor."

"Yeah, I can see that happening." I redirect my concentration back to the drip in the ceiling. "You have a knack for crazy things happening when you pass out, which is a sign that you might want to stop."

"I'll stop when you stop," he says, because he knows I'm not going to, and it makes me feel like a terrible person, even though I'm not certain he means it. Still, I should at least challenge him, but at the same time I can't give up the one thing that brings me a drop of peace in the murky lake that's become my home.

"So are you going out tonight with me after we make a pickup?" He changes the subject, glancing around at the nothingness that pretty much fills my room, except for my sketchbook that's on the floor. His gaze briefly lingers on it before he looks up at me. "Dylan said he had some shit for us to do over at Johnny's...well, he said stuff for *you* to do, since he's still pissed off at me for screwing over Trace and there's a good chance he could be there."

Johnny is the guy who supplies Dylan with large quantities of drugs for him to deal and sometimes we get drugs from Johnny ourselves. Trace is one of the guys we deal to regularly. Trace actually has a lot of money, at least in comparison to us. He also has a lot of connections, which means pissing him off is a very bad thing. About a week ago Tristan "accidentally" shorted him a couple of ounces, one of which he sold and I have no idea what happened to the other—we probably used it and I didn't even know. When Trace asked him for his thousand bucks back for being shorted the ounces, Tristan replied that he didn't have it—that he'd spent it. Tristan's dumb ass managed to get away without getting his ass kicked. He did come home with a huge bruise on his face, and I think all of us have been expecting Trace and his guys to break down the door and beat us up until Tristan pays him back.

"As much as Dylan is an asshole, I'm with him on this one," I tell him. "You're lucky Trace and his guys haven't broken down the door and beat your ass. Remember what they did to Roy and his girlfriend after they stole from him?"

"Roy was an idiot," he says. "And didn't know how to lie low."

"No, he tried to lie low," I reply in a firm voice. "But they found him and beat the shit out of him. He ended up in the hospital and almost freaking died... and they raped his girlfriend."

It seems crazy that this is the way things are, but I learned really quickly when we moved down here that there are a lot more dangers with drugs than just doing them. There's also a lot of danger through exchanges, the people I meet, the people who think I'm ripping them off. But I'm not even sure they are dangers, because most of the time I don't feel scared, knowing what could happen. The risks just exist like everything else.

Tristan seems unfazed. "A, I don't have a girlfriend, so I don't have to worry about anyone but myself, and B, I'll figure out a way to pay him back... somehow." It's clear in his voice that he has no intention of paying Trace back. Tristan has no boundaries anymore, not just with stealing and taking drugs, but with life choices; he's always pushing toward danger. Never thinking about the consequences, veering toward a short life. We all kind of hover in the same place, always a few steps away from getting ourselves killed or arrested, especially with the large amount of drugs Dylan has in his possession sometimes when he's working a bigger exchange. But Tristan never seems to know when to pull back, and a few steps is more like half a step for him. I've had to stop him more than a few times from getting into fights, doing too many drugs, mixing the wrong drugs, but it's okay. I owe him so much more, and I'll keep helping him—making sure that half a step always exists—until the day I die. It can be my penance.

"It's not worth death." I have to pause to catch my breath. Saying the word "death," talking about death, or even thinking about it, can sometimes make me feel like I'm helplessly falling, even when I'm flying. "So stop stealing shit and find a way to pay Trace back before he gets fed up."

"It's not worth death, huh?" Tristan questions, ignoring my remark about Trace as his forehead creases in confusion, and I wonder what he's on, if the drugs are just getting to him or if he really questions if it's not death.

"Not for you," I say with the little care I have left in me. "Drugs aren't worth your life ending."

"But they are for you?"

"Everything's worth death for me." I lose my breath again over the word. I need to stop saying it, but sometimes when I'm strung out, words just crash out of my mouth.

He glances uneasily at the names Lexi, Ryder, and No One tattooed on my arm. "Just stop talking about death and get up and come do this run with me."

"Where are you going?" I ask, but my voice gets washed away by the increase in the volume of the music as the drummer bangs harder on the drums and the woman singer belts out passionate lyrics that I swear to God are trying to tell me something. I become distracted by images appearing in my head, ones I've tried to put down on paper many times but can never seem to get as perfect as I want them to be. Nova with drumsticks in her hands, pounding to the beat while beads of sweat cover her smooth skin, but in the most beautiful way possible.

Tristan goes over to a corner of the bedroom and turns the music down, tipping over the stereo in the process. "You've been listening to some real depressing shit lately."

"I guess so, but does it really matter?" I ask, wiping a few water droplets off my forehead. "It sort of matches my mood anyway."

"I was just pointing it out." He picks up a dirty shirt off the floor and chucks it at my face, then gives the side of the mattress a good kick. "Now get your ass up so we can go get this shit done. I have plans later tonight."

I blink my dry eyes and force saliva down my throat a few times to rehydrate it. "I'm not sure I want to go anywhere right now."

"Why?" he asks, backing up toward the wall. "You have something better to do?"

"No, but I'm not really feeling it right now," I tell him. "In fact, all I want to do is lie back down and stare at the water stain on my wall."

He relaxes back against the wall, shaking his head. "Okay, fess up. Who the hell was on the phone?"

I turn my head toward him, my brows furrowed. "What are you talking about?"

"When Delilah gave you her phone like a week ago," he says. "You've been acting weird ever since and using more, too, which I'm not going to lecture you about, since I'm always getting pissed at you for lecturing me."

"I've been acting as weird as I always do." I sit up and pick up the shirt he threw at me. "There's nothing wrong and no one called me."

"Someone called you or else she wouldn't have given you the phone."

"It was . . . just an old friend."

He rubs his jawline contemplatively. "Was it who I think it was?"

I slip my shirt over my head and put my arms through the sleeves. "Does it really matter?"

"It seems to matter to you, which is weird because nothing ever seems to matter to you, except for the last few days," he states, moving away from the wall. He opens his mouth to say something, but then he pauses, debating. "It was Nova, wasn't it?"

"Why would you even think that?" I gather some loose change piled on the floor beside my mattress, the only money I have at the moment, and most of it came from walking around and checking car doors. If they're unlocked, then we raid them and steal anything that has value. It's the only source of income

I have other than dealing for Dylan. He uses us to deal, and in return we get drugs and sometimes cash to buy more drugs, a roof over our heads, and what more is there? It's all I need— deserve. "I haven't talked to Nova in forever," I add.

"So what?" Tristan retrieves his cigarettes from the pocket of his jeans, nudging a few quarters on the floor in my direction with the tip of his worn sneaker. "Nova seems like the sort of girl who would call after a year, and you had this look on your face while you were talking on the phone…like the conversation meant something to you."

"I'm surprised you were sober enough to see my face." I stuff a handful of coins into my pocket, then pick up the mirror that's beside the pile of coins, reach under my mattress to where my stash is, and pull out the plastic bag holding the white shards of crystal that's going to either let me numbly survive the night or kill me. "You've been on heroin so much lately, you've barely been conscious."

He rolls his eyes as he removes a cigarette from the pack, puts it in his mouth, then cups his hand around the end and lights it with a lighter he finds on my floor. "Don't be a fucking hypocrite." He blows out a cloud of smoke as he takes the cigarette out of his mouth. "You do just as much crystal as I do smack. In fact, you might even do more."

He's wrong and I want to call him out on it, but then we'll start arguing and it could go on forever. I stare down at the mirror in one hand and the bag in the other, feeling nothing other than a desire to indulge in what's inside it. It practically screams at me: *Take me, take me, take me. Forget. Forget. Forget. Everything will be fine once I erase your pain. Die. Be free from the guilt.* "Point taken." My hands start to tremble as need consumes me. *Feed the addiction. The hunger. The craving.*

"What point?" he asks confoundedly, offering me a cigarette.

I take one and set it down on the mattress beside me. "I have no idea." Nothing matters at the moment except getting a line into my system, because if I'm going to move and think and talk, I'm going to need it to fuel me. Otherwise I won't have the energy or willpower to function. One white line or maybe even two; then I'll talk and think and breathe again.

With unsteady fingers, I unseal the bag, then sink down on the mattress and balance the mirror on my lap. I pour a line across it, ignoring my reflection because I can't look at it just yet. Then I pick up a razor that's by my foot and break up the clumps with it. I grab one of the many emptied-out pens beside the coin pile, lower my head, and put the pen case up to my nostril. Then I inhale through it like it's oxygen helping me breathe, live, survive. The white powder slides up my nose, and when it reaches the back of my throat, I blow out a breath as I tip my head back.

"Feel better?" Tristan asks, scattering ashes from his cigarette on the floor before reaching out for the mirror like he wants to take a hit.

As he steals it from my hand, I catch my reflection in the scratched-up surface. Pale skin, wide eyes rimmed with red, and one side of my nose is also red, but I doubt anyone else can see the change.

I pick up the cigarette and put it in my mouth. Then I get to my feet, light the cigarette, and go out into the hall while Tristan sits down on my bedroom floor and pours himself a line. I have to step over two people passed out on the floor on my way to the living room, a guy and a girl, neither of them wearing a shirt.

Maneuvering around a pile of broken glass, I make it to the kitchen, which is basically part of the living room, only a curtain has been hung up to divide the two spaces. The place is a mess. Paper plates and cups, dirty pans and spoons, empty cereal boxes cover the counter. The sink is full of dirty dishes and it stinks like a trash can. There're empty cigarette cartons everywhere and a used syringe. I'm not even sure why I came in here. I'm not hungry or thirsty or anything really and there's probably no food anyway. I grind my jaw a few times, trying to remember why I even got out of bed. All I want to do is go back to my room and stare at the ceiling, because it was sort of becoming my sanctuary in there.

"Dylan wanted me to give you a message." Delilah unexpectedly strolls into the kitchen, wearing a skirt and a red lacy bra. She always walks around like that, half dressed, and I don't know if it's because she's just comfortable with herself or because she's trying to get someone to fuck her.

"Oh yeah?" I blink and then rub my nose, my jaw twitching as I take a soothing drag. "What does he want?"

"For you to run over to Johnny's and pick up an eight ball for Dylan to sell. You'll have to pay him for it, but he left some cash." She holds up a roll of money as she reclines against the counter, sticking her chest out. "He wants you to go, since Tristan"—she makes air quotes—"'borrowed' from him last time and never paid him back."

I graze my thumb over the end of the cigarette, and ash flutters to the floor. I nod, even though I don't want to go down to fucking Johnny's, one of Dylan's suppliers. I want to go into my room and stare at the water stains. Maybe draw. But if I don't go to Johnny's, then Dylan will get pissed, and when Dylan's pissed, everyone's miserable, since he's usually the one with the biggest stash and he has the connections to get more. "I already told Tristan I'd go with him."

"Good." She stands up straight, stuffs her hand down her bra, and rearranges her breasts. "But I'm going with you, not Tristan."

I put the cigarette out on the counter. "Who made you the boss?"

"Dylan did." She grins as she struts over to me and traces her finger up my arm while tucking a roll of dollar bills into the front pocket of my jeans. "Because the last time you two went and picked up something for Dylan, you had it finished off before you even made it home, and we don't want that to happen again, since if it does, you'll both end up out on the streets and you're too good-looking to be out there." She winks at me. "They'll eat you up in a day."

"So what are you now?" I ask, not necessarily pissed, just being blunt. "My babysitter or something?"

"Don't you wish." Her fingers travel from my arm to my

shoulder, then down my chest. "You know my offer's still on the table."

"What offer?" I honestly can't remember, and the longer I try to remember, the more I think about drawing and the water stains. And Nova. Her lips. Her eyes. God, her voice triggered something inside me. Life maybe? And I don't want life in me. What I want is to forget, to stop thinking about Nova and focus on being where Lexi is, under the ground. Lexi. I need to be thinking about Lexi, get high enough that I feel closer to her—never forget her. Always love her. No one else.

Stop fucking thinking of Nova.

Delilah's hand drifts downward until she's cupping my cock through my jeans, and I'm so numb at this point I can't even tell if I'm hard or not. Then she leans forward and puts her lips up to my ear as she presses her breasts against my chest. "You can take me whenever you want. All you have to do is say yes and I can wipe that sad look you always have on your face right off."

I don't move her hand, shove her back, or breathe. It's not like I want her. She practically sleeps with anyone now, I think because Dylan's ignoring her and fucking other women, sometimes right in front of her. But for some reason I can't seem to find the willpower to move, and when she stands on her tiptoes, ready to kiss me, I plan on letting her, knowing she'll be a really good diversion from the beautiful girl who called me out of the blue. The girl who has eyes that look blue, but are green, too. Who used to look sad but from the sound of her voice on the phone seemed happy and I wish I could be happy for her.

Delilah's lips brush mine, her auburn hair grazing my cheek as she slants her head to the side and grabs my cock harder. I'm about to part my lips and let her and the drugs potently mix in my head and erase my thoughts, but then I hear someone say something from the living room and Delilah quickly jerks away like I'm made of fire.

Her head whips toward the curtain, which is pulled back so we have a full view of the living room. "Oh, thank God." She places her hand to her chest when she sees it's just Tristan. "I thought you were Dylan."

"Would it really matter if I was?" he says as he walks into the kitchen. "He didn't care when you slept with me and I don't think he'll care about Quinton, just like he doesn't care about anything else you do."

"Fuck you, Tristan," she snaps, flipping him the middle finger as she spins on her heels and puts her back toward me. "You're just pissed because I fucked you once and then wouldn't do it again."

"Baby, don't think you're something special, because you're not," Tristan retorts, blinking several times, high as a kite, and I doubt he even knows what he's saying. I'm not sure any of us do.

Delilah slaps her hand against his chest and he stumbles back a little, tensing and looking pissed, but then the crystal kicks in and he pops his jaw and his anger unravels. He blinks his focus off Delilah and on to me. "So are we going or what?"

"You two aren't going anywhere together." Delilah rubs her eyes, smearing mascara all over her face.

Tristan's gaze cuts to her. "And who's going to stop us. You?"

She takes sharp breaths, anger rising on her face, but she's too weak to do anything to stop us. "Dylan said you two can't go together anymore. You use all the stuff before it ever makes it back here. And your dumb ass has pissed off Trace, and the last thing you need is to run into him. Even though Dylan got him to cool off, he says you need to lie low for a while, just in case. Plus, he hangs out at Johnny's sometimes. You know that."

"Yeah, but I don't give a shit. And besides, Dylan's not here to stop me, is he?" Tristan states with a crook of his brow. "So that means *we* get to decide what *we* want to do. And I'm going to Johnny's. With Quinton. Trace can kiss my ass if he shows up." He signals for me to follow him as he turns for the door. "Come on. Let's get this over with."

I hesitate, my mind briefly making it through the veil of drugs to see a real problem arising. "Tristan, maybe I should just go alone. You pissed off Trace pretty bad, and he's not a guy you want to mess around with. Remember when he and his guys stabbed that one guy for...well, I can't remember what for, but he still did it."

"I'll be fine," he says, brushing me off as he sidesteps a bucket. "If Trace is there, we'll just leave."

I want to argue with him more, because he's only thinking with his addiction, but the veil in my mind closes back up, and I lose track of why I should worry so much. "All right, let's get out of here."

"You guys are such assholes." Delilah huffs, stomping her foot and crossing her arms over her chest.

Tristan shrugs as he opens the front door, scooping up a backpack that's near the doorway. I cross the living room and step over a large glass bong sitting in the center of the pathway between the two smelly old sofas, the only furniture we have. Then I walk outside into the sunlight and it stings my eyes, which already felt like they were bleeding. Tristan mutters something to Delilah about keeping his bed warm for him while he's gone and I hear something shatter, probably the bong. Then he slams the door, shaking his head as we start across the balcony, past all the shut doors and windows covered with curtains or blankets.

"She's such a bitch," he says, slipping the backpack on.

"Yeah, but I don't know why you encourage her." I shield my eyes with my hand to block out the sunlight. "You didn't used to."

"Things change," he mutters, scratching his arm.

"Not really," I say as we reach the top of the stairway, stepping out from under the protection of the roof. The light hits me straight on and I feel like a candle melting under the sun. "Things have been pretty much the same for the last six months."

"You say that like it's bad," he tells me, trotting down the steps.

I jog down the stairway after him. "No, I say that like it's true."

He halts when we reach the bottom of the stairs. "Maybe you

shouldn't be saying anything about it at all," he suggests, grinding his teeth as he stares out at the gravel parking lot and then at the stretch of desert and run-down brick buildings to the side of us.

"Yeah, you're probably right." I decide to keep my lips sealed as we head for the street, because I really shouldn't be talking to him or giving him advice. He's probably doing all this shit because of me, because I killed his sister. I ruined his life—I ruined a lot of people's lives, something I'm reminded of every day when no one calls me or really talks to me, which is pretty much the way it's been since the accident. In the beginning I was stupid enough to believe that someone was going to say that it wasn't my fault, that it was just an accident. But that never happened. The opposite did. And now I'm here, right where I belong, and the last time I actually had a conversation about something other than drugs was with Nova.

God, stop thinking about her. What the hell is my problem?

As we walk by the bottom-floor apartments toward the parking lot, we pass by our neighbor, Cami, a middle-aged woman who likes to walk around in spandex skirts and tight shirts with no bra. She's smoking a cigarette, staring out at the parking lot, but when we walk by, she focuses on us.

"Hey, baby," she says, moving away from her front door, which she's leaning against. "Any of ya got anything good on ya?" she asks, stumbling in her heels as she blows out smoke, making a path toward me.

I shake my head. "No, I don't." And even if I did, I wouldn't give it to her.

I step to the side to go around her, but Tristan decides to stop and doesn't follow me, so I pause just behind Cami and wait for him.

"What are you looking for?" he asks, and I shake my head at him. Cami is a whore, and I mean that literally. She sells herself for money or drugs, whatever she needs at the time.

"Tristan, let's go," I say, targeting him with a look that says, *Don't go there, man.*

He looks genuinely baffled. "What?"

I nod at Cami, who seems oblivious. *No way*, I mouth.

"What do ya got?" Cami says, stepping forward. "I'll take anything. I ain't got any cash." She sticks her chest out, like she's trying to seduce him.

I don't even wait for Tristan to respond. I grab the sleeve of his shirt and tug him away. Cami yells something at us about being a tease and that we need to come back, but I keep on walking with Tristan in tow, refusing to let go of him until we reach the edge of the parking lot.

"I can't believe you were seriously considering that," I say, releasing the sleeve of his jacket.

He kicks the tip of his sneaker at the dirt. "I wasn't really . . . I was just curious what'd she say for future reference."

"You know she doesn't pay in cash, right?"

He wavers, deciding whether he really cares. "Yeah, well, it didn't hurt anything, did it?"

I opt to drop the subject and turn up the sidewalk that borders the busy street. We walk by hotels that are pretty much crack houses and by shops, heading toward another apartment complex that's about a mile down the road. It's hot, probably pushing a hundred and ten, and the heat dries out my skin, throat, and nose. The Strip, which is the main tourist area of the city, is a ways in the distance, soaring buildings and casinos that reflect the sunlight. When you walk down it at night, they're even more blinding because all the neon lights are turned on and blinking. I actually hate walking down the Strip at all. Too much going on, and it doesn't fit with all the fast motion going on in my head.

"So do you think Dylan's going to catch on that I'm ripping him off?" Tristan asks as we pause at a curb, waiting for a car to get out of the way so we can cross the street.

I rake my hand over my head. My hair's grown out and is sort of scruffy, like my face, since I haven't shaved in a while. Things like that just don't seem that important anymore. It's not like I get any benefit from looking clean. It's just a waste of my time.

"Does it really matter if he does?" I ask as we cross the street. "You don't seem like you're afraid of him."

"Who—Dylan?" Tristan snorts a laugh. "Yeah, have you seen how much weight he's lost? And he's always drunk or so doped up he can't even spell his own name."

"I think we all look like that," I say, stuffing my hands into my pockets.

"I look fine." He scowls at me. "You know, I don't get why you do that. Why you always point out where we're all headed."

"Because I don't think everyone should be headed there,"

I tell him. "Besides, sometimes I don't think everyone fully understands where they're headed."

"Well, no one really does. Not me. Not you. Not that guy walking down the street over there," he says, pointing at a guy holding up a sign that says he'll work for food.

"I think some of us do," I disagree. "I just think some won't admit it."

"You know, you're really killing my buzz," he says, annoyed. "And I know the only reason we're talking about this is because you're spun out of your mind and can't turn your thoughts and mouth off."

"I know that, but still, I really feel like I need to say it."

"Well, don't, because I don't want to hear it anymore."

"I have to." I can't seem to find the off switch to my mouth, so I just let it keep moving. "I don't get why you're here. I mean, I know you weren't the best kid ever, but still this whole drug thing...I mean, your parents care about you."

"No, they care about Ryder." His voice matches his aggravation. "And now that she's dead, they only care about her more. So I'm going to do whatever the hell I want to. And what I want to do is drugs...It makes things so much easier."

I understand what he's saying way too well. I pause, a dry, hot lump forcing its way up into my throat. "I'm sorry."

Tristan shakes his head, looking away from me and fixing his attention on the metal building beside us. "Stop saying you're sorry. Shit happened. People died. Life goes on. I'm not here because of anything you did. I'm here because this is where I choose to be and because it makes me feel better about life."

"Yeah, I guess," I mutter, not fully believing him. More bricks of guilt pile onto my shoulders and it takes a lot not to buckle to the ground.

He returns his focus to me, his eyes a little too wide against the sunlight, his forehead beaded with sweat from the scorching heat. "Now can we please stop with all the insightful tweaker talk, or I'm going to have to turn back and go do another line."

I nod, even though I don't want to stop talking, because then I'll have to think. But Tristan stays quiet, muttering shit under his breath as he picks at his arm. My eyes drift to the skyline, where the tops of the buildings and the sky meet. When the sun sets and the sky turns pastel oranges and pinks, it's actually really beautiful. It's one of the few things I can say that about anymore. Everything else seems dark, gray, and gloomy. Nothing seems beautiful, not even the stuff I saw in the past. And my future, well, it seems pretty much dead, like I'm walking toward a coffin, ready to tuck myself in and pull the lid shut. Then maybe someone will do me the favor of burying me below the dirt, where I can stop breathing, stop thinking, stop noticing how beautiful it is. The only people who will miss me are drug dealers and the people I deal to sometimes. The more I think about it, the more I just want to throw myself out in the street, hope a car hits me with enough force for my heart to stop again, because there's no point to it beating anymore. This has to be the bottom, right? There's no going back up. This is it. Yet for some reason I keep walking, talking, breathing—living.

"Did you bring your knife, by chance?" Tristan asks as we round the corner of a single-story brick building that's painted with multicolored graffiti and start to cut across the gravel parking lot to the side of it.

"Do you remember what I told you when you asked me to bring it the other day?" I say, and he shakes his head, looking stumped. "That I don't have one."

Tristan sighs as he kicks an empty beer bottle across the ground. "I'm thinking I probably should have brought..." He trails off as a sleek black Cadillac drives up and slams on its brakes, stopping right in front of us, kicking up a cloud of dust in our faces.

The windows are tinted, but I think I already know who's in there. Trace and his guys.

Tristan instantly starts to back away as the doors open up, hitching his fingers through the straps of the backpack. Two large guys get out of the back of the car, their faces very familiar, and I remember meeting them once before. Darl and Donny, Trace's pit bulls, sort of. The ones who do his dirty work.

"Shit. We have to go," Tristan says, panicking and turning to run, but I don't move. "Quinton, get the fuck out of here. Now."

Donny is holding a tire iron, and as he strolls toward us, he slams it into his palm with a threatening look on his face. I can't help but think of Roy and the many other stories I've heard about drug deals gone wrong. Broken legs. Arms. Noses. It's pretty fucking common. People get cranked up on crack and money and run on overactive adrenaline and emotion. They don't think clearly. They cheat, they steal. Hell, I've done it. I knew I could get hurt. Go to jail. Die even. Regardless of the consequences, I don't really care what happens to me. Tristan, yeah, but he's already running off. Me, I couldn't give a shit. Pain, bring it on. I deserve pain. I deserve nothing. Maybe this can be the car that runs into me and stops my heart. Besides, if I stay here, then maybe I can distract them from Tristan, give him a chance to get away. I owe him that much.

So I just stand there as Donny strides toward me, raising the iron rod like he's about to hit me, while Tristan shouts something at me, racing for the sidewalk. I could try to protect myself. Pick up something and chuck it at him, even throw a punch at him. But I don't feel like it, my heart steady in my chest, my arms resting calmly at my sides. I don't move even when he swings the tire iron straight at my face. He does it again and again, then takes a break, but only to steal the bag of crystal I have in my pocket. Then he continues striking me.

Quinton, I love you… I swear I hear Lexi's voice, but I might be tripping out.

I'm not even sure why I decide to give up at this moment. Maybe it's because I think I hear Lexi calling to me or perhaps it's that I've got so much methamphetamine racing through my bloodstream that my thoughts blur together and the good choices and the bad ones get mixed together and create confusion. Or maybe it's just that I'm tired of fighting reality and I'm finally facing my future. The future I don't have. Or maybe I've finally reached the bottom of my fall and I'm ready to walk straight on into that coffin.

Chapter Four

Nova

"Save Me" by Unwritten Law is playing from my iPod through the stereo speakers, and the trunk of the Chevy Nova is packed with all the stuff Lea and I could cram in there, the backseat packed with our instruments. The rest of our stuff we put into a storage unit. The sun is shining, the sky is blue, and there's a long stretch of road before me. It's the perfect day to be driving, but my heart sits heavy in my chest. I'm not even sure what I'm going to do when I get to Vegas. Just show up on Quinton's doorstep? Knock and say, *Hello. I'm here to save you?*

God, I sound so preachy.

Thankfully, Lea has an uncle who lives in Vegas. His name is Brandon, and he said he'd let us stay in the spare bedroom for a few weeks; otherwise we'd have to get a hotel, and we don't have a lot of cash, since we both quit our jobs for the summer and are living on our savings.

"Are you sure you're going to be okay?" I turn the stereo down, but crank up the air. It's hot and the backs of my legs are sticking to the leather seat and my hands are slippery as they hold on to the steering wheel.

Lea raises her head from the stack of papers on her lap, which she's been reading pretty much the entire drive, trying to figure out the best way to approach a drug user even though I tried to tell her papers she printed out from a random website won't necessarily help her understand *everything*, just some things. "I already told you I was, like a thousand times."

"I know." I tuck strands of hair behind my ear. "But I feel like this is all my fault."

She shakes her head and returns her focus to the papers. "What happened between Jaxon and me has been a long time coming."

"But I love you two together," I say, pulling my sunglasses over my eyes. "It hurts that you broke up."

"We were going to break up anyway," she replies, sifting through the papers. "We've been talking about it for weeks. We want two different things...He wants commitment, and he kept talking about moving in and getting engaged and me...I don't even know what I want, and until I do, I'm not committing to anything."

I can't help but think of the things I wanted from Landon, commitment and a future, and how he would never fully commit to either, which makes me wonder how long he thought about leaving this world.

I stare at the road ahead, which is lined by the desert and cacti. "It still hurts to think about it—you guys seemed like soul mates."

"I don't believe in soul mates." She clears her throat multiple times, like she's fighting back tears. "But it hurts me, too, and I don't feel like talking about it. Otherwise I'll start crying. Then you'll start crying, and I don't want to have to pull over so we can have a bawling fest, so can we please drop it for now?"

I continue to drive down the road, trying to focus on getting us to Vegas, instead of thinking about Quinton and Lea and Jaxon, or how upset my mom's going to be because I'm not coming straight home, but I think about it all. Lea and I don't speak for a while, and when I pull into the gas station just off an exit ramp to gas up, I finally decide to call my mother and tell her what's going on. I've been avoiding the call, knowing she'll worry, but I don't want to keep things from her. Plus, she thinks I'm on my way home.

"I'm going to call my mom," I tell Lea and then hand her my wallet out of my bag. "Can you put the gas in and pay?"

She puts the papers in the backseat. "Of course." She takes the wallet from me and hops out of the car as I dial my mom's number and roll down the window, because without the engine on there's no air-conditioning and it's hotter than heck.

My mom picks up after two rings and her voice is elated,

like she's super happy to hear from me. "I was just going to call you," she says. "To see when you were headed home."

"Oh." I grip the steering wheel, nervous, my palms sweating. "Yeah, about that... I'm not coming straight home."

"What do you mean?" She sounds hurt.

"I mean..." I trail off, clearing my throat. "Look, Mom, don't flip out, but I need to go to Vegas for a few weeks."

"Vegas?" she asks, now worried. "Why would you go there?"

"Because... I need to help a friend."

"What friend?" she asks, but by her disapproving tone, I think she already knows, especially since she knows I've been looking for him, not to help him or anything, but to get him to sign the release form for my video project.

I release a breath that's cramming up my airway. "You remember that guy Quinton that I told you about?"

She's quiet for quite a while, and when she speaks, she's wary. "Yeah, the one you spent time with last summer, right?"

"Yeah, that's the one... Well, I'm going to see him." I hold my breath, waiting for her reaction—waiting for her to yell at me not to go.

She pauses again, and I can hear her breathing heavily on the other end. "Why?"

"Because he needs my help." I'm surprised she's not freaking out more.

"With what?" She's not connecting the dots.

"With... with getting better," I explain evasively.

"Nova, I don't think that's a good idea," she says quickly as it clicks in her head what I'm implying—what Quinton needs help with. I told her enough about last summer that she knows about him, but what she doesn't know is about the car accident. So I tell her the details of the crash quickly as Lea heads in to pay for the gas. I make sure to tell her everything important, what he went through, how I feel about helping him—how important this is to me. When I finish, my mom's silent, and I'm anxious about how she's going to react.

"So Lea's with you?" she finally asks. My mom likes Lea a lot. I brought her home for Christmas last year, and my mom spent a lot of time talking with her and hasn't been able to stop beaming about her since.

I stare at the gas station window, where I can see Lea at the counter paying. "She is."

"How long are you going to be down there?" she asks, and I'm surprised she's made it this far without fighting it more.

"I'm not sure yet . . . It all sort of depends."

"On what?"

"On how bad he is," I say, wiping my sweaty palms on the sides of my shorts.

"Nova . . . I don't think it's such a good idea . . ." She searches for the right words, panic seeping in, afraid she's going to lose her daughter again. "I mean, you barely got over this kind of stuff yourself, and I'm worried that it'll be too easy for you to fall back into that stuff."

"Mom, I'm a lot stronger than I used to be," I assure her.

"And I have Lea here to keep an eye on me, and you know how good she is at that stuff."

She sighs heavyheartedly. "I'm still worried, and I don't think I can just let you go."

"I'm worried, too, but about Quinton," I tell her. "Mom, he doesn't have anyone else to help him, at least from what I know. And if you get really worried, you can come down and check up on me. It's only like an eight-hour drive, but I promise I'll be okay."

"You'd let me check up on you?" she asks, astounded.

"Yeah, because I know there's going to be nothing to check up on," I say. "I'm going to be okay. I can do this—I want to help him. And I need to, not just for him...but for me...This is just something I have to do, whether you like it or not." I hate adding the last part, but it needs to be done to get my point across that she can't talk me out of this.

She's silent again, and it's driving me crazy. Although I'll still go no matter what she says, I want her to support me and I wish she would relax. But I do understand where she's coming from, considering what I've put her through in the past.

My mom's still not saying anything when Lea gets into the car. She drops a large bag of Cheetos in between us, along with a bottle of water and a bottle of Dr Pepper, then shuts the door. She gives me a weird look as I start the engine and crank the air-conditioning. She starts to say something, but I hold up my finger.

"Mom, are you there?" I ask, rolling up the window.

"Yeah, I'm here." She exhales loudly. "All right. I'll let you do this, but I'm not happy about it at all. And I want you to call me three times a day at least, and if things get bad, I need Lea to tell me. Not you."

I'm a little wounded by her last remark, but at the same time I can't blame her. All that time I spent telling her I was okay, when I was dying inside—she knows how easily I can be silent when things get hard.

"Okay," I tell her, knowing she can't really force me to do anything, since I'm an adult. Calling her is just me trying to be a good daughter and let her know my plans. "I can do that for you."

"Now put Lea on the phone," she says in a stern tone.

"What? Why?"

"Because I want to talk to her."

"Okay...hold on." I hand Lea the phone.

Lea takes it, her face contorting with confusion. "What's up?" she asks me, staring down at the screen.

"She wants to talk to you," I explain, putting the car into drive. "But I don't know about what."

Lea places the phone up to her ear and says hello as I drive back onto the freeway. They chat for a while, Lea keeping her answers pretty simple. Eventually Lea hangs up and puts my phone down on the seat between us. She doesn't say anything, opening up the bag of Cheetos as she relaxes back in the seat and aiming the vent at her face.

"So are you going to tell me what she said?" I ask.

Lea shrugs as she pops a Cheeto into her mouth. "Nothing much. She just told me to keep an eye on you, which I was already planning on doing." She puts her feet up on the dash. "She really cares about you, you know."

"I know," I say, taking a handful of Cheetos. "I hate that she's worried."

"You should be glad that she does worry. It means she loves you." She says it sadly, probably thinking about her own mom and their strained relationship since her father took his own life and her mother left Lea and her sister to live with their grandmother, because she couldn't handle being a mother alone. I think she's been trying to get back into Lea's life, but Lea's struggling with it.

"I am glad." I switch lanes, then wipe my Cheeto fingers on the side of my shorts. "But I hate worrying her."

And I do. I've put my mom through enough already, but going to Vegas—to Quinton—is something I have to do. If I don't, I'll always look back and regret it, and like Lea's tattoo says, I don't want to live my life with regrets. I have a lot of them in my life and I don't want any more.

Lea and I eat Cheetos and talk about what we're going to do for the next few weeks until the city comes into view. Then Lea sits up, lowering her feet to the floor, and leans forward to look at the city sinfully glinting in the distance. "God, it's small, yet it's not."

I nod in agreement as I take in the uniquely shaped towers and buildings stretching toward the sky, and the massive billboards on the sides of the road trying to convince us of how much fun we're going to have.

"You know, I came here a few times when I was younger," Lea says. "But I never went directly into the city onto the Strip…but now I'm sort of curious."

"It looks intense," I remark, checking the GPS on the dash for directions. "This thing says we don't even go into the city to get to your uncle's house."

Lea slumps back in the seat and turns the air-conditioning up a notch. "Well, we'll have to go do something fun."

"Don't you have to be twenty-one to do things in Vegas?" I ask as the voice on the GPS tells me to make a turn in 1.5 miles.

She shakes her head. "No. I mean, you have to be twenty-one to gamble and shit, but there's a ton of other stuff we could do, like go see bands play or do karaoke. It could be a lot of fun."

I remove my hand from the shifter and extend it to her, not really wanting to go out while I'm here, but she seems sad and maybe going out could cheer her up. "Okay, it's a deal. We'll go out and have some fun while we're here."

She smiles as we shake on it. "Deal."

We let go of each other's hands and I put mine back on the shifter, tapping the brakes as I follow the GPS's instructions and make a right off the nearest off-ramp. As we pass by average-looking houses, I wonder what kind of place Quinton's living in. I have an idea, since I saw the place he lived in a year ago: a trailer in a very run-down trailer park that had a lot of druggies living in it.

My thoughts remain focused on Quinton's living situation

until I pull into a neighborhood where all the houses look identical and so do the yards. There are sprinklers watering the grass and people outside checking their mailboxes, working on their cars, walking their dogs. This neighborhood has sort of a homey feel to it, which I wasn't expecting in a place nicknamed Sin City.

"Which one is it?" I ask as the GPS announces I've arrived at my destination.

Lea points at the house at the end of the cul-de-sac, a decent single-story stucco home with a garage, and a lawn in front of it. The driveway is empty and there's a fence around the backyard, but it's short and I can easily see over it.

I park in the driveway in front of the shut garage door. "Is he home?"

Lea takes off her seat belt and cracks her door. "No. I told you he was out of town for a few days on some business trip or something, but he said there's a key under a flowerpot in the back and we could just let ourselves in."

We get out and meet at the front of the car. The first thing I notice is the heat, like I've just stepped into a sauna, only there's no moisture and it's like it's feeding on mine.

"Holy hell, it's hot." I fan my hand in front of my face.

"Yeah, desert heat," she says, walking toward the side of the house. "You got to love it."

I follow her as she wanders to the fence line and peeks into the backyard. There are a few neighbors outside in their yards and driveways, and one of them, a heavier guy with a visor on his head, watches us like we're about to rob the place.

"What if someone calls the cops on us?" I ask as she swings her leg over the fence.

She shrugs as she grabs the top of the chain-link fence and hoists herself over it onto the grass. "Then they call my uncle and he can tell them that they're crazy," she says as she lands on the other side and wipes the sweat off her forehead with the back of her hand.

I glance back at the neighbor guy still eyeing us and then put my leg over the fence and climb to the other side, brushing the dirt off on the back of my shorts. The backyard has a Jacuzzi in it, along with a flower garden and a gazebo that has a bunch of wind chimes hanging on it.

"Is your cousin married?" I ask as we round the corner of the house. "Or single?"

"He's single, thirty-four, and from what I remember, he takes up all these weird hobbies, like collecting wind chimes." She nods at the collection of them singing against the gentle, hot breeze.

"What's he do for a living?"

"He works at a bank."

"A bank." I sidestep a large flowerpot. "That sounds..."

"Boring," Lea says, grinning over her shoulder at me. "Yeah, Brandon is pretty boring, which is why it's good we're staying with him. He'll keep us out of trouble."

I smile as she strolls up to the sliding glass door. "You are the best friend ever."

"You know we're going to have to get friendship bracelets

or something and then push them together every time you say it," she jokes as she cups her hands around her eyes and peers through the glass.

"Sounds like a plan," I joke back, walking up to a flower-pot beside the door. I lift it up but there's no key under it. "Okay, no key."

"Hold on." Lea comes over and crouches down beside me. Then she rubs her hand across the bottom of the flowerpot, pulling at something. When she pulls back, she has a key in her hand.

"Ta-da," she announces, holding the key up as she picks some tape off it and straightens her legs.

"Bravo." I clap my hands.

She grins, pleased with herself, as she presses her hand against her chest. "What can I say? I'm a genius."

I glance at the sliding glass door, which obviously doesn't take a key. "All right, genius, now figure out where the key goes."

She pauses, looking around the back of the house as she taps her lip. "Huh, that's interesting."

"Is there a garage door?" I ask, stepping to the corner of the house.

"I'm not sure." She follows me. "He just moved into the house, like six months ago, so I've never been here."

I backtrack to the fence and find the door to the garage. Lea nudges me out of the way with her elbow so she can put the key in the lock. It fits and the door opens up.

"Hell yeah." She raises her hand in the air as she grins proudly.

We high-five and then step inside the garage, which

doesn't have a car in it, just shelves and boxes and a couple of four-wheelers. I can't help but think about my garage back home filled with boxes of my old stuff, a lot of it connected to Landon. I was planning on going through my things when I got there this summer, because I can now. I was going to make an album with the photos and some of Landon's sketches. I have to make sure I do it after I'm done taking care of stuff here. It's important.

After we go into the house and unlock the front door, Lea and I unload the trunk of the car and put all our stuff in the guest room at the back of the house beside the den. It's a nice place, clean carpet, tile floors, with two bedrooms and two bathrooms. The furniture is plain, but not trashy, and there are a few photos hanging on the wall in the living room, one of which Lea tells me is of her dad and her uncle.

"Your dad kind of looks like you," I tell her and then take a drink from a glass of water, parched and sweaty after being out in the heat. In the photo are two guys, one short and one tall, but their facial features are the same, one's just a lot younger— Lea's uncle. It looks like they've just gone fishing and Lea's dad is holding up a fish, looking proud of it. He actually seems really happy, all smiles and pride, and I want to ask her when the picture was taken, how long before he decided to end his life, but I'm not going to because it'll bring up painful emotions for her. I know, because whenever someone mentions Landon's name I still feel a sting in my heart.

"Thank you," she says, then turns away from the photo

and plops down on the brown leather couch. She kicks her feet up on the coffee table, picks up the remote from the armrest of the sofa, and aims it at the flat-screen mounted on the wall. "How about we watch a little *Ridiculousness?*"

I set my glass of water down on an end table, then cross my arms over my chest and walk to the sofa but don't sit down. "I don't want to seem crazy or anything, but I really want to go see Quinton before I do anything."

The television screen clicks on, and she glances outside at the sun setting, the sky a palette of colors and the city nearly glowing in the distance. "Nova, it's getting late…Maybe we should wait until morning. I mean, you haven't even called your mom and told her we got here and you know she's going to worry."

"I know." I sit down on the back of the sofa. "I was actually going to wait to do that until I talked to Quinton first…see how long I'm going to be down here, so I can give her a better idea."

She sets the remote down on the sofa cushion and turns around to face me. "And how exactly are you going to determine that?"

"I have no idea." I run my fingers through my dry, limp hair. "I honestly have no idea what the hell I'm doing. All I know is that I have to do…something."

She presses her lips together, contemplating. "From the papers I printed from the Internet, it sounds like meth addicts can be super moody."

"I think that's the case with all drugs, not just meth."

"Yeah, but meth addicts are worse."

"I sort of guessed so." Actually, I hadn't. Actually, I have no idea what I'm doing. Shit, what am I going to say to him when I first see him? Why haven't I planned this out more? *Jesus, Nova.*

"Relax," Lea says, noting my anxiety. "The papers said there're also support groups and counseling, and I'm sure there's probably something in Vegas...I'll look into it."

"Thank you," I tell her, then grow silent again, staring outside at the city glittering in the distance, wondering where he is. If he's walking around or at home. Or is he someplace worse? What if the address he gave me isn't even real and he's really homeless?

"Oh, for the love of God, Nova." She gets to her feet, snatching her keys up from the end table. "Let's go."

I quickly stand up from the back of the couch. "Right now?"

She rolls her eyes and opens the front door. "If we don't, then you're going to sit there and space off on me all night."

She's probably right, but nerves knot in my stomach. "I feel sick." I wrap my arm across my belly.

"That's your nerves." She moves away from the door and grabs my hand, giving me a gentle tug. "Now, come on. I'll drive so you can space off and overthink stuff."

"You know me too well," I say, then glance down at my tank top and shorts, which have a small stain on the hem. "Maybe I should change."

"You look great." She pulls me over the threshold and outside. "You always do." She releases my hand, reaches back inside, turns the lock, and flips on the porch light before shutting the door. Then she tucks the house key into the pocket of her shorts and heads down the cement path toward the car. "Besides, I really doubt he's going to be focusing on your looks."

"I know," I say, rounding the front of the car to the passenger side. "You're right. I'm just nervous." Really nervous, to the point where I'm going to throw up. But I force the taste of vomit back down my throat and get in the car, opening up the glove box, where I'd put the piece of paper I wrote Quinton's address on. Lea gets in and starts the engine, flipping the headlights on while I type the address into the GPS.

I examine the map on the screen. "It says it's only five miles away."

"Five miles in Vegas can take quite a while." She buckles her seat belt and so do I. "And I'm a little worried about the place we're going to."

"What do you mean?"

"I mean that there are some areas that are super sketchy."

"And you're guessing he's living in one of these areas?"

"I don't want to make assumptions. I mean, I'm sure there are plenty of drug addicts who live in nice houses and who you would never think are drug addicts, but..." She trails off, adjusting the rearview mirror.

"But he doesn't even have a phone or a job," I say, slumping back in the seat. "So I'm guessing the place he's living in isn't fancy, if he even lives in a place...I've already thought of this, but I still want to go—I need to know, Lea. I need to know what happened to the guy who made me feel things again..."

She offers me a sympathetic smile as she pushes the car into reverse. Lea isn't the best driver, and when she presses the gas she ends up giving it too much and the car jerks backward. My hand shoots out toward the dashboard and I hold on.

Hold on for dear life, knowing I'm going to have to.

Quinton

I feel like I'm dying, coming in and out of consciousness, every bone in my body bruised. I can hear voices telling me to snap out of it, but I can't seem to get my eyes to open. I can feel memories returning to me, ones I don't want to remember and one in particular I've made myself forget, yet I can't seem to stop myself from fading into it.

I'm going to die. I can feel it, through the lack of pain, the numbness in my chest, the coldness in the air. But I'm also warm, from the blood that's soaked my chest, my clothes, soaked its way from inside me to the outside. It's the feel of death all over me, and I embrace it, knowing that if I do survive, there won't be anything left for me but anguish and solitude.

I stare up at the sky as I lie beside Lexi, choking on my own tears as I hold her cold, lifeless hand. I focus on the stars, wanting to touch them until they begin to fade, one by one, my heartbeat fading with them. The sky gets darker, along with everything around me, until I can't see a thing. I can feel my breath leaving me, my chest becoming heavier but my thoughts becoming lighter. Free.

The ground below me softens, the sky dimming until I can see only blackness. It feels like I'm moving... sinking... or maybe I'm flying... I can't tell. I don't care. I just want to keep feeling this way, because it's taking the pain of Lexi's death with it. The agony... it's gone... my guilt... it doesn't exist. The fact that I ruined our future doesn't matter, because we're leaving this world together...

"Quinton...wake up, man..."

Go away...

"Quinton..." Somebody shakes my shoulder. "Seriously, wake up, man...You're freaking the shit out of me."

Leave me alone.

"Wake up!" someone shouts.

Just let me die...please...

I just want to die.

God, please just let me die.

Chapter Five

Nova

I'm not sure what to do, what to think, how to process what I'm seeing. Deep down I think I knew, but I didn't prepare myself very well for it. I should have. I should have told myself that this was what I was going to walk into, so that I wouldn't be sitting here with my jaw hanging to my knees, feeling like I want to throw up, then curl up in a ball and cry until I run out of tears. My OCD is kicking in, and the desire to count the windows on the buildings, the stars in the sky, the lines on the back of my hand, anything so I don't have to look at the horrible view in front of me, is overpowering.

"You were right," I say to Lea, dumbstruck as I grip the edge of the seat, my palms damp against the upholstery.

"I know." She frowns at the view in front of us. "I'm so sorry, Nova...I don't even know what to say."

"It's not your fault," I tell her, opening and shutting my eyes, wishing the view would disappear, but it doesn't.

"I know, but I'm still sorry," she replies, her hands gripping the steering wheel.

When the GPS first led us to the two-story apartment building, I thought it'd given us the wrong directions, since the building looked more like a very large abandoned motel than a place where people would live, but after double-checking, I painfully realized it was the right place. Half the windows are busted out, some are boarded up, and the rest have curtains hanging up to block the windows, probably to hide what's going on inside—drugs, prostitution, God knows what else. The building sits away from a road that's lined with second-hand stores, discount and smoke shops, run-down houses, some looking worse than the apartment building. In fact, I'm pretty sure it's the nicest place on the block.

Lea parks a ways back in the gravel parking lot and then turns off the headlights, like she's scared someone is going to see us. We lock the doors and leave the engine running. There are hardly any vehicles around, and the ones that are parked in the area look like they haven't moved in ages. There's a massive billboard near the entryway, but the paint is peeling off and I can't tell what it used to be an advertisement for. There are also a group of women loitering at the bottom of the stairway, smoking cigarettes, chatting and being really loud. I don't want to be judgmental, but they look like hookers, wearing tight dresses, bras for tops, and five-inch stilettos or knee-high boots.

We have the air cranked up full blast and the sky is nearly black, the sunlight about to completely disappear behind the horizon. Behind us the city flashes in the distance, neon colors and sparkling sighs, and I can almost feel the electricity in the air.

"What number did you say it was?" Lea asks as she pushes the emergency brake on.

I check the screen of the GPS. "It says twenty-two, but..."
I look back up at the building, squinting to see if the doors
have numbers on them. There are lights above some of the
doors and I can tell some have numbers, but not all of them.

"Maybe we should come back in the morning," Lea suggests, biting her fingernails as she eyes the group of women
near the stairway. Lea has never been part of the drug world,
and even though she's gone to parties, they've been mellow
parties with kegs and wine coolers, where people hang out and
dance, not get stoned and either pass out or trip out of their
minds.

I want to say yes to her suggestion and tell her we should
go home, but at the same time I can't help but think of the
what-ifs. Like what if I walk away right at this moment and
something bad happens to Quinton tonight? Or what if he
vanishes overnight? Plus, knowing he's probably right there,
in one of the apartments just in front of me, makes it hard to
walk away. What if I miss my chance like I did with Landon?
What if I leave and never get the courage to come back? What
if something bad happens?

Shit.

Nova, stop it.

Stop thinking about the past.

Focus on the future.

"Okay." I pry my fingers off the edge of the seat, then
reach over my shoulder to grab the seat belt. "I'll come back in
the morning when the sun's up."

"*We'll* come back." She pops the emergency brake. "I don't want you coming here alone, and I promised your mom I'd take care of you."

"I feel like a child," I admit, buckling the seat belt. "And you're my babysitter...I feel like my mom should be paying you or something."

"She just loves you," Lea says as she starts to put the shifter forward. "And I'm happy to do it...It's not like I have anything better to do."

I hesitate. "Lea, are you sure you don't want to talk about what happened with you and Jaxon?"

She bites her bottom lip as she fights back the tears. "Not yet...I just can't yet, okay? Especially not here."

"Okay...well, I'm here when you're ready." I sit back, fidgeting with the leather band on my wrist. I feel restless but attempt to hold still as she starts to back the Chevy Nova out of the parking lot, cranking the wheel to the side. I start to settle down as she gets the car turned around, but then I see a guy walking up beside the car, heading for the apartments with a large bag of ice in his hand.

"Wait a minute..." I mutter, leaning toward the window. "I know him."

"What do you mean you know him?" Lea asks, pressing on the gas.

I don't respond, too fixated on an old memory walking just to the side of me, like a ghost. Even in the dark, I recognize Tristan's blond hair and facial features immediately, although his cheeks are a little sunken and either his pants are just really baggy or he's lost a lot of weight. Still, I know it's him.

He looks like he's in a hurry, smoking a cigarette as he strides for the apartments, his lips moving like he's talking to himself.

"Stop the car," I say, reaching for the door handle.

"Nova, what the hell!" Lea exclaims as I crack the door open before she can even get the car stopped. She taps on the brakes, and I push the door open all the way and swing one of my legs outside. But then I pause when the seat belt locks and jerks me back against the seat.

"Shit," I curse and press back against the seat to unbuckle it.

"What are you doing?" Lea asks with wide eyes as she holds her foot on the brake, keeping the car halted at a crooked angle.

"I know that guy." I push the door open the rest of the way as Tristan starts to take notice of us—or the car, anyway. He pauses to admire it as I land just outside the car with an ungraceful stumble but regain my balance quickly.

He grazes his thumb across the cigarette, sprinkling ash on the ground before putting it back between his lips. "Hey, what kind of car is that...?" He trails off as I step forward and the lights from the motel and the street give him just enough of a glow to see my face. "Holy shit, Nova," he says with a bit of a startled laugh, his lips parting and his cigarette nearly falling out of his mouth. He quickly plucks it from his lips and positions it between his fingers, continuing to gape at me. "Where the hell did you come from?"

I point back at my car. "I drove here," I say, not ready to tell him the real reason. Tristan, while nice for the most part, is also in as deep as Quinton is, and the last thing I want to do is declare to him why I wanted—*needed*—to come down here.

"I can tell that..." He looks at the car with appreciation. The lights around us fall across his face and I'm even more aware of how different he looks: tougher, rougher, harder, drowning in more darkness, and I wonder what exactly he's been doing to get to this place. "Is that your car?" he asks.

"Yeah, it's mine." I wrap my arms around myself, even though it's not cold. It's almost like a defense mechanism as old feelings press up like shards of glass and vivid memories of the time I spent with Tristan swarm through my mind. "It was my dad's... or used to be, anyway."

His brows knit. "You didn't drive that back in Maple Grove, did you?"

I shake my head. "No. I always rode around in Delilah's truck."

"Yeah... she actually got rid of that a few months ago," he says. "Sold it, you know, so she could have some cash."

I don't say anything, because I can't think of anything to say. Things are awkward and uncomfortable because I know him, even kissed him, yet at the same time I don't know him. I've spent time with him, but the person I got to know doesn't look like he exists anymore. That Tristan is part of my past, and I wonder how hard it's going to be with Quinton, seeing a different side of him.

Can I do this? Was I naïve to believe that I could? Am I even strong enough to do this? You couldn't save Landon, but did you even try hard enough?

"Nova, are you okay?" The sound of Lea's voice brings back some of my strength because I remember that I'm not alone.

I glance over my shoulder at her. The engine's still running, the exhaust puffing out smoke, but she's gotten out of the car and is looking over the roof at me with concern on her face.

"I'm fine," I assure her, but it's only partly true, because I'm fine yet I'm terrified. I wish I could say that I was braver, that I was walking into this with confidence and certainty that I was the right person to be helping Quinton. But I'm not. I want to be, though.

I return my attention to Tristan, who's glancing back and forth between Lea and me with a quizzical look on his face. He starts to open his mouth, but I casually interrupt him.

"Is Quinton around?" My voice comes out surprisingly evenly, and I think maybe, just maybe, I'm going to be okay.

"Yeah, he is, but…" Tristan glances down at the bag of ice in his hand and then slaps his forehead with his hand, the one holding the cigarette, and the cherry falls to the ground. "Shit. I forgot I was supposed to be bringing this to him." He rushes off toward the apartments, acting as though he didn't just burn himself.

Just how numb is he? I hurry after him, across the gravel parking lot, even when Lea calls out for me to wait.

"Can I talk to him?" I ask as I catch up with Tristan. "I really need to."

He blinks and looks at me as we walk past a beat-up car that has four flat tires. "If you can get him to wake up, you can."

I hear the sound of gravel crunching behind us as Lea rushes up, panting to catch her breath. "Jesus, Nova, thanks for leaving me."

"Sorry," I apologize, but I'm distracted by what Tristan said. *If I can get him to wake up, I can?* My heart shrivels inside my chest, yet it still beats intensely. "Is he...? What's he on?"

"Nothing at the moment, really." He waves at the group of hookers/women as we approach them, and one of them whistles back at him.

Another one, with really long legs and bright blue hair, struts forward with a grin on her face. "Hey, can I get a taste?" she asks Tristan, tracing her neon-pink fingernails up his arm.

"Maybe later." Tristan flashes her a smile as he keeps walking, seeming preoccupied as he clutches the bag of ice and mutters something under his breath. When we reach the bottom of the stairway, he unexpectedly stops and so do I, causing Lea to run straight into my back.

"Look, Nova." He glances up at the balcony above us. "I'm not sure you want to go inside there...It's not really your thing."

"I'll be fine." I grip the railing as my own voice echoes in my head. *You won't be fine. What if what you see is bad? More than you can handle?* "I just want to talk to Quinton."

"And that's great, but like I said, he's not awake right now." He shifts his weight, his blond hair falling into his eyes, which are blue, but look black because they're so dilated.

"Well, can I wake him up?" I ask. "I really, really need to talk to him."

As he assesses me, for the briefest of seconds I see the guy I used to know: the one who was a decent guy, who wouldn't hurt anyone, who talked to me, hung out with me. But the look quickly vanishes as he glances coldly at Lea. "Who's that?"

"A friend of mine." I slant to the side to block Lea from his death stare.

His eyes fasten on me. "Is she cool?"

I understand his code meaning: *Does she care that there are drugs around?* "Yeah, she's fine."

Lea steps forward and rolls her eyes as she gestures at herself. "Do I look like someone who's going to narc on your little drug nest? Seriously, paranoid much?" She sounds calm, but I can feel the tenseness flowing off her.

Tristan scans her eyes, framed with kohl liner, her black tank top and red-and-black shorts, the tattoos on her arms and the piercings in her ears. "I don't know...Are you?"

She crosses her arms and elevates her chin, radiating confidence. "No, I'm not."

Tristan scratches his head, looking torn. I notice small dots on his arms, some ringed by tiny bruises. I know what they are and so does Lea, and when Tristan glances up at the top floor again, Lea aims a pressing look at me.

I'm sorry, I mouth, and give her hand a squeeze. The dampness of her skin gives off just how nervous she is, and it makes me feel even worse. I look over at the Chevy Nova parked crookedly at the back of the parking lot, about to tell her to go back and wait in it—or go back home—but Tristan interrupts my thoughts.

"Yeah, you can go in and see if you can get him to wake up," he says, looking back at me and lowering his arm to the side. "But I'm warning you—it's pretty bad."

"What's pretty bad?" I wonder as I follow him up the stairs. I quickly whisper over my shoulder to Lea, "You can go back and wait in the car."

"Hell no," she hisses, glancing over her shoulder at two loud guys who have appeared at the bottom of the stairway. "I feel less safe in there. Just go . . . I want to get this over with anyway."

"I owe you big-time," I whisper.

"Yeah, you do," she agrees quietly.

Tristan pauses at the top of the steps and moves aside so we can step by him. "He got his ass beat a couple of hours ago, and he's been passed out ever since."

"Quinton got beat up?" I'm stunned as fear pulsates through me.

Tristan nods. "Yeah, it happens sometimes."

He says it so casually, like it doesn't matter, but it does. Quinton matters. And suddenly nothing else matters but getting to Quinton. I rush up the last few steps, urging Tristan to get a move on with a motion of my hand. "I need to see him." I know it's sort of a demanding thing to do, but I don't really care. He's just walking around with a damn bag of ice in his hand while Quinton could be seriously hurt, and he doesn't even seem coherent enough to fully grasp how absurd it is.

And the fact that he doesn't seem coherent makes me worry even more, because what if Quinton's dying or something—I doubt Tristan would even be able to tell.

"All right," Tristan says, as calm as can be, and then signals for me to follow him as he heads to the left. "I'll lead the way."

Shaking my head, I follow him across the balcony and past the apartment doors. The entire place reeks like cigarette smoke mixed with weed, and it throws me back to a place I don't necessarily want to forget, but that I don't like to remember either.

There's a ton of beer bottles and buckets of cigarette butts around the fronts of the doors, old shoes, shirts, plates of rotting food, and one door is surrounded by a lot of trash bags that smell awful. There's even a plastic chair and table in front of one of the doors, with a guy slumped over it, passed out with what looks like a joint still burning in his hand.

"Is that guy going to be okay?" I nod at the guy as the smoke burns at the back of my throat and nose.

I remember.

God, I do.

It smells and tastes just the same.

Feels the same.

The numbness…the way it momentarily takes everything away.

Stop remembering.

Forget.

Remember who you are now.

As much as I fight it, I remember everything. The feelings of being lost, drifting, numb, yet content at the same time.

Detached, floating, flying, running away from my problems. I was sinking, in mud, in drugs, in life. And Quinton was there, sinking right beside me, holding my hand as we went down together, but he told me I was too good for it—that I was better than the things I was doing. He did what he could to get me to stop sinking, even though he wanted to sink himself. That day he left me in the pond, he showed me that aside from the drugs, he was a good guy. He didn't take advantage of my drifting, my confusion, my mourning.

Tristan pauses near the table and follows my gaze to the guy with the joint. "Oh, that's Bernie, and yeah, he'll be fine. He does that sometimes." He plucks the joint out of Bernie's hands, and I think he's going to smoke it, but instead he puts it out in the ashtray. When he catches me staring at him funny, he shrugs. "What? It's not my thing anymore." He starts down the balcony again, glancing over his shoulder at me. "Not really, anyway."

It takes a lot not to stare at the track marks on his arms and keep my eyes focused ahead. Lea mutters something under her breath, staying just behind me with her arms wrapped around herself. Tristan starts humming some song as he strolls past door after door. I don't recognize it, but I wish I did for no other reason than that it would be a distraction. I could sing the lyrics in my head, find solitude in music, like I've done many times.

When I check on Lea, she has her eyes fixed on pretty much everything, taking in a world she's never been in. Hell, I've never even been in it, not like this, anyway. This is so different from the trailer park—much more dangerous-looking.

Its own dark place hidden from the world and the light and I'm not sure what it'll take to get Quinton out of here, but I need to find that out.

I take slow breath after slow breath, forcing myself not to count them or my heartbeats or how many steps it's taking me to get to the door. How many stars are in the sky or how many lights there are on a casino just across the street.

Finally Tristan stops in front of one of the doors and looks back at the parking lot, like he's checking on something. I'm proud of myself for not running to numbers to calm myself down, but when he opens the door, my pride crashes and shatters like the pile of glass on the floor just inside the door.

"Welcome to our palace," Tristan jokes as he shoves the door open. The doorknob bangs against the wall behind it, causing the really bony guy slumped on the couch to let out a grunt as he turns over. I think I recognize the intricate tattoos on his arms, most in black, but some in crimson and indigo, but I'm having a hard time placing him.

As I enter, stepping over the threshold and out of the light of the porch, the first thing I notice is the smell. It stinks. Not just like weed or cigarette smoke, but like garbage, rotting food, dirt, grime, sweaty people, and there's this really musty smell, like a humidifier is on nearby, yet I can't see one anywhere. It's all mixed together and it stings at my nostrils. I wonder if this is how the trailer smelled and I was just oblivious to it—if I was oblivious to a lot of things.

On the floor are three 1970s lamps with beads hanging off

the shades, one of which is tipped over but still on. There's a
large blanket with a tiger on it hanging over the window and
the ceiling fan is on, but it's missing one of the blades and it
makes this thumping sound as it moves. There's no carpet on
the floor, and there are holes in the walls, water stains on the
ceiling, and crack pipes on the floor. It reminds me so much of
the trailer they used to live in, only much shittier (and that's
putting it nicely). I'm both repulsed by it and drawn to what's
hidden beneath the surface, the crevices, the pipes on the floor.
My senses are heightened because I know that just one or two
hits and I'd probably feel twenty times more subdued at the
moment, instead of so anxious I feel like I'm going to combust.
At least if it were weed, but Delilah told me on the phone that
they were into meth now.

"So this is our place," Tristan says, switching the bag of ice
to his other hand as he weaves between the two old sofas. Then
he gestures at the person on one of them. "And that's Dylan…
You remember Dylan, right?"

I slowly nod, trying not to look so stunned, but I can't
help it. Yeah, Dylan was always a little scraggly-looking, but he
looks like a skeleton now, his bald head showing every bump
and divot in his skull and his arms as scrawny as mine. And
Tristan looks worse under the dim light of the living room, his
skin pallid and his hair really greasy and thinning. There's a
red mark on his forehead from the cigarette, and he has a few
scabs on his cheeks and neck. Only two things run through
my mind at the moment. One, what the hell is Quinton going

to look like? And two, what the hell would I look like now if I hadn't walked away from this life?

"And that's the kitchen." He nods at a ratty curtain draped over a clothesline.

I don't say anything because there's nothing to say. I follow him across the living room, noting that the pungent smell in the air is amplified as I get closer to the curtain. It makes me wonder what the hell's behind it, but also lucky that I don't have to see, since it's probably going to push at my anxiety even more.

As Tristan starts down a narrow hallway, I peer over my shoulder at Lea. She's horrified, her enlarged eyes looking around at the glass bongs, the roach clips, the ashtrays, and a syringe on the floor. When her gaze meets mine, I can tell she's realizing the extent of what I went through last summer. And although I don't think I ever made it this far, I still was hovering over the fall that could lead to this, and this could have become my life—I could have ended here.

"So try not to freak out," Tristan tells me as he halts in front a shut door near the end of the hallway.

My body goes rigid. "Why would I freak out...? God, Tristan, how bad is he?"

"Personally, I think he looks worse than he really is." He grips the doorknob, pressing his other hand to his chest, the one holding the bag of ice, and the bag knocks against his stomach. "But I'm not sure if you'll agree."

My muscles ravel into even more knots as he opens the

door, and my breath hitches in my throat at what's on the other side of it. A room about the size of a closet with clothes and coins all over the linoleum floor, along with a mirror, razor, and a small plastic bag. And just beside the doorway, there's a lumpy mattress on the floor, and Quinton's lying on it.

Quinton.

His arm hangs lifelessly over the side of the mattress and his eyes are shut, his body motionless, and the leaky ceiling is dripping filthy water on him. And his face…the bruises…the swelling…the cuts…If I couldn't see his scarred chest rising and falling, I'd think he was dead.

"Oh my God." I cover my mouth with my hand, tears stinging at my eyes, my gut twisting in knots.

He looks dead. Just like Landon. Only there's no rope, just bruises and cuts and a room full of the darkness that's consumed his life.

"Relax." Tristan sets the bag of ice down on the floor just inside the doorway. "I already told you he looks worse than he is."

"No, he looks as bad as he is," I argue in a harsh tone, my heart plunging into my stomach as I push my way into the room and stop when I get to the mattress. "What happened to him?"

"I told you. He got beat up," Tristan replies, standing in the doorway right in front of Lea.

"And why didn't you take him to a hospital?" Lea asks in a clipped tone, giving Tristan a hard look that makes him lean back a little.

"Um, because hospitals draw attention, especially when

you've got all kinds of shit running in your blood," Tristan says with zero sympathy, and I realize I don't like this Tristan very much. The old Tristan I knew was a lot nicer, but this one seems like an asshole. "And the last thing we need is more attention drawn to us."

Lea glares at him as she crosses her arms. "Wow, what a friend you are."

"I'm not his friend," Tristan points out. "I'm his cousin."

"And that changes things because?" Lea asks with irritation.

"What the fuck is your deal?" Tristan retorts, stepping toward her.

They start arguing but I barely hear them, their voices quickly fading into the background as I focus on Quinton. I want to help him—it's what I came here to do. But this... I don't even know what to do with this. He's hurt, bleeding, unconscious. I don't know how long he's been like this, what he did to end up like this, what kind of drugs he has in his system, or if he'll act like Tristan when he wakes up.

I need to do something.

I carefully kneel on the mattress, and it sinks beneath my weight. He's changed since I last saw him, his jaw scruffy, but more defined, since he's lost weight. His hair's grown out a little and he looks shaggy and rough. He's shirtless, and the muscles that once defined his stomach and chest are gone, his lean arms now lanky. The only things that are really the same are the indistinct scar over his top lip, the large scar on his chest, and the tattoos on his arm: *Lexi*, *Ryder*, and *No One*.

Before, I wondered what they meant, but now I'm pretty sure I know. Lexi was his girlfriend, Ryder was his cousin and probably Tristan's sister, and No One is Quinton. How can he think of himself as no one? How can he think he doesn't matter? God, it's like I'm back with Landon again and I'm looking at him withering inside himself.

"Nothing I say or do matters in this world, Nova," he says to me as he leans back on his hands, staring at a tree in front of us. "When I'm gone, the world will keep moving."

"That's not true," I say, stunned by his declaration. Sure, he gets depressed sometimes, but this is dark and heavy and hurts me to hear. "I won't be able to keep moving."

"Yes, you will," he says, sitting up and cupping my cheek with his hand as we sit at the bottom of the hill in his backyard. The sun gleams down on us and there's not really a point to what we're doing other than to be with each other, which is fine with me.

"No, I won't," I argue. "If you die, I'll die right along with you."

He smiles sadly and shakes his head. "No, you won't; you'll see."

"No, I won't see." I scoot away from his touch, getting frustrated. "Because you're not leaving before me," I say. "Promise me you won't. Promise me that we'll grow old together and that I'll go first."

He starts to laugh like I'm amusing, but it's stiff and his smile doesn't reach his eyes. "Nova, you know I can't promise that when I have no control over life and death."

"I don't care," I say, knowing I'm being irrational, but I need to hear him say it. "Just tell me that you'll let me go first. Please."

He sighs tiredly and then scoots across the grass, getting close to me and placing his hand back on my cheek. "All right, I promise. You can go first."

I can tell he doesn't mean it and I want to cry, but I don't. I just keep silent, stewing in my own thoughts, fearing to press him—fearing I'll make him mad at me. Fearing the truth. Fearing that whatever's going on in his head, I won't be able to handle it or help.

I blink from the memory and focus on Quinton. "My poor Quinton," I utter under my breath, like he belongs to me, even though he doesn't. But at that moment I wish he did and I could just pick him up and take him out of here. Clean up his cuts and feed him because he looks like he hasn't eaten in days. I become hyper-aware of just how much I care for him and want to make him better—help him. And this time I'm not going to silently watch him slip away.

Hesitantly I reach for him, but then pull back, fearing I'll hurt him, and instead lean over him with my hands to my sides, clenched into fists. "Quinton," I say softly. "Can you hear me?"

He doesn't respond, breathing in and out, his chest rising

and sinking. I dare to touch his cheek, gently cup it in my hand, feel how cold his skin is. "Quinton, please wake up... I'm so sorry...for not seeing...for not being able to see..." I struggle for words through the abundance of emotions surfacing. Regret. Worry. Fear. Remorse. Pain. God, I feel his pain, hot beneath my skin, flooding my heart, and I wish I could pull it out of him. "Please, please open your eyes," I choke.

My only response is the softness of his breathing. I check his pulse with my other hand and it's there, murmuring against my skin. I try to tell myself there's still hope, that I can get out of this, but looking around...looking at him, taking in the silence that's almost as quiet as death...I'm not so sure anymore. And it hurts, almost as much as if I'd lost him, just like I lost Landon.

Quinton

I'm pretty sure I'm dreaming. Or maybe I'm dead. I'm hoping for the latter, but I don't think it's the correct assumption because this feels different from the first time I died. If I'm dreaming, it's a beautiful dream, one where I'm with Nova and we're happy. I'm surprised I'm seeing myself with her. Normally I'd stop my thoughts from going there, but I'm not awake enough to care. Plus, I feel really good, better than I have in a while. Everything feels light. Breathless. Hazy and weightless. My memories of my past are fading. I can no longer feel the blood on my hands or the weight of guilt on my shoulders. Something wonderful is taking over. I'm not in the darkness, locked within myself. I've been swept up by light and I feel like I could do anything at the moment as I lie on my back, gazing up at the sky. Nova hovers over me, cupping my cheek, and her skin is so damn warm and she smells amazing. And her eyes... bright blue with specks of green, her skin dotted with freckles, and her full lips that look so delicious I want to taste them... and I'm going to, because nothing matters at the moment. It's not real, which makes it easier to take what I want—admit what I want.

I lean up, not even thinking about what I'm doing, and press my lips to hers. It hurts my mouth, but the pain is worth it—it's worth everything just to taste her again. I could do it forever, and I want to, but when I slip my tongue deep inside her mouth, she pulls away, her eyes widening and swarming with confusion. I open my mouth to tell her to come back to me, because I want her—need to kiss her again—but then her lips start moving and the haze from my brain gradually starts to lift.

"Quinton, can you hear me?" she asks, her voice soft, distant. Or maybe I'm the one who's distant.

"I..." It hurts to talk, my throat too dry, and the brightness of the sun is stinging at my eyes.

"Are you okay?" she says, and the sunlight dims as the blue sky changes into my shitty bedroom ceiling, cracked and stained with water. That stupid drip comes into focus, haunting me again.

I suddenly realize that I'm in my room. Awake. And Nova's here. With me. My thoughts start racing as I try to recollect what happened. I was planning on those guys beating me to death. Why didn't that happen? Because it was too easy? Do I deserve not to be let off so easy—do I deserve worse than death? But if that's true, then why's Nova here?

"What are you doing here?" It's painful to talk, but I force the words to leave my mouth. "Or am I dreaming?"

She repositions her hand on my cheek but doesn't pull away, the startled look in her eyes diminishing. "You're not dreaming... You were unconscious but... Are you okay?" She seems nervous, and it reminds me of how innocent and good she is and how she shouldn't be here in the crack house that I call home.

"Why are you here?" I ask, my voice feeble as I try to sit up, but my arms aren't working and I fall right back down on the mattress.

"I came here to see you," she replies, absentmindedly touching her lips, and I wonder if I really kissed her or if I was imagining it.

She stares at me with her fingers on her lips and it's uncomfortable because she's *really* looking at me. I've been so used to people looking through me, as if I were a ghost, seeing the drugs, the person that I am now, the worthlessness all over me, instead of who I used to be. I've forgotten what it's like to be really looked at, and for a split second I enjoy it. Then she looks away and I feel like I'm dying, my brain registering the pain in my legs, arms, chest—everywhere. And I'm crashing. Badly. My hands start to shake, my heart rate picking up as soon as I realize this.

"Go put some ice in a plastic bag," she says, snapping her fingers at someone.

I hear a mutter and then Tristan steps into my view. He glances down at me and the haziness in his eyes lets me know he's high on something, but I'm glad he's at least here and it doesn't look like he's been beaten up. "Dude, you look like shit," he tells me with a dopey-ass grin.

"I feel like shit," I mutter, managing to get my hand up to my face to rub my eyes. "You look like you got away."

"I did, and you should have run with me, you dumbass... I thought you were for a while until I realized I was alone." Tristan chuckles under his breath. "Wait until you see yourself in a mirror."

His amusement seems to piss Nova off, and she gets to her feet, tugging the bottoms of her shorts down, fury burning in her eyes. "Go get a fucking bag to put the ice in," she says, not yelling, but her tone is cold, abrupt, harsh, and she sort of shoves him. This isn't the Nova I remember at all, and she kind of scares me.

She seems to scare Tristan, too, who surrenders with his hands in front of him and backs toward the doorway. "Fine. Jesus, Nova. You don't have to get crazy about it."

"You haven't even begun to see me get crazy," she snaps, pointing at the door. "Now go get a damn bag."

After Tristan leaves, she turns to the doorway and says, "What am I going to do?"

I can't see who she's talking to, and it makes me wonder who the hell is in here. Delilah? I doubt it, since I don't think she'd be asking Delilah that question.

"I don't know," someone replies. I still can't see who it is, but I can tell the voice belongs to a female and I hate how excited I get over the fact that Nova's not here with a guy.

Suddenly, a girl with black hair and big blue eyes steps in. "He looks..." She assesses me, then looks at Nova. "He looks like he needs to go to a hospital."

"No hospitals," I croak. "I don't have the cash to pay for that." And I don't deserve to heal so easily. I should suffer for getting up and running away from my death.

Nova stares down at me with reluctance. "Quinton, I really think you need to go to a hospital." She kneels back down on the mattress, sweeping her long brown hair to the side as she leans over me. Her fingers gently enfold my wrist and, moving slowly, she bends my arm so I can get a good view of my hand. It's twice the size it normally is and my skin is purple and blue. Even where her fingers are, the skin is swollen and raw, and it seems like her touch should hurt, but all I can feel is heat—her heat. God, I've missed her heat. I've spent the last year wrapped up in coldness, feeling the numbness of drugs and sex with random women, and now she's here and I feel like I'm burning up.

"It's just a bruise," I say, not looking at my hand, but at her.

I want to hold her, hug her, kiss her, touch her, but I also want her to go away. Stay. Leave. Right. Wrong. Lexi. Nova. Guilt.

Guilt.

Guilt.

Guilt.

It was all your fault.

As my past strikes me in the face, I jerk my hand away from her, not carefully, and this time I feel the pain, but I don't react to it. Instead I finally struggle to sit up on the mattress. As soon as I'm upright, sharp pains stab at my side, making it hard to breathe. I gasp, clutching at my side as I hunch over.

"What's wrong?" Nova asks with genuine concern, and it only makes it harder to breathe.

"Nova, just go," I grunt, trying to focus on my breathing, but it's like I'm being punched over and over again…My thoughts drift back to earlier today…

Donny strikes me with the tire iron, over and over again. I fall to the ground. I'm not even sure why I fall, other than that I'm tired of standing. I'm ready to give up and I do as he slams the heavy metal bar into shoulder, my rib cage, kicking me, punching me, beating me repeatedly.

I can see it in his eyes that he wants to kill me, and I welcome it as I lie in the gravel, the rocks piercing my skin, the sky blue above me.

"Go ahead." I choke on the blood gushing up in my mouth as I stare up at him. "Kill me."

He smiles, then hits me again with the bar, and I feel one of my ribs crack as the metal slams against it. It sucks the air out of me, causes blinding pain to erupt through my body. But I feel nothing. I'm numb. Dead.

I give up.

He tosses the bar to the side and rolls up his sleeves, switching to hitting me with his fists. And when he aims one of them at my head, I sprawl my arms and legs out to the side, making sure he finishes me off. Just do it. I'm done.

"You act like you want this," Donny says with eagerness and confusion on his face, and then his fist collides with my cheek.

"Maybe I do," is all I say, the taste of blood filling up my mouth. I do—I know I do.

"God, you crackheads are such worthless pieces of shit," he says with a smile. "Nothing to live for. No one to care whether you live or die."

He says it like he's not a crackhead himself, and I wonder if he is, or if he just deals, sells shit to people, helps fuck up their lives for cash. I wonder if he has something to live for. Someone who cares about him. What would that be like, to have someone like that, like I did once with Lexi?

Or Nova. I blink the thought from my head and try to force it out as he moves to hit me again, with a look on his face that makes me wonder if he's going to kill me.

Good, *I think, yet for the briefest of moments I feel conflicted. I'm not even sure where the feeling stems from. Myself or thoughts of Nova. Or the simple fear that this could be it—that this time there's going to be no ambulance to show up and revive me. Paranoia sets in.*

What the fuck.

"But I'm going to let you live," the guy says as he swings his fist down to strike, anger burning in his eyes, which are bloodshot. He's high and I know there's little control inside him, that even though he says he's going to let me live, he could easily take it one swing too far and probably wouldn't even realize it until it was too late. "So you can tell your little pussy friend who just took off that he better watch his back."

He slams his fist into my ribs again, and the pain erupts through my body. I want to shout at him to not do me the favor of letting me live. To finish me off. But instead, as he brings his arm up to hit me again, I do something I wasn't expecting. I get up and run, like a fucking wimp, running away from death, running away from what I deserve.

Fuck, what am I doing? Why didn't I tell him to finish me off? He probably would have if I'd made him angry enough. But instead I ran. Chose life. To come back to this? It's time to nail the damn coffin shut.

"Quinton, are you okay?" The sound of Nova's voice jerks me back to the present, and I get angry because she's fucking with my head. Even after nine months, she consumes my thoughts almost as much as Lexi. She makes me hesitate with stuff, and I don't like it.

I look at her, getting pissed off because she's here when I thought she'd let me go—she should have. Plus, there's barely any drugs left in my system, and I feel like I could fucking claw someone's eyes out.

"Nova, just go away," I say, moving my legs off the mattress. My knees are stiff and my joints ache. I'm also missing a shoe and my foot is cut up and scraped raw on the top.

Nova sits down beside me, shaking her head. "Not until I help you... Quinton, I want to help you."

For a second my heart skips a beat, but then the scar on my chest burns, telling my emotions to shut the hell up. I need to stop reacting to her, and I need to get a line in my system so I won't even feel any of this—feel her.

"I don't want you to help me." Trying to appear more confident than I feel, I push to my feet and stand up. My knees promptly begin to wobble, but I fight the compulsion to fall to the floor. "Now, I'm asking you to go."

She glances at her friend, who briefly scrutinizes me, seeing what I really am, what Nova won't see. "We should probably listen," she says to Nova, apparently seeing something she doesn't like, and I wish Nova would get on the same page.

Nova smashes her lips together so forcefully the skin around her mouth whitens. "No." Her eyes lock on me. "I'm not going until you let me help you."

I start to spastically shake even more and try to blame it on the fact that I need to do a line, but it's not just that. It's her. Her eyes. Her words. The simple fact that she's right in front of me, just within arm's reach, yet I can't touch her. I'd be leaving my own self-made prison if I did. I'd be trying to escape from the bars I built around myself for a reason, made of guilt, the foundation formed by a promise I made to never forget the love of my life, whose life ended because of me.

"You can't help me," I snap. "Now just get the fuck out before I make you get out."

She flinches as if I've slapped her, yet it seems to bring more determination out of her as she scoots closer to me. "I'm not going anywhere, so you might as well let me help you at least clean off those cuts you have all over you—they're going to get infected."

The idea of her taking care of me like that both pleases and appalls me. I want her to stay, which means there's only one thing I can do. Fighting the impulse inside my body to grab her and crush my lips against hers, I get up and limp toward the doorway, dodging around her friend. I head across the hallway to Delilah's room. The door's wide open and the room is unoccupied, which is what I'm looking for.

"Where are you going?" Nova chases after me, but I slam

the door right in her face. Like the asshole that I am. I lock it, and she starts to bang on it, shouting for me to open up, but I ignore her and flop down on the dirty mattress. Then I reach down between it and the wall where I know Delilah hides her stash and take the small plastic bag out. There's barely enough for a line in there, but it'll have to be enough for now, at least until Nova stops banging on the door.

I can hear her talking to someone on the other side as I scrape the remaining crystal out of the bag and onto the Tupperware bin beside the mattress. It sounds like she's crying, but I could be wrong and honestly I don't care. I only care about one thing, knowing it'll make everything feel better and then everything—the fight, Nova—won't matter.

There's a pen on the bin and I pick it up as someone knocks on the door. They say something, but I don't hear them as I lean down and suck the tiny white crystals up my nose, feeling the gnawing ache in my body slowly evaporate.

"Quinton, please open up," Nova says through the door with one soft tap of her hand. There's a plea in her voice that rips at my throat, but the white powder entering my system quickly heals it. Sure it's only temporary, but all I'll need is another hit once the wound starts to open again. I'll never have to feel again if I follow the process.

Nova says something else, but I cover my ears with my hands and ball up on the mattress until her voice fades out.

And I fade with it.

Chapter Six

Nova

I can't stop crying. The tears started flowing the moment Quinton locked himself into that room. I didn't know what to do, so I tried everything I could. I begged. I pleaded. I sobbed as I pounded on the door. But he wouldn't listen and it hurt me to think about him broken and beat up on the other side, doing God knows what while I couldn't do anything to stop him, all because of a door. A stupid door with a lock that I couldn't break.

Finally Lea dragged me out of there, and I can barely remember what happened over the next few hours, other than that I ended up back at her uncle's house in the guest room bed with a blanket over me and I feel so exhausted.

"We should have never gone there," she says as she lies down on the bed beside me. "That was bad, Nova. Like really, really bad."

"It was the ugly part of life," I agree, my tears subsiding. "But it doesn't mean we shouldn't have gone there... He needs my help, Lea."

"He needs more than your help," she replies, tucking her arm under her head. "He needs to go to a hospital and then rehab or something."

"I know that." I rotate to my side and stare out the window

at the stars in the sky, and the view calms me. "But I don't know how I can get him to do that, so I'm doing the only thing I can think of right now."

"I'm worried about you," she admits. "I don't think you should go back there."

"I have to," I whisper. "Now that I've seen him...seen how he's living, seen the condition he's in, I can't walk away." I thought maybe my feelings for him would have changed, that maybe last summer was just an illusion built around weed, but it's not. And I realized that the second I saw him lying in that bed, and when he kissed me, half out of it, it only heightened my feelings. And I didn't see Landon this time. I just saw a broken guy I wish I could just hug better.

"Nova, please just think about it," she says. "Think before you go back. Promise me you will. I think you're going to get in over your head...And those papers I was reading...Helping meth addicts is complicated. You need to understand what you're getting into and if you really want to get into it."

"Okay. I promise I'll think about what I'm doing." But I already know what the answer will be. I'm going back because I'm not ready to give up on him, not when I've barely gotten started. I have to figure this out, somehow.

"And read the papers," she adds, fluffing the pillow and getting situated.

"Okay," I promise again, wondering just how much insight papers from the Internet can give, but I guess reading them won't hurt. At the moment I'll do anything I think can help.

It gets quiet, and I close my eyes, ready to fall asleep, wishing upon wishing that I could see a way through this.

❧

"If you were stuck on a desert island," I say to Landon as he draws line after line in his sketchbook. I scoot forward on the bed, pretending I'm scratching my foot, when really I just want to be closer to him. "What's the one thing you'd want there with you?"

He frowns down at his drawing, a self-portrait, his face half shadowed, his hair shorter on one side, and his cheekbone shaded to look sunken in so it looks like he's wearing the mask from The Phantom of the Opera. *"I'm not sure…maybe a pencil." He stares at the pencil in his hand and then looks at his drawing. "But then again, if I couldn't have both a pencil and paper, there really wouldn't be any point to taking one and not the other." He sets the pencil down on the paper and rubs some smeared graphite off his hand with a thoughtful look on his face, while I pretend not to be sad over the fact that he didn't say he'd want me on the island with him. "But then again…" He looks up at me and his honey-brown eyes burn with intensity. "Maybe I'd just take you." He strokes his finger across my cheek, leaving a smudge there, I'm sure. "Having you there could have its perks."*

I crinkle my nose like it's an absurd idea when really my stomach is fluttering with butterflies. "How would

that be a perk? I'm not resourceful in intense situa-
tions...I'd probably do more harm than good."

He shakes his head, tracing his finger up my cheekbone to a lock of my hair. He twirls it around his fingers
as he sets his pencil and sketchbook to the side. "No way,
Nova Reed. You'd be a lifesaver."

"How do you figure?" My voice sounds breathless
and I hate it because it gives away everything that I'm
feeling—the effect he has on me. And even though we've
kissed and touched each other, I'm still not certain where
he stands—how he feels about me.

"Because...you save me every day," he says.

My forehead creases as I stare into his eyes, searching
for a sign that he's joking, but he looks so serious. "Save
you from what?"

He pauses, searching my eyes, but for what, I'm not
sure. "From fading."

His words hit me square in the chest and I open my
mouth to say something, but no words come out, just like
always whenever he says something so sad. Finally I manage, "I still don't get what you mean."

"I know," he says with a sigh, unraveling his fingers
from my hair. "It doesn't really matter...I was just trying to say that if you and I were trapped on an island,
I know you'd end up being the one to save us, because I
know you'd never give up and it'd make me not want to
give up either."

I'm not really sure if it's the answer I want to hear or how it connects to me stopping him from fading in the real world. I could ask him, but he silences me with his lips, kissing me softly, but with passion behind it, gripping my waist. And before I can think too deeply about what he means about wanting to give up, he gently pushes me down on the bed, lying on top of me. He covers my body with his, and I melt into his embrace as he kisses me until I've forgotten about everything except him and me and the brief warmth engulfing our bodies.

May 17, day two of summer break

Nova

When I open my eyes, the sunlight blinds me and I'm sweating from the heat. No one bothered to close the curtain last night, and without any mountains around, the heat of the sun is intense. I throw the blanket off and blink as I gradually sit up. I'm so exhausted that all I want to do at the moment is give up. Curl up in a ball, throw the blanket back over my head, and sleep until the next day, maybe longer. But I can't help thinking about the dream I had last night. At the time I didn't think anything of it, and honestly, I'm surprised I even remember it. *I know you'd never give up and it'd make me not want to give up either.*

It hurts, thinking about Landon, because he did give up and leave me. In the end I wasn't a lifesaver like he thought. I was just a distraction from his pain and I didn't save him. I don't want to be a distraction this time around. I want to do things differently. But how? How can I make sure Quinton doesn't end up like Landon?

After thinking about it for a while, I do something I haven't done in a long time. I sneak out of bed, grab my laptop, and go sit out on the sofa to watch the video Landon made right before he ended his life. I'm not even sure what the point is. Whether I just want to see him again, or analyze the video. Watching his lips move, the pain in his eyes, the way his inky black hair falls across his forehead, it takes me back to that night when I woke up on the hill. Just after he made this video, I would find him hanging from his bedroom ceiling. Music would be playing, like it is in the video. I often wonder if, had I woken up just a little bit sooner, I would have caught him making the video, instead of right after he hanged himself. Could I have stopped him? Was he waiting for me to wake up and stop him, but I took too long and he gave up?

Finally I shut off the video. I have such a fucked-up mentality over his death, but since there will never be any answers, there will always be a ton of questions.

I swallow hard and cup my hand around my wrist, remembering the one time I almost gave up, too, almost left the world, left my mom to find me bleeding out in the bathroom with a ton of questions she'd never have answers to, like

Landon did with me. Part of me really wanted to end it all, to stop burying the pain inside me, but part of me was scared of the what-ifs. What if I did go through with it? What if I just ended my life? What would happen to the people who cared about me? My mom? What would I miss? It was one of the darkest times in my life, and it's permanently branded on my body, a scar put there by my own hand, reminding me never again. I'll never give up again.

When I return to the bedroom, Lea is still asleep on the other side of the king-size bed, her face turned toward the opposing wall, her breathing soft, and the blanket is pulled up over her. I quietly put the computer away and get ready to go, not wanting to wake her up and argue with her about going back home. Plus, I need to talk to Quinton alone. I get dressed in a pair of red shorts and a white shirt and pull my hair into a ponytail to keep the heat from melting it to my skin. Then I read through some of the papers Lea printed out that talk about helping a drug addict: intervention, talking to the addict, getting him into rehab. They're very technical and most are like clinical instructions on how to handle drug addicts. What I don't get, though, is where the information is on how to deal with their mood swings. Or the hopelessness that comes with trying to make someone see that he needs to get better, trying to find the right thing that will bring him back. Or how about how to get his family to come down and support him, because that's what he really needs. He needs people who know him and care about him, like I needed my mom when I decided I wanted to heal.

I don't know much about Quinton's family other than that his mom passed away when he was born, and even though his dad raised him, it was pretty much like he raised himself. I wonder if I could find out more about his dad...Maybe he'd want to help Quinton. I mean, Quinton is his son and I know if my father had been alive when I was doing drugs, he'd have done anything to help me. But I can't count on it, because not all people are like my mom and dad and willing to do anything for their child. Still, it wouldn't hurt to look into it, if I can get someone to either give me his father's phone number or tell me his name and where he lives so I can get him.

I write Lea a note, telling her that I'm going out for coffee and will be back soon. I hate lying to her, but at the same time I hated seeing how terrified she was last night. I put the note on the pillow beside her, then write on the back of my hand *no regrets*. It's something Lea and I say to each other all the time, and it's going to remind me today not to regret anything I do, right there on my hand, just in case I even think about trying to take something that I'll regret taking later.

I tuck my phone into my back pocket and head out to the car, locking the front door behind me on the way out. It's so hot I feel like I'm melting into a steaming puddle, the heat leaching the air out of my lungs. I walk swiftly to the car and hop in, but curse when the black leather seat burns my legs. I start up the engine, then find Quinton's address on the GPS, along with the nearest coffee shop, because I'm going to need a caffeine boost if I'm going to make it through this.

"You can do this, Nova," I say as I back down the driveway and turn onto the road. I continue to repeat the mantra in my head all the way to the coffee shop. I order two coffees, not even sure if Quinton drinks coffee or how he takes it, but I make a guess. Then I crank up a little "Help Me" by Alkaline Trio and drive to Quinton's apartment, trying not to get too upset at the sight of it in broad daylight. But I can't help it. The sun only makes it look more tragic and fills me with even more hopelessness, but I still park the car. Then I take my phone out of my pocket, flip the video recorder on, and let out a deep breath before I aim the screen at myself.

"Why am I talking to you...? I really have no idea, other than that I find it therapeutic," I say to the camera. "Because when I'm talking to you, I can say what I'm really feeling... and what I'm really feeling is...well, it's a lot of things. Like for starters, I'm scared, not just for myself, but for Quinton. That place he's in...it's horrible. I knew people lived like this from movies and stuff, but seeing it with my own eyes...it's terrifying." I pause, glancing at the building. "And I also feel hurt...I mean, he was so, so upset with me last night for being here and all I want to do is help him...The only thing that can get me past that is remembering...remembering how much my mom wanted to help me and how much I shut her out. I didn't want help, but looking back, I think deep down I really did want it. I just couldn't see past all the dark stuff... until I watched Landon's video...the one he made right before he committed suicide...In a way, that video woke me up. I'm hoping that Quinton is the same way—that there's something to wake him up. I have to believe there is. Otherwise there's no hope left. And I'm not ready to accept that yet." I pause, taking a deep breath before I add, "So here goes. I'm going back in." I stop talking and click off the camera, putting the phone back into my pocket. Then I get out of the car, making sure to grab the coffees and lock the doors.

The area is eerily silent, like everyone sleeps during the day and comes out only at night. I'm sort of glad, though. It makes walking to the stairs, going up them, and walking to the door so much easier. The hard part comes when I get to the door. I stare at the cracks in it, breathing in the stale air. I'm not sure what to do next, or if I even want to do anything next.

What do I do?

Finally, I knock on the door, softly at first, but then I hit it a little harder when no one answers. All I get in return is more silence. I glance back at my car, growing nervous. Should I go? But when I look back at the door, all I can picture is Quinton on the other side, bruised and broken—lost. Just like I was at one point in my life.

I'm not sure what to do, and my legs start to feel like rubber as I stand there. Finally, I sit down on the ground and lean against the railing, knowing it's probably filthy. But filth doesn't matter at the moment. I can handle getting the back of my shorts dirty. I set the coffees down beside me, read *no regrets* written on the back of my hand, then touch my exposed scar.

Remember.

I float back into the memory of how bad things were when I fell toward rock bottom, leaning my head back against the railing and staring up at the sky through a hole in the canopy roof above me.

I can't feel my body. I think I've drunk so much that I've managed to drown myself. Because that's what I feel like. Submerged in water, only it's hot, scorching, yet at the same time my body is connected to the heat so I can't do anything but let it burn my skin. Slowly.

I want out of it. My body. My thoughts. I want to be above water again or maybe at the bottom. I'm not sure. I'm not sure what I want anymore. What I'm supposed to be doing. So I keep wandering around helplessly, kissing guys I shouldn't be kissing, not focusing past anything but taking the next step, and even that seems difficult.

Maybe I should just stop walking.

I go into the bathroom at my house and don't lock the door because Landon didn't lock the door and I want to figure out why he didn't. Did he want me to walk in, or did he just forget... Was he just too out of it? I don't know.

I don't know anything anymore.

I sink down on the cold tile floor, tears staining my eyes and cheeks. I've been crying all night, feeling guilty, aching from the inside, but now suddenly I feel nothing. Emptied. Like all my emotions were drained out through those tears and I'm not sure any feelings are ever going to come back. Maybe I'm broken. Maybe Landon took what was inside me with him. Maybe I don't even have blood left in my veins.

God, I miss him. Is this what he was thinking right before he left? That he missed someone? Or that he didn't have life in him? That he felt broken?

I have to know—need to understand—what he felt like when he decided it was time to go forever. Because sometimes it feels like I'm heading to that same place, where giving up seems easier than taking any more steps.

I reach up toward the counter and feel around until I find the drawer handle. I pull it open and without looking in it, I feel around until I find a razor. My fingers don't shake when I take it out. I kind of expected them to, like they would freak out over the fact that I'm going to do this.

I am.

I bring my hand back toward me and stare at the razor in my hand. I'm not even sure how sharp it is or how exactly to do this. It doesn't look very sharp, and the pink handle makes it look almost harmless. I dare touch my fingertip to the edge of the razor and press down. Nothing. So I slide it up, and it slowly splits the skin of my finger open. Dots of blood trickle out and onto the floor around my feet. I stare at them, feeling the burn in my finger, but not really feeling it, which makes me think I might be able to go through with this. Is that what Landon did, too? Did he test what the rope felt like around his neck? Did it burn? Was he afraid? Was he thinking about how he was going to miss me? How much I'd miss him? How much it'd hurt for me to see him like that? Was he thinking at all? I'm not sure. I'm not sure about anything anymore.

I stretch my arm out in front of me, see the vein. It's faint and small, so I pump my fist repeatedly until it's purple and bulging like it's angry. Like it's shouting at me to stop. Don't do it. I can't stop. Not until I understand.

I bring my knee up and rest my arm on top of it, my forearm up. I pump my fist over and over again as I move the razor closer, feeling nothing, not until the blade comes into contact with my skin. I feel a hint of cold and I shiver, but I shove the sensation aside and press the blade down. It stings as the skin tears open. I feel it, along with the warmth of the blood dripping out, but I still don't understand what he was thinking . . . what made him go through with it—what made him end his life.

I push the razor down harder and start to graze it along my skin. Cutting my skin open. Letting the blood out. Letting the pain out. It's trailing down my skin, like a weak river, and the line across my wrist is opening up, but it's not nearly open enough, just a faint cut, something that will barely leave a scar. I need to do it more.

I slice the razor back and forth over my skin, each movement bringing on more pain, yet at the same time I'm letting it out. I'm starting to feel light-headed, like I'm swimming into dark water, drowning. How far can I go? When do I stop? How much is enough?

Suddenly someone knocks on the door. "Nova, are you in there?" my mom asks.

"Go away!" I shout, my voice off pitch and trembling.

"What the hell are you doing in there? Are you okay?" she asks, worried.

"I said go the fuck away!"

"I will not. Not until you tell me what's wrong... I thought I heard you crying in there."

When I don't respond, the doorknob starts to turn and then the door opens. Her expression falls and her eyes widen as she takes in the sight of me, razor in my hand, blood all over my arm and the floor. She's going to freak out, and all I can think is: Am I glad she walked in? Am I glad I left the door unlocked? Am I glad she stopped me?

I blink from the memory, breathing in and out, telling my pulse to settle down, to remember, but to not let the memory overtake me. Sometimes, when I really think about it, I tell myself that I didn't lock the door that day because I wanted someone to walk in on me, wanted them to find me before I bled out—that I never intended to kill myself. I'm not sure if there's any truth behind it or not. My head was in too weird a place at the time, and thinking back, it's hard to decipher what I was truly feeling. But my mom did walk in on me—she did open the door—and I didn't die. I was madder than hell at her, too, yelled and screamed, not even sure why I was so mad. But I got over it, and in the end, right in this moment, I'm so glad that she did.

Getting to my feet, I walk forward and knock on the door to Quinton's apartment again. I do it ten times just to be sure that no one is going to answer, and then, even though I'm afraid to do it, I grab the doorknob. I'm not sure if it's the right thing to do, but I'm not even sure there is a right thing to do, so I do what I know.

Summoning a deep breath, I turn the doorknob, but it's locked. As I let go and my arm falls to the side, a piece of my hope burns out. I back away from the door and sit back down. All I can do now is wait for Quinton to come to me.

Quinton

The pain's starting to dwindle, or maybe it's still there in my body but my mind is focusing on other stuff. Like the sound of the wind just outside, or how cold the wall is against my back, though my skin feels hot, or how my hand itches to draw yet I can't move my fingers enough to pick up a pencil.

"You are so jacked up right now," Tristan remarks as he lowers his nose to the mirror and sucks up another line. He throws his head back and sniffs, putting his hand to his nose as he releases a euphoric breath. He's done at least three more lines than me, pushing that boundary he's always pushing.

"So are you." I lean forward from the wall and steal the mirror from his hand. I don't hesitate, putting the pen to my nose and sucking the white powder up in one deep, wonderful breath. Then I set the mirror down on the floor and rub my hand across my nostrils, sniffing as my nose and throat absorb the adrenaline rush.

"True," Tristan says, drumming his fingers on the tops of his knees as he glances around my room, like he's searching for something, but he's not going to find it, since there's nothing in here. "I think we should do something."

"Like what?" I massage my bruised hand. My fingers are crooked and I still can't straighten them, but there's no pain for the most part. One of my eyes is also swollen and I can barely see out of it, but everything's good because I'm soaring right now. "Because I can't do anything that involves using my hand or my foot or my ribs either."

He snorts a laugh as he starts tapping his foot, so much energy buzzing through him I think he's going to lose it. "Isn't that what we were trying to do here? Numb out your pain so you can move?"

I consider what he said and remember that was the point behind doing so much today. "Let me see if I can," I tell him.

Then I bend my knees, put my good hand down on the floor, and push up. It feels like it hurts yet at the same time I feel at peace with the ache inside me as I stumble to my feet. My left leg tries to buckle, so I put all my weight on the right one and brace my hand on the wall.

"I think you got it," Tristan says, standing up from my mattress. "Now we can walk over to Johnny's and get some more, pretending we're making a pickup for Dylan or something."

"We don't have any cash for that," I point out, then glance at the pennies on my floor. "Unless you think he'll accept pennies."

He shakes his head and then smiles as he takes a roll of cash out of his pocket. "Yeah, we do."

"Where did you get that?" I ask, leaning my weight on my arm as I try to support my body.

He shakes his head and stuffs the money back into his pocket. "I'm not going to tell you, since you'll be all weird about it."

I frown at the money that I'm pretty sure belongs to Dylan, the money that Delilah gave to me to make the pickup that led to my ass getting beat by Trace's guys. "Did you steal that off of me yesterday, because that wasn't mine. It was Dylan's."

"Can we just go?" he asks, and I know he did—he took the money and has no plans to give it back—yet I don't say anything because in the end that money is what is going to get us more drugs. "Forget about where the money came from. I'll make sure to pay Dylan back, but let's just get to Johnny's because we're running low."

"Do you think that's a good idea? After what happened yesterday? Because I really don't feel like getting my ass kicked again, and this time I don't think I'm going to be able to run away." I rest my head back against the wall and roll my eyes a few times, trying to stop them from drying out. "You know, the guy who beat the shit out of me made a threat that you were going to get it, too."

"So what? I can handle whatever they bring," he says with a stupid amount of confidence that's going to end up getting him hurt, I can feel it. "Besides, if they come here, then I'll run, unlike you..." He considers something, looking perplexed. "Why didn't you at first? It makes me think you're crazy."

"Maybe I am."

"Maybe we both are."

"Or maybe we both need help," I say, but I only really mean him.

"I don't need to hear that shit from you, too," he states with an exaggerated sigh.

"What do you mean me, too?" I ask, lifting my head back up to look at him. "Who else has been telling you that?"

"My parents," he replies with a shrug.

"I thought you haven't talked to them since we bailed out on Maple Grove?"

He does another line, sucking air through his nose multiple times as he puts his head upright. "I made the stupid mistake of calling them a few months ago to see if they could lend me some money. I used Delilah's phone, and apparently my mom cared enough to save it in her contacts—although she didn't care enough to say yes to lending me the money." He mutters something under his breath that sounds an awful lot like "Stupid bitch." "Then she randomly called about a day or two ago...told me I should come home and get help...said they missed me or some shit, like they suddenly decided they were going to start caring."

"Maybe you should go home," I say, thinking of my own father, wondering what he's doing and if he ever thinks about me. I haven't talked to him since I left Seattle, but then again, I haven't tried to call him and I'm not sure if he knows how to get ahold of me. If he does, though, I think I'd rather not know, because that means he can call me but chooses not to. The truth can hurt a hell of a lot more than just thinking about the fucked-up possibilities. "I mean, if they want you to get help, then why not? It obviously means that they care about you."

He laughs sharply. "They don't care about me. Trust me."

"Then why would they call you?" I ask, wishing he would go, get better, live a good life. "I'm sure they care about you— that they miss you...You're probably hurting them a lot..." I almost say, "all things considered," since they've already lost one child. But I can't do that—say it aloud. Remind him and myself of what I've done.

He ignores me. "You know what? Maybe you should go home," he retorts as he pinches his nostrils with his fingertips.

"This is my home," I say. "I don't have anywhere else...I fucked that up a long time ago."

It grows quiet between the two of us, which happens a lot when one of us brings up the past, even if we're both forcing euphoria into our bodies. The past can always momentarily hinder the high, although we have gone into some really deep heart-to-hearts about it when we're both soaring on adrenaline, but we never remember exactly what we said when we crash back down to reality.

He starts messing around with his shoelaces even though they're tied while I reach for a shirt on the floor. But as I bend over, my ribs ache in protest and I stand right back up, letting out a groan.

"What's wrong?" Tristan asks, his attention darting from me to the door to the window to the ceiling.

"I think I broke one of my ribs."

His eyes land back on me. "Well, you know what they say the best cure is for broken ribs," he says, picking up my shirt for me. "More lines."

I take the shirt from him when he offers it to me. "I'm pretty sure no one says that."

"I just did," he says in all seriousness. "Now, are you going to come to Johnny's or what?" He's practically bouncing, glancing all over my room, drumming his fingers like he can't sit still.

I try to put my shirt on, but get only one arm in when I decide that I can't move my body enough. I give up and toss my shirt aside. "There's no way I can get that on," I say, trying to figure out a solution, but thinking too deeply about one thing gives me a headache. "I'll just walk over there without a shirt on."

He nods as he opens my bedroom door. "That's a good idea. Then maybe you can hook up with that Caroline chick. She has a thing for you and she's hot. Plus, she's got connections."

I shake my head as we walk down the hall. "I'm not hooking up with anyone today."

He gapes at me like I'm insane. "Why the fuck not?"

I scratch at my arm, right over the tattoos, even though it's not itchy. "Because I don't feel like it."

"You will when we get a few more lines in you," he assures me as he knocks a glass bottle out of the way and it crashes and breaks against Delilah's shut door.

I exhale, not believing that's going to happen, because the real reason for my hesitation isn't going to go away anytime soon. Even with adrenaline storming through my system and my mind and body in a state of artificial contentment, I still can't stop thinking about Nova...how she showed up last night.

Showed up to see me.

I'm still trying to process it. That someone would actually want to come see me, actually care enough about me to take the time to do so. And what did I do? I ran away. Shut the door in her face. I feel bad, yet at the same time I don't, because I want her to be here, yet I don't. I'm very confused, and I feel guilty for even being confused about my feelings for her, so I force myself to stop thinking, allow the drugs to wash the thoughts away, and keep walking in the direction I'm going, to more drugs.

The whole house is quiet, but that's normal. Dylan took off sometime last night and hasn't been back since. When

Delilah came home last night, she was on something that was making her pretty happy, so I took the opportunity to tell her I'd finished off her stash. She didn't seem bothered by it, and by the time she wakes up, she probably won't remember I took it. And if she does remember, I honestly don't give a shit. We all do it to each other—steal from one another. Put our addiction before anything else.

When we enter the living room, Tristan grabs his bag, which is by the front door, while I struggle to jam my feet into my boots. I don't bother lacing them because it would take too long trying to do it one-handed; then I limp toward the door, focusing on taking step after step because that's as far as my mind will allow me to look into the future—all it can focus on.

"You gonna be able to make the walk?" Tristan asks as he grips the doorknob.

I nod as he cracks the front door open and lets a single ray of sunlight in. "I'm good... The pain's wearing on me, but that'll be fixed soon enough."

He looks a little lost. I feel the same way but focus on what I do understand. We're getting closer to Johnny's—to more crystal—and the idea takes over my mind. Shrugging off his confusion, Tristan opens the front door and starts to step outside, but he quickly slams to a stop and I end up running into him, smacking my head against the back of his.

I clutch my nose and stumble back. "Jesus, Tristan, a little warning next..." I trail off at the sight of Nova sitting just outside our door, leaning against the balcony railing, the sunlight and city her backdrop and she outshines them both. For the briefest moment I feel like my old self, aching to run back to grab my sketchbook and pencil and draw her. But running would hurt, and I can't draw because my hand's all fucked up. Plus, turning back would mean turning away from my next hit.

Nova gets to her feet, picking up the two coffees beside her, then stretches out her legs. "Hey."

It's such a casual word, but it doesn't fit the environment or situation at all, and neither does she. "What the hell are you doing here?" I ask, sounding like a dick, when really all I want to do is run up and hug her, let her warmth spill all over me.

Tristan steps aside and gives me a strange look, like he doesn't understand what I'm doing.

"I came here to see you." She holds my gaze, and it throws me off, scares me, confuses me. She steps forward, looking straight at me, like Tristan doesn't exist, like we're the only two people in this world. When she's right in front of me, she extends her hand and hands me a coffee. "I got this for you."

"What about me?" Tristan asks.

"I forgot to get you one," Nova says without looking at him. "But I'm sure you'll live."

Tristan makes a face and then winds around her, taking his cigarettes out of his pocket. He lights up and then rests his elbows on the railing, staring at the parking lot. "Quinton, make this quick. We gotta go."

I'm not even sure what he means by "make this quick."

Make what quick? Make talking to her quick? Make drinking the coffee quick? Make fucking her quick...God, I wish it were that one, and for a second the crystal in my body makes me feel like that idea is okay.

Nova glances over her shoulder at Tristan and then turns around and leans in toward me. "Can I talk to you alone for a little bit?"

I shake my head, staring at the coffee, knowing I should take a sip, but I'm not thirsty and my jaw hurts. "I need to go somewhere."

"Please," she says. "I came all the way here to see you."

My eyes lift to hers. "I didn't ask you to...and if you would have told me you were planning to come here when you called, I'd have told you not to."

"I still would have come," she admits with a shrug. "I needed to see you."

"Why?"

"Because it's just something I need to do."

I pick at the label around the coffee. "And what if I said that I'm not going to talk to you? That it'd be a waste of your time?"

"I'd say you were lying," she replies, trying to act calm, but I can tell by the way she fidgets with the hem of her shirt that she's uneasy. "Just like you're pretending to be an asshole to try to get me to walk away."

"But I'm not going to talk to you," I say simply, but on the inside I shudder because she's so right it scares me how much she understands me.

"But you already are," she retorts, and the corners of her mouth quirk. "Since we're standing here talking right now."

I rub the back of my neck, stiffening as I massage my tender muscles. "Nova, I'm not in the mood for this," I say, because she's the one thing right now standing in the way of my getting to Johnny's house. And when I get there this—my confusion and this entire conversation—will be a vanishing thought in my mind. "Please just go away and leave me alone."

She shakes her head. "Not until you talk to me."

"I'm busy," I lie, wishing she'd go, but also wishing she'd stay. Wishing I could stop thinking about Johnny's and meth, but even thinking about not thinking about it sends my fear and anxiousness soaring.

"I only need, like, an hour," she replies without missing a beat. She pauses as I deliberate what she's asking and I can't believe I'm even considering it. "Please," she adds. "It's important to me."

Tristan's taken an interest in our conversation, and he shakes his head at me, like don't even go there, but I want for a moment, just for a second, to remember what it was like to be with her, talk to her, feel the presence of someone who cared about life and who maybe could care for me. Just an hour. Do I deserve an hour? I don't think so, yet I want it. But at the same time I don't because it's an hour I have to spend away from lines of crystal, and crystal always makes it easier to think. It's like a tug-of-war. Go. Stay. Nova. Johnny's. Feeling. Sedation. Thinking. Silence. Meth. Meth. Meth. *I want it.*

"Nova, I don't think…" I trail off as her expression falls and then I say something that surprises all three of us. "Fine, you have an hour." But I'm not sure how much that time is going to stick. I remember all the times I talked to Nova and how lost I got in her and how time just drifted by.

She cups her hands around her coffee and nods, not smiling, not frowning, just blowing out a stressed breath. "Can you go for a drive with me? I'd rather not stand out here and talk."

I'd rather she not be standing out here either, not just because it's a crack house, but because I'm worried that Trace and his guys could randomly show up to make good on their threat, and I'd hate myself forever if she were here when something like that went down.

I nod, even when Tristan huffs in frustration. "I think I can do that," I tell her, but I'm not so sure.

As I start to follow her across the balcony, Tristan shoots me an irritated look and then says to me, "If you're taking off, then I'm going back inside. I'm not going to wait around for you."

I'm torn because I know what he means by "going back inside." He's going to go finish off the last of the heroin he was going to use this morning before he decided to do lines with me because he thought it'd help me feel better enough to move. "Can't you just wait, like, an hour? I don't want you mixing shit." I say it to him all the time, because he's always trying to overdo it, making crazy cocktails, almost eliminating that half a step he has left between life and death.

He rolls his eyes. "I'll be fine."

"Just wait an hour and I'll be back here and we can go down to Johnny's..." I trail off, noticing Nova is listening intently just behind me. Leaning in, I lower my voice. "Then we can go down to Johnny's and get spun out of our minds and an hour won't even matter."

He considers this with an undecided look on his face and then reluctantly gives in. "I'll wait an hour." He points a finger at me. "But only an hour, and then I'm walking over there without you and you can figure out how to get high by yourself."

"Okay." I cross my fingers, hoping he can't keep track of time.

He rolls his eyes again like I'm a burden to him and then squeezes past me and goes into the house. Then I shut the door, still not fully grasping what I'm about to do or why I'm doing it.

"You ready?" Nova asks, eyeing my cut-up chest and then scanning my bruised face, wincing when she sees my puffy eye.

I shrug. "Yeah, I'm good. Let's go."

"Do you...do you want to put a shirt on?"

"I can't...I think one of my ribs is broken or bruised."

Her lips part in shock. "Quinton, I—"

"So we better hurry." I cut her off as I start across the balcony, limping. "I have to be back in an hour...It's important that I am." Besides, whatever is said in the next hour isn't going to be real because right now my thoughts aren't real. None of this is. Not her. Not this apartment. Not the pain in my beat-up body.

She hurries after me, her sandals scuffing against the concrete. "Why?"

"Because it is," I reply evasively. "Do you have the time, by chance?"

She picks up her pace and moves up beside me, taking her phone out of her pocket as she reaches the stairs. "It's twelve twenty-three," she says.

"Can you let me know when it's around one?" I ask her, knowing that if I don't I'm going to forget to keep track of the time. "I want to make sure I'm back in time."

"Sure." She stuffs the phone into the back pocket of her shorts and starts down the stairs. I follow her, trying not to look at her, watch her, but I'm drawn to the way she moves and how different it is from the way she used to. She carries her shoulders higher, exuding positivity in her movements and her eyes that reflect the sunlight. It's amazing to watch, and for a moment I get wrapped up in it, the way her expression is filled with confusion, the way her hair blows in the hot breeze, how she bites her lip nervously. But then we reach the bottom of the steps and Nancy, one of our neighbors who like to wear bras for shirts, is standing there, drinking a beer.

"Hey, baby," she says to me. We've hooked up a few times, done a few lines, and she's always trying to get me to shoot up with her. I always decline, though, just like I do with Tristan, because I fucking hate needles. Not because they hurt or any shit like that. But because needles helped me come back to life, the doctors jabbing all sorts of shit into me.

I connect needles with reviving from death and always hate them because of this.

I blink my thoughts away from needles and stare at Nancy for a moment, assessing the way she's looking at me like she wants to hook up again. I look like shit, but Nancy doesn't care, just like I don't care about much of anything. We're the perfect match in this fucked-up world, yet I can't get the girl beside me out of my head. She's more overpowering than perfection, and I'm not strong enough to fight it.

Still I try for a moment, smiling at Nancy. "Hey, gorgeous," I reply as I consider just kissing Nancy and destroying this entire connection with Nova. Right here. Right now. End it. Go on living my life exactly like I am now.

Nova looks at her and then me and makes the connection, but doesn't say anything, turning toward the parking lot and heading to her cherry-red Chevy Nova parked just across the lot. The car looks so out of place in my world—too nice and shiny. And Nancy bats her eyelashes at me, her chest popping out of her top, her eyes glossy from the rush she's feeling. She's part of this world. So easy. So simple. I should just do it—kiss her— but I'm too much of a selfish asshole, wanting both worlds, and end up following Nova out to her car. We climb inside and she starts the engine and turns up the air-conditioning.

"So where do you want to go?" she asks, scrolling over my body, her eyes lingering on my stomach. "Are you hungry?"

My jaw ticks and my stomach screams, *No food!* "Nah, I'm good. I'm not even hungry."

She looks unconvinced. "Are you sure?"

I nod with certainty. "Yep, I'm sure."

She grips the steering wheel, staring out the window at the sky, like she's making a wish, and if she is, I wonder what it is. Then finally she puts the car into drive and heads out onto the main road, pausing at the curb.

"Put your seat belt on," she says, buckling up herself.

Not wanting to have that argument with her again, I do what she asks. As soon as I'm fastened safely in, she drives down the road toward the main area of town. "Infinity" by The xx plays from her iPod, but I know the band and song title only because I can see the screen. I remember how into music she is and how I've been listening to music a lot over the last nine months because of her.

"So what have you been up to?" she finally asks, turning the music down slightly.

I shrug, unsure how to respond to her question. Plus, I'm trying to restrain myself from saying much, since everything that comes out of my mouth is going to be unreal and driven by drugs and she deserves better than that. "Nothing much. I've pretty much just been wandering around."

She nods like she understands, but I don't think she does. How could she? "I did that for a bit, too, at the beginning of the school year," she says.

"But not anymore?" I question, examining her smooth skin dotted with perfect freckles, full lips, bright eyes, soft hair... *God, I want to draw her.* "I'm guessing no because you look good."

"I feel good for the most part. And lately I've known exactly what I want to do."

"And what's that?"

"A lot of things. Graduate. Play the drums." She hesitates, fleetingly glancing in my direction. "See you."

I suck in a breath as another drop of crystal drips down my throat and starts to soothe me, relax me, allow me to deal with being here. "But why? You don't even know me... There's a lot that you don't get."

"You could always tell me the stuff that I don't get," she suggests as she turns the car off the main road and into the drive-through lane of a busy McDonald's.

I swiftly shake my head, getting sick just thinking about the idea of telling her about my past, what I've done, the people I've killed. "I can't."

She straightens the wheel. "Why not?"

"Because I just can't." *Because then you'll look at me like everyone else does—like someone who's taken life.* She'll think less of me, maybe even pity me, and I don't want that. I've seen it enough.

She's silent as she pulls up to the drive-through menu and rolls down her window. "You know, I've thought about you a lot over the last several months," she admits, reading the menu, seeming casual, but her chest is rapidly rising and falling, and I can tell she's struggling to breathe.

I don't know how to respond, and even if I did, I don't get the chance because she starts to order some food. I space out, my thoughts running a million miles a minute. All I want to do is ask her questions, find out why she's here, but at the same time I want to get out of the car and run back to the only place that I can call home. I almost do, but I lose focus, watching her as she rattles off her order. Then somehow I end up with a hamburger on my lap and some fries.

Then she pulls around to the front of the building and parks the car in a spot of shade beneath a tree.

She leaves the engine on as she opens up her chicken sandwich and takes a bite. "It's really hot here," she says. "God, how can you stand it...? I feel disgusting." She fans her hand in front of her face.

"You look beautiful, though." I let it slip out, my mouth and thoughts barely under control anymore.

She blinks, slowly, her eyelashes fluttering. "Thank you." She takes in a gradual breath before rotating toward the window. She starts eating fries, her forehead creased, like she's confused as hell, and so am I. I'm not even sure what's going on anymore. Why we're here. What the point is.

"Nova," I say as another drip hits me and I can focus again. "What do you want from me? I mean, you show up here out of the blue and you just want to hang out? It doesn't make any sense."

She chews the bite of food and then shuts her eyes. At first I think it's because she's going to cry or something, but when she opens them, her eyes aren't wet with tears.

"I came here to help you," she confesses, looking directly

at me, intensity radiating from her expression. "I...I called because I wanted to find out about you signing that release to use the video. I've actually been looking for you for a while, but it's been really hard to track you down."

"Okay..." I pick at the fries, not even close to being able to eat them, my jaw too sore from grinding my teeth and my belly too queasy from the crystal I devoured before I left, so I immediately set them back down. "But I don't get why you think you needed to come down here to help me. I'm fine and I don't get why you don't get that or why you'd even think differently."

Her bluish-green eyes unhurriedly scroll up my body with zero indication that she believes in any way that I'm okay. "Because Delilah told me something on the phone... about you."

I stiffen, my pulse accelerating, my lungs tightening, stealing my air away. "What did she tell you?" *What the hell have I told Delilah? God, I have no idea.*

She deliberates something with caution, wetting her lips with her tongue and licking some salt off them. "Do you remember the concert we went to together?" she asks.

"Of course... How could I forget?" It's actually one of the few things I can remember. The sun, the smell, her, Nova, all over me.

Her lips curve slightly upward like she's happy that I can remember. "Yeah, I've never been able to forget either, all that time that we spent together, how I was... and how I just ran off in the middle of it all."

"It was good that you did," I say, and I mean it. "You never should have been hanging out with us to begin with—you never belonged in our world."

"I know it was good that I left when I did," she agrees. "And I learned something about myself, not then, but later on, after I got better." She gazes off at the gas station in front of us as a car backfires. "I've spent the last few months learning a lot about myself, and I discovered that I want to help people, you know. I've missed a lot of chances of being able to help because I was too afraid to see the truth or I couldn't take care of myself enough." I'm not sure what she's getting at and I'm about to ask her, but when she looks at me, something in her eyes stops me. "I want to help *you* get better." She says it like it's as easy as breathing, but it's not. It's harder than finding a bottom in a bottomless pit.

"You can't," I say, very aware of the tattoos on my arm—*Lexi, Ryder, No One*—and the fact that she can see them. Permanent reminders that I can't be helped—that I shouldn't be helped. But Nova doesn't know what they mean, since I never told her. If I did, she wouldn't be here. "Nothing you can say or do will ever be able to help me—I'm not helpable."

"Yes, you are, and I know I can help you." She rotates in her seat and brings her knee up on it. "If you'll just let me, you'll see that."

I almost laugh at her because she doesn't get it. How could she, when she doesn't even know anything about what's going on? "You don't even know what you're talking about—you don't even know me at all. You can't help someone you don't know, and besides, I don't even want to be helped. I'm fine right where I am." *I belong right where I am. Everyone knows it. My dad. Lexi's parents. Tristan's mom.*

> *"I wish it'd been you who died," I hear Tristan's mom sob. "I wish it'd been you—it should have been you."*
> *I blink, fighting back the tears as I lie in the hospital bed, surrounded by people who hate me. "I know."*
> *She starts to sob harder and runs out of the room, leaving me alone with my guilt consuming me, and all I want to do is feel death again.*

I tear myself away from the memory as Nova's quivering hand slides across the seat and takes hold of mine. Heat. Warmth. Comfort. Fear. All these things surge through me, and all I can do is stare at our hands, fingers tangled, connected. It's been a long fucking time since I've felt a connection, the last time being with her last summer.

"I went to therapy for a while," she divulges as she clutches my hand. Her fingers are trembling, and I notice that just below the scar on her wrist is a tattoo: *never forget*. I wonder what it means, what she doesn't want to forget. "It was kind of helpful... It made me realize that I was running away from my problems instead of facing them. All the stuff I did... the drugs, how I cut my wrist, all of it was because I wasn't dealing with Landon... my boyfriend's death." She says it like it's so easy to talk about and I have no idea what the fuck is going on. I mean, I remember her telling me her boyfriend had taken his own life, but she was bawling her eyes out and now she looks so calm. I remember the scar on her wrist, too, but she never flat-out said she did it herself until now.

"That's good," I say, not sure what else to say. What I want to do is just hug her, feel her, be the kind of person to comfort her, but I can't do that to her—offer her this revolting ghost version of myself. "I'm really glad for you."

"It is good," she agrees, stroking the back of my hand with her finger. The feel of her skin on mine makes me shudder, and I don't know why. I'm numbed by drugs. I shouldn't feel anything, yet I do. I feel everything. The heat of the sun. The slightest variation in our body temperatures, the soft coolness of the air as it hits my cheek. How much I want to kiss her.

"It made me realize who I was and what I wanted out of life...I want to live, and I mean *really* live, not just go through life in a daze. And I want to help people who are going through the same thing I went through...people who won't ask for help when they need it." She pauses. "I actually spent a lot of time volunteering for a suicide hotline, helping people."

"That's really great." I'm happy she's made a life for herself, one where she can use her good heart to help people. "I'm so glad you moved on from all this shit..." I glance down at my bruised and scarred chest and my scraped-up hand, markings of who I am now. "I've always told you that you didn't belong in our world."

"I don't think anyone really does," she says with all honesty. "I just think that sometimes people *think* that they do."

I press my free hand to the side of my head as it begins to throb. She's messing with my head and it's giving me a headache. It's like her words have a hidden meaning, yet I can't figure it out what it is.

"I don't agree with that," I say, still holding her hand even though I know I should let go. *Just a little bit longer. Just a few more minutes of warmth before I step into the cold.* "I think that sometimes people do terrible things and deserve to rot and die."

She winces, her breath catching, but she quickly gathers herself and scoots closer to me on the seat. "You didn't do anything terrible."

I clamp my jaw tightly and pull my hand away. "You have no idea of the things I did...what I've done."

"So tell me," she says, like it's that easy, when it's not. "Let me understand you."

"You can't—no one can. I already told you this. No one can help me who's alive, anyway." Remorse skyrockets through me as I accidentally let the truth slip, but there's no taking it back. Sometimes, when I'm really high, at that point where I almost feel detached from my body, I think that maybe Lexi can help me, even though she's dead. Sometimes when I get that far gone, she doesn't feel dead—or maybe it's that I don't feel alive—and I swear she can hear my thoughts, almost touch me. She tells me that it's okay. That she forgives me and loves me, like she did yesterday when I was getting beaten up. But the comfort is only brief, since when I come out of my daze, I realize that it wasn't real and that no one will ever forgive me. That I'm a junkie who killed two people and there's no changing that.

"Quinton, you're not alone," Nova says, her eyes watering as she inches closer to me, looking like she feels sorry for me. I want the look to go away so goddamned bad I'm considering shouting at her, but then she gets close enough that her bare knee touches the side of my leg. "And if you'll talk to me, you might be able to realize that. That you're not alone. That people care…that I care."

Heat swelters me—her heat. I feel it. It's been a long time since I've felt anything, and I want to jump out the door and run, yet I want to melt into her, too. I can't think straight. I need her to stop this. Need her to stop trying.

"What if I told you I killed someone?" I say, hoping that maybe it's what will finally cut the ties…the connection between us that needs to be severed. "Would you still want to understand me then? Would you still care about me?"

She winces and I think, *There you go. Now are you scared? Now do you want to understand me?*

"I don't believe that," she tells me, quickly composing herself.

"But I did," I say in a low voice, leaning in. "I took two lives, actually."

"Not on purpose, I'm sure." She barely seems worried, and

it annoys me because I don't understand the reaction. Everyone around me told me what I fuckup I was, how much I messed up, how much I ruined everything. And she's just sitting here, looking at me like it's perfectly okay.

"No, but it was still my fault." My voice cracks, revealing that I'm not really okay with talking about this, just pretending.

"Not necessarily," she insists and then shifts so she's pretty much sitting on my lap, her knees on mine, her back against the dashboard so she's looking at me straight on and I seriously forget how to breathe. The sensation is so intense that it actually hurts, in my chest, my gut, my heart, what's left of my broken, insignificant soul. "I think that maybe you think it was your fault, but I know that sometimes blaming yourself is the only way to deal." She places her hand on my cheek, and I feel a spark of life inside me, one I thought had burned out a long time ago.

"That's not what I'm doing...I don't even deal with it." I pause, wondering how she got me to say that aloud when she doesn't even know what the heck I'm talking about. I've been so shut down for months, and now she shows up and I can feel that pull to life again. I've taken a breath again, and it's time to return to my drowning because I can feel the painful prickle of memories surfacing. What death felt like on my hands; Lexi's blood, my own, the guilt, all still memories decaying inside me.

"I need to go back." I ball my hands into fists to keep from touching her and I stare out the window, avoiding her overpowering gaze. "I'm done talking. I just want to go back now."

She hesitates and I expect her to argue, but instead she puts the car in reverse. "Okay, I can take you back, but can I ask for a favor before I do?" she asks.

I squeeze my eyes shut, holding my breath, wishing I could stop breathing altogether. "Sure."

"Can I come visit you tomorrow?" she requests in a soft tone. "I'm not going to be here for very long, and I'd like to see you and talk to you a little bit more before I have to go."

I should tell her no, save her like she's trying to save me, but even in my cracked-up head I can't bring myself to let her go just yet, so I greedily say, "Yeah, if you want to, but I hope you don't." I open my eyes and watch her reaction.

She smashes her lips together, battling her nerves. "But I do want to see you. I really, really do."

I'm not sure what to do with that, so I decide to do nothing, shutting myself down, and it's easy because seconds later I'm thinking about something else, getting home, getting to Johnny's, getting my next hit. Then nothing will matter. Not this. Not the future. My past. What I did.

It'll all be gone.

❧

I don't say much to her on the ride back to my place, but she talks lightly about music, how she's been playing again, and I love hearing her talk that way. I love hearing her happy. It makes me almost want to smile, and I haven't wanted to smile in a really long time, but I don't think I quite get there.

Then we're pulling up to my building, and the slight elation I was feeling deflates into the darkness that engulfs the place where I live. My mouth begins to salivate, knowing what's waiting for me as soon as I get Tristan and get to Johnny's. I want it more than sitting in this car, more than eating, breathing, living.

"So when should I come over tomorrow?" she asks, the tires of the car grinding against the gravel as she stops the car a little ways from the building.

"Whenever you want," I tell her, because it doesn't really matter. I know I'm going to be up all night and all day after I get enough lines in my system. Then I start to get out of the car, ready to get inside my apartment. Ready to forget all of this. Ready to be free again from my emotions, my conflict, my memories. I'm ready to return to my prison.

"Wait, Quinton," she calls out, and I pause, turning to look at her.

Her lips part, like she's about to say something, but then she shuts her mouth and scoots over toward me. I freeze up, wondering what she's doing. Then she opens the glove box and takes out a pen and tears a corner off an envelope. She jots down some digits and then hands the paper to me. "This is my number, just in case you need to call me for something."

I stare down at the paper in my hand, baffled that she gave it to me. "I don't have a phone."

"I know," she says, tossing the pen down on the dashboard. "But Delilah does, and I want to make sure you have that just in case."

I try not to get worked up over the fact that she gave her number to me, like she actually doesn't mind if I call. Like she wants to talk to me. No one has given me their phone number in a very long time, and I'm not sure what to do with it. Part of me wants to throw it away and get rid of the temptation to call her, but instead I find myself putting it in my pocket. Then I start to get out of the car, and she leans over and gently places a kiss on my mouth. I'm not sure why she does it, if it's simply a friendly kiss or if she's experiencing the same kind of pull I am. But the kiss feels twisted and wrong in a way, because I'm high and I wonder if she can taste it on me—the decay inside me. But in another way the kiss feels so damn right, like if I was living a normal life, one where I hadn't gotten in a car accident, and I'd simply broken up with Lexi and met Nova, we would have kissed like that all the time.

I'm so sorry, Lexi. For forgetting you. For living. Moving forward in life, while you remain motionless.

Thoughts of Lexi stab at my mind, yet I still kiss Nova back, slipping my tongue into her mouth, getting a brief taste of her before I pull back. "I'll see you later," I whisper against her lips and then lean back and take the food when she hands it to me, feeling like I'm leaving a piece of myself behind. But I shove the sensation aside and go back to my apartment, where I belong.

When I open the door, I'm flooded by a musty cloud of smoke, and my senses of taste, sight, smell, and touch, go haywire. God, I need to feed my addiction. Now. In fact, waiting to get back to my room seems nearly impossible.

Delilah and Dylan are sitting on the sofa, heating up some crystal on a piece of aluminum foil. Delilah is fixated on it, cuddled up to Dylan's side, watching him drag the lighter back and forth and create smoke. They both have bags under their eyes, and I wonder how long it's been since they've slept... I wonder how long it's been since I've slept.

"Where the hell have you been?" Dylan asks, glancing up from the piece of aluminum foil. He looks down at the McDonald's bag in my hand, confused because we rarely eat. "And where did you get that?" He's got a fresh bruise under his eye, and there's dried blood on his lip.

"From McDonald's," I say, heading for my room, not wanting to talk about Nova to either of them because it feels wrong to talk about her in such a crappy-ass environment. "What happened to your face?"

"You and Tristan happened to my face," he says, irritated. Then he hands the aluminum foil and lighter to Delilah as he gets to his feet, scooping up something I didn't notice before on the coffee table. A small gun. *What the fuck?* "Do you want to tell me what happened with Trace... why you look like you got the shit beat out of you?"

I stop near the curtain that shields the kitchen from the living room and flex my bruised fingers as I eyeball the gun, trying not to look alarmed, but it's a fucking gun, for God's sake. "He sort of kicked my ass." I pause, deciding whether I should ask. "Where did you get that?"

Dylan glances unconcernedly at the gun in his hand. "I got it the other day to protect myself."

"Protect yourself from what?" I ask as Delilah's attention lazily drifts up from her crystal. Her eyes widen as she spots the gun in Dylan's hand, and when she looks at me, she appears horrified, very unlike herself, since usually she pretends she doesn't give a shit about anything.

"Baby, put the gun down," she says, her voice quiet—scared. She's scared, and I am, too, honestly.

"Fuck you," Dylan snaps at her, and then he looks at me. His expression is stone-cold as he ambles toward me, the veins in his neck bulging, anger simmering in his eyes about ready to burst. "I had to get this after you two fucked up and now we're all on very thin ice." He points his finger at the bruise below his eye. "You see this fucking thing right here? I got this because I was jumped by Trace and his guys." He jabs a finger roughly against my chest. "Because you two worked for me and messed him over...like it's my fault you're dumbasses." He leans forward, his breath hot on my face. "Do you know how stupid you are to mess around with Trace?" He steps back and rakes his hand over his bald head, his other hand at his side, grasping the gun. "Jesus, I knew this was coming, and I'm sure it isn't over with yet. The guy's a relentless douche."

"You don't know anything for sure...Maybe Trace is satisfied now that he beat the shit out of me and you," I say, knowing it's a stupid thought process and that there's no way that could be possible, but Dylan is all worked up with a gun in his hand. I glance over at Delilah as she gets up from the couch, watching us with caution. At first I think she's going to come over and try to talk him down, but then she eyes the door like she's going to run.

"Yeah, because that's the way the world works," Dylan snaps, swinging the gun around while he turns in a circle. Delilah freezes in place while I realize just how severe this situation is: that he's high and he's got a gun and I'm standing right here in front of him. The question is: do I care? I'm not sure.

He stops spinning and lowers the gun. "You two better stop fucking up," he warns in a low tone. "I have a lot riding on connections and I don't want you messing up any more of them."

My heart is thudding in my chest as I think about how ruining his connection with Trace is only part of the problem. Tristan has also been stealing drugs and money from Dylan, like he did the other day. But as far as Dylan knows, I was the last person with the money. Does he know it's gone? Does he think I took it? Will he shoot me if I tell him it was Tristan? Do I care? Jesus, my thoughts are racing a million miles a minute, flowing in a crooked stream through my brain. I'm losing control and I need to get out of here.

Dylan tosses his gun onto the coffee table, making both me and Delilah jump. I seriously expected it to go off, but it doesn't, and the air starts to cool, although Dylan still looks like he's going to hit me, his jaw set tight, his fist clenched, his arm kinked and ready to strike.

But then he settles down and backs away, putting up his hands. "Take care of this mess—fix things with Trace. Get him drugs or pay him back—do whatever you have to to make this good again. And pay me back that fucking money you two were supposed to use for the exchange at Johnny's before your dumb ass got beat," he says in a voice that carries a warning. "Or else you're out of the house. You and Tristan both. I'm tired of your shit."

I want to tell him that this apartment doesn't belong to him, since we're renting it together, but the gun is lying on the table, so instead I nod, even though I have no idea how I'm going to do either of those things. Then I go back into my room without saying another word. Tristan is waiting there with a mirror out in front of him along with a spoon and a syringe and a small plastic bag filled with crystallized powder. He's just staring at it with his knees pulled up to his chest and his arms wrapped around his legs.

When the door creaks, he glances up, looking relieved, and as soon as I see what he has in front of him, our emotions match. "Thank God," he says. "I thought I was going to lose my mind if I had to wait a second longer."

"We have a huge problem," I announce as I kick the door shut behind me. "Did you know Dylan has a gun?"

Tristan nods his head distractedly as he stares at the spoon. "Yeah, he made a point to show it to me yesterday when he threatened me and told me that I needed to patch things up with Trace and to pay him back the money we took."

Anger flickers when he says "we," but I quickly simmer down, remembering I owe Tristan more than I'll ever be able to pay him back for killing his sister. "You should have said something. He completely blindsided me with it just now."

He shrugs, glancing up at me. "Sorry, I forgot."

I want to get mad at him, but at the same time I sort of understand how he could forget—how easily our spun minds can make things disappear. "So what are we going to do about it? I mean, he's super pissed and I guess Trace gave him a shiner—kicked his ass like he did mine."

"We'll look for the gun when he's asleep or something and get rid of it," Tristan suggests, stretching his arms above his head as he blinks tiredly, probably ready for his next boost of adrenaline.

"Okay, but even if we do that, we still have to worry about Trace coming to kick your ass."

"If he does, then he does," Tristan says indifferently, his hands flopping onto his lap.

I bend down and lower myself to the floor beside the mattress, moving slowly because my body still aches. "I think we need to take care of it." Not for me, but for him.

He rolls his eyes. "Just because Trace threatens us doesn't mean he's actually going to do anything about it."

I look down at my banged-up body. "You really think so?" I ask.

Tristan grunts unenthusiastically. "Fine, I'll figure out a

way to pay him back or something. Or better yet, we could just find where Dylan hides his dealing stash and give him that."

"Yeah, I don't think pissing Dylan off is going to help this situation at all." I bring my knee up and rest my arm on it. "We just need to find a way to pay Trace back what you owe him." I glance at the spoon and mirror on the floor and the bag of crystal. "And I'm guessing we need to find a way to pay Dylan back, too, since I'm assuming you already spent that money you stole from him."

"I'll figure something out," he says, still looking like he doesn't give a shit, like he doesn't care what happens to him, and it makes me angry, not at him, but at myself. Because deep down, I have to wonder why he's here in this shithole. That maybe part of the reason is because I killed his sister and he couldn't handle the pain, just like I can't. "I'll go break into some houses and get some cash. I should be able to scrounge enough up over the next week or so."

I'm not so sure, but it's a start. "We should get started, like, tonight."

Tristan nods, and I rack my brain for a better way to get him out of this, one that I know for sure will work. What I want to do is call his parents and tell them to come get him. I'm not sure how well that'd go over, though, considering they hate me and Tristan probably would get really pissed and refuse to go with them. And what if they said no?

"Where'd you get that?" Tristan asks as he catches sight of the bag of food in my hand.

I blow out a stressed breath as I glance down at the bag and remember I have other problems, too, at the moment, like how determined Nova looked to spend time with me—be with me. "Nova made me take it." I set the bag down beside my feet and lift my hips to take the piece of paper with her phone number on it out of my pocket.

Tristan scratches the back of his neck and then collects the spoon from the floor. "Yeah, she seems to care about you, doesn't she?" He rotates the spoon in his hand as I grab my empty wallet and tuck the paper inside it, deciding to hold on to it for a while.

"She cares about everyone," I mumble as the awkwardness between us rises.

"Yeah, but she really seems to care about you," he says, watching my response with interest.

"Maybe." I remember her words in the car, how she said she wants to help me. Me, the fucked-up druggie loser. I take the spoon away from him and toss it aside, then pick up the mirror and the plastic bag full of crystal. The crystal is calling to me, promising me that it'll let me forget everything that happened today with a simple taste.

Tristan drops the spoon back onto the floor and steals the plastic bag from me, opening it up, then dipping his finger in the white powder. "So how did it go with Nova?" he asks distractedly. "I mean, what does she even want?"

My hands start to quiver with my need to feel the taste of

it—to forget everything that's happened today. Nova. Dylan. Trace. Lexi. Ryder. Everything and everyone. "To help me."

His concentration is diverted to me. "*What?*"

"She says she wants to help me." My eyes are glued on the bag in his hand, not on his words, not on Nova anymore. Everything is slipping away, which is why I love it—need it to survive.

He studies me, skimming the tattoos on my arm. "Why?" He says it like he can't understand, and neither can I. I'm worthless. He knows it. I know it. Everyone knows it except for Nova.

"I have no idea." I pick up the spoon and fiddle with it to keep myself busy, bending the handle back and forth. Focus. "And I don't want to talk about it anymore."

He arches his brow as he glances at the spoon in my hand. "Do you want to try that? Because I'm telling you, it's so much better than what you're used to. In fact, we could do a speedball."

"I've already told you I'm not going to do that... I hate needles and mixing drugs," I say, chucking the spoon on the floor. "I just want to get spun."

He scoots off the mattress and onto the floor in front of me, putting the mirror between us. "Then let's get spun."

So we do, and for a moment I forget my past, my future, how Nova made me feel something today. I forget about the heavy cloud hanging over us. How much bad shit could go down at any moment.

I forget about *everything*.

Chapter Seven

May 19, day four of summer break

Nova

It's been a long three days, filled with visits to Quinton that seem to be leading nowhere. We have the same conversations, and he won't open up to me at all. I'm not sure how to bring up to him that I know about the accident, so I just keep dodging around it, lying to him. But bringing up memories like that is complicated and painful. I know because every time someone would even mention Landon's name after his death, it'd feel like a part of me died inside.

When I'm not over there with Quinton, I spend my time hanging out with Lea. We haven't gone to the Strip yet, but we chatted about going out this weekend when it's late and all the lights are on, just as long as her uncle doesn't mind that we come home late. He actually just got home from his business trip last night and chatted with Lea and me for a little bit. He seems nice and even cooked us dinner while he asked us about our plans while we are here. Lea was vague about the details, telling him that we were here to see a friend.

It's late morning and I'm sitting in the guest room at Lea's uncle's house with the computer screen aimed at me so I can see myself as I get ready to record before I head over to Quinton's for my daily visit. I have the curtain pulled shut to avoid any glare. My brown hair is wavy and runs down to my shoulders and the blue studs in my ears match my tank top. I have shorts on and no shoes. "It's been three days of going over to see Quinton, and the time I spend with him feels so short and the time in between feels so long because I'm always worried about what he's doing when I'm gone." I lean forward in the chair, getting closer to the screen. "I still hate going over there, though, because it's so terrifying…his place. I'm not even sure why. If it's because there's so many rough people walking around doing things that are bad and illegal or if it's the fact that if I didn't change paths, I could have ended up there." I pause, considering my next words carefully. "What's really hard is that sometimes I can see myself there, sitting beside Quinton on the shitty mattress in his room. I can picture myself there getting high beside him, connecting with him, and life is so different. Less stressful." I make a guilty face. "Maybe that's not the right word, because it is stressful in a different way, but it's like you're so wrapped up in drugs that you can't register the stress until it's too late and everything's falling apart. I don't want to get sucked into it again, but it's so easy, and even though I won't tell Lea this"—I lower my voice and lean closer to the screen—"there's been a few fleeting seconds where I think why not? Why not just join him again? What's stopping you?

Which makes me wonder if maybe I'm not the right person to save Quinton." I raise my arm in front of the screen and get a shot of my scar and tattoo. "But then I look down at this and I remember that place, where I was so lost, drifting, drifting, drifting. I could have died and it wouldn't have mattered," I say. "But right now it does matter because I want to live."

I sigh, knowing I'm rambling at this point. "Honestly, I don't know what exactly I'm trying to say with this recording, other than to get my thoughts out." I faintly smile. "Sort of like a diary." I click the camera off and shut down the computer. I slip my sandals on and grab my bag, ready to head out, hoping that I can continually remember, never forget just how bad things can get, because it's what keeps me going.

Later that day I pull up to Quinton's apartment building. Even though I've been here four times, I still get extremely nervous just thinking about walking up to Quinton's door. And when I get there, I always wonder about everything that could be going on on the other side of that cracked door. If he's doing drugs right at this moment. If he's okay. If he's overdoing it. If he's alive. I hate to think it, but he looks so bad, so scraggly, so beat up that I have to wonder if he'll even answer the door or if one time I'll come over here and he'll be dead. I know it's really messed up to go to the dark possibilities instead of the lighter ones, but when you've seen as much dark as I have, it's hard not to automatically think of the bad.

Thankfully, today, when I knock on the door, I get a brief respite from the dark when Quinton answers. I feel even better when he quickly steps out, so I don't have to go inside. He's got a wrinkly black shirt on and cargo shorts that are frayed at the bottom, and his hand is still bruised but not as swollen. His hair is shaggy and he's starting to grow a stubbly goatee.

"Hey," he says as he starts to shut the door, but then he gets this really weird look on his face, like he's torn. Then he holds up a finger. "Can you hold on for a second?"

I nod, barely able to keep up with him as he rushes back inside, leaving the door wide open. The sunlight heats up my back as I stare inside the stuffy apartment, the air laced with smoke coming from a lit cigarette on an ashtray on the coffee table. Delilah's passed out on the sofa in the living room, her arm draped over her stomach as she sleeps on her back. I haven't talked to her yet and I'm sort of glad because I have a feeling that conversation isn't going to go very well. Not just because she's been a bitch to me on the phone, but because if she does decide to be nice to me, I know I could possibly be swept up in being her friend. And being her friend means getting high. And I'm still not sure how I'd respond if I were actually offered something.

As I'm watching the smoke snake around the room, Dylan unexpectedly strides out of the hallway and over to the coffee table. He looks like a skeleton, but they all do really: bony arms, bald head, his cheekbones shaded, bags under his eyes. He also seems distracted, oblivious to me as he hunts the room for something.

At first, anyway.

But as I instinctively take a step back, his eyes elevate to me. I've never been a fan of him. He was too intense and treated Delilah like shit. Plus, he seemed angry all the time, no matter what was going on.

He looks calm now, though, which might be more frightening than when he's angry. "What are you doing here?" he asks as he picks up a tiny bag off the table.

"Waiting for Quinton," I answer quickly, stepping back until my back brushes the railing.

He winds around the coffee table toward me. "No, I mean what the fuck are you doing here in Vegas?" He halts at the doorway, staying in the shadows, clutching the bag in his hand. "Weren't you, like, going to college or something?"

"Yeah, but it's summer break," I explain nervously. "So I decided to come down here for a while."

"To see Quinton?" he asks, giving me a look like he thinks I'm a moron. "Interesting."

I nod, not saying anything, hoping he'll leave, but all he does is stand there and stare at me. It's really starting to creep me out when Delilah sits up on the sofa. She says something, but her speech is so slurred I can't understand her. Then she stumbles over to Dylan, her red hair tangled around her pale, thin face, her cheekbones hollowed out. She's wearing a T-shirt that barely covers her thighs and, like Tristan, she has a few sores on her arms. She also has a massive bruise on her cheek, like she's recently been in a fight. That's when I notice Dylan's knuckles are covered in scabs like he scraped the skin on something. Delilah's face, maybe. I have to wonder.

"Baby..." She trails off as Dylan turns around and gives her a gentle shove toward the sofa.

"Go lie down," he calls over his shoulder in an icy tone.

She keeps herself from falling by grasping the back of a chair. "I...need..." She blinks around the room, and despite everything we've been through, all the crappy moments we shared, my heart twists inside my chest.

"What's she on?" I ask, inching forward, preparing to help her.

Dylan turns around and slams a hand on each side of the doorframe, blocking my way in. "That's none of your damn business."

I stand on my tiptoes and glance over his shoulder at Delilah. "Delilah, are you okay?"

She stumbles over a glass pipe on the floor as she makes the rest of the short walk back to the sofa and then flops down on her back. "I'm fine...go...k..." She waves her hand at me, shooing me away.

"You don't look fine," I say, wondering what it would take to get Dylan out of my way.

Dylan leans to the side, shielding her completely from my view. "She said she was fine. Now back off," he growls in a low voice.

I tip my chin up and meet his sullen eyes. I think about saying something like "Fuck off," which is completely out of character for me, but at the same time being here isn't really me either.

I never manage to find my voice, though, and instead Dylan just ends up smirking at me for a painfully long minute. When I see Quinton emerge from the hallway, I exhale deafeningly, and Dylan seems pleased about the fact that he was making me nervous.

Quinton glances at Delilah, who's lying on the sofa with her eyes shut, as he makes his way across the room. He doesn't say anything as he pushes Dylan aside and squeezes between him and the doorway. Dylan glowers at him, and Quinton seems edgy, even placing his arm around my back and hurriedly guiding me away from the door. "You ready?" he asks.

"Yeah…" I peek over my shoulder at Dylan, who's watching us walk away, lighting up a cigarette. It creeps me out even more, and I scoot closer to Quinton, feeling a little safer being near him.

Dylan stays that way until we're halfway across the balcony and then goes back inside the apartment, shutting the door behind him.

I turn around and focus on walking. "Is Delilah okay?" I ask Quinton.

He shields his eyes from the sun with his hand. "She's as okay as the rest of us."

"She seemed out of it."

"That's because she was."

"What's she on?"

He hesitates, his hand on my back tensing. "You really want to know?" he asks, and I nod. "She's on heroin."

"Do you...?" I inspect his arms, noting they're sore-free, but I want to be sure. "Do you do it?"

He shakes his head with no hesitancy. "Not my thing."

"Oh." I'm not sure if that makes me feel better, because he still does drugs. "What about Dylan?" I ask as he guides me around a man standing in the middle of the balcony, smoking. "What's he on?"

"His asshole-ness," Quinton begrudgingly says.

"So he doesn't do drugs?" I ask, astonished by the idea.

"No, he does," he replies, slowing down as we approach the stairs. "But high or not, he's always a dick."

It's a lot to take in—maybe too much. Everything around here is so dark and it hurts to walk around in it, even if I'm only visiting. I can still feel it taking a toll on me. The heaviness. The fear. The temptation. So much could go wrong just from my being here.

But you need to be here. You need to save him. Like you didn't with Landon.

Quinton withdraws his hand from my back and we start down the stairs. "So where are we going today? Or are we just chilling in your car again?" He seems twitchy, his brown eyes really large and glossy and his nose red. It makes me sad to see it, how he's hurting himself.

"Do you want to go somewhere else?" I ask, holding on to the railing.

He shrugs as we reach the bottom of the stairway. "I'm down for wherever, just as long as I'm back by, like, five."

I want to ask him why, but at the same time I fear the answer, so I keep my lips sealed. We climb in the car and I start up the engine and crank the air, trying to think of a safe place to go. "There's this good restaurant my friend Lea told me about," I say. "We could go get something to eat there."

He waves me off. "Nah, I'm not really hungry."

"Okay." I try to think of somewhere else, but I don't know Vegas very well.

"I know somewhere we can go," Quinton says with a thoughtful look on his face, his honey-brown eyes temporarily lighting up. "But you're going to have to trust me."

It takes me a minute to respond, because even though I want to trust him, I'm not sure I can. "Okay, but where is this place?"

"It's a surprise." He gives me a smile, but it's difficult to see it because I don't think it's real, but rather created by his high. But I play along, because it's all I can do. Pretend that it's real. Pretend I'm okay with everything. "Okay, but you got to give me directions."

He motions to me to drive forward. "Get going and I'll guide you there." He winks at me. "Just relax. You can trust me, Nova."

Even though every single part of me screams that I can't, I force myself to drive forward, letting him guide me, hoping I'm not going to do something stupid and make a wrong turn. Because one wrong turn can lead to a lot of damage.

Quinton

Dylan's been acting strange lately, even though we managed to pay him back with some money we stole from a house the other night. He seems more violent and erratic than he has in the past. I think all the smack is starting to screw with his head a little bit, so I don't like it when I walk out and he's paying so much attention to Nova. I shouldn't have left her out there alone, but the moment I saw her, my heart leaped in my chest, way too excited to see her. Such a wrong reaction, and I had to go back and get enough crystal for a hit or two if I need it, if I get to feeling too much while I'm out with her.

I'm actually probably way too high to be doing anything, yet somehow I find myself out and about. It's like one minute I'm back in my room, absorbing as much intoxicating crystal as I can, feeling my heart rate speed up to the point where I feel like I'm flying—feel like I could do anything, and then suddenly I'm driving in the car with Nova, flirting with her like we're on a date.

Stupid.

Stupid.

Stupid.

Yet at the same time I'm perfectly content with being stupid—with being near her, because I'm soaring.

High.

Confused.

After I get her away from the apartment and Dylan, I tell

her to drive and she does, trusting me, which she shouldn't, yet it pleases me in the most fucked-up way possible. By the time we're pulling up to the building, I can tell I'm going to mess this up badly. I can feel it, yet I'm too spun out of my mind to care.

"So this is where you wanted to take me?" Nova asks, with a baffled look on her face at the sight of the dated motel that I found one day when Tristan and I were looking for a place to crash after we got caught shoplifting and had to find a quick place to hide. The thing is, I'm still not even sure if we were ever being chased or if paranoia had set in.

I take off my seat belt because she always makes me wear it whenever I'm in the car with her. "Yeah. I know it looks a little sketchy, but we'll be okay," I tell her, and when she still looks skeptical, I add, "Trust me, Nova." My thoughts laugh at me, deep down knowing I'm not trustworthy, but it's like I can't get my emotions to link with my thoughts and my thoughts to link with my mouth, so I'm just saying stuff, cruising through the motions without thinking of the consequences.

She swallows hard, but then unbuckles her seat belt, and we get out of the car. I meet her around the front. I don't know why, but I slip my arm around her waist, and again I don't know why, but for some reason she lets me. It's so hard being near her when I feel this pull toward her, yet I also feel this push away from her, driven by my guilt.

"You seem in a really good mood today," she notes,

glancing up at me with those gorgeous eyes that I've been sketching every day despite the battle of my inner thoughts.

I shrug and pull my hand away, giving in to the push and the guilt. "I'm just in a normal mood."

She doesn't say anything else as she follows me through the door that's marked as an exit. She instantly stiffens as she steps into the dust and the darkness and the debris on the floor. The walls are caving in and there's spray paint on the wall and I get her reluctance, but at the same time I know she'll appreciate why I brought her here.

"Just follow me." I slip my fingers through hers, surrendering to the pull. "I promise when we get to the top, it'll be worth it."

Her eyes widen as she angles her chin back and looks up at the hole in the ceiling that stretches through five floors. "Is it safe to get to the top?"

"Of course," I say, but I'm not really sure. "Just follow where I walk."

She nods and then moves to the side when I do, tracking my footsteps, clutching my hand, her skin damp. It briefly registers through her nervous touch that she's trusting me to keep her safe, and so when I reach the place where Tristan and I climbed up through the holes in the walls to get to the top, I instead go to the right to the stairway, because it's safer.

"So this place used to be an old hotel?" she asks as she takes calculated steps, making sure to stay close to the wall.

I put my hand on the wall as the stairs creak below our feet. "I think so. At least that's what the sign said outside. I'm guessing, though, that it was probably a casino, too, since most of the hotels here are."

She glances at an open room that still has orange shag carpet and brightly painted yellow walls with a rainbow pattern down them. "Yeah, they even have slot machines in the gas stations. It's weird and noisy. Plus, everyone's always smoking," she says, and when I pause, she quickly adds, "It doesn't bother me, but my friend Lea can't stand the smell of cigarettes."

I start walking again. It's amazing how a single sentence can remind me just how far apart we are, even if part of me doesn't want us to be that way. "Is Lea the girl who was with you the first day you showed up at my place?"

She nods with her head tipped down, hair veiling her face, her attention focused on the floor as she chews her lip, and all I can think is how perfect she is and how much I want to draw her. As soon as the thought surfaces, it makes me feel like I'm cheating on Lexi, thinking about doing that with someone else, and I seriously almost turn around and bail out, wishing I could go back to my room and do more lines.

"I met her at the beginning of the school year," Nova continues as she sidesteps a large chunk of Sheetrock. "She came up to me and introduced herself when I went to this center for people who've lost a loved one to suicide."

I look over my shoulder at her. "She's lost someone, too?"

"Her dad," Nova explains as she holds on to my hand,

and the fingers of her other hand wrap around my arm. "Even though it's not quite the same as what I went through, we really connected, sort of like I did with you for a while there."

I stop walking, moving, breathing. Time stops. She ends up nearly running into me, stumbling over her feet, but catches herself by jabbing her fingertips deeper into my arm and putting her hand on the wall beside us.

She grips my arm as she stares up at me. "What's wrong?"

"What do you mean you connected with me?" I ask, my voice coming out a little sharper than I planned.

"Last summer," she says timidly. "That time we spent together—I thought we sort of connected. Not like in a hey-we're-best-friends way, but..." She releases my arm to drag her fingers through her hair. She must have gotten dust on her hand from touching the wall because the movement leaves a streak of it in her hair. "But I could talk to you about stuff that I wasn't able to talk to anyone else about. Stuff about my dad and Landon."

I reach up and brush my hand across her hair, trying to get the dust off her head, and I hate how excited my heart gets when her breathing speeds up, all from me touching her. "Nova, I'm pretty sure that was the weed that let you talk openly like that, not me."

She shakes her head, her tongue slipping out of her mouth to wet her dry lips, and all I want to do is back her into the wall, pick her up, and devour her. But the wall would probably crumble under the slightest pressure, and I'm not sure we'd survive the fall.

"I don't think that's what it was," she says. "And I'm going to prove it to you."

My face contorts with confusion. "How?"

She motions me forward. "Just get us to somewhere where the floor doesn't feel like it's going to give out and I'll tell you."

I'm not sure what she's up to, but I'm curious, so I start up the stairs again, holding her hand, guiding her around the holes in the floor, trying to focus on the bigger picture of all this, but I can see only three steps ahead.

When we reach the top of the stairway, I open the door and sunlight spills over us like warm water. Stepping to the side, I hold the door ajar and let Nova through.

She steps out into the sunlight, glancing around at the massive signs on the rooftop. Ones that I'm guessing used to belong to casinos that are closed down now. Some are made up of light bulbs and others are just painted. Some are cracked, others are warped, and they all sort of create this maze.

"Wow…" She pauses as she takes in everything. "There are no words. This is amazing." She glances at me, her big eyes making me feel like I'm falling into her. Part of me wishes that were really happening, but I think I'm tripping out.

"Yeah, it is," I agree, nodding, then point to a stack of bricks near a large VIVA LAS VEGAS sign. "Can you go get one of those bricks? Because if the door shuts, we're locked up here."

She pulls a wary face, but then zigzags around the signs, ducking and maneuvering around them as she crosses the length of the roof and picks up a brick. I try not to smile at how much she struggles to carry it, either because it's too heavy for her or because she doesn't want to get dirty. She sets it down in front of the door and I gently let the door go, holding on to it until I know the brick is going to hold. Then I hop over a smaller sign that's fallen over in the way and head over to the ledge of the roof and climb up onto it. I sit down, hanging my legs over the side. Nova doesn't follow me right away, so I pat the spot next to me and tell her to come over without looking at her, wondering just how much she trusts me. I secretly wish she'd just run away, but at the same time I want to hear what she has to say—why she thinks we connected last summer.

Of course she sits down, because she's sweet and innocent and sees some sort of good inside me. I honestly don't get it, because whenever I look into a mirror, which isn't that often, all I can see is a skeleton, the remains of a once-good person, who ruined everything and who will always ruin everything. Kind of like the view in front of me of old buildings, stores, houses, that I can tell used to be beautiful before things changed—life changed—and they were all forgotten, lost like the sand in the wind, left to crumple in the shadows of the city, the area no one wants to see, yet I prefer it.

"You think you're not good enough," she says, situating herself beside me, her legs dangling over the edge. "But you are."

"What?" My head snaps in her direction as I try to rewind and see if maybe I was really thinking my thoughts aloud.

"When you're in that dark place," she says. "At least that's how it was for me. It was almost like I thought I didn't deserve to be happy."

I relax a little, understanding that she's just thinking aloud. "And that's why you did drugs?" I ask.

She shrugs. "One of the reasons. But, honestly, there were many . . . like the fact that I wasn't dealing with my boyfriend's death . . . What are your reasons?"

She expresses herself so easily and I'm not sure how to respond. There's no way I can explain to her why I do it—all the dark reasons. "Why would you think I even have a reason?" I ask. "Maybe I just do it because it feels good."

"Does it feel good?" There's a challenge in her eyes that makes me fear what she's going to say after I answer.

"Sometimes, yes," I tell her straightforwardly. "I mean, I don't know how it was for you, but it helps me forget stuff."

"What kind of stuff?" she asks interestedly as she tucks her hands under her legs.

"Stuff I've done." I pop my neck and then crack my jaw. "But why are we talking about this?"

She plays with a loose strand of her hair, twirling it around her finger as she gets lost in her thoughts, staring down at the abandoned stores and houses five stories below us. "Is this why you brought me here? To show me the view?" she wonders, eluding my question.

I look her over, wondering what's going on in her head. Is she seeing the same view as me? Does she find it repulsive? Or can she still see what it used to be? "Yeah. I stumbled across it once and I liked it." I tear my eyes off her and focus on the view. "It's like Vegas used to be out here, before all the madness took the city over."

"Was it ever not full of madness?" she asks, pointing over her shoulder at the city gleaming against the sunlight and stretching toward the hazy sky. "Because every time I think of Vegas, I can only see that."

I shrug, swinging my feet back and forth. "I'm not sure, but I can picture it, even if it's not true." I put my hand up and motion at a cluster of single-story homes kitty-corner to our right. "Imagine, just a bunch of normal houses, no casinos, no people packing the sidewalks. Everything is painted in warm colors, the grass is green, the fences straight. Trees grow in the yards, bright flowers surround the houses, and people are just hanging around outside and taking life slow." I point to the left at an oddly shaped stucco building with old signs hanging on the side. "Imagine the stores and shopping areas were like that, instead of crammed so close together, all carrying the same overpriced souvenirs. Imagine the quiet, ordinary, simple life. A place that's not busy and where your thoughts don't have to race to keep up with it." I shut my eyes and savor the scent of freedom in the air. "Imagine breathing again."

She's quiet for a while, and I wonder if my tweaker rambling has frightened her off, but when I open my eyes, she looks relaxed as she observes me, turned just at the right angle so the blue sky and sunlight are her only background and her hair is dancing around her face in the gentle breeze. A strand of her hair falls from behind her ear and lands near her chest, and I remember what it was like to touch her there, feel her, do whatever I wanted with her.

Beautiful. That's the word that pops into my head, and for a fleeting moment I just want to hold her and for her to hold me and for me to not have to think about Lexi and Ryder and what I did to them.

"You paint a beautiful picture," she says, interrupting my thoughts. "It makes me want to live in this place."

"Well, it might not exist," I utter quietly. "I was just making up what I see."

"You should draw what you see sometimes," she suggests with a faint smile at her lips. "I bet it would turn out beautiful."

"I'm just rambling," I mutter. "It doesn't really mean anything."

Intensity burns in her eyes. "You'd be surprised what your words can mean to someone."

"I never say anything important," I state truthfully. "Everything I do or say gets forgotten quickly."

"That's not true... You said a lot of stuff to me last summer that meant something. Like when you told me I was too good to be doing drugs."

"That's because you were—are."

"Everyone is," she insists, scooting closer to me. "But you were the one to actually say it aloud."

"It still doesn't mean that what I said mattered," I argue,

wanting to inch away from her, but I can't seem to find the willpower to do so. "You just remember it because it happened during an intense part of your life."

She studies me momentarily and then looks back down at the scenery below us. "Do you remember the pond?" she asks.

That question hits me straight in the heart and makes it slam inside my chest. "How could I forget?" I say, grinding my teeth. "It wasn't one of my finer moments."

Her attention whips back to me. "Are you kidding me?" she asks in shock, which seems so out of place that I have to look up at her to see if she's being real or joking.

"No...I'm being serious," I tell her, fighting the emotions buried inside me—the guilt I feel for leaving her that day. "I should have never left you there like that. I was—am—such a douche."

She gapes at me like she can't believe what she's hearing. "You are not in any way, shape, or form a douche for leaving me there. You pretty much saved me from doing something I'd always regret and that probably would have kept me in that dark place a hell of a lot longer." She says it with so much passion, like she's been thinking about this a lot, and I don't know what to say to her, so instead I stare silently at the ground. Finally, she places her hand on my face and cups my cheek, forcing me to look at her. "You helped me so, so much, whether you want to believe it or not."

Emotions I've worked hard to bury clutch at my heart, and it hurts like needles are lodged in my skin, all connected to my guilt. "I didn't do anything but watch you do stuff you shouldn't."

"And you kept reminding me that I shouldn't—you kept trying to make me see what I was doing."

"But I didn't stop you."

"Because you couldn't." She traces her fingers across my scruffy jawline. "You were—are still—obviously going through some stuff, and you did the only thing you could for me at the time. You kept me out of getting into too much trouble, you listened to me ramble, and you didn't take advantage of my vulnerability when a lot of guys would have."

"A lot of guys would have kicked you out of the house in the first place, before you did anything," I snap. "Just because I didn't fuck you when you were sad doesn't make me a good guy."

She flinches but then composes herself, slanting closer to me, her hand firmly in place on my cheek. "Yes, it does. It makes you a great guy."

The more she says this, the angrier I get, and the sharper the needles become. She needs to stop saying good things about me. I'm not good. I'm a terrible person, and she needs to accept that just like I have and everyone else has.

"No, it doesn't." I lean in to her, our breaths mixing and creating heat, our eyes so close I can see her pupils dilating.

She nods, whispering, "Yes, it does, and I'm going to think that no matter what you say."

I want her to shut up, to be afraid of me, so I don't have to feel the emotions she's triggering. All the work I did today, all the shit I shoved up my nose so I wouldn't have to think the thoughts racing through my head, and now she's saying shit that's making me think them anyway.

I'm not a good guy. I deserve nothing. I deserve to be rotting under the ground. I deserve pain. I deserve to suffer, not sit here with her, being touched by her, loving being touched by her.

"Quinton, I'm sick of this," my dad says. "It's time for you to move out... I don't want you around anymore. Not when you're like this."

"Nova, stop talking about shit you don't get," I growl, and it should scare her, yet it seems to fuel her with determination.

"But I do get it," she snaps, equally harshly, and I swear to God it seems like she leans in, too, giving in to the pull like me. Our foreheads touch, and I can smell the scent of her, vanilla mixed with a hint of perfume. "I do get how much it hurts." She pounds her hand against her chest. "How much you think about all the other paths your life could have taken if you would have just done this or that. I get how much you want to forget about it all. How much you hate yourself for not doing things that would make it so they were still here!" She shouts at the end, her eyes massive, her breathing ragged, and my body is trembling from the emotion emitting from her and being absorbed into my skin, like I can connect with everything she's going through.

We're so close that our legs are touching and there's only a sliver of space between our lips. I could kiss her, but I'm too pissed off. At her. At myself. But dear God I want to kiss her, just to get a small taste of the life flowing off her, to feel her, breathe in her warm scent. It's an amazing feeling, like for a moment she's become more powerful than the meth.

But then she says, "You and I are so alike."

That makes me jerk back, and her hand falls from my face. "No, we're not, and don't ever say that again." I swing my legs back over to the roof and get to my feet, bumping into one of the signs. "We're not the same, Nova. Not even close."

She rushes after me and cuts me off halfway to the door with her arms out to the sides. "Yes, we are. We were both using drugs and this life to escape our feelings—the stuff that happened to us. The terrible stuff that happened to us."

I shake my head, my buzz flying away in the wind like loose powder. "You have no idea what the fuck you're talking about," I say, looking away from her. "You did weed for, like, what? A couple of months. Weed's nothing, Nova." I encounter her gaze. "You have no idea how dark stuff can get." I pause, rage erupting inside me, and for a moment I think about saying it aloud. What I did. How I killed my girlfriend and cousin—the entire story about how I killed two people, so hopefully she'll realize the full extent of it and leave me.

She swallows hard, but manages to keep her voice even. "So what? Just because I haven't done anything harder doesn't mean I don't get things—don't get death. I get what you're going through."

"No, you don't." I get in her face, hoping to scare her back, but she stands firm. "You lost your boyfriend because he chose to leave. I crashed a goddamned car and killed my fucking girlfriend and cousin—Tristan's sister—I took their lives. And everyone fucking hates me for it." I wait for the disgust in her eyes to appear, the disgust I've seen countless times, whenever anyone hears my story.

But she completely blindsides me and looks at me with sympathy. "Everyone doesn't hate you. How could they, when it was an accident?" Her voice is loud, but it cracks. She's not even shocked. Yeah, I told her I killed some people, but I didn't tell her who, yet it seems like she already knew. "I know it wasn't your fault...I read the newspaper article."

Suddenly it makes sense that there was no shock factor for her. She already knew about my messed-up, twisted past, what happened that night. How I was responsible for two people's deaths. She probably even knows I died.

Something about the idea of her digging up my past elicits a dark and sinister feeling inside me. It makes me furious and not I-just-need-to-get-another-hit furious. She was the only one who didn't fully know my story and now she does—now she knows what I am, down to the very last details.

"The newspaper doesn't know jack fucking shit. Yeah, maybe the police report said it wasn't entirely my fault, but ask fucking anyone." I cup my hand over my upper arm, because I swear to God I'm feeling the pain again of when I put the tattoos there, sharp pricks, the burn, the pain I deserve—I deserve so much more. "Ryder's parents, Lexi's parents. You can even ask my father and they'll all tell you that it was my fault... He even blames me for my mother's death..." I trail off, losing my voice, as I remember all the silence between my father and me—how, growing up, I could always feel the distance between us, because every time he looked at me, he probably thought about how my mother died bringing me into this world. It makes me realize just how long I've felt this blame, just not as bluntly. "They'll all tell you I'm a piece of shit that should be fucking dead instead of everyone else." I'm on the verge of tears. But they're tears of rage more than anything, and I need to find a way to get them to stop. Find a way to get Nova to stop looking at me like I'm an injured dog that she just kicked and gave more pain to. Find a way for her to stop pitying me and get on the same page as everyone else.

I know what I do next is so fucked up there are no words to describe it, yet I can't find the will to care inside my junkie body, which only sees life from delusional angles created by substances that let me see things how I want to. So I reach into my pocket and take out a plastic bag.

"You want to see how alike we are?" I say, opening the bag, watching her and her reaction. "You want to see what you're trying to save?"

She tries to remain calm, but I catch the flicker of fear in her eyes and I think, *There you go. Be afraid. Finally.* I dip my finger into the powder, coating it with just enough to give me a bump, and then I put my finger up to my nose. I expect her to look away, but she doesn't. Her gaze is relentless, confused, disgusted, curious. All sorts of messed-up shit. And it should be enough for me to put the stuff away, because I've obviously gotten my point across, but now that it's out, I want it. So I breathe it in like it's heaven, or a make-believe version anyway. Once it crashes against the back of my throat, it makes hurting Nova the slightest bit easier, and when she walks away, I feel twistedly satisfied, like I accomplished something, when I didn't. I haven't accomplished anything in a very long time. But the thing is, it doesn't matter. None of this does. And when I walk back to my place—because I'm sure she's going to leave my sorry ass—I'll take hit after hit and barely remember or feel anything at all. At least not in a way that matters.

Nova

I have to walk away while we're on the roof because it's too hard to watch. He follows me down, staying a ways behind. I think he thinks I'm going to leave him, because as soon as we step outside, he starts off toward this back area that leads to a stretch of desert, instead of toward my car.

"Where are you going?" I call out, taking my keys out of my pocket.

He stops just short of where the asphalt shifts to dirt and

glances over his shoulder at me. "I thought I was walking home."

I shake my head, backing up to the car. "Quinton, I can give you a ride."

A puzzled look crosses his face. "Even after what I did— even after I yelled at you? Even after what I just said...?" He trails off, like his emotions are getting the best of him again.

I need to make sure to do my best to keep him calm, because he seems pretty irrational right now, and with drugs in his system, things could get ugly—even more than they are. "Nothing you said on the roof affects our relationship. Things are still the same. Although I wish they were different—better. Now, would you please get in the car? It's hot as heck out here, and I don't want you walking in the heat."

He sniffs a few times, rubbing his nose, as he glances in the direction he was heading and then at my car. "Okay... yeah. I'll get in the car."

A small weight lifts from my shoulders as he climbs inside, but it's back by the time we're at his place, and he hops out before I even get the car to a full stop and without saying good-bye. I hate when people don't say good-bye, yet it happens all the time and sometimes I don't see them ever again.

I'm worried about never seeing Quinton again.

I start to drive back to Lea's uncle's house, but I can feel a meltdown coming on as I keep picturing Quinton on the roof, shoving that stuff up his nose. Finally, I have to vent, get it off my chest before I explode, so I pull the car into a gas station parking lot and take out my phone. Aiming the camera at myself, I hit record.

"I had to back off, even though I didn't want to. What I wanted to do was slap him, then steal that damn bag out of his hand and throw it off the roof. What happened was intense, but it was partially my fault. I was pushing him and I knew he was high—easily breakable. But I was so determined to make him see the real picture, the one he can't see, that I kept going. I tried to force him to admit things that clearly he can't admit—that sometimes accidents just happen. But then I let it slip out that I'd read the article about the accident and that only seemed to piss him off...and then he..." I trail off, wincing as I recollect him putting that crap up his nose like he was inhaling a piece of chocolate. "He doesn't even see what he is right now, and it sucks because I've been in that place and I want to get him out of it, like I got out, yet I know that he's got to be on the same page—realize things. And I'm still not quite sure what's going to do that for him."

I lower my head onto the steering wheel, still aiming the camera at myself. "How do you get through to someone who doesn't want you to get to them? How do you save someone who doesn't want to be saved? God, he reminds me so much of Landon...and I'm worried that one of these days I'm going to show up a few minutes too late again and all I'll have left is a video." The breath gets knocked out of me as I choke on my emotions and have to pause to catch my breath. "But Quinton has to want to be saved, since he hasn't given up yet...I just don't think he can admit it yet. I need to make him some-how...need to make him realize that not everyone in the world hates and blames him like he thinks they do." My voice wobbles as I recollect how he looked when he told me that everyone blamed him for the deaths. The self-hatred burning in his eyes. "What I need is a better plan—help maybe. Because what I'm doing right now isn't working very well...I just don't know where to go to find it."

I take a moment to gather myself before I sit up and turn the camera off. Then I drive down the road back to Lea's uncle's house, listening to "Me vs. Maradona vs. Elvis," by Brand New, and the memories of the last time I listened to the song almost cause me to bawl my eyes out. It was the first time I got high and Quinton and I kissed. It was a kiss so full of emotions that were—still are—practically indescribable, and I'm pretty sure I'll never experience a kiss like that again. I'm not even sure I want to.

By the time I get to the road that leads to the house, I'm bummed out. The urge to count the mailboxes on the road is becoming uncontrollable and I give in. I make it to eight before I tell myself to shut up and be stronger, but that only makes me feel more anxious and helpless. I feel drained, and Lea instantly knows something's wrong when I walk inside the house.

"Okay, what happened?" she asks from the kitchen. She's cooking something that smells an awful lot like pancakes and it makes my stomach grumble.

I drop my bag on the sofa and head into the kitchen. "It was a rough day," I admit to her.

She's standing over a griddle, and there's batter on the counter, along with eggshells and a bowl. "Do you want to talk about it?"

I plop down on one of the stools around the island, prop my elbow on the counter, and rest my chin in my hand, breathing in the scent of pancakes. "I don't know...maybe...but I already kind of talked about it to a camera."

She flips one of the pancakes over with a spatula, steam rising in the air. "Yeah, but it might be better to talk about it with a human maybe." She smiles at me.

I note how quiet the house is. "Where's your uncle?"

"He went out on some business dinner or something. He called and said he'd be home late. Why?"

"Just wondering." Honestly, I didn't want to talk about Quinton and was going to use that as an excuse, that her uncle was here and I didn't want him to hear. But I guess I can't use that excuse, so I lower my head into my hands, confessing my day to her. "Quinton and I got into a fight and some stuff happened that's confusing me."

"Like what?"

"Like...like he did drugs in front of me."

"Jesus, you didn't do any—"

"Do I look high to you?" I cut her off as I raise my head back up.

She assesses me with wariness. "No, but I'm not an expert."

I sigh. "Well, I promise I'm not. You can even take me to get a drug test if you want to." I don't really think she will, but I say it hoping it'll make her feel better.

She relaxes a little, turning back to the pancakes. "Well, I don't think you should go over there anymore. There's too much temptation at that house."

"He didn't do the drugs while we were at his house," I clarify, but stupidly, because really it doesn't matter where he did them. The fact is he still did them. "And it wasn't like how you would think. He didn't do it because it was all fun and games and he wanted me to join him. He did it to piss me off so he could prove that we weren't like each other and that I don't understand him. He wasn't offering drugs to me—he wouldn't even let me take any if I asked."

She frowns, the pan sizzling. "Are you sure about that?"

I nod, but I'm not 100 percent sure. The Quinton I saw today, the one at the end of the conversation, wasn't the same as the guy I first met, who always told me I should stay away from drugs. "Besides, it's not like I want to do them," I say, omitting that I have thought about it a few times because she'd probably flip out and make it a bigger deal than it is, because I haven't done anything yet. "I was just being honest with you about what happened. If I weren't telling you this, then we'd have a problem."

She slips the spatula under a pancake and flips it over. "I honestly don't know what to say to you because I don't understand any of this."

"And that's fine," I say, sitting up straighter. "You don't have to say anything. Listening helps a lot."

She turns off the heat and reaches for a plate in the cupboard. "I think you should go down to this clinic that helps people who have people in their lives that are struggling with drugs."

"Where is it?"

She sets the plate down on the counter and begins piling the pancakes on it with the spatula. "Down on the east side of town."

"Okay, maybe I'll drive down there tomorrow," I tell her, figuring it can't hurt. "Do I need an appointment or something?"

"I'll give you the information after we eat." She sets the spatula down on the counter. "Completely off the subject, but do you want me to cook some bacon and eggs with these pancakes?"

I force a grin, and just trying to be happy makes it feel almost real. "Bacon sounds good... God, it's like I have my own little housewife, cooking dinner for me."

"That means you need to be a good little wife and go bring in the bacon." She snaps her fingers and points at the fridge. "It's in there in the bottom drawer."

I get up from the stool and cook the bacon while she washes up the pan and bowl she used to make the pancakes. Then we sit down and eat at the table and it's so normal. By the time we're done, I feel a little better. It worries me because feeling better allows me to realize just how down I was. I wonder how far is too far. How far do I allow myself to sink to get to Quinton?

Chapter Eight

May 20, day five of summer break

Nova

I wake up the next morning and watch Landon's video while Lea takes a shower, because I don't want her to know I'm doing it, because she'll worry more about me. I hate that I watch it, but I can't help it. Something about studying it makes me feel like I'm going to be able to help Quinton not come to that point. Like if I watch it enough, I'll see something I didn't see before. But I still haven't figured out what that is yet.

After I watch it, I get dressed and go down to the clinic, like I told Lea I would. I really don't know how helpful it's going to be to listen to other people talk about what they're going through trying to help addicts, but at this point I'll try anything because I feel so helpless.

I pick up a coffee and a bagel on my way there, then park my car in the closest parking garage. The building is in an area that looks almost as sketchy as Quinton's house. But I do my best to ignore that and go inside. There's a meeting going on for people who have family members and friends who are drug addicts, and I take a seat in the back, sipping my coffee and listening, feeling a little out of place because I barely know

Quinton and everyone else seems to be related to the person they're here for.

I listen for a while to people expressing how they're feeling, how sad, how hurt, upset, heartbroken they are. A lot of them are parents and keep talking about how it feels like they've lost a child, like drugs have killed them. One man in particular with brown hair and brownish eyes that sort of remind me of Quinton's starts talking. Even though I know it's not Quinton's dad up there, I could easily picture him being that person. It makes me wonder if Quinton's dad feels like this like he's lost a child. He has to.

But according to Quinton, at least from what he said yesterday, his father blames him for the deaths that happened in the car accident. But I don't—can't believe this. It has to be something he created inside his head. I wonder if Quinton ever actually talked to his father about any of this—if his father even knows where he is.

It gives me an idea, but it's going to be a hard idea to pull off because it's going to require me getting a phone number for Quinton's dad. And I doubt he'll give it to me.

Although I think I might know someone who will, if I can work it right. So after the meeting ends, I drive over to Quinton's apartment. The sun is blaring down and the temperature has to be pushing 120 degrees. It's so hot that I don't even want to get out of the car, but part of that might be me avoiding going inside.

After a few minutes pass by, I force myself to get out and

into the heat, keeping my sunglasses on to protect my eyes from the brightness. The apartment area is quiet, as usual, as I make my way across the vacant parking lot and up the stairway. That guy Bernie, who was passed out the first time I was here, is back at the table outside his door, awake this time and rolling a joint right out in the open, which reveals just how blasé this place is about drugs and makes me wonder what the hell goes on behind all the closed doors.

"Hey, sweetie," he says to me as he checks me over with his bloodshot eyes. He's not wearing a shirt, and his thin chest is tinted red from the sun. "Where'd you wander over from?"

I have on a black tank top and denim shorts, and his appreciative gaze makes me feel very vulnerable and exposed, so I hurry, wrapping my arms around myself.

"Hey, if you're lost, I can help you find your way home," he calls out with a chuckle. "I'm pretty sure the place you're looking for is my bedroom."

"Creepy pervert," I mutter, rushing past closed door after closed door, breathing freely only when I'm standing in front of Quinton's. As I lift my hand to knock, I keep my fingers crossed that Dylan's not the one who answers it, since he's about as creepy as that Bernie guy.

Thankfully, after three knocks, Tristan opens the door, barefoot and with a cigarette in his mouth. His blond hair is a little ruffled, like he just woke up, and his gray T-shirt and jeans have holes in them. "Hey," he says, seeming a little uneasy, glancing over his shoulder at the filthy living room with a nervous look on his face. "Quinton's not here right now and he's not supposed to be back until really late."

"Actually, I'm here to talk to you," I tell him, trying to shrug off the fact that it seems like Tristan's covering for Quinton and that Quinton might even be here but avoiding me.

His nervousness turns to befuddlement as he pulls the cigarette out of his mouth. "Why?"

"Because I need to ask you something." I nervously peer over at the Bernie guy, who's watching us as he smokes a joint, and then look back at Tristan. "Look, can we go somewhere and talk?"

He gives me a look that's sort of harsh for the Tristan I used to know. "Just talk to me here."

I suck in a slow breath through my nose, counting down backward in my head, telling myself to stay calm. "I'd rather talk to you somewhere more private."

He stares at me with this bored expression like I'm annoying the crap out of him, so it surprises me when he says, "Okay."

He flicks his cigarette over my shoulder and over the railing, and then he goes back into the house. He leaves the door cracked just enough that I can hear him talking to someone who sounds an awful lot like Quinton. When he opens the door again, he has an old pair of sneakers in his hand and he steps out, shutting the door behind him.

He pauses to put the shoes on, glancing up at me as he ties one of the laces. "You know, despite what he'll say later on, it's going to hurt Quinton that you came here to see me," he tells me, fastening the lace and standing up straight.

"I'm not so sure about that," I say as we walk across the balcony. "I think he sort of wants me to leave him alone...In fact, I think you're covering for him right now."

He glances at me with curiosity. "Do you really believe that? That it won't hurt him that you came here to see me?"

"Yeah," I tell him with honesty. "I do."

"Well, it will," he says as we head down the stairs. "But don't tell him I told you that."

I keep quiet until we reach the bottom of the stairway, processing what he just told me. "Why are you telling me this?" I ask.

Tristan gives a shrug, looking around at the bottom floor like he's searching for someone or something. "I don't know. Because it's the truth and you deserve the truth."

I'm not sure what to make of what he says, and the more I examine him, the more I notice how agitated he is: drumming his fingers on the sides of his legs, his jaw moving all over the place. He's high and it saddens me, but even though I hate to think it, I wonder if this will make it easier to get some information from him.

We head over to my car, not saying anything. The sun has heated the leather seats up, so when I climb in they burn the backs of my legs as I sit down. I hurry and turn on the engine while Tristan buckles his seat belt.

"So where are we going to?" Tristan rubs his hands together with a playful look in his eyes.

"I don't know...Is there somewhere you had in mind?" I

place my hands on the steering wheel, but instantly withdraw them when it burns my hands. "Crap, that's hot."

He thinks about it briefly and then points to our left, where the city gets darker, more run-down, and that makes me uneasy. "Yeah, there's a bar a little ways down the street that we can go hang at," he says. I'm wary about going to a bar around here, and it must show because he adds, "It's totally low-key and safe. I promise."

"Okay," I reply, but I'm not sure I trust him or his massive pupils and spastic jaw. But I want answers about Quinton's dad, so I go with it, hoping I'm not making a big mistake. Hoping whatever lies ahead for me will be worth the risk.

Quinton

I think I made a mistake. Or at least that's what my overriding brain is telling me. That I need to chase down Nova and tell her to stay with me, not go with Tristan, tell her that I'm really here and that I was just upset about the roof thing and had Tristan lie for me. The problem is, they're already gone, because I hesitated. Torn between what's right and what the drugs tell me I want.

I'm pacing the floor of the living room like a madman, wondering how things went this way. One minute I told Tristan to cover for me and tell Nova I wasn't here because I didn't feel like talking to her after the whole roof incident. In fact, I planned on never seeing her again.

And that's what I told Tristan.

The next thing I knew, they were leaving together. I'm fucking pissed, but a lot of that anger is directed at myself for caring so much that I can't just let her go, that I want her this bad. Knowing she's out with Tristan has made me painfully aware of this, and so I did the only thing I could think of to try to turn it off.

I do line after line, trying to kill the emotion out of me and the crushing guilt attached to the emotion. But for some reason, today crystal is adding fuel to the fire—adding to my emotions. I'm not sure what to do with all the pain and the anger. It's been a long time since I've felt this way, and all I want to do is ram my fist through a wall. I stop pacing, pick up a hollowed-out ballpoint pen, and do another line off the cracked coffee table. After the sensation of it hits my body and slams into my heart and mind, I head toward the wall to punch a hole in it like I wanted to, but the front door suddenly swings opens. I do a U-turn and find Dylan shoving Delilah into the room.

"You stupid fucking whore," he says, shoving Delilah into the apartment, and she lands on her back, her head just missing the corner of the coffee table. "I told you not to mess shit up, but you couldn't keep your mouth shut, could you?"

"I'm sorry." Tears stream from her eyes as she sits up and struggles to get her feet under her. She has only one shoe on. It causes her to roll her ankle, but she manages to get up by supporting her weight against the sofa.

"Fuck you and your sorry." Dylan slams the door hard enough that shit falls down in the kitchen, and I hear glass break. "You're always sorry, yet you keep messing up."

I've seen them fight before—actually, a lot. But they've been getting worse lately. A lot of yelling. A lot of shoving each other around. I really think Dylan might be losing it, his inner demons, whatever they are, slipping through the cracks. This seems even worse than what I've seen before, but that might be because I'm beyond tweaked out. My mind is racing a thousand miles a minute so that I can't even keep up with them and everything's just one big fucking pileup.

Delilah's sobbing and her cheek is inflamed like he hit her and Dylan is hyped up, eyes bulging, veins defiant under his skin. He looks like he's tripping on acid and maybe he is. Whatever it is, when he storms toward her with his hand up, something snaps inside me. Here I am freaking out because I want a girl that I can't have—don't deserve—because I lost my girlfriend—killed her—and he has his girlfriend right here. He can have her whenever he wants and he's choosing to hit her.

I see red, and before I realize what I'm doing, I jump between the two of them. It might not be the brightest idea, since Dylan might be going a little crazy and he's always carrying that stupid gun around in his pocket, but I don't care at the moment. He's pissing me off, not even realizing what he has. Plus, I'm so jacked up I can barely hold my head still, my fingers twitching, and I think I might have done too much or something because my heart and mind feel like they're going to explode.

"Hey, back off," I say, not shoving him back, but I do stick out my hand, causing him to walk straight into it and trip backward.

"Are you fucking kidding me?" he snaps, rage flaring as he regains his balance and barrels toward me.

I slam my palms against his chest and push him back again. He seems to be really struggling to keep his footing, tripping sideways and bumping into the wall. I figure he's high and that I should be able to get him away, but suddenly he gets a second wind, racing toward me and swinging his fist.

I don't have time to duck, and his fist collides with my face. My jaw pops as I stagger into Delilah and accidentally knock her to the ground. She starts to wail, crying out something that sounds a lot like "Please don't hurt him." I'm not sure if she's referring to me or to Dylan, but it doesn't matter. Dylan smirks at me, and the anger I was feeling when they walked in magnifies, combusts, bursts. I barrel back at Dylan, my adrenaline pulsating as I raise my fist, and I ram it into his face. His lip splits open and blood splatters everywhere.

Things sort of blur after that.

He makes threats of kicking me out as he spits in my face. "You're fucking done."

I tell him to go to hell as I shove him back with so much anger and adrenaline inside me it scares the shit out of me. "Fuck you. You have no say in who gets to stay in this house. It's all of ours."

His face reddens. "I do get the say because I'm the one who

controls everything. Without me and my connections, no one would have any money or drugs to survive. I bring in the drugs to deal. I built this." He points around the apartment like he's claiming a prize.

"And what a fucking prize that is." I ball my hands into fists, wanting to wring his neck, kick him out of the house. My anger is searing so viciously through my body, I'm shaking as my blood roars in my ears.

We keep arguing about this shitty apartment and life, getting in each other's faces, breathing down each other's necks. I've never felt so much rage in my life, besides maybe the time I realized I had been brought back to life while everyone else was dead. It feels like I might do anything at the moment. I'm out of control. He's out of control. I'm not even sure what would have happened, but Delilah steps between us and shoves me away from Dylan.

"Leave him alone!" she cries, spinning to face me.

I gape at her with my hands out to the sides. "Are you kidding me? He was about to hit you."

She quickly shakes her head, adjusting her shirt back into place and smoothing her hair down, like fixing herself fixes the problem. But her cheek is still swollen and her eyes are still stained with mascara. "We were just fighting, Quinton. That's all."

I want to argue with her, but she takes Dylan's hand and leads him around me and to the hallway. "Come on, baby. Let's go put some ice on your face."

Dylan glares at me, his cheek puffy where my knuckles

collided. "I want you and Tristan looking for a new place. I mean it. I'm done with you two," he says.

"You're always done with us and yet we never leave!" I yell, and he narrows his eyes at me as Delilah tugs him down the hall.

I blow out a breath, not even realizing how nervous I was, how much tension was in the air until it's gone. I cup my cheek where he hit me, feeling the hot pain spread up my entire face. I'm not sure what to do, not just about the living situation or Dylan but also with myself. I'm not sure of anything anymore. What just happened—that fight. It wasn't me. What I did on the roof—being rude to Nova like that. It wasn't me. I used to never get in fights or yell at girls. But then again, I'm not who I used to be anymore. But who the fuck am I exactly? This person inside me, the one who survived the accident and is now all doped up and barely living, doesn't feel right. He feels damaged and distorted, ugly and tangled. Gashed and split open. Vulnerable and unstable. And I'm not sure if it has to do with Nova randomly showing up or if I'd feel like this anyway, regardless of who was around. But it seems like only a week ago I was more stable, which has to make me wonder just how much she affects me, how much fighting her affects me.

I drag my ass back to my room and flop down onto my mattress, the overload of adrenaline I was feeling dwindling. For a brief second my mind slows down to reflect on how I got to this place. How I could get to such a low. How I created this monster within me—what I would be like if it died. But then I glance down at the names on my arm and remember.

I got here because I'm no one.

I shouldn't even be alive.

Nova

I follow Tristan's directions to a small bar on a corner a few miles away. Right beside it is a place called Topless Hotties and Drinks and across from it is a massage parlor, but I have to wonder by the half-naked lady painted on the glass window just what kind of massages they give.

Tristan doesn't seem to be made uncomfortable by any of this. In fact, he seems right at home as he climbs out of the car and lights up.

"So they have the best Jäger bombs here," he tells me as he opens the tinted glass door at the front of the building. He holds it open for me and I enter, cringing at the dark, smoky atmosphere.

"I don't really drink anymore," I tell him and breath eases from my lips as a waitress walks by in a uniform that looks like it was bought at Victoria's Secret.

Tristan gives me a weird look like he doesn't quite understand the concept. "Sure. Okay." Then he leads me out into the open bar area, which has tables and chairs on one side and a few pool tables on the other.

There's a jukebox in the corner playing "Leader of Men" by Nickelback. All the waitresses are dressed similarly to the one we ran into when we walked in, wearing lingerie-type outfits.

There are mostly guys hanging out in here—go figure—but thankfully, there are a few women patrons here and there, so I don't feel too out of place. Although I do feel very uncomfortable about the half-dressed waitresses.

"Do you want to play some pool?" Tristan asks, angling his head and checking out one of the waitresses not so discreetly.

I shrug. "I've never played before."

"Really?"

"Yeah, really."

He muses over this, intrigued. "Well, I think it might be time to break that cherry," he says with a sly expression that makes me wonder if he knows I'm a virgin. If maybe Quinton told him about the little incident in the pond. But for some reason, I just can't seem to picture Quinton doing that.

"Sounds good." I play along, knowing that if I want to get information about Quinton's dad from him, I'm going to have to stay on his good side.

He grins and motions for me to follow him, stopping briefly to order a shot of vodka at the bar. He asks me if I want one and I shake my head. He gives me a weird look but doesn't press.

Once he slams it down, he looks even more relaxed, and part of me wishes I could take a shot, too. But I'm afraid one shot may lead to five shots and that may lead to so much more. Plus, I have to drive.

Tristan gets two cues from the wall, hands one to me, then racks the balls up. He waves at some guy with a long beard as he rounds the table to get ready to break the balls and I have to wonder...

"Just how often do you come here?" I ask, leaning my weight on the cue as I prop it vertically against the floor.

He shrugs, lowering his head and slanting over the pool table while aiming the cue at the balls. "I don't know...like once or twice a week." The cue jerks forward and the tip slams against the ball. It springs forward and hits the others, scattering them around the table. He stands up straight, smiling proudly as two solid-colored balls go into the pockets. "I think it's going to be payback time for making me lose at darts all the time."

"I didn't make you lose at darts," I tell him. "I'm just better at it."

He gives me a cocky grin and moves around the table, setting up his next shot, which he makes. This happens two more times, and each time he looks cockier. When he finally does miss a shot, it barely fazes him.

"Go ahead and give it a try," he says, gesturing at the table.

I almost smile because this feels so normal, like how things used to be, only he's high and I'm sober. I step up to the table and try my best to hit one of the striped balls, but fail epically. I frown as not a single ball except the white one moves.

He laughs at me and it's the first real emotion I think I've seen, real happiness fleetingly slipping through the drugs taking over his system.

"I'm glad you think this is funny," I say, and I mean it. It's good to see him laugh.

"Oh, I do." His laughter dies down, and he studies me from across the table with his blue eyes, which used to be so much brighter. He cocks his head to the side as if he's deliberating his next move and then he sets down his cue and strolls around the table, coming over to the side I'm standing on. "Here, let me help you."

He reaches for me, and I instinctively step back. "But it's your turn."

"I know," he says. "But this can be more of a lesson than a game."

I pout. "Am I that bad?"

He suppresses a laugh. "Just let me help you."

I let out a loud breath. "Okay."

He grins and then steps up to my side. "Face the table," he says, and I do, turning around. He puts an arm on each side of me, and his chest presses against my back as I lean down. He moves with me, showing me how to hold the cue correctly by putting his hands over mine and guiding them into the right position.

His closeness makes me nervous, especially when his warm breath caresses my cheek as he dips his head forward. I think he's going to say something, maybe kiss my cheek. I wonder if I'd let him—how far I'd go to get what I need in order to help Quinton. I'm not liking my thoughts very much right now, but thankfully, I get to escape them when all Tristan does is help me aim the cue and then shoot it forward. This time a lot of balls scatter and one even makes it in.

"See? Not so hard, right?" he asks, his hands leaving mine.

I shake off my jitteriness and turn around. "No, but now that you've showed me how, you've made it harder for you to win."

He chuckles as he rubs his scruffy jaw. "For some reason I doubt it."

"Yeah, me, too," I agree, stepping around the pool table to make my next shot, which I miss. He laughs amusedly.

We play for a little bit longer, and of course he kicks my ass, which he comments on a few times as we find a seat at a table so he can order another drink. After the waitress leaves to go get Tristan his Jäger bomb and me my Coke, he grabs the saltshaker and starts rotating it between his hands.

"So are you going to tell me what you wanted to talk about?" he asks, setting the saltshaker aside and leaning back in his chair. He places his hands behind his head, elbows bent outward. "Because I'm guessing it wasn't about pool."

I shake my head, picking at the cracks in the table. "I wanted to ask you something about Quinton."

He pretends to be nonchalant, but I can tell he gets tense because he starts grinding his teeth. "What about him?"

I fidget with the band on my wrist, trying to figure out where to begin. "Well, I was sort of wondering about his dad?"

His eyes fasten on mine, shadowed with irritation. "What about him?"

God, how do I say this? I mean, I don't want to bring up his sister at all, but how do I avoid it and still get what I want? "Does he ever talk to him?"

Tristan lowers his arms onto the table. "Nope, at least not that I know of." He reclines in the chair as the waitress arrives and puts our drinks on the table, and he waits for her to leave before he speaks again. "They don't get along at all." He drops the shot of Jäger into the taller glass and then picks it up. "In fact, it's pretty much why he ended up in Maple Grove—because his dad kicked him out of the house."

I want to ask him if Quinton's dad knows about his drug use, but since Tristan's high I'm not sure how well that'd go over. "Yeah, but if he knew where he was living, do you think he'd want to talk to him?" I take a sip of the soda. "Help him?"

"Help him with what exactly?" There's a challenge in his eyes, daring me to say "drug use" aloud.

I stir my straw around in my drink. "I don't know...I was just curious...if they talked or if someone's told him anything about the situation."

He takes another large swallow of his drink, staring at me over the brim of the glass. "And what situation is that?"

I'm obviously pushing the wrong buttons and I don't know any way around it, so I decide to be blunt. "Look, I know I'm making you mad right now, but I really want to help Quinton, and I just think that maybe if I could get ahold of his dad and tell him what's going on, it could maybe help him get better. But I need you to give me his name and number in order to do that."

"Who said I was getting mad at you?" he asks calmly and then finishes off the rest of his drink.

He's being an ass, but I know for a fact it's not really him, but this ghost, drug-addict version of himself. He doesn't say anything else to me and gets up from the chair to take the empty glass to the bar. I wait for him to come back, but instead he starts hitting on our waitress, a leggy woman whose top is see-through when the light hits her at the right angle.

Tristan seems to be going out of his way to make it obvious that he's hitting on her, even going as far as groping her breast. The woman giggles in response and starts coiling a strand of her hair around her finger. The longer the scene goes on, the more awkward I feel, and finally I get up from the table, deciding this was a bad idea and that I need to come up with a better plan. I throw a five on the table to cover my drink and then leave the musty bar. When I step into the sunlight, I breathe freely, but the feeling that I failed crushes my chest.

By the time I make it to my car, I'm panting and struggling not to count the poles in the parking garage. I grab the door handle, my hand trembling.

Inhale... exhale... inhale... exhale...

"Nova." Tristan's voice floats over my shoulder. "Are you...?" His feet scuff against the pavement as he steps toward me. "Are you okay?"

I'm on the verge of crying and the last thing I want to do is turn around and let him see that fact. "Yeah, I'm good." I lift my hand to discreetly dab my eyes with my fingers and pull myself together before I turn around to face him. "I'm just not feeling very good all of a sudden."

There's speculation in his eyes as he looks me over. "Maybe we should get going, then."

I nod and am about to climb into the car when I spot a tall guy, with sturdy arms and broad shoulders, wearing black pants and a nice button-down shirt, strolling toward us, with his eyes on us. He has this strange look on his face, like he's found something he's been dying to get his hands on and finds it amusing.

"Well, well, well, look who I finally ran into." Tristan tenses just at the sound of his voice, then gradually turns around. "Trace, what's up?" There's a nervous laugh under his stressed tone.

Trace stops just short of us with his arms folded. He's probably in his mid-twenties, tall, with a very sturdy body and intimidating gaze. He also has brass knuckles on his hand and a scar on his cheek, just a light graze, but it screams drug lord to me. As soon as I think it, I shake my head at myself at the absurdity. There's no way that could be going on—no such thing.

"You know, you're a hard person to track down," Trace says broodingly. "I show up in the parking lot and you let your friend take the blow. Then I go over to your shitty-ass house and Dylan takes the blow for you that time, although if you were there he probably would have ratted you out." A small smile touches his lips, as if he's entertained by Tristan's nervous manner. "Things would have been a hell of a lot easier if you would have just stepped up instead of being a fucking coward."

Tristan deliberately inches to the side, placing himself between Trace and me. "Yeah, sorry about that. But you know how things are... You're high and shit and you just do stupid stuff."

"High on my drugs," Trace says, ambling forward and cracking his knuckles. I'm not sure what to do—stay put? Get in the car? But I can feel the tension in the air, so thick it's smothering. "Drugs you owe me money for." He stops in front of Tristan, towering over him, and Tristan isn't that short, which means the guy is tall. "I'm going to make this real easy on you. Give me the money you owe me, plus interest, and I'll let you walk."

"I don't have the money right now," Tristan mutters with his head tipped down. "But I'll get it to you. I just need some time."

"Time, huh?" That's when the Trace guy looks at me for the first time, but it feels like he noticed me long before. "And who's this lovely thing right here?"

I'm not sure if it's a rhetorical question or not, but I opt to keep quiet, cowering behind Tristan. My pulse is racing so fast I feel light-headed and woozy, like I might pass out.

Tristan stands up straighter, sweeping his hand through his hair. "That's none of your business, so leave her alone."

"None of my business." His low laugh reverberates around us. Then suddenly his hand shoots out and he grabs the bottom of Tristan's shirt. "Right now, everything you do is my business until you pay me back." He pats Tristan's cheek roughly with his free hand. "Got that?"

"Yeah, I got that," Tristan says though gritted teeth, afraid to budge.

Trace lets him go, and Tristan stumbles back toward me, bumping into the front of my car. "Good." Trace seems to have calmed down, and I start to relax as he turns away to leave, but then he unexpectedly spins around and rams his fist with the brass knuckles into Tristan's gut. I hear the wind get knocked out of him as Tristan collapses to his knees, gasping for air. I start to rush for him, but Trace's eyes land on me and the dark warning stops me in my tracks. He looks back down at Tristan crumpled on his knees and then raises his fist again. This time his knuckles collide with Tristan's cheek. I hear a pop as Trace pulls back again, preparing to hit him again. I cry out for him to stop, but he slams his fist forward again and I watch in horror as he punches Tristan in the stomach again. Tristan's legs shake, wanting to collapse as he hunches over, struggling to breathe.

Finally, Trace lowers his hand, the brass knuckles and his hand splattered with Tristan's blood. "You have one week to pay me back or you won't be walking away. Got it?"

Tristan nods, not saying a word, and the Trace guy turns and heads back out of the parking garage, taking his cell phone out of his pocket.

I rush for Tristan and help him get to his feet. "Oh my God, are you okay?" I ask as he wiggles away from me.

He wraps his arm around his stomach as he stands up straight. His face is twisted in pain, blood dripping out of his nose, and the entire side of his face is red and swollen. "Just peachy."

I eye him over with concern. "Maybe I should take you to the hospital." I reach out to touch him, but he leans back.

"No hospitals," he says sharply. "I'm fine."

"You don't look fine."

"Well, I am."

I shake my head, irritated by his stubbornness. "What was that about?" I cast an anxious glance in the direction of the exit Trace wandered off through.

"Just an old debt," Tristan says, supporting his weight against the car, working to breathe properly.

"For drugs?"

He shrugs as he wipes some of the blood off his nose with his hand, then winces from the pain. "Sometimes I do stupid shit."

I remember how last year I saw Dylan, Quinton, and Delilah dealing drugs to those guys. "You guys deal drugs now?"

He looks like he wants to roll his eyes at me, but resists the urge. "You seem surprised."

"I am a little," I admit. *Or maybe I just didn't want to see the truth.* "Is Quinton in trouble, too?"

He shakes his head. "Nope, just me and my own stupidity." His voice lowers when a couple of people walk by us, heading to their car.

"Are you going to be able to pay that guy back?" I ask.

"Of course." Tristan brushes me off. "In fact, I need to get back to the house and get a few things done that will get me extra cash."

I want to ask him what those few things are, but I fear the answer. "How much do you owe him?"

"Don't worry about it," he says. Then, keeping his hand on the hood, he starts around the car to the passenger side.

"Are you sure…because I could maybe help you. Loan you some money or something."

"I said I'm fine, Nova." He opens the door with his arm still across his stomach.

I grab the handle of the door. "Well, if you ever need any help with anything…I'm here."

We climb into the car and Tristan gives me a cold look. "What? Are you going to save me, too, Nova? Pay off my debt and drag me out of this hellhole along with Quinton?" He rolls his eyes. "Because things don't work that way, especially when people don't want to leave that hellhole they live in."

"I…" I have no idea how to respond to that. Even though I offered to help him with his debt, I don't have a lot of money. And when it comes to getting him out of that hellhole, I can't even handle Quinton, let alone someone else.

"I didn't think so," Tristan says coldly, facing the window and dismissing me as he lifts the bottom of his shirt up to his bleeding nose and tries to wipe away the blood still dripping out.

Shaking my head, I reach into the glove box and take out a napkin. "Here," I say, giving him the napkin.

"Thanks," he mutters and then presses the napkin to his nose.

I back out of the parking spot and head toward his house. I try to talk to him, but he doesn't seem too interested, staring out the window the entire time as he drums his fingers on his knee to the beats of the songs. By the time I park the car, I expect him to get out without saying anything like Quinton did the last time I dropped him off.

But as he grabs the handle to get out, he pauses and then pulls away. "You got your phone on you?"

"Yeah. Why?"

He turns his head toward me with a reluctant look on his face, sets the napkin down on his lap, and extends his arm toward me. "Let me see it."

I retrieve it from my pocket and give it to him, watching as he punches a few buttons on the touch screen before giving it back to me. "His name's Scott Carter and he lives in Seattle." He reaches for the door handle again. "I'm not sure if that's still his number, since the last time I talked to anyone from the house was over a year ago, when Quinton used to live there, but that's your best shot."

"Thank you, Tristan," I say as he cracks the door, stunned he actually gave me the information. "And if you ever need anything—help getting yourself out of trouble—please, please ask me." I want to say more, but I don't know how much good it'll do.

"Whatever. I'm only giving the number to you because you asked. Not because I want your help with anything," he replies, pushing the door open all the way and ducking his head to climb out. "And I don't think it's going to help Quinton at all. Trust me when I say that he's only going to quit doing what he does when he wants to quit. I know because that's how I roll, and it's hard to quit something that makes you feel so fucking good." He says it so causally, and before I can respond, he's shutting the door and walking away toward his crappy apartment, moving slowly because he's in pain.

I stare at the phone in my hand, Tristan's words replaying in my head, wondering if he's right. If maybe it won't do any good. If I'm trying to search for a solution to a problem that can't be fixed, one that's so much bigger than me, something that I saw today in the parking garage.

Still I at least have to try. Because the last time I didn't try, someone wound up dead.

❧

When I arrive back at Lea's uncle's house, it's midafternoon and I'm exhausted, more than I have been in a long time. But I try to stay positive and hopeful as I tell Lea my plan and ask her for her help in calling Quinton's dad.

"I don't know what to say to him," she states as I sink down on the sofa beside her, exhausted. She collects the remote from the armrest and aims it at the television, muting it. She turns to me on the sofa, bringing her leg up on the cushion. "Parents are, well, parents, you know. And I don't think he's going to respond well to a friend of Quinton's calling him and telling him his son's a junkie."

I wince at the word "junkie." "Well, do you have a better idea?" I ask.

She considers it for a minute or two. "Call your mom."

"What?"

"Call your mom and ask her to call his dad."

I slump back in the sofa, wondering if that's a good idea or not. "You really think that's the best way?"

She kicks her bare feet up on the table. "You remember how before we could help with that suicide hotline we had to go through that screening process and training?" she asks, and I nod. "Well, you haven't gone through the training process of being a parent yet," she jokes.

I snort a laugh. "That's kind of a good thing." I twist a strand of my hair around my finger, thinking. "But I get your point."

She offers me a small smile and pats my leg. "Call your mom and ask her."

I sigh and retrieve my phone from my pocket, dialing my mom's number. I start out with a light conversation, telling her in vague detail how my last couple of days have been. Then I dodge around to telling her my idea about getting ahold of Quinton's dad and asking him for help.

"And you think I should be the one to call him?" she asks in a hesitant tone.

"Yeah...I mean, you are a mom and get things that I don't," I tell her, thinking about the parents I saw at the clinic. "I'm sure you understand this on a level I can't even begin to understand, especially considering the hell I put you through."

I swear it sounds like she's crying. What I don't get is why. I didn't say anything overpowering. Just the truth.

"You're acting so grown-up right now," she says, and I can definitely hear her sucking back the tears. "Give me the number and I'll see what I can do."

"Thanks, Mom," I say and then tell her the name and number, making sure she understands that I'm not 100 percent sure it's still Mr. Carter's number. She says she'll try it and call me back in just a bit. Then I hang up, and Lea and I head into the kitchen to get a snack.

"So how do you think it's going to go?" I ask Lea as I open the fridge door. "Do you think his dad is going to freak out?"

She shrugs as she searches the cupboards. "I'm not sure."

"Yeah, me either," I say, grabbing a bottle of water before closing the fridge and turning around. "Although I'm sort of worried he'll go through denial—my mom did for a while."

She takes out a box of crackers, shuts the cupboard, and hops up on the counter, letting her legs hang over the edge. "What I'm wondering is how Quinton will react if his dad suddenly gets ahold of him. I mean, I honestly don't think he's just going to give up everything because of that."

"Yeah, me neither…but I have to try." I squeeze my eyes shut, picturing Quinton: the weight he's lost, the emptiness in his honey-brown eyes after he did drugs, the anger in his voice. "I have to try everything I can think of before I can even start to give up—I have to know I tried everything this time." I open my eyes as Lea starts to say something, but my phone rings from inside my pocket and cuts her off. I take it out and glance at the screen. "It's my mom," I tell Lea and then answer it. "Hey, that was quick."

"That's because I couldn't get ahold of him," she says, and my hope plummets.

"It wasn't the right number?" I ask, opening up the bottle of water.

"No, it was, but he didn't answer...I left a message, though. We'll see where it goes—if he calls me back or not."

She sounds so doubtful. My shoulders slump forward, my mood sinking lower as I lean back against the fridge. "Do you think he'll call you back?"

"Maybe," she says uncertainly. "If he doesn't in a day or two, I'll try calling him again...but Nova, I don't want you to get your hopes up that this is going to fix everything. Trust me, as a mother I know that even if a parent wants to help, it doesn't mean the child will accept it."

"I know that." I sound so depressed and I know it's probably worrying her.

"I love you, Nova, and I'm glad you care so much about this, and I'm not trying to get your hopes down," she says. "But I'm worried about you."

"I'm fine," I assure her. "I'm just tired." I take a swallow of water, my throat feeling very dry against the lie. I know I'm more than tired. I'm stressed and lost and overwhelmed.

"Yeah, but..." She struggles and then finally just says, "You sound sad. I think it might be time to call it quits, come home, and let me get ahold of the boy's dad so he can take care of him."

"I promise I'm fine," I insist. I can feel Lea's gaze boring into me. "I'm not ready to give up and come home yet."

"You don't sound fine," she points out. "You sound like you're in that place again...that one where I...and I just..." She's on the verge of crying. "And I don't want you to go there— I want you to be happy. Do things that make you happy."

"I am happy." I force a light tone, even though the sound of her voice is breaking my heart. "In fact, Lea and I were just about to go out and have some fun exploring the city."

She pauses, sniffling. "That does sound fun, but I'm not really sure there's a whole lot for twenty-year-olds to do in Vegas."

"We're going to karaoke," I tell her, ignoring Lea's withering stare as she sets the box of crackers aside and hops off the counter. "And to see the sights...It should be fun."

My mom's still undecided, but gives in. "Please just be careful. And call me if you need anything. And I'll call you if I hear from his dad." She pauses and I think she's done until she adds, "And please, please take care of yourself."

"I will do all those things," I tell her; then we say our good-byes and hang up.

As I'm putting my phone into my pocket, Lea walks over to the foyer and starts putting her sandals on. "Where are you going?" I ask.

She pulls her hair up in a ponytail and secures it with an elastic on her wrist. "You told your mom we're going into the city, so we're going into the city," she says, and I gape at her. "I'm not going to let you lie to her," she adds. "And besides, we need to go out and do something. I'm going stir-crazy."

Despite the fact that I'm not in the mood for crazy city stuff, I get her point and agree to go, hoping that maybe I can have fun, despite the fact that my thoughts are lost in Quinton and my mother now. I hate worrying her like that. She's all I've got and the last thing I ever want to do is make her sad.

But I also can't forget the sadness and pain in Quinton's eyes, which I've seen in someone else's eyes before. Someone I cared about. Someone I didn't try to save, and in the end I lost him. And I refuse to lose anyone ever again, no matter what it takes.

Chapter Nine

May 21, day six of summer break

Nova

After Lea and I had a somewhat fun night walking up and down the Strip, watching all the lights, listening to the music, and absorbing the atmosphere, I felt a lot better. We didn't make it to karaoke, but made a deal to go out again in a few days and give it a try.

I'm feeling pretty good the next morning, knowing my mom's trying to get ahold of Quinton's dad, telling myself to be positive, but then I get to Quinton's house to see him and no one answers the door. But I can hear people inside, ignoring my knocking. It reminds me of all the times I asked Landon if he was okay, he said yes, and that was that. I couldn't change anything.

My hope starts to extinguish as I trudge back to my car, feeling so helpless because no matter what I do—whom I talk to—Quinton's actually the one who has the power in this situation. He can shut me—anyone—out and there's not a goddamned thing anyone can do about it. Plus, I'm worried. After seeing what that Trace guy did to Tristan, I fear that they might be in a lot of trouble. And I don't know how to fix it or if I can fix it. How many things can one person fix?

God, I wish I could fix it all.

I turn to my videos for comfort, getting my camera phone out of my pocket, needing to vent.

"I keep having this dream where Quinton and I are back in the pond, kissing and touching, and I'm seriously thinking about letting him slip inside me, take me over, own me," I say, staring at myself on the screen, the backseat my background; the black leather makes me look pasty. "And this time my head's in the right place and when he's about to, I embrace it, ready to give that part of me to him. But then suddenly he stops it, like he did the first time. But instead of pulling away and swimming to the shore, he starts to sink under the water. I want to help him, but I can't seem to pry myself away from the rock, and I just stay there in the water, watching him help-lessly go under, his honey-brown eyes locked on me the entire time, until they disappear and I can no longer see him. Then the dream shifts to the roof and he's standing there soaking wet with a noose in his hand and white powder on his nose. He keeps shouting at me to help him, but I just stand there and watch him as he walks over to the edge and gets ready to jump. When he starts to fall is when I start to scream and then I'm always jerked awake, gasping for air and panting…"

I glance up when I notice movement by the stairway, hop-ing someone maybe came out of the house, but it's just a woman walking around in her robe smoking and talking on her phone.

So I continue with my video diary entry, looking for some-thing to keep me distracted while I wait. *Always waiting, but nothing ever comes.* "The dream's been happening every night since I saw him sniff that powder up his nose and I just stood there and let him. It's become one of those rewind moments where I want to go back, rip the powder out of his hand and tell him to stop it, even if it pisses him off. But I know way too well that life doesn't come with a rewind button and some-times you just have to admit your mistakes, learn, and do bet-ter the next time…if there is a next time…" I pause, choking back the images of Landon filling up my head. *I can't go there right now.* "I'm trying to do better…My mom still hasn't got-ten ahold of Quinton's dad, but she's still trying. And trying is something, right?" I don't sound too convincing as I say it. In fact, I sound confused and lost.

My hope is starting to burn out and I keep having to relight it over and over again even though I don't have a match.

I need a match, but I don't know where to find one.

May 22, day seven of summer break

Quinton

I've been avoiding Nova, even when she comes over to my apartment and bangs on the door. It's been two days in a row she's done it, two days since she and Tristan wandered off together. I honestly thought she'd give up, especially after Tristan told me she saw Trace threaten him and hit him. I thought it'd scare her enough to stay away—I wish it had. But it didn't.

I'm struggling with my worry for her, along with the fact that I'm trying to pretend it doesn't bother me that she went off with Tristan, even though it does. And pretty fucking bad, too, since I can feel the annoyance through the meth. It makes me want to do more. But at the same time I want to maintain a balanced high and not go completely crazy and lose my temper like that because the last thing I need to do is hurt someone. But not overdoing it is complicated, since it's a lot easier to overdo it than underdo it.

I've been leaving the apartment a little more lately and that seems to be helping a little, keep me distracted, moving, instead of staying still and staring at that stupid water stain on the ceiling. Ever since Tristan informed me that Trace demanded he get him paid back, we've been doing whatever we can to scrounge up money. We've been breaking into the neighbors' houses and stealing whatever we can that has value, which usually isn't a lot, since no one around here owns much of anything, besides drugs, and they don't keep a lot of those around, since they devour them.

"I hate to say this, but I'm a little worried we're not going to be able to come up with enough money," I say as Tristan digs through dresser drawers. We're in one of the few houses on our street, although it barely qualifies as a house. The roof's got duct tape and mold all over it, the walls are just Sheetrock, and the back door is a piece of plastic, which allowed us to easily tear through and slip inside after checking through the windows to make sure no one was home.

Tristan has this needy look in his eyes that he sometimes gets when he hasn't shot up for a while. "Yeah, sort of…but I know we'll figure something out—we'll get enough money to pay him back, just like we did with Dylan." He pauses, wavering. "We could maybe even borrow some from Nova if we have to."

"We're not doing that," I say harshly. It still annoys me as much now as it did two days ago when he told me she offered to help out. "She doesn't need to get involved in this."

"Fine." Tristan takes something out of the dresser drawer. "Jesus, would you relax? Every time I mention her name you get all crazy." He looks down at the small plastic bag in his hand, which has maybe a gram of crystal in it. "Shit, this sucks. There's hardly anything in this."

I flick the bag with my finger. "You could probably make like fifty to seventy-five bucks off this by selling it."

Frowning, he shakes his head. "While that kind of helps the owing-Trace-money problem, it still doesn't help that I need a fix."

"It does too," I say. "You can take a small fix of that and still sell the rest."

"This isn't what I want." His fingers curl around the bag and he grips it tightly.

It sounds like a car pulls up, so I quickly go check out the window, nervous we'll get caught. But it's pulling up next door. Still, I'm uneasy.

"You need to stop doing that shit." I draw the hood of my jacket over my head. It's hotter than hell outside, but I want to stay as covered up as possible just in case someone comes home, because they'll be less likely to identify me that way. "Seriously. Lay off the fucking smack, Tristan." I'm being a hypocrite—I know this. But I feel this need to try to protect him like somehow it makes up for killing his sister. "It's only going to get you into more trouble than you already are."

He glares at me as he searches through the next dresser drawer, which is filled with clothes and empty cigarette packs. "Why are you so sure that doing crystal is better than doing smack?" He gives up on the drawer and turns toward the lumpy mattress on the floor. He hands me the bag of crystal and then kneels down on the floor and looks underneath the mattress.

"I don't think it's better—none of this is better. I just think smack's a little more dangerous than crystal. I mean, look what it's doing to Dylan—he's going crazy," I tell him as he drops the mattress back down on the floor, dusting off his hands. "You putting that stuff into your veins with a needle is bad, and besides, you totally pass out when you're on it." I follow him as he gets to his feet and goes back into the living room/kitchen/bathroom that we walked through when we first entered the house. "Someone could beat the shit out of you and you wouldn't even know until you woke up with bruises all over your body. And at the moment someone does want to beat the shit out of us."

"I know all this," he insists as he wanders back toward a floor lamp beside a couple of overturned buckets and a large plastic bin that acts as a kitchen table nestled in a corner of the room. "And Dylan's been going crazy since before he started using heroin. He has a lot of issues, you know."

"Like what?" I ask, trailing after him, looking under the bin, checking if there's anything of value hidden under it.

"I'm not sure about all of them," he says, digging through a box on the floor, which has a few light bulbs in it, a sheet, and a lighter. "But when we first started hanging out, when he was normal, he'd talk about how crazy his mother and father were. Although he never gave me any details, I got the impression it really affected him."

I peek under the buckets, too, searching anyplace I can think of where people would hide their drugs or anything else of value. "Well, I'm getting a little worried...that he might be losing it more than we all can handle."

"You always worry."

"And you never worry," I tell him, dropping a bucket back on the floor when I see a dead mouse under it. I shake off the nastiness and move away from the bucket. "Sometimes I wonder if you see the bigger picture of how much shit we're in if we can't come up with the money to pay back Trace."

"We'll come up with the fucking money…we've already got, like, two hundred." He nods at the bag in my hand. "Plus fifty more if we can make a quick sale with this." He tucks the bag into his pocket. "And if I have to, I'll find where Dylan hides all his shit he uses to deal. Now, there's an easy way to come up with money."

I shake my head. "Don't go there yet. Not when he's acting crazy and has a gun," I say. When he doesn't respond, I step in front of him and add, "Tristan, promise me you won't do something that stupid. It's not going to fix the problem. It'll only make it worse."

He scowls at me but says, "Fine." He bends over and looks down into the lampshade, then reaches up and pulls the chain to turn the light on, but it doesn't so much as make a click. "You know, you need to stop worrying all the time about what I do."

"I can't stop worrying about what you do," I say as he muses over something, then takes the shade from the lamp and chucks it on the floor. "I feel like it's my job."

"Why would it be your job?"

"Because I'm the one who put you here…because I killed your sister." Wow, I think I'm a little more out of it than I thought. Either that or Nova might be making me crazy still, despite the fact that I'm shutting her out. All this making me talk about shit has made me say something aloud that I'm not sure Tristan or I am ready for.

He pauses in the middle of unscrewing the light bulb and searches my eyes. "Fuck, how much have you had today?"

I glance down at the bag in my hand and then shrug. "I don't know... maybe a little more than I usually do, but not that much."

"Are you still tripping about the Nova thing? Because I already told you, nothing happened between us. She was actually just asking stuff about you."

"I know that... It's not about that... I just worry about you overdoing stuff sometimes."

He squints and examines me closely, then pats my arm. "Just relax, okay? What I do isn't your fault."

"It sure feels like it is," I mutter as he goes back to unscrewing the light bulb. My hands are shaking with my nerves, my palms sweaty. I can't believe I'm saying these things aloud, but the more I do, the harder it is to turn off my mouth.

"You really need to stop blaming yourself for everything." The light bulb comes off. He removes the bottom of it, and his eyes light up as he sticks out his hand and dumps out something that was stuffed inside the light bulb. A small plastic bag inside it falls out, but it barely has anything in it.

He curses and throws the light bulb on the floor, where it

shatters. "Dammit!" he shouts, his sneakers crunching against the broken glass as he starts to pace the length of the floor. "I thought I was going to score with that find."

Outside, the sky is graying. We've been here for a while— too long. "Let's just take what we got and go. The last thing we want to do is get busted and be on someone else's shit list."

Tristan glares at me, the look fueled by his craving for his next hit, but gives in and stuffs the bag into his pocket. "Fine, but I'm only selling one of these bags, and I'm going to go find someone who will trade me a bag of this for what I'm craving."

"We need the money," I remind him, following him to the piece of plastic tacked to the doorframe on the back of the house. "And besides, I hate when you do that shit."

"Okay, Mom." He rolls his eyes as he ducks and squeezes through the plastic, stepping outside.

"I'm just trying to look out for you." I lower my head and wiggle through after him, putting the bag away in my pocket as we cut across the backyard, taking a shortcut over a fence to our apartment.

He keeps walking, zigzagging around sagebrush, but he shoots me a quick perplexed look from over his shoulder. "You know, you've always been kind of weird with the whole heroin thing, but you've gotten a little more preachy the last week, and I'm starting to wonder if it isn't just a coincidence that it started happening a lot more when Nova showed up." There's insinuation in his eyes as he turns around and walks backward across the sandy backyard toward the space of desert behind it.

"It's not because of her." I maneuver around a cactus, eyeing our building in the distance, wanting to get back so we can stop talking and just do some crystal.

"It would make sense if it was." He whirls around in the sand and walks forward. "That her goody-two-shoes act would wear on you since you've been spending time together...I can see it affecting you."

"How so?"

"I don't know...You're just different." He shrugs. "Less determined to give up on life because you want her and wanting her means being around to have her."

I tensely massage the back of my neck as we reach the border of the parking lot. "I don't want her. She's just determined to come around."

"You want her just as much as you did last summer. It's why you've continued to draw her even after you two hadn't seen each other for almost a year and why you were flipping out the other day when I went out with her," he says determinedly. "You're just fighting your want a little harder right now for whatever reason."

I want to disagree with him again, but the lie gets stuck in my throat, because I do want Nova. A lot. "Want and deserve are two different things." I draw my hood off, the sun and heat bearing down on me. "Just because you want something doesn't mean you get to have it. Trust me..." I start to get worked up, thinking about how much I want Lexi and Ryder to be alive, how I'd die over and over again if they could be alive right now. "Besides, Nova's too good for me and I don't deserve her, so this entire conversation doesn't even matter..." I kick at the rocks as I trudge along, my chin tipped down. "Nothing fucking matters anymore."

He grows quiet for a while, reaching for the cigarettes in his pocket. "You know, I've often wondered what you saw the day you died that would make you feel like you don't deserve anything."

"I saw nothing, other than that I had to come back because some idiot doctor thought he'd save a worthless life," I say, sounding harsher than I'd planned.

"Jesus, relax." He surrenders, holding his hands in front of him, pulling a *whoops* face, knowing he's pushed the wrong button.

I shake my head. "And besides, me dying has nothing to do with why I think I don't deserve anything. It's because two other people died."

He starts to slow down, and this strange look crosses his face. He opens his mouth, and he looks like he's struggling to say something super meaningful that could potentially free me from this internal misery. I'm not even sure what he could say that could do that and perhaps there isn't anything. Perhaps I'm just hoping there's something.

He never does say anything, instead offering me a cigarette. But the strange thing is, for the briefest moment, I saw something—felt something. Hope that perhaps something could change how I feel.

I have no idea where the hell the feeling stemmed from, whether I've done too many drugs for one day, or if Nova's getting into my head even more than I realized. And the truly terrifying part is, part of me wants to go back to her, start answering the door, keep letting her get to me.

Let the hope build.

But the other part of me wants to shatter the possibility into a thousand pieces and keep heading to a young death, let myself rot away quickly until I finally stop breathing forever, like I should have done two years ago.

Chapter Ten

May 23, day eight of summer break

Nova

Time is starting to blur together. Every day is the same. It's been four days since I've seen or talked to Quinton, and I feel like I'm going to explode from the lack of moving forward. I'm trying to keep my plummeting mood hidden from Lea and my mom, but it's hard when they can both read me like an open book.

"Are you sure you don't want to come to lunch with us?" Lea asks as she collects her purse from the computer desk in the guest room. It's the weekend, and she and her uncle are going out to get something to eat. "I might go shopping afterward."

I shake my head as I lie down on the bed and drape my arm over my head. "I'm really tired. I think I might just take a nap."

"You're probably tired because you keep waking up in the middle of the night," she says. "You're a freaking restless sleeper lately."

Because I keep dreaming of the dead and the soon-to-be-dead if I can't figure out a way to help Quinton. "Yeah, I know…I have a lot on my mind."

She looks at me suspiciously, like she can read through my life; like she knows that really, once she leaves, I'm going to go over to Quinton's for the second time today and see if I can get someone to answer. "Nova, I know you've been watching Landon's video."

I'm not sure how to respond, and thankfully, I don't have to because her uncle peeks into the room, interrupting us.

"You girls about ready?" he asks. He's an average-height man, with thinning hair and welcoming eyes. The kind of person who looks friendly, and he is. He's usually wearing business attire when I see him, but today he's wearing jeans and an old red T-shirt.

"Nova's not coming with us," Lea says, slipping the handle of her purse over her shoulder. "She's *tired*." She gives me a look that lets me know I'm going to get a lecture when she gets home.

"Oh, that's too bad," he says, stepping into the room. "I

was going to take you to Baker and Nancy's. I hear they have excellent steak."

"Maybe next time," I tell him. "I really think I need to get caught up on some sleep."

"Well, if you change your mind, call Lea and you can meet us," he says, backing toward the doorway.

"All right. Sounds good," I say, then roll over and rest my head against the pillow.

I hear Lea's uncle say something to Lea as they leave and it sounds an awful lot like "Are you sure she's okay? She looks really down." I can't help but wonder just how down in the dumps I look, if a stranger can notice this.

A few minutes later the house gets quiet. The air-conditioning clicks on. The sun glistens through the window. I'm starting to like the quiet because it eliminates all the worried looks and questions I keep getting. If I had my way, I'd avoid talking to my mom until I could pull my shit together, but like she's read my mind, my phone suddenly rings and I know without even looking who it has to be.

I probably wouldn't answer it, but she might have information about Quinton's dad, so I reach over to the nightstand and pick up my phone.

"Hello," I say, rolling onto my back and staring up at the ceiling.

"You sound tired," my mom says worriedly. "Have you been getting enough sleep?"

I wonder if she's been talking to Lea about my lack of sleep or, worse, if Lea's told her about my watching Landon's video, although I'm guessing it'd probably be the first thing my mom would ask me about if she knew.

"Yeah, but I think it's the time change." It's a lame excuse, since the time change is only an hour and I've actually already gotten used to it.

"Well, make sure you get enough rest." She gives a heavy-hearted sigh. "And make sure you're not overdoing it."

"Okay, I will." I feel the lie burn inside my chest. "So have you heard anything from Quinton's dad?"

"Yeah…" She's reluctant, and I know whatever happened is bad. "It didn't go very well."

"What happened?" I ask, sitting up in the bed.

"I just don't know if this is going to work," she says. "If he'll do anything to help his son."

"Why not?" I get so upset I nearly yell.

"Honey, I think this might be deeper than we realize," she says in the gentle motherly tone she uses when she knows I'm on the verge of cracking open. "I mean, I only talked to him for a few minutes, but I got the impression there's a lot of problems there. Not just between the two of them but with Quinton, and that his dad would rather avoid the problem."

"I know he has problems." I drag my butt off the bed and look around the room for my purse. "That's why I'm here trying to help him."

"Yeah, but… his father seemed so upset on the phone and not for the right reasons…" She trails off and then clears her throat, like she's getting worked up. "Look, sweetie, I know you're really determined to help him, but maybe he needs more help than you can give him."

"Do you think his dad will come down here and help him?" I ask, picking up my purse from the back of the computer chair and getting my car keys out of it. "If you talked to him a little more?"

"I'm not sure... but I can keep trying while you're here," she says persistently. "Please, Nova, come back home."

"Not until I know for sure his dad will help him." I walk out of the room and to the front door. "Look, Mom, I got to go. I'll call you later, okay?" I don't wait for her to respond. I know I'm being rude—worrying her. But the thing I was counting on—Quinton's dad—has just been lost.

I need to see him now. Need to look at him. Need to save him.

Somehow.

❧

I'm starting to hate the sight of that door. The one with the crack. The one that keeps Quinton on one side and me on the other. The divider. If I were strong enough, I'd kick it down, but I'm not, so all I can do is keep knocking on it.

"Would someone just open the damn door!" I shout, feeling like I'm going to lose it as I hammer it with my fist. "Please!" My voice echoes for miles like it's the only thing that exists.

I sink onto the ground, frustrated, feeling beaten down.

I want to give up, but I keep seeing Landon's face that night we lay on the hillside, the last time I ever saw him. There was something in his eyes—I saw it. Sadness. Pain. Internal misery. It's a look that will haunt me until the day I die, no matter how much time goes by. I don't want to learn to live with it again, and if I walk away from Quinton now, I'll have to, because I've seen the same look in his eyes before. And I won't let him die like I did with Landon.

So I sit there on the scorching-hot concrete, letting my skin scald, staring at the door, the only barrier between the truth and me. And I refuse to budge until it opens. It finally does. It's getting late, and the horizon is fading behind me, but the door opens and Tristan walks out wearing an open button-down long-sleeved plaid shirt and jeans, like it's not sweltering hot out here. He startles back when he sees me and scrapes the heel of his foot on the concrete, splitting the skin open. He doesn't seem fazed at all, though, ruffling his messy blond hair, and then he yawns as he stretches out his arms and legs.

"What are you doing out here?" he asks calmly, lowering his arms to his sides.

His calm attitude irks me, and I scowl up at him, hungry and thirsty and cranky, a bad combination. "I banged on the door for a while. Why didn't you answer?"

His eyes lift to the sky as he contemplates what I said. "I didn't hear anyone knock…Quinton has his music up. Maybe that's why I couldn't hear it."

I can hear music playing from somewhere inside, but still.

"Can I talk to Quinton?" I ask. His lips part and I hold up my hand, silencing him. "And don't tell me he's not here, because you just let it slip that he's the one listening to music."

His lips tug up into a half-smile. "I was actually going to say yeah, come on in. You shouldn't be out here by yourself this late anyway. It's not safe." He offers me his hand. "Especially when the sun's about to go down completely."

"Oh." I take his hand and let him pull me to my feet, uncertain if I'll really be safer inside. "You make it sound like a bunch of vampires live around here and they're going to come out and drink my blood at sundown," I joke lamely because I'm tired and thirsty and hungry. I've been sitting outside for probably a couple of hours and I think the back of my neck is sunburned.

Tristan's blue eyes gradually scroll up my long legs, my shorts, my tight white tank top, and conclusively land on my eyes. "Not vampires, but I'm sure there are plenty of people around here who would love to get a taste of you," he says as he shuts the door behind us. He has this look in his eyes, glazed and incoherent, like he's here in body but not in mind, and I think I might have my hands full.

It takes me a moment to find my voice. "I'm not even sure how to respond to that," I say, squirming uncomfortably.

"You don't have to respond. I'm just rambling," he tells me with a shrug and then turns toward the kitchen, stumbling over the hem of his jeans when he steps on it. "Do you want a drink or something? We've got vodka and…" He searches through the cupboards, but they're all empty. He shuts the last one, walks over to the counter, and picks up a mostly empty vodka bottle. "And vodka."

I smile with apprehension. "'No thanks. I don't drink that much anymore. Remember, I told you that at the bar."

"Oh yeah. Sorry, I forgot." He unscrews the cap of the vodka bottle and sniffs the contents, but doesn't drink. "It's hard to keep track of stuff sometimes, you know."

Even though the floor is covered in sticky puddles, wrappers, even a used syringe, I dare step into the kitchen. "Yeah, I do know how that feels way too well, because I've been feeling it every day since I got here. I think this place is starting to crack at my sanity." I'm tired and being way too blunt.

He screws the cap back on and he briefly appears vexed, but it fades. "Okay, not to steal your line or anything, but I don't even know how to respond to that."

"You don't have to respond," I say as he tosses the bottle back onto the messy countertop a little too hard. It sounds like it breaks, but he doesn't do anything about it. "You know me. I'm just saying how I feel."

"Saying how you feel. How nice of you to share that with me. I feel so honored." He rolls his eyes and strolls back into the living room, toward the sofa covered with pieces of aluminum foil and lighters. His sudden shift in attitude throws me off and I debate whether to say anything about it, whether I want to open Pandora's box or not.

"What's wrong?" I ask, following him into the living room. "You're acting kind of rude right now. Is something up? Did something happen with that Trace guy?" I notice he doesn't have any bruises on him or anything, so he hasn't recently been beaten up, but I need to check to make sure he's okay. "Because my offer still stands if you need help."

He looks at me like I'm an idiot as he stuffs his hands into his pockets. "Nothing's wrong. And what happened with Trace isn't your business—it's mine." He picks up a lighter that's on the coffee table and flicks it. "And I'm not acting rude—I'm acting like myself, Nova."

"No, you're acting kind of cold right now... You were nice the other day," I say. "Or at least civil, but now..."

He chucks the lighter across the room, then whirls around near the sofa, shooting me a dirty look. "I wasn't nice to you the other day. You asked me to talk to you and I had nothing better to do so I did. Plain and simple." He picks up another lighter and starts restlessly flicking it. "And if you'd just stop coming over here, you wouldn't have to deal with my moodiness, but you seem to be on some pointless save-the-crackheads mission that you clearly can't handle, but won't admit."

His words blaze under my skin, and between my anger and exhaustion, I say something I regret as soon as it leaves my lips. "I don't have to deal with your moodiness at all, since I came over here to see Quinton, not you."

Rage consumes him, and suddenly he's striding toward me, reducing the space between us in an instant. "Well, if you don't give a shit about me, then leave," he growls. He's so close I can see my reflection in his eyes, can see the fear in the reflection of mine.

"I'm sorry." My voice shakes as I shuffle back and gain space. "I didn't mean that."

"Yeah, you did," he snaps hotly, matching my move and stealing the space right back. "You don't care about me even though you've known me for longer than Quinton, even though you hardly know anything about him."

"That's not true," I say, refusing to cower back. "I do care about you." *I can only handle so much, though, and this is too much. All of this is becoming too much.* "I just…" Shit, I'm starting to get worked up, ready to crack, break apart. "I can only handle so much, and Quinton seems to really need my help."

I can see in his eyes that it strikes a nerve. For a fleeting instant his shield crumbles and his hurt is visible, but it swiftly builds back up and he's annoyed with me again.

He throws his hands in the air exasperatedly. "Whatever, Nova. You show up here with your judgmental eyes and think that everything you say matters, like you can save Quinton just by talking and calling up his dad. You think you can fix everything, like helping us with our drug dealers. Like you have a fucking clue how any of that works." He points his finger at me and starts for the hallway, walking backward, his dazed blue eyes fastened on me. "I don't have to deal with this shit." Then he vanishes down the hall, leaving me in a room that smells worse than dog shit.

I press my fingers to my temples and let my head fall forward. I swear to God, it feels like I've walked into a minefield and one wrong step and I'll set off a bomb. Only the steps are words and the bombs are moody, strung-out people, either high or craving to get high.

It doesn't help that I'm cranky, too. I seriously consider going out through the front door and back to my car, driving off into the sunset, not stopping until I reach it, forgetting about all of this, like it would be that easy, when it wouldn't. Besides, I couldn't even reach the sunset if I tried, since it doesn't really exist. It's just an illusion that paints the world with its pretty colors just before night comes and covers it all up with darkness. It reminds me that walking away, pretending Quinton doesn't need my help, isn't going to get me anywhere, other than maybe to another video, recorded moments before he dies.

So I end up going down the hall toward Quinton's room. As I pass by the shut door of the room Quinton locked himself in the first time I came here, I hear people arguing behind it. Their voices are muffled so I can't tell what they're saying, but it sounds like things are heated. It makes me a little nervous, and that feeling only grows when I reach the end of the hall. Quinton's door is cracked and the one to my right is wide open. What I see inside makes me seriously wish I had picked the delusional sunset.

Tristan is sitting on the floor just inside the room with a rubber band around his bony arm and he's flicking his vein with his finger as he opens and closes his fist. It reminds me of when I slit my wrist open, only he's preparing to sink the syringe that's beside his foot into his skin.

As if he senses me watching him, he glances up and our eyes lock. It frightens me how cold and empty his are. Before

I can say a word, he moves his foot and kicks the door shut in my face, and suddenly I understand his erratic behavior a little bit more. It hurts, more than I thought it would, and opens my eyes a little to a much bigger problem. If I save Quinton, help him, there are still so many others slowly killing themselves, like Tristan. It feels like such a lost cause. One I can't change, but desperately want to.

I squeeze my eyes shut, telling myself to stay calm. *Shut it out. Focus on one thing at a time. Breathe.*

But the yelling in the room gets louder, and I hear something crash against the door and shatter. My eyes shoot open and I turn around as the sound of crying flows through the door, and then it opens up. Dylan strolls out wearing a white tank top and a pair of jeans held up with a frayed belt. He glances at me frigidly as he shuts the door, giving me no time to see what's going on inside.

"You looking for something?" he asks, relaxing causally against the door like nothing's going on at all.

I shake my head, my nerves bubbling inside. "I'm just here to see Quinton."

He points at something over my shoulder. "His room is that way, not over here."

I hesitate to turn around and do only when the crying stops. I feel Dylan stand there behind me for a while until finally he goes back into the room.

I free a trapped breath, my muscles unraveling. "What is wrong with that guy?"

"Delilah and him fight all the time." Quinton appears in the doorway of his room, wearing only his boxers. I can see every scar, every sunken-in area, the weight he's lost, the sheer lack of health. His eyes have dark rings under them and they're filled with the same unwelcome look that was in Tristan's eyes. "I feel bad for her and tried to help her once, but she won't leave him..." He shrugs. "I don't know what else to do."

"Maybe I should go in there and talk to her," I say. "See if I can, I don't know, do something."

"Always trying to save everyone."

"Everyone I care for," I say, meeting his gaze.

He gives me an indecisive look and then sighs, submitting. "What are you doing here? I thought we ended stuff the other day on the roof." He says it like he seriously believes that he thought our fight on the roof was the end of things.

It takes a tremendous amount of energy to shrug off his asshole comment. "We didn't end things," I say. "We just had a fight and now I'm here to apologize."

"Apologize for what?"

"For making you mad. That is why you've been avoiding me, isn't it?"

He cocks his head to the side, looking at me like I'm a foreign creature. "No, you didn't make me mad. You just made me realize that I don't want you hanging around...that it's not good for me to be around you."

"But I want to be around you, and you told me you would let me visit you before I go home, which is soon." The last part is a lie because I honestly have no clue when I'll head back—when I'll be able to accept that things may never change. Give up hope.

He studies me even more closely, seeming conflicted and a little irate, and all I want to do is step to the side and let the wall block me from his unrelenting gaze. "You can stay and hang if you want to," he says as he reaches for a pair of jeans on the floor. "But I . . . I have to do a few things first."

"Like what?"

He doesn't respond, but he does take out a tiny plastic bag filled with white clumpy powder. He holds it up and raises his eyebrows inquiringly, like he's testing me, daring me to give him a reason to send me away, back out to the other side of that cracked door.

I feel myself curl into a ball inside, but outside I stay tall. "Do you have to?"

He nods with need in his eyes, and I force the lump down in my throat and don't say a word when he starts to open the bag and then shuts the door. At least he does me the courtesy of not doing it in front of me this time.

I stare at the cracks in the wall as I wait, tracking them with my gaze, not counting them even though I desperately want to. Then the bedroom door swings open, the one Dylan went in. But he's not the person who steps out.

Delilah is.

She's wearing a see-through shirt and her shorts look more like boy-cut panties. Her auburn hair is matted and her cheek

is a little swollen. But she seems more alert than the last time
I saw her.

She starts to head in the opposite direction from me, ashing her cigarette on the floor, but then pauses when she sees
me. "So the rumors are true," she says, sniffling, her nose red,
and I'm unsure if it's because she's been crying or because she
just snorted something.

"What rumors?" I lean against the wall, and she stands
across from me, relaxing against the door.

She shrugs, taking another drag of her cigarette. "That
you're here in Vegas."

"Yeah, I got here a little over a week ago," I tell her. "And
you saw me the other day."

"Really?" She stares at the ceiling as she tries to recollect.
"I don't remember that."

"That's because you were out of it," I reply, folding my arms.

She sizes me up, and I can see the hatred in her. "Why did
you come here?"

"To see Quinton." I ignore her rude attitude.

Smoke circles her face as she exhales. "Why?"

"Because I want to try to help him," I explain to her.

"With what?"

I glance up and down the hallway, at the garbage on the
floor, the used syringes, the empty alcohol bottle. There's no
carpet on the floor. The ceiling is cracked. The entire place looks
like it's about to collapse. "With getting out of this place."

She laughs snidely. "Yeah, good luck with that." She puts

the cigarette between her lips again and breathes deep. "No one around here wants to be saved, Nova. You should remember that, since you were once in this place."

"But I got out."

"Because you wanted to." She grazes her thumb across the bottom of the cigarette, scattering ash across the floor. "We're all here because we choose to be here."

I elevate my eyebrows. "Even you?"

She frowns. "Yes, even me."

"Then why were you crying a few minutes ago?" I don't really think that has anything to do with drugs, but I'm trying to get her to talk about it. Despite the fact that she can be a bitch most of the time, she was my friend once.

"I was upset about something," she says, dropping her cigarette to the floor. "I'm allowed to be upset."

"I know that." I move toward her. "Why's your cheek all swollen?"

She narrows her eyes at me. "I walked into a wall."

I don't believe her at all. "How the heck does that happen?"

She shrugs, pressing the tip of her shoe to the cigarette, putting it out. "I was tripping out. Thought I could walk through walls."

"Are you...are you sure it had nothing to do with the yelling?"

"Yeah, I'm sure," she snaps, shuffling forward and grabbing hold of my arm. "Don't you dare speculate that Dylan hit me. Because he didn't."

I flinch as her fingers dig into my skin. "I never said he did."

She huffs, releasing her hold on me, and flips me off. "Fuck you. You don't know me. Not anymore." Then she stomps off down the hallway, throwing her arms in the air.

"Delilah, wait," I call out as I hurry after her. "I wasn't trying to make you mad."

She spins on her heels, her face red with anger. "Then what were you doing?"

"I just." I squirm uneasily against her heated gaze. "I just wanted to make sure you were okay."

"I'm fine," she says through clenched teeth.

"If you ever need anything, you can call me," I say in a pathetic attempt to help her.

Her mouth is set in a thin line. "I don't…won't ever need anything."

The helpless feeling inside me magnifies and nearly drowns me as she turns and walks away, leaving me standing at the end of the hallway. I feel like banging my head on the wall, surrounded by a ton of people who need help but don't want it. And I'm not strong enough to help all of them at once. What am I supposed to do? Keep trying until I break? Walk away and always regret not staying? Because I know that's where this will go. I'm already becoming obsessed with the what-ifs again, just like I did after Landon died. And maybe I'll eventually get over it, heal. But at the same time, I want this to turn out well. I want just for once not to have to lose someone because I couldn't do things right—ride my bike fast enough or wake up a few minutes earlier and convince the person I love that life is worth living.

"What are you doing?" The sound of Quinton's voice startles me and my heart speeds up.

I spin around. He's standing in the doorway again with jeans on, sniffing profusely as he puts a shirt on. His eyes are much warmer and more coherent, like he's killed the monster that was emerging in him, or just put it to sleep.

"I was talking to Delilah." I walk back down the hall to him.

"And how did that go?" he questions, stuffing the plastic bag into his pocket.

"Not very well," I admit. "I'm worried about her, not just because of the...well, you know..." I seek the right words, but I'm not sure there are such things. "Not just because she's on drugs, but because she's with Dylan."

"But you can't help her if she doesn't want help." There's an underlying meaning in his tone.

"But I can try," I reply, straining a small smile. "What kind of person would I be to give up on people?"

"The normal kind," he says with honesty.

"Well, I've always known I wasn't normal."

"No, you're not." There's a mystified look on his face. "But it's a good thing, I think." He continues to stare at me for a moment, looking more and more lost, until finally he crouches down to grab a handful of change off the floor. "So where are we going tonight?" He stands back up with a ghost smile on his face. So hot and cold. So up and down. So much like Landon.

"Where do you want to go?" I ask as he stuffs the coins into his pocket.

He presses his lips together, scanning his room, the floor covered in coins and on his mattress a blanket and his sketchbook. "You just want to hang out around here?"

"I'd rather not, if that's okay."

"It's probably not the best place for you, is it?" He frowns, like he just realized where we were standing.

"Or for you," I dare to say, pressing a point.

He swallows hard, and I can see the monster vanishing, probably because he's just fed it. "You're too nice to me," he ultimately says, and that's when I think I see a glimpse of him. The Quinton I first met. The sad one, but still nice, still caring; a good guy who just needs help fighting his inner demons. Who needs to let go of his past.

I force myself to be positive. "Just wait. I've got a whole lot more niceness for you that you haven't even seen yet," I say, playfully nudging him with my foot.

He shakes his head, but fights back a smile, his honey-brown eyes flickering with a hint of life, and the sight makes me want to throw my arms around him and hold on to him— hold on to the life I see there in his eyes. "How about we go sit in your car and talk?"

I work to keep my arms to my sides and nod, pushing

myself to look past all the problems around me, even though it feels like maybe I shouldn't—that maybe I'm the one who needs to open her eyes. "I think that sounds like a great idea."

∾

I'm not sure how much crystal he did, but by the time we make it to the car, a burst of energy kicks in and his talking goes into hyper mode. "So how are you liking Vegas?" he asks as we climb into my car, parked in the parking lot in front of his house.

It's such a formal question that it takes me a moment to answer. "Good, I guess."

I get comfortable in the seat, rolling down the window and letting the warm air in as he tips his head back against the headrest. "Have you done anything fun?"

I scoot my seat back a little so I can stretch out my legs. "I went to the Strip the other night."

"I hear it's intense." He rubs his eyes and then blinks as he gazes up at the ceiling.

"Yeah, lots and lots of lights and people…Do you go down there ever?"

He shakes his head. "Nah, it's not really for me." His eyes land on me, and through the dark I can almost pretend that he's sober. "Too many people."

"You don't seem to like the city," I note, rotating in my seat to face him. "Yet you live here and you used to live in Seattle, which is pretty big, isn't it?" I tense when I feel him tense, worried that maybe bringing up Seattle wasn't the best thing.

But he relaxes. "Yeah, but cities haven't always bothered me."

"What changed?"

"Me," he says, scratching at his arm where I know his tattoos are hidden. "I just decided I like the quiet...I already have too much noise in my head, and the last thing I need to do is add more."

"And yet you're here."

"I'm here because I have nowhere else to go."

"Not even back to Seattle." I hope I'm not about to break the thin ice I'm already walking on.

"I'll never go back to Seattle," he replies disdainfully, cracking his neck and then his knuckles. "There's too many fucking memories there."

It grows quiet as he stares at the building in front of us with a contemplative look on his face, like he's considering if he wants to bail out and go back in. Before he can, I take the opportunity to say something that I hope doesn't make him angry, that I hope makes him understand that I understand him more than he thinks I do.

"You know, I used to feel that way about Maple Grove," I divulge. "Especially since it's where my boyfriend died. His house was actually across the street..." I swallow the lump in my throat, preparing myself to say the one thing I'll always hate saying aloud. "Where I found him...after he...well, he took his own life."

Silence stretches by. I hear cars whizzing by on the streets. Their headlights illuminate the rearview mirror.

"I'm sure that had to be hard for you," he utters quietly, his breath becoming ragged.

"It was really hard," I admit. "Especially because I blamed myself for his death."

He turns his head toward me with his brows furrowed. "Why would you blame yourself over that? He chose to do it. You didn't make him." He pauses, composing his erratic breath.

"Yeah, but at the same time, I saw signs that I sort of ignored because I was afraid to admit they existed. Afraid he'd get mad at me…I was afraid of a lot of things, and I'll always regret that fear for the rest of my life."

"Yeah, but even if you weren't afraid and you said something to him," he says, not looking at me but staring over my shoulder out at the darkness, "it doesn't mean things would have happened differently. He still might have decided it was time to let go."

"Yeah, but I'd at least be able to sit here and say that I did everything I could." I press a point that feels really important now. "That I didn't give up before it was over."

"Is that what you're doing with me?" He looks at me. I think he's aiming to be rude, but his uneven voice gives away that he's getting emotional.

"Maybe," I tell him honestly. "Does that make you afraid?"

He shakes his head, holding my gaze. "No, because I know you're just wasting time."

"I don't agree with you." I refuse to blink away from his intense gaze. "No time is wasted when you're trying to help someone."

He's baffled by my words, his lips parting as he scratches his head. "So what? You're going to continue to hang out at this place in the hopes that you're going to save me?" He gestures at our surroundings. The neighborhood has started to come to life, people standing outside on the stairway of the building, walking around the front. "You really want this to be your life? Because even I sometimes hate it. Plus, it's dangerous and you shouldn't even be hanging out here." He falters over his words like he didn't mean to let the last part slip out. "But I deserve it. You don't."

"Well, I don't have to stay here all the time," I say, getting an idea as I start up the engine. "No one does. Everyone has a choice of where they want to be. You. Tristan, especially after seeing what that Trace guy did to him."

"Tristan will be fine...I'm taking care of him." He slides back in the seat.

"Are you sure? Because I can help—"

He cuts me off. "I'm not letting you get involved in this shit, so drop it, Nova."

"Okay...but I just want you to know that I'm here if you need anything."

"I know that." His expression softens. "And I want you to know that I don't want you getting involved in anything that's part of this." He gestures at the apartment building. "I want you safe."

I shift the car into drive. "I know you do."

We exchange this intense look that makes it hard to

breathe. But then he clears his throat a few times and sits up straight as I start to back the car up. "What are you doing?"

Getting you away from your crappy apartment. "I just need a soda. I'm freaking thirsty."

"There's a gas station just down the road where you can get one," he says, pointing over his shoulder at the road. "It only takes, like, a minute to drive there and a few minutes on foot."

"I'll just drive there." I crank the wheel to turn the car around. "And then we can keep talking."

"But doesn't our conversation keep going in circles... you trying to help me when you can't? It's kind of a lost cause," he says as he guides his seat belt over his shoulder and clicks it into the buckle.

I flip on the headlights as I pull out onto the road. "No time with you is a lost cause. It's actually very valuable."

I hear his breath hitch in his throat, and when he grips the door handle, I worry he's going to try to jump out, but he startles me when he says, "Nova, you're freaking killing me tonight." His voice is just a whisper, choked up, full of the agony he keeps bottled up. "You got to stop saying that shit to me."

My heart races inside my chest. "Why?"

He lowers his head and rubs his hand roughly across his face. "Because it means too much to me, and stuff shouldn't mean things to me... It messes with my head."

"Well, I'm sorry, but I got a whole lot more meaningful stuff waiting for you," I tell him, unsure where the hell this conversation is going to go.

He stares down at his lap. "I can't take it anymore. Please just talk about something else besides me." He glances up at me, and the lights on the side of the street are reflected in his eyes, highlighting his agony. "Tell me something about you," he begs, slumping against the seat with his head turned toward me. "Please. I want to hear something about you."

I turn my head and our gazes collide. I want to cry because he looks miserable, like he's silently begging me to put him out of it. God, what I'd give to know the right thing to say, something that could take away his pain. The problem is I know from experience there's no right thing to say that can take away the pain. There's nothing that can save him from it. He just has to learn to live with it and not give it so much power over him.

"Like what?" I ask, fighting to keep my voice balanced.

"I don't know." He shrugs. "You said on the roof that I was easy to talk to last summer and I said it was because you were high, so prove me wrong right now. Talk to me about something—something about you."

I consider what he said as I tap the brakes, stopping at a red light. Something about me. Maybe something that will help him see that people can be helped. "I watched Landon's . . . my old boyfriend's video, the one he made minutes before he killed himself." I don't look at him when I say it because I can't, but his elongated silence says that I've stunned him. The light turns green and I drive down the road, heading toward the gas station on the right side.

Finally he says, "When?"

"I already told you he made it right before he died," I say as I pull into the gas station. "I actually had the video file forever, but I was too scared to watch it. I had it there on my computer and then on my phone all last summer, but wouldn't... couldn't watch it."

"No, I mean when did you watch it?" he asks as I park the car in front of the gas station doors and beneath the fluorescent glow of the signs.

I turn off the engine. "It was the day I took off from the concert," I tell him, our gazes locked. "The morning after you left me at the pond."

"And did it make you feel better?" he questions. "Knowing what he thought before he..." His voice cracks and he clears it, putting his hands at his sides.

"Yes and no," I answer honestly, and when he looks at me funny, I explain. "Yes, because it helped me see what I'd really become—what I was turning into. Even though it was right in front of my eyes, I couldn't see it, and his words reminded me of what I used to be and what I wanted to be again."

He absorbs my words like they're oxygen, breathing in and out. "And why do you regret it?"

I shrug, but everything inside me winds tight as I stare out the windshield at the store lights, letting them burn against my eyes so I won't cry. "Because I still ended up confused over why he did it...He never did give a real explanation, and honestly, I'm not even sure one exists. Plus, it hurt to watch him like that, you know." I look over at him, and even though it's hard, I hold his gaze. "Watching him hurt like that and knowing that soon his pain was going to end—that he was going to die soon and I couldn't do anything to stop it. That I missed my chance...I never want to miss my chance again."

"I'm not going to die, Nova," he says. "If that's what you're getting at."

"You don't know that," I say, looking back at him, seeing spots from staring at the lights. "What you're doing...it could kill you."

"Well, it's not going to," he insists. "Trust me, I've been trying to die for a very long time and I can't make it happen, no matter how hard I try."

The hope inside me poofs out, and before I can even get myself together, tears flood my eyes. Quinton's honey-brown eyes become Landon's, and abruptly it feels like I'm sitting in the car with *him* and we're just talking, but I can feel that he's sad and I'm just watching him getting sadder and sadder and not doing a goddamned thing about it—watching him die.

"Why would you ever say something like that?" I say as hot tears drip from my eyes. I want to hit him, but at the same time I want to hug him. I'm conflicted, so instead I just sit there and cry and he just sits there and watches me like he doesn't care. But then the tears start streaming down my cheeks and splattering on the console, and when he sees them falling, it's like he suddenly realizes I'm crying and that he played a part in it.

He leans over quickly and wraps his arm around me and

pulls me against him, crushing our bodies together. "God, Nova, I'm so sorry. Fuck. I'm such an asshole...I don't even know what I'm saying half the time...Don't even listen to me."

I let him hold me as tears soak his shirt, and he kisses the top of my head, whispering apologies. For a fleeting moment, it's not me and this warped version of Quinton in the car. It's me and a different Quinton I wish I could meet, the one from before the accident. I'm not really sure what he's like, but I've gotten enough glimpses of him that I can picture a loving, genuinely good guy. And he's the one holding me right now, rather than the one who made me cry.

Eventually I suck the tears back and return to reality. I start to retreat, but he keeps his arms around me, pressing on my back, and I notice his arms are trembling.

"I'm so sorry," he says, and he's shaking like he's scared. "I should have never said that."

"It's fine." I move back enough to look him in the eyes. "You're probably just tired, right?" I offer him an excuse, hoping he'll take it and we can let this go.

"Yeah...tired," he says warily because we both know that's not the case.

I lift my hand to wipe the tears from my cheeks, but he grabs my hand. Then he moves forward and I instantly tense as he brushes his lips across my cheeks where the tears stain my skin.

"Tired or not," he says between kisses. "I should never make you cry. Ever. I'm a horrible person who you should just stay away from," he whispers through another kiss. "God, I don't deserve to be here with you. You should just take me back home."

"No, you do deserve to be with me." My eyes shut as his warm breath touches my cheeks and his chest brushes against mine with every breath he takes. Emotions surface...how much I care for him...how much I wish he could be in my future...my life...healed. I'm painfully reminded of why I came here. Why I needed to help him. And it's painful because I know how hard it is, how hopeless it's becoming, but how worth it it is because of the glimpses like these.

"What can I do to make it better?" he whispers against my cheek. "I'll do anything that you tell me to."

I know I shouldn't say it, but I can't help it. "Stop doing drugs." I stiffen, waiting for him to shout at me, but all he does is lean back, keeping his hand on my hip.

"I can't do that," he says softly, almost sounding disappointed, but maybe that's just me reaching for hope.

"Why not?"

"Because I can't."

I want to press him more, but he's shutting down, the life dying in his eyes. I know that once it's gone, he'll ask me to take him home, so I let him go and search for a way to keep him here beside me.

"Hey, know what we should do?" I say as he sits back in his seat.

He drums his fingers on his knee as he stares at the gas station. "What should we do, Nova like the car?" he asks, giving me a sideways half smile. It's been a while since he's used my nickname, and memories of last summer flow through me so powerfully it makes me light-headed.

"We should play twenty questions again," I tell him. "Like we did last summer."

"That's what you really want to do?" he questions with a crook of his brow.

I yawn as my fingers wrap around the door handle. "Just as soon as I go get a soda."

He studies me, looking torn, but then gives in. "All right. Go get your soda and we'll play twenty questions for a little bit."

I get out of the car, not feeling happy, but at the same time not feeling like I'm drowning in hopelessness. Although I do worry that by the time I make it back to the car, he'll be gone. So I rush to buy a soda and when I step back outside, relief washes over me when I see him lying on the hood of my car, smoking a cigarette, staring up at the stars in the midnight sky. The street is fairly quiet and there are no other cars parked nearby. The only noise is coming from the gas station radio speakers and it's set on the oldies station, playing soft tunes. It's almost like we have the quiet he was talking about on the roof. It'd be a perfect moment if I didn't know what's going to happen when I take him back to the apartment. Still, I climb up on the hood with him and take a swallow of soda as the scent of cigarette smoke encircles me.

"What are you thinking about?" I ask him, looking up at the night sky, feeling calm inside as I stare at the constellations.

He puts the cigarette up to his lips and inhales. "Thinking about my first question," he says, blowing out a cloud of smoke.

"Oh yeah?" I say, twisting the cap back on my soda. "Who said you get to go first?"

He slants his head to the side. "You're not going to let me go first?" He's almost playful.

I smile. "I'm kidding. You can go first."

He thinks about it for a moment while sticking his arm to the side and ashing his cigarette onto the ground. "If you could be one place in the world, where would you be?"

"Honestly?" I say, and he nods. "I think I'd be all over the world, videotaping everything."

"Everything?"

I nod. "Everything. There's just so much to see, you know, and sometimes it feels like I'm just sitting around, missing everything."

He turns to his side and props himself up on his elbow, cigarette smoke circling around us. "Then why don't you just go?"

"For a lot of reasons," I reply, rotating the soda bottle in my hand. "One being that I need to graduate first . . . It's important for my future."

"Yeah, I can see that . . . needing a degree if you have a future," he says with a frown, and it stabs at my heart.

"You could have a future, you know," I say, hoping I don't set him off again.

"No, I can't." He lies down on his back and fixes his eyes on the stars, growing quiet.

"Okay, my turn." I pivot onto my hip, rest my head on my arm, and set the soda bottle against the windshield. "What were you like before you started doing drugs?" It's a brave question, but I want tonight's game to actually have a point. I want to get to know him more. Understand him, so I can maybe understand what will help him.

He winces like I've slapped him and lets out a sharp cough. "I'm not going to answer that question."

"That's not fair. I always answer yours, even the one about my dad's death, which is hard to talk about."

"When did I ask you about your dad?"

"Last summer," I remind him. "When we were in the tent and we...and we kissed a lot."

More memories swarm around us as I remember, and I can tell he remembers, too, because he touches his lips and gets this really strange look on his face. Then he swallows hard and flicks his cigarette onto the ground. He finally answers my question. "I was normal. Just a normal guy who thought about college and who liked to draw and wanted to be an artist. Who hardly got into trouble, and who had only been in love with one girl...a normal, boring guy." He sounds so conflicted, like he misses that guy, but at the same time he doesn't want to.

The song switches to one I know, even though I'm not into oldies. But it's one my dad used to listen to, "Heaven" by Bryan Adams, and it makes me think of the good times in my life, when I used to dance around the living room with my dad, listening to music, and everything felt so easy. I wish I could capture some of that easiness now and spill it over Quinton and me.

"I like the sound of that boring guy," I utter softly. "I hope one day I can meet him."

"You won't, so you should go find another one." He sits up like he's ready to go, but instead he stretches his arms above his head. "What do you see in me, Nova? What keeps you coming around? I mean, I'm not that nice to you, at least not always. I have a shitty life and do shitty stuff."

"All of that's because you're hurting, though, something I get really, really well." I sit up and bend forward to meet his eyes, which are wide and full of panic. "I see a lot of things in you, Quinton. I'm not going to lie. You sometimes remind me of Landon and that's part of the reason why I think I'm so drawn to you," I say, and when his expression falls, I quickly take his hands. "But that's not the only reason...When I'm around you, sometimes it seems like you and I are the only two people who exist and nothing else matters, and for someone who overthinks everything, that's really hard to achieve."

I can tell he sort of likes my answer because his pulse starts slamming against my fingers. "Is that all?" he asks, and I shake my head, wondering how long it's been since someone said nice things to him.

"No way. I'm just getting started." I hold on to him tighter. "Last summer you made me feel things...things I thought I'd never feel again after Landon died. And it's not because I was high. Trust me. I haven't felt that way again, not until I came back here to see you."

"I'm a junkie, Nova," he mumbles. "I shouldn't make you feel anything."

"You're not a junkie," I argue, tightening my hold on his hands. "You're just someone who's really, really lost and hurting and won't admit it and drugs take that all away for you."

He's starting to look scared, panicky, his eyes sweeping the area like he's looking for a place to run, hide, and get high. So I clutch him tighter and move on.

"If *you* could do anything right now," I say quickly. "What would *you* do?"

"Get high," he replies, meeting my eyes, and his are so full of anguish it steals the breath out of me. "What about you? What would you do right now if you could?"

I think he thinks I'm going to say I would save him, and I want to, but I'm not going to say it because I need a break from the repetitiveness and so does he. We both know why I'm here and I'm not forgetting why I came. I'm just trying to work my way into his head the only way I can think of. By trying something that's easy and uncomplicated. Because we need easy at the moment.

"I would dance," I answer, then let go of his hand and slide off the hood of the car. I know I'm being goofy, but it's all I've got at the moment, so I stick out my hand. "Will you dance with me, Quinton?"

He glances warily at the speakers on the trim of the gas station, at the vacant pumps, then over to the street. "That's really what you want to do? Right here? Right now?"

I nod with my hand still out. "Yep. Now, will you grant me my request?"

He considers this, and there's hesitation in his eyes, but he still gets down off the hood and takes my hand. The contact gives me a brief break from all the crappy stuff surrounding us. Easy. We're going to do something that's really, really easy. I know it won't erase all the hard stuff. But sometimes taking a break from the complicated stuff is enough to get me through the next step and the next one. One step at a time. One breath at a time. One heartbeat at a time.

One life at a time.

I reach out to put my hand on his shoulder, but instead he pushes me back and spins me around. "You know you're getting in over your head, right?" he says, jerking me to him and crushing me against his chest.

I'm breathless as I put my cheek up to his chest and feel his heart racing beneath it. "Where'd you learn to dance like that?"

"From my grandmother...She taught me right before I went to my first dance in middle school," he says, breathing into my hair as he rests his chin on top of my head and we begin to sway to the music.

"Was it because she wanted to teach you?" I ask. "Or because you wanted to learn?"

"Sadly, it was because I wanted to learn," he says. "I thought knowing how to dance would make my crush want to dance with me."

I press my cheek to his chest. "But she didn't want to?"

"Nah, but I wasn't the kind of guy girls wanted to dance with," he says. "I was too shy at the time."

I try not to smile, but it's hard. "I was shy too at one time."

"I can see that," he says thoughtfully.

I pull away slightly and tip my chin up to look him in the eyes. "How? I'm not shy anymore."

The corners of his lips quirk. "Yeah, but sometimes you get embarrassed over stuff you do and the shyness comes out," he says, and when I frown he adds, "Don't worry. It's only happened a couple of times, back when we first started hanging out. And besides, I like it."

I press my lips together and return my cheek to his chest, and he puts his chin back on top of my head. "Well, I'm glad you do, because I don't."

"Well, I do." He keeps dancing for a moment, leading me in a slow circle. Then I feel him swallow hard and he says, "I guess you learned another thing about the old me—that I used to know how to dance."

I smile to myself because he didn't used to know how to dance—he still does. And as we rock to the rhythm, I stay silent, telling myself that if he can still dance, then the old Quinton's still burning somewhere inside him, and now that I've seen a glimpse of it, I don't want to ever let it go.

So I hold on to him tightly as we sway to the song. I shut my eyes and feel every aspect of the moment, the heat in the air, the warmth of his body, the way my body seems in tune with his. No regrets. This is one moment I will never regret. I don't care that we're in a shitty gas station parking lot and that we both smell like cigarette smoke. I want it. Want this. Want him. Right now. I know it's not the right time at all, that there are so many things wrong, things hidden deep beneath the surface, but I just need to touch him a little bit more. So without opening my eyes, I kiss my way up his neck and across his scruffy jaw, and find his lips. I'm not sure what I expect him to do, but he opens his mouth and kisses me back deeply, with passion and heat. He manages to keep us moving and at the same time presses our bodies closer, until we're almost one person. I can feel everything about him. His heat. His breath. The slight gasps he makes every time our lips barely part. And with my eyes shut I can pretend that I'm with the old Quinton, the one I'm trying to save.

And part of me wishes I never had to open my eyes again. Part of me wishes I could stay just like this. Forever. Just he and I. Just contentment. The easiness. It makes me want to create more moments like this. I just need to find a way for him to let me.

After we're done dancing, we climb back on the hood and chat a little more. He seems to unwind as time goes by and I'm guessing that he's reached a sort of peaceful balance in his high, one I remember well because it's what drew me to drugs in the first place. Then it starts to get late, the noise dying down so severely it seems like the city has gone to sleep.

I yawn, stretching out my arms as I stare up at the stars. "It's so late."

"I know. We should probably get back," he says, sitting up and hopping off the hood. "It's late and I hate the thought of you being around here at night and driving back to wherever you're staying."

I slide toward the edge of the hood and he helps me down by taking my hand. "I'll be okay. Lea's uncle lives in a pretty good area."

"Still, I worry about you." He seems uncomfortable saying it.

"All right. I'll drop you off and get home, then."

He nods and lets go of my hand. Then I take him home and give him a kiss on the cheek before he gets out of the car.

"Nova," he says before he climbs out, his back turned to me, his feet out of the car and on the ground. "I wish you'd stop coming here."

My heart sinks in my chest. For a moment I thought I saw promise that things might change between us—that he'd stop fighting me so much. "You really want me to stop?"

It takes him a few seconds to answer. "What I want doesn't matter . . . What's right does."

"It's not wrong for me to see you." I nervously fiddle with the key chain dangling from the ignition. "And I'm not ready to stop seeing you . . . Are you ready to stop seeing me?"

His head lowers, but he still doesn't look at me. "I can't answer that right now."

"Well, then, let's stop talking about it until you do," I say, and he starts to get out of the car without saying a word. "I'll see you tomorrow?"

He pauses as he's closing the door. "Yeah...I guess so."

It's not much, but it's enough to lift me a little bit out of my slump. "Bye, Quinton. I'll see you tomorrow."

He doesn't say anything and shuts the door. Then he goes back up to his place and I wait until he's inside before I take out my phone and angle it at my face.

There's very little light, but I can still make out my outline on the screen, which is enough. "So I got this idea tonight," I tell the camera. "It might be stupid, but it's all I got. It's called fun. And I'm not talking about getting-drunk-and-partying type of fun. That's the last thing Quinton and I need. I'm talking about the plain, easy kind of fun. The dancing, music, laughing, playful, peaceful kind of fun...the kind we shared tonight. It seemed to help him relax, not putting pressure on him, pretending that we were just two people hanging out... and I can pretend as long as it can get me somewhere...I just hope I can keep getting to him...keep learning about him... understand him." I pause, biting my lip as a guy walks out of Quinton's apartment, strolls up to the railing, and stares down at my car. He flicks his cigarette over the edge and then rests his arms on top of the railing. The light over the door hits his back, making it hard to see his face, but it sort of looks like

Dylan. If that's the case, then it's time for me to go, before he ruins my vaguely decent night.

I shut the recording off and toss my phone aside, feeling a little bit lighter as I drive away. I just pray to God that when I return tomorrow morning, the Quinton I had toward the end of tonight is still thriving.

Chapter Eleven

May 26, day eleven of summer break

Quinton

I'm changing and I don't like it. I'm feeling things and I don't like it. My self-destruction plan is becoming complicated and I don't like it. I don't like anything at the moment, yet I keep doing the same things over and over again. Keep seeing Nova. Letting her affect me—change me.

But I can't seem to help it.

Dancing with her was...well, it was amazing. Touching her like that—kissing her like that—it should be forbidden, especially after making her cry like I did. I made a silent vow to myself the second Nova dropped me off that day when we were on the roof and I showed her one of the ugliest sides of myself and made her cry. I vowed I'd never hurt her again and that I'd stay away from her, but I suck at the last part.

I don't know how to shut it off—turn away from her—without feeling like I'm going insane. She's taking me over, almost as potent as the drugs, but unlike with drugs, I'm very conflicted about my emotions. The last time I felt something was at that concert, and I ultimately made a choice to shut myself down, not let myself have Nova, not drag her down. Not feel anything. Create my own prison. But Nova seems to know how to get through the bars and pull me out like she did last summer. And the emotions I tried to kill with drugs have burst to the surface again. Sometimes I think I should embrace them. Sometimes I think I should run from them. Sometimes it makes me angry and I worry I'll fly off the handle one of these times and say something to hurt her again.

Fortunately, that hasn't happened yet. I've seen Nova every day for the last four days and managed not to flip out and make her cry, but that's partially because I always make sure I'm at the perfect high whenever she comes around. Her visits are starting to become a routine. Like today. I wake up at around noon or one, get my morning boost, get dressed, and then wait around and draw until she shows up. I almost get excited knowing she'll be here to see me. All of this stuff seems good, but there's one huge problem. The more time I spend with her, the guiltier I feel about Lexi. I'm leaving her behind to rot in her grave, deciding that I should live instead of putting myself into a grave like I should have been.

I'm not sure what the hell is wrong with me. What kind
of person would just move on from the girlfriend he killed? So
I try to fight it—my feelings for Nova—but she consumes my
thoughts, takes over my life, even my drawings. I'm actually
drawing a picture of her when she shows up today. It's one of
her sitting on the edge of the roof where we chatted that day
I yelled at her. The perfection I saw as she looked at me and I
explained my love for the scene below. It's an amazing drawing
that makes me sad to see, that I've gotten to that place where I
can put so much effort into drawing another girl.

The last thing I want is for Nova to see it, so when she
enters my room I quickly shut my sketchbook. "Hey," I say,
tossing it aside onto the mattress.

She's all smiles, two cups of coffee in her hands as she
materializes in my doorway, wearing a blue dress that shows
off her legs, her hair done up so I can see the freckles on her
face and shoulders. "So I have a plan for today." She sticks out
her hand, offering me a cup of coffee, looking so happy even
though there's a mirror on my floor that's coated in white resi-
due, like she can see past all that stuff, like how I've treated her
in the past, like the scar on my chest that marks the terrible
thing I did.

I take the coffee from her. "Who let you into the apartment?" I ask, stretching my arms above my head and blinking
a few times to hydrate my eyes. I did a line about a couple of
hours ago, so I'm good right now, but not overflowing with
adrenaline.

Her upbeat attitude sinks. "Dylan."

My arms fall to my sides. "He didn't say anything to you, did he?"

She shrugs, picking at the edge of the coffee lid. "It's not really what he said, so much as how he stared at me for about a minute before he let me into the house...Delilah was passed out on the sofa and he made a smartass remark about liking her better that way. I think he likes getting to me...and I hate seeing Delilah like that."

Of course she does, because she worries too much about everyone. "I'm sorry," I say, wanting to wring Dylan's neck. He's been acting like a dick more and more every day, insisting we need to move out. Tristan and I actually sneaked into his room and searched it for the gun, but I think he keeps it on him all the time. I'm a little worried about where this all might be headed, and the last thing I want is for Nova to get involved. "I don't think you should come up here anymore."

She quickly shakes her head, her eyes widening. "No, I can handle creepy Dylan...Just please don't make me stop seeing you."

"I didn't mean stop coming to see me," I correct her and take a small sip of the coffee. It's been a long time since I've had the fancy Starbucks kind, and it tastes better than I remember. "I just meant that maybe you shouldn't come up to the house anymore. We can just meet in your car."

"But how will you know when I show up?"

"We can set a time."

"But you say you have a hard time keeping track of time." She drinks her coffee as she waits for me to respond.

If I do, I'm pretty much making a commitment to see her—to keep seeing her. Go against everything I feel inside me, which I might be able to do if I can keep the right amount of drugs in my system, the balance that keeps me stable—functioning. "I'll try my best to be out there every day by noon." It's the best that I can do.

"That sounds good to me." Her perfect lips curve up into a small but portrait-worthy smile. "So do you want to hear my plans for the day?"

I rotate the cup in my hands. "Sure."

Her smile brightens as she sits down on the mattress beside me, and I tense as her body heat flows over me. "We're going to have a fun day of not talking about our problems and not arguing," she says.

I tense at the word "fun." The night of the accident, Lexi wanted to have fun. Although Nova and Lexi aren't alike at all. In fact, Nova's probably talking about calm, carefree fun, while Lexi always loved impulsive and dangerous. "I don't think I can have fun."

She bumps her shoulder against mine, smiling. "Of course you can."

I suck in a slow breath through my nose, telling myself to be calm. "No, I can't."

Her forehead creases. "Why not?"

"Because I just can't."

"Quinton, please just tell me," she pleads. "Otherwise I'll go crazy trying to figure out why…like I always had to do with Landon."

Shit, she's making this hard. She played the dead boyfriend card. Plus, she's staring at me and her eyes are so big and beautiful they nearly swallow me whole.

"My girlfriend…Lexi asked to have fun the last time…" Tears sting at my eyes, and I tip my head back to stop them from falling out. The water stain is right above me, which used to annoy me all the time, but oddly, for the last few days it's stopped dripping, although the stain itself has grown. "The night she died." I lower my head when I get myself together and look at her.

She's quiet as she chews her bottom lip, her hands on the tops of her legs, her fingers delving into her skin. At first I think she's uncomfortable, but then I realize her eyes are watering and she's fighting not to cry. "Landon never wanted to have fun." Her voice is so soft when she says it but lacks so much emotion, like she feels hollow. It nearly kills me to hear the emptiness in her voice. It's a weak spot—she's a weak spot.

Tristan was right. She does change me. I'm just not sure if it's for the better or for the worse, because I have a hard time dealing with the emotions she summons out of me, the feelings she manages to pull out of me, even through the layers of drugs.

I cover her hand with mine and she stiffens. My heart leaps inside my chest and nearly strangles me as desire pours through me—the desire to make her happy. I blow out a breath as I realize where my thoughts are headed. "What kind of fun were you thinking of for today?"

She perks up, the tears in her eyes receding. "Go out to the city. Ride some roller coasters. Laugh. Have fun." She says it like it's the easiest thing to do in the world.

I scrunch up my nose. "I'm not sure I even remember how to do that, unless I'm tweaked out, but I don't think that's part of the fun you're referring to."

"No, it's not." She flinches as I say it, wounded by my words. "And I'm going to show you how to without being high," she says, letting it go as she holds out her hand like she wants me to take it.

"You know I'm high right now, right?" I hate to say it, but it's the truth and I don't like lying to her.

"I know, but maybe you could try not to do anything while we're out." I can see the nervousness in her eyes, the fear of rejection. I picture her crying in the car and how I never want to be the cause of that again, so I take her hand.

"I'll do my best, but I can't promise you anything," I tell her straightforwardly, not trying to hurt her, but she needs to know where I stand. That despite the fact that I'm changing in other ways, I have no intention of quitting. That I'm just toning it down while she's here to visit me. That if I were sober, I probably couldn't even be around her because the memories of Lexi would drown all the air out of me instead of part of it. That I'd have to feel every emotional sting, feel what it's like to live, breathe, let my heart beat exactly how a normal heart should. Let go of Lexi and choose to live.

She nods and I let her lead me out to the car. Our fingers leave each other's only when we get into the car and I'm sober enough that I can feel the connection leave me and also sober enough that it hurts a little when I realize I want the connection back.

Nova immediately starts up the engine and cranks up the air-conditioning. "You know, I bet the amount of people who go to the hospital for heat exhaustion is pretty freaking high around here." She wipes the sweat from her forehead with the back of her hand. "I feel like I'm melting."

"Well, you look pretty melt-free." I pause as she looks a little confused and I feel a little confused. *Maybe I'm not as sober as I thought.*

"I'm not exactly sure what you mean." She reaches for her iPod on the seat. "But I'll take it as a compliment." She scrolls through the songs, searching for the perfect one. I've noticed this is her routine, and if I pay really close attention, I can get the feel of her mood based on the song choice.

Music clicks on and I have to glance at the screen when she sets the iPod down because I'm unfamiliar with the song. "'One Line,' by PJ Harvey...never heard of her." But I swear to God Nova's trying to send me a message with it, a positive one about the kiss we shared in the parking lot.

"That's because you're music-deprived," she teases as she

reaches for her sunglasses on the dashboard and puts them on. I wonder how she can do it. Sit here with me and pretend to be okay with everything. I think about what she told me in the car, about her boyfriend, how she wants to save me like she didn't save him. Maybe that's why.

"I'm not that music-deprived," I say, buckling my seat belt as she presses on the gas and drives forward. "I'm just not as awesome as you." And now I'm flirting. Great. It's going to be a very interesting day, which I'm sure I'll suffer for later when it all seeps into me.

She bites back a smile as she pulls onto the road. "You know, I've been getting even more awesome at my own music," she says, maneuvering into the right line and heading toward the city just in the distance. "I've even started to make up some of my own beats."

"That's really awesome." I drum my fingers on the door to the beat of the song to let some of my energy out in the most discreet way possible.

"And I've even played up on stage a few times."

"Really?" I remember that time we stood in the crowd at the concert and I got lost in her getting lost in the music.

She nods, looking a little bit proud. "Yeah. I mean, it was hard at first, considering Landon bought me my first set of drums. But I worked through the pain, made new memories, got my love back for it." She grins at me as she pulls the visor down. "And now I rock at it."

"I bet you do."

"You know, I still owe you a show."

My eyebrow crooks upward. "A show?" Too many dirty images flash through my mind and it pushes a rush of adrenaline through me, or maybe that's from the drip in the back of my throat.

"Yeah, I told you I'd play for you one of these times," she says, tapping on the brake to stop at a stoplight. "And I haven't yet."

"One day, maybe," I say, but I wonder just how far our future's going to go, how long she can watch me like this. Even though I'm sitting here with her, I have no plan to change what I do. "How about today?" she suggests as the light turns green and she starts moving with the traffic again.

"You want to play the drums for me today?" I ask, glancing around at the sides of the streets and the tattoo parlors, souvenir shops, and secondhand stores that shift to casinos as we veer farther into the main area of the city.

She nods, flipping her blinker on to change lanes. "I mean, if you want to." She moves the car over into the turning lane. "I have my drums stashed at the place where I'm staying."

I make an excuse. "Yeah, I don't think anyone's going to be cool with a crackhead hanging out at their house."

"The owner's never home until after six," she states, turning into a parking garage.

"What about your friend Lea?"

"What about her?"

"Won't she be mad at you for showing up with me?" I ask,

unbuckling my seat belt as she pulls into an empty parking space.

"She'll be okay with it," she tells me, pushing the shifter into park. "She knows how much I care about you."

No matter how many times she says it, her words always strike me hard in the chest and knock the wind out of me. It's like she senses it, too, because she quickly says, "Sorry, I'm being too meaningful already, aren't I?"

I rub my hand over my head and then to the back of my neck, gradually exhale. "No...it's okay...Let's just go try to have some fun."

Sober fun.

Does that even freaking exist?

I'm not even sure I believe in fun anymore, but I'm about to attempt to find out. Thankfully, I still have enough crystal in my system not to crash completely, although the rush could fade before the day's over, especially if I get worked up over something. I'm worried. Not just about myself, but about Nova.

Worried she'll get to see the real monster that lies inside me and it'll crush our fun day into a thousand unfixable pieces.

Nova

We walk up and down the Strip talking and laughing. Well, I do most of the laughing. Quinton rarely laughs, but I do manage to get him to smile a few times. We go to the New York, New York casino to ride the roller coaster that winds around the outside of the building. While we're waiting in the fairly long line, he admits he's a little scared of roller coasters.

"When I was about twelve or thirteen, I was sitting next to some kid when I was on one and he barfed his guts out," Quinton admits. We're standing across from each other, a bunch of people around us, but as we talk, making eye contract, it feels like it's just him and me. I didn't know eye contact could be so powerful until today, and I become highly aware that Landon didn't make eye contact a lot, like he was always looking off somewhere else.

"Ew." I pull a disgusted face. "Did any get on you?"

He nods, looking utterly disgusted. "Oh yeah, it was nasty."

"My dad and I used to ride roller coasters together," I tell him, moving forward with the line. "I haven't gotten on one since he died, though, because it sort of makes me sad."

"Really?" he asks, surprised.

"Yeah, this is me getting back in the saddle."

"Are you sure you want to share that moment with me?" he wonders, uneasy as he hunches back against the railing that the line weaves around.

I nod and then daringly reach toward him and take his hand in mine, intertwining our fingers. "I'm glad it's you and no one else."

He stares at the floor, muttering something that sounds an awful lot like "Meaningful." But he doesn't let go of my hand until we climb into our seats. We get buckled in and the guy comes around to check that we're fastened securely. Then I hold my breath as the car inches forward and climbs the track to the outside. The sun is blinding, but I refuse to look away, wanting to feel this moment, knowing that when the car drops, I'll feel a fleeting moment of freedom, something I've needed since I got here. And I hope that maybe the ride can do the same for Quinton.

Quinton tips his knee in when we reach the top, pressing it against mine. I'm not sure if he realizes he's doing it or if he's doing it on purpose to comfort me or himself, but I embrace the touching, holding my breath as we fall. Together. We twist and turn and hang on, people shouting all around us. My hair whips in the wind, air flows over my body, and I feel like I'm flying. It's the most liberating feeling and I wish I could just stay on that damn roller coaster forever. Because it's plain and simple fun. So effortless, like how I wish life could be.

By the time we get off, Quinton looks like he's on the verge of laughing, but he never does let it all the way out. Still, it's good to see his eyes hued with a hint of happiness.

"Jesus, my heart's racing," he says with excitement as he presses his hand to his chest. He reaches over and takes my hand in his, then places it over his heart. "Do you feel it?"

I nod, forgetting to breathe. "So's mine."

Without really seeming like he realizes what he's doing, he puts his hand over my heart, which is racing more from his touch than anything else. He doesn't say anything, just feeling my heartbeat, while I feel his. Both alive. Both feeling the simple yet meaningful moment while people dodge around us, trying to leave the ride, giving us strange looks, because they don't get what we're doing. I feel sorry for them, that they can't get how amazing it is to feel someone else's heartbeat, to know they're still alive.

Maybe it's because I get that that I do what I do next. Or maybe it's just that I simply want to kiss him. Who knows. But for whatever reason, I find myself standing on my tiptoes and pressing my lips against his. He hesitates at first, his lips not moving against mine for a fleeting moment. But then he sucks in a sharp breath and suddenly he's kissing me back. Our tongues tangle, our bodies press together, our hands squished between us because we still have our palms over each other's hearts. His free hand finds the small of my back and he pulls me closer, devouring me with his tongue, stealing the breath right out of me. Everything I felt last summer for him crashes through me and spills over my soul. The rush of emotion is so compelling my heart accelerates and my legs buckle. I nearly start to fall, but Quinton holds me up, gripping my waist as he backs me up against the railing. The bar presses into my back as his hands wander all over my body, fingers delving into my skin. With every breath I take, my chest crashes into his and the heat of his body mixes with mine and the heat of the desert air, making my skin damp with sweat. I'm breathless. Lost. Consumed. The people and the dings of slot machines around us start to fade away. It's like we've flown off somewhere else. I wish we could stay that way forever, but eventually he pulls away, nipping at my bottom lip. Gasping for air, he rests his forehead against mine and doesn't say anything. Neither do I. We're both confused over what happened. At least I know I am. As much as I feel for him, the fact that he's on crystal right now makes my feelings conflicted. Is it wrong to be with him when he's like this? Can he even understand his true feelings? Can I understand my true feelings? Because they're getting intense. More than I think I realized.

"So now what?" he finally asks, breathless and wide-eyed, his hand on my chest trembling.

It takes me a moment to gather myself before I can lean back to glance up at the clock on the wall. "How about we grab a bite to eat and then go back to where I'm staying so you can see me play?" It seems like such a mundane thing to do after that kiss, but it's all I can come up with through the emotional fogginess created by his touch.

He gives me a half smile, seeming a little dazed. "That sounds good." He's being so cooperative, and between that, this entire day, and that kiss, hope flashes inside me as bright as the sun. And for a stupid moment, I actually believe this is all going to turn out well. That having fun and hanging out can help someone want to get better.

But there are clouds in the distance that match the ones in his eyes, the ones that belong to the thing he wants the most—to feed his addiction—telling me that hope is about to fade completely, and it does about thirty minutes after we leave the city. We're about halfway to Lea's uncle's house when Quinton starts to get squirmy and agitated. Finally, he reaches into his pocket and when he does, he flips out.

"Shit," he curses, balling his hands into fists.

"What's wrong?" I ask, turning down the music.

He shakes his head, his jaw set tight. "I forgot to bring something with me."

I smash my lips together with my eyes on the road, focused on getting us through traffic. "Drugs? I thought you weren't going to do any while we were out?"

He gets testy, scowling at me. "I said I would try, but I can't do it." His tone gets clipped. "I never thought I could."

I grip the steering wheel tightly as the simplicity of the day dissipates. "So you lied to me?"

"I said I would try," he snaps, the monster inside starting to take him over. "And I went without it for a few hours, but I can't do it anymore...I need to go home now." He takes his cigarettes out and starts smoking.

"I can't turn around right here." We're on the freeway, so that's not even possible. And even if it were, I'd still try to get out of it.

His hands are quivering as he holds the cigarette between his fingers. "Nova, I'm trying not to lose it here, but things are going to get really ugly really fast if you don't turn around this fucking car."

"Quinton, I—"

He pounds his fist against the door. "Take. Me. Home. *Now*." His voice is low and carries a warning.

I want to cry. I want to scream at him. But I can see the ugliness—the hunger—rising in his eyes and it frightens me. So I do something I'll always hate myself for. I take the next exit and turn the car around, heading back toward the house, feeling our happy day dwindle, like the sunlight in the sky.

Quinton

I messed up badly. Not just with that damn kiss. In fact, I'm confused right now over the kiss and whether I regret it or not. And that confusion is causing a stir inside me and I forgot to bring a few lines with me, so I can't calm the stir down. I've never done that before. Always remembered the thing that keeps me thriving. But Nova distracted me with the promise of a good day, smiling at me, making me get lost in her again. Kissing me like I'm the air she needs to breathe. It's so fucking wrong, yet it feels so right at the same time.

And now I'm crashing. Hard. And ruining that beautiful day Nova tried to create.

By the time we arrive at my place, I'm sweating, panting, my hands split open where I stabbed my nails into them, and I can't feel my mouth from grinding my jaw. I feel like shit, but there's only one thing that's going to make it go away and I concentrate on that: the small plastic bag hidden under my mattress. The single thing that makes life bearable, makes the confusion bearable.

But the tension coiling inside me tightens when I notice a

black Cadillac in the parking lot and a large man standing outside it, leaning against the door, smoking a cigarette. It looks like the car that pulled up when I got jumped and the man smoking looks like Donny, the guy who beat the shit out of me. It's been only six days since Trace made a threat, but for some reason I'm not surprised they're early.

Shit, Tristan.

"Thanks for hanging out with me," I say quickly, grabbing the door handle. My thoughts are going haywire as a bunch of thoughts surface at once. *I hope it's not Trace who's here. I hope Tristan's not in trouble. I hope no one's found my stash.* The last thought is so selfish, yet I can't control it. My addiction controls me at the moment.

"Wait—what's wrong?" Nova asks, noticing my sudden jumpiness. She tracks my gaze to the car and Donny, her forehead creasing. "Who is that guy?"

"No one," I say, my fingers fumbling to get the seat belt undone.

"But you seem nervous," she replies, looking at me with concern. "Does this have anything to do with that Trace guy?"

I hate that she knows enough about my drug life that she knows who Trace is. "Everything's fine, Nova. You just need to go." I don't make eye contact with her as I climb out of the car. When I go to shut the door, she calls out my name, making me pause, briefly pulling me back to her.

"Quinton, wait. I can tell something's wrong," she says with a plea in her tone. "So just tell me."

"Nova, let it go," I say, lowering my head to look into the car at her. "You can't be here right now. It's too dangerous."

"It is about that Trace guy, isn't it? Tristan didn't pay him back in time?" She worriedly flicks a glance over at Donny. "Jesus, Quinton, this is bad."

"I know it is," I say, looking at Donny, who's taken notice of us and turned in our direction. He has his weapon of choice in his hand. A tire iron, and my body aches as I remember what it felt like to be beat by it.

"Do you need to borrow money?" she asks as I look back at her. "Because I have, like, fifty dollars on me if you need it."

God dammit, Nova and her sweetness. It's killing me because she just needs to stop caring and leave. "Fifty dollars isn't going to do any good, and I already said I don't want you involved in this." I shut the door, hoping it'll end there.

But she gets out of the car and shouts over the roof, "But I want to help you."

"God dammit, Nova!" I shout as Donny starts to stroll toward us with a smirk on his face. I panic. Not because I'm worried anything's going to happen to me. It's all about Nova. "Get back in the fucking car!" I yell at her from over the roof.

Donny pats the tire iron against the palm of his hand like he did the first time he beat the shit out of me, but he's not looking at me, he's looking at Nova. This is so fucking bad. And all my fault.

"Trace wants to see you," he calls out as he approaches us, his black boots scraping the dirt.

My muscles wind into painful, guilty knots, connected to

Nova. I think of Roy and what Trace did to his girlfriend, how he raped her. I have to get her out of here. Now. She should never have been here to begin with. I should never have let her into my life like this. What the hell was I thinking?

I hurry around the front of the car, startling Nova by how quickly I arrive on the other side, right in front of her. I grab her arms roughly and yank her to me, our bodies crashing together. "Please, if you care about me at all, you'll get in the car and drive away. Right now," I whisper in her ear.

She clutches my arm, and I can hear how fast her heart is beating. "What's that guy going to do you?"

"Nothing," I say, lying to her and myself. "He's just here to get Trace's money."

"But do you have it?"

"Part of it," I say, which is the truth. Tristan and I have managed to collect half of what we owe Trace.

"Is that enough for him to leave you alone?"

"Yeah, for a little while," I lie, but it's the right thing to do, because if I don't lie she's not going to leave. I hear the sound of Donny's boots crunching close behind us, and I know he's getting closer. "Just get in the car." I kiss her cheek, pleading. "And go home."

She holds her breath for a moment and then nods. I relax as she pulls away and turns for the door, but then I feel the presence of Donny behind me and I immediately tense. Just having someone like him so close to Nova is enough to make me feel like I'm going to lose it.

"You need to go inside," Donny says from right behind me. "Trace wants to talk to you. He's up in your apartment with your lovely little friend that got you into this mess."

Nova's eyes dart over my shoulder and widen. I quickly turn around and step in front of her, blocking her from his view. "I'm headed up there now." I glance over my shoulder and tell Nova, "Go."

"No, you should bring the girl," Donny says. He purposefully moves the bottom of his shirt up a little and I see something tucked in the front of his pants, sparkling silver. A gun. He's got a fucking gun and he wants Nova to come with us.

It hits me all at once. Hard. The entire situation—how much bigger this is than I realized. And Nova is here to witness it. Just the idea of something happening to her nearly crushes the air out of my chest. I don't even want to think about it—can't think about it. Yet images press their way into my head, like shrapnel. I can picture myself back on the side of the road, lying beside Lexi, covered in her blood, only it's not Lexi's eyes staring up at me, but Nova's bluish-green ones. And again I'm the one who hurt the girl I love...Shit, it that what this means? Does this fear of losing Nova mean that I love her? The revelation makes me hate myself more than I already did. Hate myself for being here. For allowing myself to feel this way toward another girl. God dammit, why did I let myself keep breathing, keep living, feeling, loving? Lexi's dead and I might be falling in love with someone? This is how I repay her for crashing the car that night and killing her? I break my promise to her and forget her enough that I let myself feel love for Nova? I let Nova take her place?

I'm so angry at myself that I almost forget the situation until Trace's guy rams the tire iron against Nova's beautiful car, scraping the cherry-red paint.

"Get in the fucking house!" he shouts, his calm demeanor suddenly gone, uncontrollable rage in his eyes.

I shove all my feelings aside and sober right up. I'm very aware of Nova's presence. Very aware that everything I do for the next few minutes is going to matter, unlike the last few years of my life. But once I fix this—get her out of here— everything can be over and nothing can matter again.

"I'm going in the house," I tell him calmly, folding my fingers inward and digging my fingernails into my palms as I glance down at the gun. If I have to, I'll go for him, if it means she'll have time to get away. "But she's going to leave."

He laughs at me. "Like hell she is." He steps forward and reaches to my side, trying to get to Nova, and I don't even think. I just smack his hand out of the way. His eyes flicker with fury and his hand starts to lift, not in my direction, but in Nova's. He's going to hit Nova and it's going to be all my fucking fault. I'm going to destroy the girl I love again. I'm such a fucking screwup again.

I need to do something to get her away from this. I rack my brain, looking for an answer. I remember how he took the drugs out of my pocket and I see the rings of red around his nostrils that are rings of gold at the moment. I could bribe this guy with drugs, but I doubt what I have in my room's going to make him happy.

I need something bigger.

Something that will make him forget about everything, even if it's for a minute or two, enough time for Nova to get away.

"I know where Dylan keeps his stash and he has a couple of ounces. If you let her go, I'll show you where it is," I blurt out, which is a total lie, but it's all I can think of at the moment. It's a viable lie, too. Dylan's a dealer and he has a large stash—somewhere. But I have no clue where he keeps it, whether it's even in the house or how much he has. It doesn't matter, though. All I'm looking for is getting him away from Nova and then letting whatever's going to happen happen. Let him beat me. Hurt me. Kill me. I don't care, just as long as I know she's safe.

The guy pauses, the tire iron still lifted. "How do I know you're not full of shit?"

I shrug, pretending to be calm, despite the panic inside me. "You'll just have to come with me and see. If I'm lying, then you'll still get to kick my ass, like you were planning on anyway." *Just let her go. Please just let her go.* "But if I'm not, then you could have the stash for yourself. No one would have to know." It's like tempting a dog with a bone. As a drug addict, I understand that the need—want—is more powerful than anything else.

The guy seems wary, but then gives in, lowering the tire iron. "Let's go, then," he says and starts toward the house, all the anger leaving his body. Part of me thinks he was only going after Nova to fuck with my head. Still, she's free to go and that's all that matters.

I start to follow him, but Nova grabs my arm and pulls me back. "Quinton, don't go," she says. I don't even look at her, shaking her hand off me and moving forward. But she relentlessly enfolds my arm again.

I shoot her a cold look from over my shoulder, knowing that the only thing that matters at the moment is getting her into the car. "Get in your car and go." My voice is low.

Her eyes are filled with horror. "Quinton, I—"

"Get in your fucking car and go, Nova!" I shout venomously. "Leave, like I've been telling you to do from the start!"

She starts to cry, tears rolling down her cheeks, and I want to comfort her, but I know it'll make things worse if I do.

"I'll be fine," I say in a low voice. "I'm going to go pay this guy back and then everything's going to be fine." I feel like such a dick for lying to her, but I'm doing what I have to to get her away from this.

"But how will I know if you're okay?" she asks, glancing at the guy.

"I still have your number and I'll call you later," I tell her, touching my back pocket, where the piece of paper with the phone number on it rests inside my wallet. "I promise." Another lie, but I don't feel bad because I can see in her eyes that it works.

She leans forward and gives me a kiss on the mouth. I

barely kiss her back, even though I desperately want to. But I make myself hold on to the image of Lexi, like I should have been doing the entire time—make myself suffer for loving Nova and putting her into this mess.

Everything is all my fault.

"This is all your fault," Ryder's dad says to me while her mother sobs in the background. "Dammit, you shouldn't have been driving that car so damn fast."

My dad stands in the background, watching him yell at me, letting him vent, because everything he says is right. It is my fault. I was driving too fast. "Why couldn't you have just driven slower?" he asks, and then he starts to cry, sorrow haunting his face, and even though I want to cry, I don't because I don't deserve to. I don't get to hurt like they're hurting, because I put the hurt there.

I caused this.

As Nova drives away, I feel strangely calm, sedated, dead inside. I turn to Donny, who's waiting for me just a few strides away. I could run, out into the desert or down the street. But then I'd be bailing out on Tristan. I've already fucked up on paying Lexi back for killing her. The last thing I need to do is fuck up on paying Ryder back.

So I follow Donny upstairs, listening to him ramble about what he'll do if I mess this up. Maybe if I weren't crashing so badly, I'd feel the pain of what lies ahead for me a little bit more. I'm only half focused on it, the need to get a hit or two taking up the other part of my mind. But when I step inside the apartment, reality sort of just crashes over me, like a violent waterfall. The entire place is trashed, even more than it normally is. There's broken glass all over the floor, holes in the walls, the table in the kitchen has been tipped over, along with the sofas, like someone went on a rampage.

I can also hear loud crying in one of the back rooms and a lot of banging. It sounds like someone is being tortured.

I glance at Donny, who's still got his tire iron out. "Where's Tristan?"

A sly grin curves up on his face. "I'll tell you just as soon as you show me where the drugs are."

More violent water crashes over me because I think they've already done something to Tristan. The water's about to push me down, bury me alive. Yet I somehow keep walking, keep breathing, keep living this piece-of-shit life.

Donny follows me down the hallway and toward my room. I pause beside Delilah's door, the crying and banging coming from the other side.

"Your friend Dylan gave up his girlfriend pretty easy to get himself out of this mess," Donny says, nodding toward the door. "Something you maybe should have considered."

I force back the vomit in my throat as the crying gets louder and louder, then suddenly stops. How did I get to this place? How did I think living this life would be better than being dead?

Donny nudges me along and I go into my room, feeling this strange numbness wash over me, like my mind's trying to shut down. As I'm getting the crystal out from under my mattress, I notice that a small area of my roof has caved in, right where the water stain used to be, and now there's a giant hole in its place. Everything's falling apart and I don't want to fix it anymore.

I get what crystal I have left and toss it to Donny. "Here you go."

He catches it and then stares down at the small quantity in his hand. "Are you fucking kidding me? You said you had a few ounces." He holds up the bag. "This is barely a fucking line."

I shrug. "I guess I miscalculated how much I had."

He clutches the bag in one hand and the tire iron in the other. "You said you knew where Dylan's stash was."

"I lied." I'm surprisingly composed.

He stares at me for a moment, baffled that I'd screw him over, although I have no idea why, since that's what everyone seems to do to everyone else around here. His bafflement shifts to anger, his face tinting red as he raises the tire iron to hit me. I'm disappointed that he doesn't grab the gun, because it'd be over more quickly. But instead he hammers his fist into my face. I don't even flinch as he collides with my jaw. When I fall to the floor, I don't get up, even when he kicks me in the rib cage repeatedly, steps on my hand, stomps on my face, asking me why I seem to enjoy getting my ass kicked. I keep waiting for him to pull the gun out, but he never does. I wonder if he knows just how much I want this to all be over, that that's why

I don't run. Maybe he can see it in my eyes that I want to die and that by not killing me he's making this even more painful. I don't know, but what I do know is that when he walks away without killing me, I feel disappointed. I lie there for a while on the floor before I finally sit up, my lip bleeding, my whole body feeling exactly how it did the first time Donny beat me up.

After a while Delilah appears in my doorway, her shirt ripped and her shorts unbuttoned. Her face is smeared with mascara, her lip is split open, and large welts cover her arms and thighs.

"You should go," she says numbly. "Dylan's not going to let you walk out of here breathing, if you're here when he gets back."

I put one of my hands down on the floor and ungracefully push myself to my feet, my body aching in protest. "Where is he?" I ask, hunching over.

She shrugs, her face emotionless. "He took off after he offered me up, but I'm sure he'll be back."

I brace my hand on the wall for support, feeling sorry for her. "Do you need any help with anything?" It sounds so lame when she looks so broken and I can barely stand.

She laughs, but it sounds hollow. "You've got other problems to fix," she says, turning her back to me. "Before you showed up, Trace and a few guys took Tristan out back. And he was barely coherent, since he just shot up."

"Shit!" I hobble out the door, pushing her out of the way as I stumble down the hall. The pain in my body is blinding, but I know it's going to be minimal compared to the internal pain I'm going to feel if anything happened to Tristan. If I'm too late again, like I have been in the past. Always too late.

I limp across the balcony for the stairs, past memories swarming through my head like bees as I run into the unknown again, not knowing what waits for me ahead.

"Lexi, God no!" I cry out to the stars. "Please don't leave me."

I drag my ass down the stairs, my heart knocking in my chest, my skin coated with sweat. My legs are so sore it feels like they're going to give out on me and my hand might be broken, but physical pain is nothing. I've felt a lot of it over the last few years and it's the most bearable part of life.

Her body goes limp in my arms, her head slumping against my chest, which is split open, spilling out blood—life.

I look into Lexi's eyes, but there's nothing left inside them, and I know that pretty soon nothing will be left inside me, so I lie down on the ground with her and take her hand, allowing myself to bleed out.

The Cadillac is gone, but I'm not sure if I'm relieved or not, since it means that whatever they were going to do to Tristan, they've probably already done to him. I limp off toward the back of the apartment building, my arms and legs sore and stiff, my movements lethargic.

Everything is stilling inside me—I can feel it. Darkness sets in as my life slips away. I can feel myself being pulled somewhere and I swear I can feel Lexi with me, so close, yet at the same time so far away. Don't leave me. But she is, or maybe I'm leaving her. I feel myself being pulled back, people calling out my name. I hear the beeping of machines, feel needles sinking into my skin, giving me life, and I hate them for it. I want them to take it away...

I round the corner and see someone lying on the ground, arms and legs sprawled out, unmoving. *Hang on.* I rush up to Tristan and I shudder at the sight of his face, slit open and bleeding onto the rocks below his head. His eye is so engorged it blends in with his face and his arm is scraped raw. The only good thing about the sight is that he's breathing, and when I check his pulse, it's erratic and unsteady, but I'm not sure if it's because he's on smack or because he's been beaten up.

"God dammit, Tristan," I say as he rolls over, groaning about needing it to go away while his body trembles. "Why did you have to screw Trace over?"

"I...don't...know," he mutters, pain straining his voice, and his syllables are all messed up so it's hard to understand. "I...fucked up. And I tried to fix it—give them money. But it wasn't enough."

I'm not sure what to do, but I know I've got to get him out of here, in case the guys come back or Dylan shows up with his stupid gun. I'm not even sure where the hell they went, if they're planning on returning, or if they're done here. The entire situation is a mess and I need to get Tristan up and out of here, because from the look of him, if there's a next time, he won't make it out alive.

I drag my fingers roughly through my hair, looking around at the desert behind me and then at the stores and old houses to the side of our building. I need to find somewhere we can hide out for a little while, someone who might let us stay with them. I need a lot of things at the moment, like a line or two, because I feel like I'm melting under the pressure, heat, and emotions inside me. If I'm going to handle this—keep it together enough to help Tristan—I can't be crashing.

Blowing out a breath, I lower my hand and reach down and grab hold of Tristan's arms. "All right, we've got to get you out of here," I say, then lift him as best I can and try to get him to his feet, grunting and cursing as he puts most of his weight against me.

I manage to get him standing, but I'm not sure if he's even aware of it—if he's aware of anything going on right now or if he's got too much smack in his system, or whatever he was on when they showed up. I get his arm around my neck and then support most of his weight as he drags his feet and struggles to walk back toward the front of the building.

I can barely walk myself, and I end up going to Nancy's, since it's close and she's a somewhat decent person and I know she'll probably let us crash at her place, although I'm sure we'll owe her for it. But I'll figure out that part later. Right now I just need to get Tristan inside and a few lines into my body because it's screaming at me to feed this; otherwise I'm going to break. And I can't break yet.

Tristan leans against me as I knock on Nancy's door. She doesn't even look surprised when she answers it. She's wearing a robe, her hair pulled up, and she easily lets us in.

"I knew he was going to get into trouble one of these days," she says as she shuts the door behind us while I help Tristan sit down on the torn sofa in the living room. When I move my arm away from him, he collapses to his side and presses his puffy cheek to the cushion. It's actually oozing out blood on her plaid seventies-themed couch, but she doesn't seem to mind.

"Do you have something to clean his cuts up with?" I ask Nancy as she stands near the back of the couch, watching Tristan with fascination. Her pupils are dilated and ringed with red and she keeps sniffing. I know she's on what I want and I wonder if she has any she'll share, but then again, if she does, it probably won't be without a price. But I don't really care. I just want it. Need to breathe again. Forget everything that's happened over the last couple of minutes. Hours. Days. Forget who I am and what I'm feeling. Things are so much easier that way.

She tightens the tie around the silk robe she's wearing. "Let me get some towels," she says, then strolls off to the bathroom at the back of the house. I wait for her in the small living room that's dark because she has curtains hanging up and no lights on. There's a pot steaming on the stove in the kitchen and a pile of dirty dishes in the sink, and it reminds me a lot of our place. As soon as I think it, another problem smacks me in the face.

Shit, where are we going to live?

When Nancy returns she has a wet rag in her hand and a plastic bag with a small amount of crystal in it. Tiny crystals my body yearns for, and my thoughts and worries drift from my head as my senses instantly heighten. Wanting. Wanting. Needing. Wanting.

Now.

I almost snatch the bag from her hand, but resist the urge with all the control I have left in me, worried that if I do, she'll kick us out. She sets the wet rag gently down on Tristan's forehead, and Tristan groans as he presses his hand to it, taking sharp, raspy breaths. Then she sits down on the floor in front of the coffee table that's scratched up and has old magazines stacked in the middle of it. She looks at me and I can see the want in her eyes, but I'm not sure exactly what it is she wants—the drugs or me. Still, when she pats the spot on the floor, I more than eagerly sit down, then watch with hunger as she pours the crystal onto the coffee table and picks up a razor.

"You look like you could use this," she says, eyeing me as she chops up the clumps and forms two lines that are small enough they'll barely give me a boost. I need more and I can't help but think of the stash up in my room. Gone. No more. What am I going to do?

I fight to keep my hands to myself. "I could."

She stops chopping up the clumps and swipes her finger across the edge of the table, cleaning off the remnants of crystal and then licking her finger clean. My heart thrashes inside my chest as I watch her, wanting to taste it myself. When she leans in, I sit perfectly still, knowing what she wants— knowing I can taste it on her if I let her kiss me. She touches her lips to mine, and for a moment I tense, thinking of Nova and the revelation in the car. How I realized that I love her. But something bigger overtakes me, the hungry beast inside me stirring awake and wanting to kill every emotion out of me. Everything's moving so fast as my body and mind crash and spin out of control. I need to pull myself back together, so I slip my tongue inside her, kissing her back, hating myself for it, but self-hatred is all I am anymore.

When she pulls away, she lets me have a line, and then she sniffs the last one herself before taking my hand. She pulls me to my feet and leads me back toward her room.

"I need to keep an eye on Tristan," I tell her, looking back at him on the sofa with the rag draped over his face, his chest rising and sinking. "Trace and his guys beat him up pretty bad."

"He'll be okay for a few minutes," she assures me, her eyes fixed on mine as she walks backward, guiding me with her. "I have more back in my room. If you'll come with me, I'll share it."

I hesitate, glancing back and forth between Tristan and

her. Tristan or her. Tristan or drugs. My feet follow her as I tell myself that Tristan will be okay for a few minutes and that once I get a few more lines in me I'll be able to focus on helping him, instead of needing a hit. When we get back to her room, she gently pushes me down on the bed, then takes my shirt off and runs her fingers up my chest and along my scar.

"You never did tell me where you got that scar," she says, pressing her hand over my heart, just like Nova did at the roller coaster.

I gently shove her hand away, unable to stand her touch being connected to thoughts of Nova. "I put it there myself," I lie, wishing she'd just get the damn drugs.

Her brows furrow as confusion masks her expression, but the look evaporates as she leans in and kisses me again. I move robotically, letting her kiss me, letting her fingers wander all over my body as she gasps and moans, wanting more. Guilt consumes me. Devours me. And I almost yell at her to stop. But she pulls away on her own and removes her robe. She only has a bra and panties on, and she smiles at me as she goes over to her dresser to get more from her stash. I know that when she comes back, I'll have to pay for each line I take. And I know I'll take more than a few, even though I don't want to pay for any of them.

I lower my head into my hands and wait, feeling my pulse throb, my lips quivering, my mind aching as I feel myself sink further to the bottom, feeling any life left inside me dissipate.

Chapter Twelve

Nova

I'm about to lose it. Or maybe I already have. I'm not even sure how I made it back to Lea's uncle's house, since I tried to count the cars on the road as I drove. I should never have been behind the wheel, too unstable to drive.

Yet somehow I made it home alive. But not in one piece, since my mind has cracked open and split apart. All I can think about is Quinton and that he's in trouble and how I just left.

I should never have left.

"Nova, are you okay?" Lea hops up from the sofa and rushes up to me as I walk into the house. She slows to a stop, her eyes widening as she takes in the sight of me. I have no idea what I look like, but by the look on her face, I can tell it's bad. "Jesus, what happened?"

I just stare at her, unable to get my lips to function or to process any words. I can barely move, the only motion inside me is from my beating heart and my lungs as they take in breaths, but even that seems like a lot of work. I'm about to fall apart, right here in her uncle's living room. I am crying, breaking down. I need to stop it somehow.

"I want to play my drums," I finally say, because it's all I can think of at the moment to keep myself moving without crumbling.

Lea gapes at me. "What?"

"I need to play my drums." I feel a little better saying it. I push my way past her and head back to the guest room where I'd stuffed my drums in the closet.

She chases after me. "Nova, what the hell happened today?" she says concernedly. "And don't tell me nothing, because you look like you just saw someone die."

I think I might have. I throw open the closet and start taking out the pieces of my drums, the cymbal, the snare, the stool I sit on. I'm running away from my problems at the moment. I know this, but I just need something to drown out all the dark thoughts racing through my mind.

Lea keeps chattering something about calling my mom, but I lose track of her words as I set up the pieces in the corner of the room. Once I get everything positioned, I open up my laptop and go to my iTunes app. As soon as I sit down on the stool behind my drums, I reach a state of calm. Silence. Solitude. I feel at peace. I pick up my drumsticks and it makes me feel like I'm alone, just myself, no one else. Lea's withering stare from the doorway blurs away. Memories of today and two years ago blur away. Time fades. I fade. It's a beautiful place to exist, and the feeling only grows as I reach back and turn on "Not an Addict" by K's Choice. I only have to wait during a few lyrics and then I get to come in, touch the sticks to the drums and press on the pedal, create the beat, feel the rhythm, the passion, as the lyrics and tune drown me, just like I want them to. I picked this song for a reason, because it feels like the song gets what's going on around me. Simple words, beats, notes, vibrations, can be so overpowering it feels like I've entered another world, not this fucked-up one where I keep messing up everything and losing everyone around me.

My foot moves on the pedal in sync with my other hand as I run away from my problems. I get completely swept away to a place that used to exist when I was younger. When I'd spend time with my dad and my mom, when death wasn't such a huge part of my past, when drugs and darkness weren't a part of my life, when it seemed like everything was full of light and hope. When I didn't realize just how hard things were and that caring about people meant hurting when they were hurting. Worrying about them. Growing frustrated because they can't see how they're killing themselves, dissolving themselves away, refusing to breathe no matter how much I try to breathe life into them. And the hardest part of all is that I get what it feels like. I know how hard it is to breathe again, and it makes me understand, even though I don't want to, that Quinton might not give in and let me help him breathe. That maybe all of this was pointless and no matter how hard you try to save someone, it might not turn out the way you want it.

I didn't save him.

Like I didn't save Landon.

I messed up again.

I crash the drumstick one last time against the cymbal as

the song ends, and then the tears come pouring out of me as reality crashes back into me. I slip off the stool and fall to the ground, sobbing hysterically, letting every ounce of emotion pour out of me. What I saw today. That guy had a gun. A tire iron. And I just walked away.

I continue to sob, losing track of time. When I finally do look up, Lea's on the phone. It takes me a moment to process whom she's talking to. My mom. When I realize this, something snaps inside me and I get to my feet. Lea must see something in my eyes because she runs out of the room.

"Lea, hang up the phone!" I shout, chasing after her, seeing my opportunity to help Quinton any more slip farther and farther away.

She locks herself in the bathroom and won't open the door, even when I bang on it so hard it sounds like it's going to break.

"Lea, please don't do this!" I cry, falling to the floor. "You can't do this! You're my friend."

It gets quiet and moments later the door opens. Lea stands in front of me, her hair pulled back, her eyes watery like she's been crying.

"It's because I'm your friend that I'm doing this." She crouches down in front of me with the phone in her hand. "Nova, this whole save-Quinton mission is destroying you."

I shake my head, rocking back and forth as I kneel on the floor. "No, it's not."

"Yes, it is," she insists, getting to her feet. "Now, start packing. Your mother's flying down here to drive us back up to Wyoming."

And just like that, all my hope is taken away. It's over. And once again, I didn't do anything right.

I manage to get to my feet, and then I lock myself in the bedroom, opening up my laptop and turning on Landon's video again. I set it down on the bed, then lie down and curl up in a ball, watching it—watching him fade away right in front of my eyes.

Quinton

I hate myself, but it's easier to bear because I've got drugs in my system and my mind's not quite connected to anything that's happening around me. This room is just a place and Nancy is just a person and I'm just another junkie loser fucking someone I don't care about because I want to get high again. And when I'm done, I hate myself even more. I'm nothing but a shell, ready to crack, ready to crumble, and I'll start the whole process over because I can't seem to get to that final step where I fully give up.

"I'm going to go get a drink of water," Nancy says after I slip out of her, her skin damp.

I nod, feeling hollow as I put my boxers and jeans back on. "Okay."

"Don't go anywhere," she jokes as she walks from the room.

I almost laugh. Where the hell would I go? I don't have any money, any drugs, any place to live. I have absolutely nothing and decide that this is rock bottom. This is my own prison of hell and I'm locked inside it.

God, I just want it to all be over.

I'm drowning in my pain, deciding that it might finally be time to give up, that I've slammed into rock bottom, torn apart and left to bleed out, when I hear a deafening scream from the living room. I suddenly wonder if I was wrong and that maybe rock bottom was within reach, but I needed to take a few more steps to get there. I get up and hurry out of the room. As soon as I catch sight of Tristan on the sofa, I'm thrown back to the mental state I lived at right after the accident, the one where I had to painfully feel the consequences of everything I'd done, when everything was so raw and heavy that it felt like it was killing me.

Tristan's skin has turned sheet white, his lips blue, and he's foaming at the mouth as his body shakes. For a moment I just stare at him, feeling pounds and pounds of weight stack on my shoulders.

"What's wrong with him?" Nancy asks, covering her mouth and backing away with tears in her eyes.

Guilt and fear are about to smother me, but I fight to keep breathing. "Get me a phone!" I shout, running up to the side of the couch.

"Why?" Nancy cries as she backs into the wall.

"Because I'm going to call an ambulance." I kneel down beside Tristan, my hands shaking, my pulse frantically beating. There's so much foam coming out of his mouth and his chest is barely moving, yet his body is moving so much. "I think he's..." Holy fucking shit. "I think...I think he's OD'ing."

My words tumble out of me and reality swallows me up in one large breath. This is my fault. I should have been taking care of him better. I owed it to him. But instead I was too caught up in my own problems, like Nova. "Fuck!" I should never have gone out with her today.

Regret.

Remorse.

Blame.

I've felt it all before and I feel it again, like needles under my skin, stabbing their way to the surface. Everything's falling apart and it's all my fault.

The next few moments move in clips. Nancy gets me her cell phone and I call an ambulance. But she tells me to wait outside, that she's got too many drugs inside her house. I tell her she's fucking paranoid, but she flips out, so I carry Tristan outside while he fights to breathe, his skin getting paler and paler, his lips bluer. I stop when we reach the edge of the parking lot, and by the time I set him down, his chest has stopped rising and falling altogether.

I feel myself break apart as I push on his chest and put my mouth to his, giving him CPR, trying to breathe for him, live for him, keep him from leaving, like everyone else left.

One more breath.

One more.

But it's not working—he won't breathe on his own. I feel like I'm dying with him, only I'm not. I'm still kneeling here on fucking concrete while everyone keeps dying around me and I just sit by and watch, motionless, unable to stop it. I fucking hate it. I hate being here. I can't do it. Can't feel death again.

"Why do you keep doing this to me?" I cry out to the sky as tears stream down my face. I can't take it anymore. I can't. "I don't want to live! Please just take me instead!" I'm not even sure if I believe in God or if he exists, but I swear if he does, he hates me. Or maybe it's just me that hates me.

Tears fall from my eyes, and I start breathing for Tristan again, refusing to give up. Fighting. Refusing to accept another death. "Come on," I beg through my hopeless sobs. "Please, please, just breathe."

Please, please don't die.

Chapter Thirteen

May 27, day twelve of summer break

Nova

I have about twenty-four hours to figure out if Quinton's okay before my mom's flight lands and I have to go home. He never called me like he said he would, and I at least need to know if he's okay before I bail out on him, let him go, knowing I'll probably hate myself forever for walking away.

I try to call Delilah's phone, but she doesn't answer, so I drive over to Quinton's house. Lea argued with me about it for a while but gave up and got in the car with me, despite my protests that she shouldn't go over there. If she knew the entire story of what happened, she probably would have put up a bigger fight, but I didn't tell her, knowing this.

It's a rare cloudy day and I'm grateful to get a break from the sunlight. Although when we pull up to the building, the gray sky over it makes it seem much more ominous.

Warning flags are all over the place when I get to their door. There's a hole in it and the front window is cracked. But it's not even just that. I have a bad feeling, like I did the morning I woke up and found Landon dead in his room. I knew something was about to shift and not in a good way.

"Nova, would you just relax?" Lea says as I cup my hands around my eyes and peer in through the window of Quinton's apartment. The curtain's falling down on one side and I can see right into the living room. The place is a wreck, more than it usually is. One of the sofas is tipped over, there's an abundance of garbage and glass on the floor, and there are more holes in the walls, Sheetrock all over the linoleum. The lamps have been bashed to pieces and the ceiling light is on the floor.

"No...something's not right." I glance over my shoulder at her. "I can feel it."

"You're not telling me everything," she says, putting her hands on her hips. "Something happened yesterday—something bad."

"Everything's fine," I lie. I'm not even sure why I'm lying

at the moment. My mother's already headed down here. Everything's ruined. But saying it all aloud makes it feel so real.

I put my face up against the glass and try to see inside again. There's someone lying on the sofa that's still upright, arm hanging over the side, head turned to the other side so I can't see his face. But from the bald head, bony body, and tattoos, I'm guessing it's Dylan.

I step back from the window and glance out at the parking lot and the two vehicles out there, one of which is mine and one of which has four flat tires. The Cadillac that was here yesterday is gone. I don't know what that means or if I can handle what it means—whatever happened between Trace, Tristan, and Quinton.

"Nova, I think we should go," Lea says, glancing down the balcony with worry in her eyes as Bernie walks out of his apartment.

She's probably right. We shouldn't be here. I'm putting us at risk by making us stay, when I have no idea what happened yesterday.

"I just need to know if he's okay." I move back in front of the door and try the doorknob, but it's locked, so I knock on the door. "I think he might be in some trouble."

She picks at her fingernails nervously. "This entire place is trouble, Nova. You should have never been hanging around here." She catches my arm, startling me. "And if that's true, then you need to stay out of it." She targets me with a stern look. "Focus on the bigger picture and how dangerous this is."

She motions around us, her gaze lingering on Bernie, who's watching us. "All of this is."

I jerk my arm away from her, more roughly than I meant to, but I don't apologize as I slip my fingers through the hole in the door, trying to reach the lock, refusing to walk away until I know Quinton's not dead.

I manage to get to the lock and the door opens up. "Thank God," I mutter.

"Nova, please don't go in there," Lea begs, but I'm already over the threshold and she doesn't follow me in.

It's stuffier than normal, but that could be because all the garbage and dirty dishes from the kitchen are scattered all over the place. Whatever the reason, the air is so heavy and potent that it knocks the breath out of me.

"I'm not going in there," Lea calls out from the balcony and I'm glad because I don't want her to.

I leave her standing outside and walk over to the sofa, broken glass crunching under my sandals. When I get there, I lean over and determine that it is Dylan lying there with a rubber band tied around his arm and a needle on the floor just below him, along with a spoon and a lighter. I hate that I feel it, but I'm glad he's passed out on drugs because I don't want to deal with his creepiness today.

Swallowing the burn in the back of my throat, I head for the hallway and go to Quinton's room. For the briefest second, I flash back to the moment I walked into Landon's room and found him hanging from the rope. I'm not sure why, other than maybe because my stomach and mind feel like they're in the same place now. The place where I know something bad is about to happen—or has happened.

Quinton's not in his room, though, and I'm not sure if I feel good about that or not, because I didn't find him dead behind the door, but he's still missing.

His sketches are all over the place, torn up, crinkled. There are some of me and some of a girl I think must be Lexi. His mattress has been flipped over and slashed and a few holes have been put in his wall. There are coins scattered all over the place and shards of mirror all over the floor.

I pick up a few of his drawings, fold them, and tuck them into my pocket. Then I leave his room and peek into the room at the end of the hallway, Tristan's room. Or at least the room I saw him shooting up in. It looks to be in the same condition as Quinton's: completely trashed, stuff ruined and thrown all over the place, and a dresser tipped over, the contents of the drawers dumped out.

I turn around, feeling the hope inside me dim a little, feeling my oxygen fading. I need to get out of here and breathe in some fresh air, get my thoughts together—pull myself together, before I have another meltdown like yesterday. So I hurry down the hallway, but slam to a stop when one of the doors on my left swings open and someone steps out.

I jump back, startled, but slightly relax when I realize it's Delilah. "Shit, you scared me," I say, pressing my hand over my heart.

She gives me a dirty look, her swollen eyes stained with mascara and her cheek puffy and red like she's been struck there. Her auburn hair is tangled, she has on an old T-shirt that goes to her midthighs, and she's barefoot and walking around on glass, but it doesn't seem to bother her.

"You should be scared," she says in a strained voice, her legs wobbling, and she braces her hand on the door.

Shaking my head, I move to leave, not wanting to get into this with her, but she quickly rushes toward me and throws her arms around me, hugging me way too tightly.

"Oh, Nova, this is so bad." She starts to cry into me, and I have no idea what to do or if I want to do anything.

Awkwardly, I pat her back. "What's bad?" I ask. "Delilah, what's wrong?"

"Everything," she cries, her shoulders heaving with each breath as she grips me. "Everything's so fucked up."

"Why? What happened?" I ask, my muscles stiff under her hold.

She shakes her head and tightens her hold on me, so it feels like I'm suffocating. "We all screwed up."

Fear courses through my veins. "Who screwed up?"

"Me." She sniffs. "Tristan...Quinton. *Everyone.*"

I'm not sure what state of mind she's in, so I choose my words carefully, even though all I want to do is shout at her to tell me what the fuck happened. "Delilah, what happened exactly...? Where are Quinton and Tristan? Did...did Trace do something to them?"

"Who knows," she says, still soaking my shirt with her tears as she shrugs. "He could have killed them for all I know...I haven't seen them since yesterday when everything went to shit...when I..." She glances at her arms and legs, which are covered in bruises. She blinks and then looks at me, her hysteria calming. "Either living out on the streets somewhere or dead in a ditch." She says it with so little compassion and it infuriates me.

I jerk back. "You're lying."

"Believe whatever you want, but I'm not." She hugs her arms around herself as she collapses to the floor on her knees. I have no idea what's wrong with her, whether something actually happened or she's just on something. And as much as I'd love to help her, I need to find Quinton.

I crouch down in front of her. "Delilah, when Quinton left here, was he okay?"

She shakes her head. "No, they beat him up." Then she turns to her side and curls inward, into herself, her tears drying, but her sadness amplifying.

I shut my eyes, counting my inhalations and exhalations, sucking air in and blowing it out of my lungs. What does that mean? That he's beaten up but still alive. "You don't know where he went?" I ask, feeling completely hopeless at this moment. Like I've drowned and I'm sitting at the bottom of a lake, still breathing, but there's no way back to the surface.

"No." She brings her knees to her chest, balling herself up more on the floor, which is stained and covered in sharp pieces of glass, a death trap, yet she doesn't care. "Just go away. Please. Before Dylan wakes up and takes his anger toward Quinton out on you."

Part of me wants to press her for more information, but the other part wants to get the hell out of this house and go find Quinton. "You should come with me, Delilah. Get out of this house."

"Would you please just fucking go!" Delilah shouts. "I'll be fine." She mutters the last part like she's trying to convince herself.

I'm not sure if it's right—leaving her in that kind of state. Right and wrong. Whom to help? It feels like there's a really thin line between the two at the moment. When Delilah shuts her eyes, looking like she's drifting off to sleep, I stand up and head out of the apartment, but my body and mind ache with each step.

Lea's not there when I walk outside. When I glance down at the car, I can see her sitting inside, staring up at the balcony, where Bernie is shouting over the railing something about Jesus saving everyone. He's tripping out of his mind and Lea's probably scared out of hers. I should be, too, but Quinton is consuming my thoughts. My mind is racing a thousand miles a minute as I rush toward the stairs, pushing Bernie out of my way when he grabs my arm. He staggers to the side, nearly toppling over the railing, and starts shouting that I'm not going to be saved.

I pick up my pace as I reach the stairs. My thoughts speed

up, and I start counting my strides as I jog across the parking lot. I'm halfway across it when it hits me. All of it. The fact that I may never see Quinton again—may never know if he's alive again. That the moment I walk away from this apartment, that's it. I've given up. It's over and I have to accept that I may never see Quinton again. That I'm going to have to feel that sense of loss again. The responsibility of not stopping it.

All I want to do is count and not hear the thoughts. I want them to shut the hell up.

Two large breaths.

Five heartbeats.

Too many rocks on the ground.

One guy in the background, shouting for the world to hear, but he's saying things and doing things no one wants to hear or see, so everyone ignores them.

One step.

Then another.

Taking me farther away from this place.

Delilah's lying on the floor, broken and beaten.

Quinton and Tristan could be dead somewhere in a ditch.

Gone.

Two people dead. Two people I knew. That makes four people I've lost.

Four. And only one of me.

I make it to the front of my car before I collapse to my knees, and tears spill from my eyes as hopelessness drowns me, pushes me down to the ground. I grasp at my throbbing chest as I see the bigger picture open up in front of me: just how many people need saving. And how it's pretty much impossible, since I can't even handle one person.

I didn't help Quinton. I didn't save him. I didn't do anything. Just like I didn't save Landon.

And now Quinton could be dead.

Dead…

Dead.

Dead.

Dead.

The word echoes in my head, but all I can hear are my sobs and the quietness around me. Like no one but me exists anymore.

Like I've lost everyone.

Quinton

"Did she leave?" I ask as Nancy walks back into the room, letting her robe fall to the floor, wearing nothing but a pair of lacy panties.

"The girl? Or the crazy asshole screaming upstairs?" she asks. "Bernie is losing his mind."

"I don't care about Bernie… I just need to know that Nova left." When I saw her pull up, I just about lost it and went out to her. But what good would it have done? I'd just be giving her a reason to keep coming around to this place, seeing me, dragging herself down.

It's better for everyone if I disappear.

I shove down the emotions prickling inside me, the ones I've been working really hard to bury over the last twenty-four hours. I focus on drawing along the piece of crinkled-up paper I found on the floor, lines and shapes that mean more than I'll ever admit.

"She left," Nancy tells me, climbing onto the mattress beside me. She rests her head on my chest. Her touch brings me nothing but coldness, but it matches the deadness inside me so I let it be. "She was crying for a while out in the parking lot, though."

I swallow the lump in my throat, refusing to look at my drawing of Nova and me dancing out in front of the gas station. So perfect. So real. I wish I could have that moment back again, and the one in front of the roller coaster, when we felt each other's heartbeats. But I know I'll never be able to. No more goodness. No more light in my life. What happened to Tristan reminded me what I'm supposed to be—what I deserve.

"She's really pretty." Nancy pushes up from my chest and looks down at the drawing. "I wish someone would draw me like that."

I know she's hinting at me to draw her, but I won't. It took a lot for me to draw Nova, and I only got there because she means something to me. But after I'm finished with the drawing, I'm going to destroy it and force myself to forget about everything that's happened between us. I'm not going to feel anything for Nova anymore. I'm going to go back to holding on to Lexi, like I should have been doing this entire time. If Nova doesn't know where I am, then I can't give in to the pull I feel toward her and she can't give in to the pull she for some reason feels toward me. She'll be safer if I stay away. And even though she can't see it now, she'll be happier never knowing that a piece of shit like me fell in love with her.

Now I just need to figure out a way to forget her—forget about life. About my emotions...the love I'm fairly certain I feel for her. I just want to escape it all and go back to living my promise to Lexi, continually seeking forgiveness from her, knowing I'll never get it and that eventually I'll die and never have to feel a thing again.

"How's Tristan doing?" I ask, trying to distract myself from where I am and who I'm with. "You called the hospital, right?"

"Yeah. It was a pain in the ass to get them to release any information, but the nurse was spacey and I told her I was his aunt," she says. "They said he's still in recovery."

"I still wonder what he took," I say, knowing it's beside the point. No matter what he took, he almost died and I almost wasn't there to help him. "He was always mixing shit."

"Does it really matter? What matters is that he's going to be okay."

"Yeah, I guess," I mumble. "And at least his parents are headed here and hopefully they'll take him home with them." I really hope they do. It took a lot for me to make that phone call, but after the paramedics got him breathing again, I knew I had to do it—had to help him the only way I could. So when the ambulance drove off, red and blue lights flashing, I made a call I didn't want to make and everything that I expected to happen did. His mom blamed me when I told her Tristan overdosed, said it was my fault because I was a bad influence on him and that he was doing drugs because he lost his sister and that he was hurting inside. And she's right.

Everything is all my fault, and I just want to stop feeling it, go back to killing myself one hit at a time.

"And you'll go with him?" Nancy asks as she leans back against the wall and observes me. "When he goes back home?"

I keep drawing because it's the only thing that's keeping me hanging on. Motions. Simple lines. A task to keep my thoughts centered. "No... I don't have a home."

"Then what? You'll just stick around? With me?"

I don't answer, and silence drifts by. I can tell I'm making her uneasy. I'm not even sure whether she wants me to say yes or no, but she keeps wiggling around and then finally she crawls down to the bottom of her mattress. "Are you about ready to try this?" she asks.

I force the nervous lump down in my throat, continuing to move the pencil across the paper. "You sure that it'll help me forget everything?"

She smiles at me as she returns to my side with a box in her hand. "Baby, it'll make you feel like a god." She opens the box and starts to take my hand.

I jerk away. "But will it help me forget?" I need her to say yes before I commit. "I want to forget. All of this."

She pulls out a folded-up white piece of paper and a syringe. "Sweetie, this will give you all of your heart's desires and more. You're not even going to be able to think about forgetting because you're not going to be able to think."

I nod, still focusing on my drawing, nervous, thinking about the last time needles entered me. All they did was fuck me up more by bringing me back to life. Hopefully, this time it'll take my life away. "Okay, I'll do it."

She smiles elatedly. "You won't regret it." She removes a spoon and a lighter from the box, along with a rubber band, then starts working to melt the smack with the lighter. I keep drawing through the entire process, trying not to think about it, because if I do I'll chicken out and then I'll be left stuck in my thoughts and I need quiet.

When Nancy says she's ready for me, I take the lighter from her hand, then lean over to the side, hold the paper out, and light it on fire. I watch it burn into black ash that flutters to the floor, feeling my memories fade with it, and soon I hope they'll be gone. Lexi. Nova. Tristan. My guilt. Me.

"Give me your arm," Nancy instructs as I sit upright on the mattress.

I stick my arm out onto her lap, trembling with nervousness, not just because of the needle, but also because of what this means. That I'm going to forget about everything and fully accept that this is what my life will be until I can finally rot away.

"Lie back down and get comfortable," she tells me, and I

obey, lying down on the lumpy mattress, which smells damp and smoky.

Her cold fingers brush my arm as she ties the rubber band and then flicks my skin a few times. "Try to relax."

Easier said than done. But I try my best and take a deep breath. Then another. Then start sucking in air by the lungful. She shifts toward me, and then the tip of the needle stings against my arm. I almost back out, shout at her to stop, but I keep silent and then the needle's sinking deep into my skin.

"Come back to us, Quinton," someone whispers. "Open your eyes."

"No…" I mutter with my eyes shut. "Just let me go…please…"

"Don't give up on us yet." I hear the beeping of machines trying to breathe life into me—life I don't want. I want to stay cold. Feel nothing. Disappear into the stars.

"Please just give up on me," I beg, but they continue to pump life into me, and I know that as soon as I open my eyes, I'll have to accept that I'm alive and that Lexi's dead. I wish they'd just let me go. I want to let go. I want to give up, tear my chest open, let it bleed out, but they keep sealing it up.

The needle plunges deeper into my vein and seconds later the smack enters me, potent, toxic, burning through my bloodstream, scorching its way to my heart. I feel a rush where I think about everything all at once, and then suddenly I'm falling into the darkness and I can't remember a single thing. I drift farther from everyone still living and move closer to the people who have left me. The pain disappears. My thoughts and memories disappear. Everything disappears, and I disappear right along with it.

Chapter Fourteen

May 28, day thirteen of summer break

Nova

"So it's been two days since I lost Quinton," I say to the web camera. My eyes are really large, and there are bags under them because I've barely slept at all. My hair's pulled up into a messy bun and I'm still wearing my pajamas. I feel like I'm tottering on the edge of falling and clawing to hold on. "And I'm not going to lie. I feel like shit, which you can probably see from watching this video..." I trail off, not wanting to concentrate on my looks too much, but I don't want to concentrate on the other stuff I have to say either. I drag my fingers down my face as a loud breath slips out of my mouth. "God, I don't even know what the point of recording this is, other than to tell you that I'm giving up—that I can't see hope anymore…so I'm giving up." I choke and immediately want to take it back, but I can't because it's really happening. "My mom's here to take me home. I could have fought her more, but I think it might be time. Not to give up but to let go…because I can't handle it like I thought I could…But God it hurts…knowing that I'm about to walk away and he might be out there somewhere, hurting or even dead…"

"Are you ready to go, sweetie?" My mom sticks her head into the guest room of Lea's uncle's house, where my stuff is packed and ready to go.

I shut the computer. "I guess so."

She gives me a sad look as she enters the guest room. "Look, Nova, I know that you're really disappointed that you didn't get to help your friend, but we can't make people do things they don't want to do. Sometimes you can't help people no matter how much you want to."

I get up from the chair and bend down to unplug my computer. "I get that, but sometimes it takes another person to wake you up from what you're doing and make you realize that you want help."

"Yes, but you can do it by yourself, too," she says, rounding the foot of the bed. "Like you did."

I start to wrap the cord around my hand. "I didn't do it by myself."

She looks puzzled. "What do you mean?"

"I mean I had help," I say, putting the balled-up cord in my laptop bag. "From Landon."

She's even more lost, so I decide to explain. "I watched his video, the one he made before he... before he killed himself, and he said some stuff that sort of woke me up and made me realize I didn't want to do drugs anymore... made me see what my life had become." I think Lea's been trying to make me see what it's become now, but I'm fighting to open my eyes and accept everything.

She pushes up the sleeves of her shirt. "Why didn't you ever tell me that... that you watched his video?"

I shrug as I slide my laptop into the bag. "Because I wasn't ready to talk about it back then."

"But you are now?"

"I guess." Honestly, I'm not really sure why I'm telling her unless it's because I'm emotionally drained. "But you should probably know that I told Quinton first, which I think says a lot about how much I care for him," I say, zipping up the bag. She opens her mouth to protest, but I cut her off, holding my hand up. "Look, I know you don't get it and I don't expect you to, but just trust me when I say that I care for him and I probably won't ever completely stop caring about him... He'll always be a part of me."

"Nova, I understand that you care about him," she explains, picking up my duffel bag from the floor. "I just don't want you to be unable to move past this. I don't want to see you pulled under like you were with Landon's death, and Lea said things were getting really bad."

"They were...are," I admit as I slide the handle of the laptop bag over my shoulder. "But it's going to be hard to get over this when I have no idea where he is, and I was the only one looking out for him, so no one's going to even try to find him anymore."

She walks up to me and puts an arm around my shoulder. "Well, we can still keep working on his father. Maybe if we tell him what you told me happened...that he might be hurt and in trouble, he might want to help him a little more," she says, heading toward the door and guiding me with her. "And maybe we can get Tristan's parents involved, too."

"I don't think that'll work," I tell her as we go into the living room. "I think they blame Quinton for Ryder's death."

"Yeah, but I'm sure they care about their son," she says. "And maybe if they go looking for him, they'll find Quinton, too."

"And what if they won't? Or what if they do and they find Quinton and make things worse?" I'm wary of her optimism, partly because of what I said and partly because I'm worried there's no Tristan and Quinton to find.

"I don't think they will," she assures me, giving my shoulder a gentle squeeze. "And it's their son, too, who's out there, and as a mother, I know that despite any angry feelings I'd have, I'd want everyone to be safe."

I start to cry because I have no hope at the moment. My mom hugs me while I cry, letting me feel the pain because she knows it's better than keeping it trapped inside. Whether she realizes it or not, she helps. It's so nice to have so many people in my life who do, and it hurts to think about Quinton, who has no one, just wandering around waiting to die like he told me that night. I wish I could stay and search for him, but my mom loves me too much to let me stay, and deep down I know that I'm not strong enough at the moment to take on such a huge task. I thought I was when I started this. Thought I could handle this. I'd been doing good, helping at the suicide hotline. But the problem is that I have huge, massive feelings for Quinton, ones that remind me of my feelings for Landon. They make this so much more personal and trigger too much instability inside me.

It's one of the hardest things to do, getting into my car and driving away from that noisy city, knowing that he could be out there lost in a sea of people who barely acknowledge his existence, who don't want to see the ugly, dark, messed-up part of life, so they pass by without giving it a glance, like the lost part of the city Quinton showed me. Forgotten by the brighter side of town.

As my mom drives the Chevy Nova down the freeway, I watch the city behind us, turning on the song Quinton and I were listening to that night we danced in front of the car, the one good time when everything seemed like it was going to be okay—when I thought maybe, just maybe, I was helping him. I mutter the lyrics underneath my breath as the buildings and hazy sky slip farther and farther away until Vegas disappears completely and all that's left to do is turn around in the seat and face the future.

Chapter Fifteen

June 30, day forty-six of summer break

Quinton

Time is becoming nonexistent. Even major events, like the apartment building burning down a couple of weeks ago. Such a big thing, but I barely remember stumbling out of the apartment in the middle of the night, while flames engulfed the building.

No one really knew what happened. Someone said they'd heard gunshots coming from where Dylan and Delilah were living. I'd seen them a couple of times since the whole thing with Trace. Dylan and I even got into a fight. But he was too high to really do anything and so was I.

I wondered if maybe one of them started the fire, but I didn't stick around to find out—I couldn't. The cops and fire trucks showed up, and that was Nancy's and my cue, along with everyone else's who was doing illegal shit there, to bail out and take to the streets.

And that's where I've been living ever since. Sleeping behind Dumpsters, in vacant buildings when we come across them. We sometimes crash at people's places when we have the opportunity, but that's rare.

All we really have left is the clothes on our backs and a limited amount of drugs that we buy after stealing stuff when we can, and sometimes Nancy prostitutes herself out, when we're running really low.

I'd hate my life at the moment, if I could feel hate, but I can't feel anything except the hungry monster living inside me. He's taken over every part of me and almost killed off the old Quinton entirely.

"Don't shoot up right here," I warn as I pace the alley between a strip club and a pawnshop. There's a stack of crates at the back, concealed by a Dumpster, and it's where Nancy I spent last night after the cops showed up at the vacant warehouse we'd been staying at for the past week.

"Why the hell not?" Nancy asks, glancing up at me with starvation in her eyes as she searches her backpack, looking for the one thing that can feed her hunger. Just seeing the look on her face—seeing the need—makes me salivate.

"Because first off, the last thing you need to do is pass out in an alley," I tell her. "Then I'll have to stay awake and keep an eye on you."

She laughs at me from the ground, this hysterical laugh that she gets when she's super sleep-deprived. "Is someone a little greedy?" she asks. "Afraid you're going to have to watch instead of taste?"

I stop pacing and glare at her. "Can we please just go somewhere more private?" I glance nervously down at the end of the alley, at people walking by. Always looking over my shoulder, worried someone might show up. I'm not even sure who I think will show up. Maybe deep down it's that I want someone to—a blue-green–eyed girl I still think about no matter how much numbness I put into my veins. I don't even know if she's in Vegas anymore or if she went home. And that's how it should be. I should know nothing about Nova Reed. "Somewhere we can just lie down and enjoy getting high?"

Nancy sighs and then zips her backpack up before getting to her feet. "Where the hell are we supposed to go?" she asks with irritation as she glances up and down the alley.

I rub my hand down my face as I start pacing again. It's been too long since my last hit. I can feel emotions surfacing, sharper than the needle, more potent than heroin. I need to silence them. Now. Before I melt into the ground. I need somewhere quiet and away from all these people.

I lower my hand to my side, getting an idea. "I think I know a place."

She nods as she puts her backpack on and doesn't even ask questions. She just follows me, hoping that I'll lead her to a place where she can pump her veins full of drugs in the hopes that she can escape whatever she's running away from. Just like everyone else. Just like me.

Escape.

It takes us a while to travel across the city and toward the less-populated side of town. Hours or maybe even an entire day. It's hard to tell. I know it's daylight when we leave and the sun has set when we arrive, but sometimes I lose track of time because I become so focused on getting to that one place where I can fly and soar through my past without having to feel it—without having to feel the guilt of everything that's happened in my life. The guilt of death. The guilt of love. The guilt of existing.

When we step inside, I'm blasted with memories of the last time I was here, with Nova, and I almost turn around. But then Nancy nudges me in the back.

"Hurry up," she says, heading for the stairs. "I'm dying here."

I move forward, stepping over the rubble and debris, trying not to think of Nova, but it's hard. The only thing that keeps me stable is the fact that when I get to the roof, it'll only be minutes before everything filling my head right now vanishes. So I keep moving, going through the motions of walking, and when we reach the roof, I feel like I can breathe again.

Nancy eagerly drops her backpack to the ground beside one of the massive signs and starts taking the spoon and syringe out. I don't help her. I can't. Despite how many times I've shot up, I still can't inject myself. The memory of needles and injections bringing me back to the life I didn't want to live is still too strong. But I always get over the phobia the moment she shoots me up. So I lie down on the ground and stare up at the stars like I did with Nova—like I did that night I died. I keep my eyes on them, waiting with zero patience until the needle enters my vein and slowly makes its way through my body, erasing everything inside me. My guilt briefly goes away and thoughts of Nova leave my mind. It feels like everyone in the world has forgiven me. I feel so much lighter as I float up to the sky, feeling closer and closer to Lexi. And I swear to God that if I could reach my hand out, I could touch her.

Almost there. Almost within reach.

Chapter Sixteen

August 1, day seventy-eight of summer break

Nova

I've been working really hard to keep busy, keep moving forward, keep going. I've been doing as much as I can to distract myself and have been spending a lot of time making video clips. I even got a real camera, or, well, my mom got it for me, I think because she feels sorry for me.

"It's amazing how fast the last couple of months moved by," I say to the camera that's positioned on the kitchen table, aimed at me while I talk and work on the photo album I'm putting together of Landon. "I'm not even sure how it happened. I blame it on my mom and not in a bad way. She's been working really hard to keep me busy, having me help her organize the house. She's even helped me create a photo album of Landon, just like I was planning on doing but never was able to start…"

I glance down at Landon's photos and sketches all over the table in front of me and at the photo album pages I'm supposed to be putting them on. "I even went and visited Landon's grave the other day...It was hard, but bearable, and for some reason it seemed to help with the obsessive need I'd been feeling to watch his video over and over again," I say as I put a piece of tape on the back of a photo of Landon and me. He's kissing my cheek and I'm laughing and, with just a quick glance, it looks so perfect. If I stared at it long enough I'd see the flaws, but I'm not going to I'm only going to remember the good.

"I still sometimes feel like crying for Quinton...not knowing where he is...The not knowing sometimes feels harder than knowing he's dead..." I unfold one of Landon's drawings of a tree and smooth out the wrinkles. "My mom somehow got Quinton's dad to go down to Vegas and look for him...although I'm a little skeptical about how hard he's searching for him, since he even flat-out said he didn't want to. But I heard my mom give him this big huge lecture where she almost completely lost it and yelled at him to be a"—I make air quotes—"'Fucking father'...I've never heard her curse like that before or get that intense." I tape the photo to the page. "When we first got home, she tried to call Tristan's parents to get them looking for him, but apparently they were already down there getting Tristan, which would have been good, except Tristan's parents are assholes...I don't want to be unsympathetic or anything, because I know how hard it is to lose someone you love, but the stuff Tristan's parents said to my mom about Quinton being responsible for Ryder's death—it's completely messed up. To put the blame on someone like that is terrible. I don't care if they're mourning. Purposely going out of their way to tell Quinton he's responsible for everything that happened is messed up...and it painfully helps me sort of understand Quinton a little bit more...although it doesn't do me any good now..." I start to choke up and quickly clear my throat a few times, telling myself to keep it together. This happens a lot, whenever I think of Quinton.

I exhale, then add another photo to the page, then turn to a clean page. "I've also learned some stuff about Quinton from Tristan, who's back here in Maple Grove as of a week ago. To make a long story short, I guess around the same time I lost track of Quinton, Tristan almost OD'd. Quinton called the ambulance and then Tristan was taken to the hospital. Then I guess Quinton called Tristan's parents, who showed up at the hospital and got him to go to rehab. I'm not even sure how they got him to agree to go, but I wish I did—I wish I could find the magic thing to bring Quinton to his senses and realize how good a person he is, despite what he thinks. That the bad stuff that happened to him was out of his control, something I've been working on telling myself, too...although it's still hard. That I could never get through to him enough to help him." I pause, taking a deep breath. "I failed. I don't give a shit what my mom says. I failed him, just like I failed Landon, and now all I can do is live with it."

I add a photo of Landon to the page, his sad honey-brown

eyes reminding me of Quinton, which is a little weird because usually it's Quinton reminding me of Landon. Landon was so beautiful, and when he left, the world lost a piece of its beauty. "Tristan wrote me a few times while he was in rehab, apologizing for anything he's done that might have hurt me and for bringing me into the whole Trace mess. I never wrote him back, because I didn't know what to say, or if I even could write him back, but he called yesterday... We talked a little bit about stuff—life. We even talked about Quinton. He says he has no idea where he could be—there are just too many places—but that he heard the building they were living in burned down. No one died, at least in the fire, because no bodies were found. But the fire was started on purpose, and it makes me wonder what the hell happened. If Quinton was there when it happened. If Delilah was there when it happened. It hurts my heart to know that all of them could be living on the streets, doing God knows what. And that there's a chance no one may find them. And poor Delilah. I'm guessing her mother isn't looking for her, considering how bad their relationship is." I sigh, feeling the hopelessness arise again. "I think Tristan might know a little more than he's letting on about all this stuff—about everything that happened—but I didn't want to push him, since he's like a newborn baby deer learning how to walk again and a lot of things could make him fall, at least from what people tell me." I pull a piece of tape off the dispenser. "I've been going to these group meetings, kind of like the one I went to in Vegas... It's sort of scary... listening to people's stories, but at the same time it's good to hear the good parts, where someone survives and conquers their addiction. It gives me a little hope that it's not over for Quinton yet." I press the piece of tape to the page so it's securing a corner of a picture. "Plus, the meetings gave me some insight into what I'm in for, since Tristan is supposed to be heading over here today. It gives me hope that his visit will go well." I glance at the camera. "Although the pessimist side of me thinks it's going to be really awkward."

I glance over at the clock on the microwave and realize he'll be here soon and I'm still wearing my pajamas. I return my attention to the lens. "I'll let you know how that one goes." I give the camera a little wave. "Until next time." Then I click the camera off and put it and the photo album stuff away in my room, on my desk, beside where I keep the few sketches of Quinton's that I took from his apartment the last time I was there. Just looking at them makes me miss him, makes me long to hold him. If I could do one thing at this very moment, that's what I'd do—hold him and never let him go.

Sighing, I turn away from the drawings and go over to my dresser. I change into a pair of shorts and a black tank top and comb my hair, leaving it down. I don't put any bracelets on the wrist with the tattoo. I never do anymore, so that I can *never forget* any of it: my dad, Landon, Quinton, where I went, how I rose, how easy it is to fall. How easily my life can swirl out of control. It's kind of what the scratch on my car is becoming—a reminder to never forget. I never did fix it after that guy hit it with a tire iron. My mom offered to pay for it, but I told her no. I know it sounds crazy, but it reminds me of the last time I saw Quinton, and even though it's a horrible, terrifying memory, it's all I have to hang on to.

When I'm finished changing, the doorbell rings. My stomach rolls with nerves and I head to the door. My mom and my stepfather, Daniel, are out on their daily hike and they won't be home until late, which means that it's just going to be Tristan and me. I can almost feel the awkwardness rising in the air.

When I open the front door, he's standing on the edge of the porch like he was about to leave or something. The sun is blinding behind him, making it hard for my eyes to focus. The more he steps forward into the shade, getting closer, the more of his features I can see, but the glare still makes it seem like I'm looking through a camera lens. At first he looks blurry. Then I can make out his blond hair, his facial features, then finally his blue eyes. He's wearing a clean plaid shirt, nice jeans, and a pair of sneakers. He looks good. Healthy. And those track marks that were on his arms have faded, but there are a few tiny white specks that I think are scars.

"Hey," he says, stuffing his hands into his pockets.

I just stare at him, my arm holding the screen door, my body drifting toward shock or something. He's almost unrecognizable, and it makes me happy and hurts at the same time, because it reminds me of just how unhealthy he used to look and how Quinton's still in that place.

"Hey," I reply, forcing myself to stop staring. I step back and gesture at him to come in. "You can come inside."

He hesitates, nervous, but ultimately walks past me and through the doorway, and I get a whiff of cologne mixed with cigarettes, which is a lot better than the I-haven't-showered-in-weeks smell he had the last time I was around him.

I shut the door behind me and turn, studying him as he looks around the living room, at the family pictures on the wall, the floral sofas, and the television.

"I don't think I've ever actually been in your house," he states, turning in a circle before his eyes land on me. "It's nice."

"Thanks," I say, fidgety. God, I have no idea what to say or do, where to put my hands, where to look. He has this scar on his cheek, like he had a gash there once and it healed, but the scar didn't used to be there. I want to ask him about it, yet I don't think I should.

But he must notice me staring, because he touches it and says, "Trace cut me there with a knife that day when...well, you know, everything went to shit."

My lips form an O. "Oh my God, are you okay?"

He nods and waves it off. "Yeah, it's pretty much healed now."

Memories. Potent. Tearing my heart in half. Vegas. Quinton. Knife. Cuts. Drugs. I take a slow breath and let it out, telling myself to calm down.

"I'm sorry," he says, taking his hands out of his pockets and crossing his arms.

"For what?"

"For bringing up Vegas."

"You don't have to worry about bringing it up," I insist,

sitting down on the sofa, and he sits beside me. "We can talk about it…" *What am I doing?* "If you want?"

He eyes me skeptically, like he doesn't quite believe I'm being serious. "Maybe in a bit," he says. "How about we just chill for a while and see where things go?"

I nod, and we spend the next hour talking about nothing important. High school. What we used to do for fun. He does tell me a little bit about when he got into drugs, but never does explain why. He got high for the first time quite a while before his sister died. His using never had to do with her death, although being high made that easier to deal with. I wonder what the cause was but don't dare ask, afraid I might upset him.

Around dinnertime I order pizza, and then Tristan and I sit back down on the couch in the living room and eat while we continue to talk.

"So you're doing okay, then?" I ask, opening up the pizza box. "I mean with being out in the real world."

He shrugs, reaching for a piece of pizza. "Well, I've only been out for a week, so I'm still not sure…I'm still not sure about a lot of things, like what the hell I'm going to do with my life…I'm supposed to be making goals." He rolls his eyes. "I tried to tell my counselor that I didn't have goals, but she didn't seem to believe me."

"You could go to school," I suggest, picking up a slice of pizza. "It's a great place to start."

He smiles amusedly. "Nova, no college is going to accept me. I barely graduated high school."

"That's not true," I tell him. "Sure, Ivy League schools probably won't, but my college is pretty easy to get into. In fact, Lea, my friend you met in Vegas, well, her boyfriend didn't even graduate. He got his GED and still got into my college."

He picks at the cheese on his pizza as he leans back in the sofa. "I guess I'll think about it, then," he says. "But I never did like school."

"Neither did I in high school," I agree, relaxing back against the armrest with a slice of pizza in my hand. "But college isn't so bad."

He seems surprised. "You always seemed like you liked high school."

"Yeah, but I was good at faking how I felt." I take a bite of my pizza.

"Really?" There's playfulness to his tone. "I always sort of thought of you as an open book."

I roll my eyes. "You did not."

"I did too," he says. "I could always tell when you were angry or upset, which was a lot. Like that time we kissed." The corners of his lips quirk. "I could tell seconds afterward that you regretted it."

I'm not sure how to respond. I don't quite think he's flirting with me, just being cheerful, but at the same time, we're just sitting here joking around and it feels wrong.

"Well, I'm not angry and upset a lot anymore," I say, taking a bite of my pizza. "And I'm sorry about the kiss thing, but I was going through some stuff."

"I know," he says, picking a string of cheese off his chin. "And if you're not angry or upset anymore, then what are you?"

"I'm not sure," I say honestly, staring down at my pizza. "Most of the time I just feel normal, but sometimes I feel sad."

His chest sinks as he blows out a slow breath. It grows silent between us, the only sound the chewing of our pizza, as my thoughts drift to what's making me sad—Quinton. I wish things could be different. I wish he could be sitting here with us in the awkwardness, eating pizza and talking about everyday things for the most part.

"Do you still think about him a lot?" Tristan finally asks, giving me a sideways glance.

I blink my gaze off my pizza and look at him. "Think about who?"

He picks a pepper off his pizza and tosses it into the box. "Quinton."

I nod. "All the time."

"Me, too," he utters.

"Have you heard anything from his dad, by chance?" I ask, setting my half-eaten slice of pizza down on the plate on the coffee table in front of us. "My mom said he went down there for a while to look for him, but with how hard she worked to get him there, I'm not so convinced he'll really look for him."

He swallows a bite of pizza. "Yeah, he took a week off from work and went down there. I guess he put up flyers and everything..." He pauses, picking at a string of cheese hanging off the pizza. "I hate to say this, but I have to . . . No one's going to find Quinton."

A massive lump forms in my throat as I force a bite of pizza down. "Do you really think that?"

Tristan tosses his crust in the pizza box as he puts his feet up on the coffee table and leans back in the sofa. "I think he'll only be found when he wants to be found."

"And do you think he'll ever get to that point?" I tuck my foot under me, turning sideways on the sofa.

Confusion vanishes from his face as he folds his arms across his chest. "Honestly, Nova, I'm not sure. I know that if you would have asked me a few months ago if I wanted to be found, I'd have said no. In fact, my parents actually tried to call me a couple of times and I blew them off." He pauses, staring at the window across from us, where I can see Landon's house just outside. "But after almost dying . . . well, things changed a little."

"So you were glad you were found?" I ask. "Glad you're here instead of Vegas?"

He contemplates this deeply. "I'm not going to lie." His fists tighten as he crosses his arms. "Even after all that shit happened, I still crave it . . . crave the solitude drugs gave me." He pauses again. "But I prefer being here at the moment."

"Because you're sober," I say. "And can see things a little clearer now."

"Yeah, I guess that's it . . . but I don't think that helps with Quinton, since I was forced to get sober and someone would have to force him to get sober." He searches my eyes for something. "You managed to walk away from it once. How did you do it without anyone forcing you?"

I don't want to tell him, but at the same time, I'm the one who brought up the subject, so I decide to just be honest, even though it'll probably sting a little. "It was a video Landon—my boyfriend who died—made. It made me rethink what I was doing and reminded me of who I used to be." My hands shake as I pick up my soda, thinking about how watching the video this summer had the opposite effect and kind of made things worse, because I wasn't letting it go. Letting go. A really big problem for me.

"Are you okay?" Tristan asks, noting how emotional I'm getting.

I nod. "Yeah, it just gets to me sometimes... I mean, I still feel guilty for leaving Quinton down there."

He considers something for a moment while I take a sip of my soda. "I feel guilty, too, because I think he's out there somewhere, thinking what happened to me is his fault, and it's not. Just like he blamed himself for my sister's death and his girlfriend's. I think he's been spending two years blaming himself for everything." He starts picking more peppers off of his pizza and dropping them on top of the pizza box. I can tell he's trying to internally work through his thoughts. Processing something. Finally, he slumps back in the sofa. "You want to know what I think?"

I nod with eagerness. "Yeah, I do."

He pauses. Then he takes a deep breath. "I think that what Quinton needs is to realize that all of the stuff wasn't his fault—that shit just happens sometimes and is out of our control."

Easier said than done. I've heard how Quinton thinks about himself, what he thinks people think of him—how he thinks everyone hates him. I know he needs to be freed from those thoughts so he can breathe again, but I'm still not 100 percent sure how to make him see that. I spent the first part of the summer trying to get to him, make him see that he was a better person than he thought.

I stare down at the backs of my hands, worried about what I'm about to ask, but needing to ask it nonetheless. "Do you think he'll ever be able to get to that place? Be able to forgive himself for what happened? Realize that it wasn't his fault?"

Tristan doesn't say anything right away. I wonder if it's because he's actually thinking about the answer or if it's just hard for him to talk about things related to his sister's death. "I'm not sure." His voice slightly trembles, and he clears it. "I want to try, though... help him if I can find him... help him realize it's not his fault, like I should have been doing instead of injecting my veins with poison."

I bite at my lips. "So you don't blame him for... for the accident? Like your parents do?"

He shakes his head. "I've never really looked at it like that. Yeah, it kind of made me angry the first few times I saw him after I lost my sister, but at the same time, I got that it was an accident. He wasn't drunk or high or anything. Shit just happened. It was no one's fault." He pauses, rubbing his hand tensely down his face. "Besides, if it wasn't for Quinton, I wouldn't even be here right now, I don't think...He called the ambulance when I OD'd...He did CPR..." He trails off, seeming distracted by the memories. "And he tried so hard to save me even before that. Get me to stop doing stupid shit. Tell me that I was better than it...help my sorry ass when I got us into trouble."

God, what I would give for Quinton to be here and hear that. I wonder if he'd see it that way—that he saved a life. Not took one. That he did good. Helped someone. "You could tell Quinton all that," I say. "We just have to find him."

He turns his head for a moment, and I'm pretty sure he's wiping away tears. But I don't say anything, and when he turns around to me, his eyes are dry. "You know, you're one of the most determined people I've ever met," he says.

"Not determined enough," I say, thinking about how I left Vegas—left Quinton there.

"Hey." He puts a hand on my knee and I flinch. "You staying there wouldn't have done any good. Like I said, Quinton needs to stop blaming himself and realize there are people who care about him before anything can change. And even then he still has a lot of shit to work through."

"Do you think there's still hope?" I ask. "For him? That he could still get better?"

I hold my breath as I wait for the answer, and I swear it takes hours when really it's probably only seconds. He nods and I breathe again.

"I think as long as he's alive still, there will always be hope," he says softly. "And if we could get him sober, or at least give him an intervention and get him to a place where he could get sober, like my parents did with me, then maybe he could start working on forgiving himself."

It grows quiet between Tristan and me, as soundless as that day I spent with Quinton on the roof. I wonder if it's quiet where he is, if he's enjoying the quiet, or if he even realizes it is quiet. I wonder if he has a roof over his head. I wonder if he's eaten anything. I wonder if he still looks at things from an artist's point of view. I wonder if he still draws. I wonder if he still thinks about me.

There are so many things I wonder, but the biggest question I'll always have is if he's okay.

Quinton

I have lost track of time. I can't remember what month it is, what day. I can barely tell it's night. I'm down to my last pair of jeans and a T-shirt. I lost one of my shoes somewhere, but I can't remember where. I've barely had any water to drink in days, and I'm starting to feel it, a slow ache in my throat and belly, but I can't bring myself to leave the roof, so I stay up there most of the time. Nancy complains about me being a lazy-ass junkie, leaving it to her to make all the money, dealing and whoring herself out. I always tell her to go, and I wish she would, so I'd finally rot all the way into nothing, yet she always comes back and keeps me going when I'm on the verge of dying.

Nancy's been on her cell phone for a while, something she came back with the other day, telling me it'd help her with her clients, but I look at it as money wasted on the phone and the stupid card she paid for to get minutes. We're getting low on our stash, only a hit or two left, and she's trying to find more for cheap. She's yammering away in the background, but her voice is barely there as I stand on the edge of the roof, staring down at the vacant houses and stores below, the wind against my back and my arms out to the sides. I don't have a shirt on or shoes and my pants barely stay up at my hips. There's hardly anything left to me, but I'm still here, wasting away.

One more step and I could be free. One more step and I could finally just fall and crash to my death. The lights would go off. The guilt would be gone. This personal hell that I live in would end.

"Why the hell are you always standing on the edge of the roof?" Nancy weaves around the signs and walks up to me with the phone in her hand.

"Because I'm wondering if I can fly." I shut my eyes and breathe the air in, freedom just in front of me if I dare take it.

"Don't be crazy." She grabs my arm and pulls me down from the edge. "You're just tripping. If you'll relax for, like, five minutes, I can get you another hit ready and you'll feel better."

I stumble to get my balance as I turn around to face her. "But we're running out."

"I found us more," she says, backing toward her backpack in the middle of the roof and stopping near the VIVA LAS VEGAS sign. She's not wearing shoes, and some guy hacked off her hair while she was passed out so it barely touches her chin. "But do you have any cash left on you at all?"

Even though I know I don't, I still take my wallet out of my back pocket and open it up. Then I tip it upside down and dump the contents onto the ground: a few quarters, my driver's license, which I thought I'd lost, and a piece of paper. Nancy quickly gets down on her knees and snatches up the quarters, then hands me my driver's license. She picks up the piece of paper and starts to throw it to the side.

I grab hold of her arm, stopping her. "Wait a minute." I pry the piece of paper out of her hand and open it up. A phone number is scrawled on it, so I fold it back up and put it back into my wallet, before stuffing my wallet back into my pocket.

"What the hell was that?" she asks me, rubbing her arm where I grabbed her.

"Nothing." I don't say anything else as I sit down on the roof, trying not to think about whose phone number it is. I don't need to think of her—can't feel those emotions again. Can't go back to that place. *I need to stay here.*

"Okay, then." Nancy looks at me like I'm crazy, but she's pretty much on the same page at this point, ready to lose her mind if she doesn't get a bump or two. "How about we get you taken care of, and then you can relax while I go get us a better stash?" She squats down beside her bag and opens it up.

"Why do you always help me like this?" I gesture around at the roof. "Why do you stay with me when I can't give you anything?"

She peers up from her bag. "Does it really matter?"

I shake my head, because it doesn't. "Not really." Nothing does anymore.

She takes out a syringe and bites off the cap. "Then let's get you taken care of."

I lie down in front of her and wait. Moments later she's sinking the needle into my vein, and for a moment I taste freedom, but it's not as potent as it used to be, and as I feel myself falling into a state of euphoria, I find myself wishing that instead I were falling off the roof.

Chapter Seventeen

August 19, day ninety-six of summer break

Nova

I've been watching the show *Intervention* lately because Tristan makes me. I'm not even sure why he does, except that he seems to think it'll teach us a thing or two about how it goes down, just in case we ever do stumble across Quinton again. He likes to compare the episodes to what happened with him, how his parents confronted him in the hospital and his mother cried a lot. He said his dad was actually kind of a dick, but only because he cares—Tristan can see that now. I asked him if he thought that was what was wrong with Quinton's dad and he said maybe, but we might never know unless a real intervention happens.

I've also started to pack for school, even though I don't head back for a week. Lea and I have an apartment, the same one we lived in last year. We just have to sign the forms when we get there and put down a deposit. I've ordered all my books, enrolled in all my classes. Everything is set, yet it feels like so much is missing.

The sun is setting outside, another day come and gone, another day when I try not to think about Quinton, but I always do. The worst is when I close my eyes and see the look in his eyes when we kissed near the roller coaster and I stupidly believed everything was going to change. Sometimes I see the self-hatred I saw when he told me the accident was his fault. Sometimes I dream that I'm reaching out to him as he falls into darkness, but he won't reach back and take my hand. Sometimes he turns into Landon as he's falling and he starts to reach back but then at the last second he pulls away. I'm really starting to hate dreaming.

"Do I really need to take four classes?" Tristan asks as he scrolls through the list on my computer. He looks even healthier than he did during his first visit, his skin clearer and his eyes filled with a little less misery. He's actually been hanging out with me a lot, mainly, he says, because I keep him out of trouble. I'm glad. I wish I could turn it into a job or something, although the breakdowns I have when things don't go my way would probably happen a lot more frequently.

"The more classes you take," I tell him as I fold up my clothes and stack them on my bed, "the quicker school will be over."

He grins over his shoulder at me. "Now, there's some motivation."

"Glad to be of service," I joke as I put a stack of shirts into a duffel bag, the ones I'm not planning on wearing until I get to school.

"Have you asked your friend if she minds sharing an apartment with a dude?" Tristan asks as he clicks the mouse. "Especially when she's seen me at my worst."

"Crap. I forgot to bring that up," I say, zipping up the bag.

"Forgot?" Tristan questions in a joking tone as he glances over his shoulder at me. "Or are you avoiding it?"

"Maybe a little of both," I admit as I reach for my phone on the nightstand. The screen says I have one message, and for a second my heart leaps in my throat. But that happens every time my phone shows a message or a call, because for some reason I think it's going to be Quinton, but it never is.

The message is from Lea, telling me to *call her please!*

I sigh and head toward the doorway. "I'll be right back," I tell Tristan, noticing that he's left the campus website and has now opened a search engine. I don't need to see what he's searching for. He told me once that he reads through Vegas articles for information about where Quinton could be. He's says it's pretty much pointless, especially when Quinton might not even be in Vegas anymore, but he does it anyway because it makes him feel better—makes him feel like he's doing something to help Quinton the way Quinton helped him.

I go out into the kitchen, where my mom and Daniel are, getting ready for the week-long camping trip that they're leaving for tomorrow. They've got the tent, the sleeping bags, and a few Tupperware bins on the table and the floor, which they're packing with food, pans, utensils, and whatnot.

"Hey, sweetie," my mom says as she drops a box of Pop-Tarts into one of the bins. "How's the college thing going in there?"

"Good," I say, stealing a cookie from a plate on the counter. "Tristan's trying to figure out what classes he wants to take."

"That's good," she says, opening a drawer. "It's good he's going."

"Yeah, it is," I agree and take a bite of the cookie.

She smiles at me but then frowns. "Nova, are you sure you're okay with me taking off for this trip? I worry about you."

"I'm fine," I assure her. "You've seen me be fine for almost three months now."

She looks wary as she takes some plastic spoons out of a drawer. "But you look so sad all the time."

"I know," I tell her. "And I'm not going to lie. I'm sad sometimes, but that doesn't mean I need you to stay home from your trip. Besides, I'm leaving for college in, like, a week."

"I know." She drops the spoons into the bin. "But I just think about last summer and how I took off on a vacation when I knew you weren't doing very well...when you were doing drugs."

I wind around the table and walk over to her, stuffing the rest of the cookie into my mouth. "Trust me, Mom, this isn't like last summer. I'm not doing drugs. I'm just sad about Quinton, and I can be sad sometimes."

"I know." She sighs and then pulls me in for a hug. "I just wish things would have gone better for you—you've been through so much."

I hug her back as tears sting at my eyes, but I remind myself that despite the people I've lost, she's still here. Still breathing. Still alive. And so am I.

"I'm always here for you, Nova," my mom whispers. Then she pulls away, heading over to the cupboards, and starts digging through them. I wipe away the tears in my eyes and go into the living room to call Lea. I figure someplace quiet is probably best, seeing as I'm going to have to talk to her about Tristan staying with us for a while. I know I'm taking a huge chance on him, but I want to help him get on his feet.

I dial her number as I sit down on the sofa. The call ends up going to her voice mail, and I leave her a message. "Hey, you sent me that text to call you and now you're not answering... I have something important to talk to you about...about our apartment, so call me back."

I hang up and slump back in the sofa with the phone in

my hand, staring out the window, hoping she'll call me right back so I can get this over with. Landon's house is just across the street, and I remember all the time I spent in there, never knowing what to say to stop making him sad. Just like Quinton. How I woke up on that hill that night, a little too late. How I'm still not sure if I'm too late with Quinton because I have no idea where he is. I wonder if there will ever be a time when I'm not so wrapped up in the past. Yeah, I've been moving forward for the most part. I have plans to go to back to school. Continue with it. Graduate. Forward movement. But my past continues to haunt me.

As I'm dwelling in my thoughts, my phone starts to ring. I sigh, preparing myself to give Lea a speech about how we'd really be helping Tristan by giving him a place to stay.

I press talk and put the phone up to my ear. "So what's up? And why did you tell me to call and then not answer?"

There's a pause, and I can hear someone breathing. "Is this Nova?"

My heart actually stops beating for a second, and I forget how to breathe. Sucking in a large breath of air, I say, "Quinton."

"Yeah..." He seems hesitant.

The fact that I'm hearing his voice and finally know that he's still alive is the most amazing feeling ever, but at the same time so many questions run through my head. Like where is he? What's he doing? "Are you okay?" I ask, leaning forward in the sofa, growing fidgety, needing to count, but I refuse to go to that place again. It damn near broke me back in Vegas and

I'm realizing just how big an addiction it can become for me, like drugs.

"Yeah…" He pauses again, and I have no idea what to do or say that will keep him on the line with me. I feel so desperate, so out of control. He could hang up at any moment and then what? He's gone again. Missing again. "Sorry I called…I was just thinking about you," he says. "And I dialed your number."

"You were?" I get to my feet and start back toward the kitchen, biting my thumbnail as I pace the living room.

"Uh-huh…" He sounds out of it, and while I care, I care more about figuring out where the hell he is. "I was thinking about the quiet and how much we talked about liking the quiet and it made me think of you."

"I'm glad you thought of me," I say as I head into the kitchen. My mom takes one look at me when I enter and her expression falls as she drops the pan she's holding.

"What's wrong?" she asks, hurrying around the table toward me.

Quinton, I mouth as I point to the phone, and her eyes widen as she stops in front of me.

"I'm really not supposed to," Quinton says with a worn-out sigh. "I try not to think about you, but I can't stop."

"I can't stop thinking about you either," I whisper. "I think about you all the time…where you are…what you're doing…" God, I wish he'd tell me.

"I'm doing nothing," he says. "And I'm nowhere. Just like I'm no one."

I squeeze my eyes shut, fighting back the tears burning at my eyes, feeling the loss threatening again because at any moment this conversation could end. "Yes, you are. God, I wish you could just see how much you matter…to me…"

He pauses again, and fear courses through me, fear that he's hung up. "I probably shouldn't be talking about you, just like I shouldn't be thinking of you," he says. "But I've been living at our spot, and it reminds me of that time with you…I never should have done that to you."

My eyes shoot open, and I almost drop my phone as I grab my mom's arm for support. Oh my God, I know where he is. "Done what to me?" I try to stay calm.

"Everything…" His voice is sluggish, and it frightens me. "Touched you, kissed you, been near you…fallen in love with you…You're too good for me…"

Fallen in love with me? Holy shit. He loves me. Do I love him?

I quickly shake the thought from my head, needing to focus on the bigger picture. "No, I'm not," I say, sinking down in a chair at the kitchen table, still holding on to my mom's arm. She's watching me with worry. Daniel's watching me with worry. Yet it feels like it's just Quinton and me alone in this room. "Quinton, is that where you are? Are you on that roof?"

"Yeah…" he says. "I can see those old buildings below… You remember the quiet ones, right?"

"I do." I suck in a slow breath, feeling both relieved and terrified. "The ones I told you to draw."

"Yeah...but I don't draw anymore..."

My heart compresses in my chest, and I fight to keep air flowing in and out of my lungs. "Quinton, you need to come home. Your dad's been looking for you. Everyone's worried about you. Me. Tristan."

"That's not true," he says seriously, and it rips my heart in half. "No one would ever look for me...well, except for you... You were always too nice to me..."

"Your dad *is* looking for you. I promise," I tell him. "He's put up flyers and everything. People care about you, whether you think so or not."

"Stop saying that." His tone is suddenly sharp and clipped with anger.

I'm losing him. I can feel it. The finality of our conversation crackles through the air, and I hate knowing that we may never talk again. "Quinton, please just..." I trail off as the line goes dead.

I grip the phone in my hand tightly. I want to scream. Throw my phone against the wall. Cry. But none of these things would get me anywhere. I need to do something. I check my phone screen, hoping that there's a callback number. There's not. The caller comes up as "Unknown," but even if there had been a number, I doubt he would have answered. He cut the connection with me and only he can give it back.

But there is one other choice.

I rise from my chair. "I'm going to Vegas," I announce to my mom, rushing for my bedroom before she can argue.

She cuts me off, stepping in front of me before I can make it to the doorway. "Nova, we're not doing this again."

"Mom, you don't have any say in this." I try to step by her, but she sidesteps and blocks me.

"Nova Reed, I won't let you go down that path again," she says in a choked-up voice that makes me feel guilty. "You tried saving this boy once before and you broke down."

"I have to go," I tell her. "I know where he is."

She grabs my arm, making me stay put. "We'll call his father and have him go down there."

"He doesn't know where to go and I do," I say, pulling my arm away. "And Quinton needs to talk to Tristan and his dad—he needs an intervention from the people who care about him, which includes me."

"Nova, he needs to go to rehab," she says. "And his father can do that."

"I know that, but he's not going to go to rehab until we give him a reason to go. He needs a reason to keep on living, just like Landon needed, but I couldn't give it to him! But if I—we all—talk to Quinton and tell him how much we care for him and how much he's hurting us, then maybe he'll consider it! Consider choosing life!" I'm shouting by the end, but the kitchen has gotten really quiet.

Daniel is staring at me from over by the table, and my mom looks like she's on the verge of tears. I'm messing this up, because I don't want to upset anyone.

"Is that what you think?" she asks quietly. "That Landon... that he took his own life because you didn't give him a good enough reason to live?"

I shake my head, but it's not quite the truth. "No, I just said that because I was upset."

"Nova." My mom's tone is full of warning, telling me I better tell her the truth.

"Fine." I give in, throwing my hands in the air in exasperation. "Sometimes I think that, but not as much as I used to."

She gives me a sympathetic look. "Honey, what happened to him isn't your fault."

"I know that," I say, because she'll never understand what it's like to watch someone sink into depression, sink further away from you until they're gone. Just like she'll never understand what it was like to run away to get my father help only to find him already gone by the time I came back. "Just like I know that what's going on with Quinton isn't my fault." I turn for the doorway. "But it doesn't mean I'm not going to go help him—I need to. Not just for him, but for myself."

Her fingers enfold my arm before I make it out of the room. Then she holds me in place for a moment with my back turned to her, and I wonder how much of a fight I'm going to have to put up to get her to let me go.

"Fine. You can go," she says so quietly I'm not sure I heard her right. "But I'm going with you, and I'm going to call his father and get him down there as soon as possible."

I glance over my shoulder at her. "You would do that for me?"

She nods. "Nova, I'd do anything for you to help you get over all the stuff…all the bad stuff that's happened to you."

I swallow hard, then turn around and give her a tight hug. "Thank you, Mom. I love you."

"I love you, too, and you're welcome," she says, hugging me back, tears falling from her eyes and dripping onto my shirt. "But you will come back before school starts. You're not going to mess up your life. I won't let you."

"Thanks," I say again. "And I'm not going to mess up my life. I promise." We've started to pull away when I add, "Wait. What about your camping trip?"

"We can do it later on," Daniel says from near the counter when my mom looks at him. "You should go with Nova."

"Thank you," she says, and I nod, then turn back to my room, hoping that Tristan's still in the same place he was three weeks ago—still ready to forgive. I feel weird for even asking him, but I have to. After I tell him what happened, he sits quietly for the longest time, swiveling in my computer chair.

"So that's where he's living?" he asks with wide eyes as I stuff some clothes in a backpack. "On the roof of that shitty motel?"

"Yeah. He took me up there once," I tell him, heading over to my dresser and getting a brush. "And when he just called, he told me that's where he was staying—he even described it to me like he was standing right there."

He makes a disgusted face. "That place is worse than the apartment."

"I wouldn't go that far," I say, throwing the brush into the bag. "Because I'm sure he's still doing the same thing up there as he was at the apartment."

He sighs. "Yeah, you're probably right."

I zip up my bag and slip my arms through the straps. "So do you think you can come and talk to him? Tell him how you feel about when you...OD'd?"

"You want me to go to Vegas?" he asks, and I nod eagerly. "I'm not sure...My parents would freak out...and...I'm worried myself."

"Because you'd be too close to drugs and you think you'll relapse?"

He shakes his head. "No, I'm just as close to them right now as I would be down there," he tells me. "I can think of three places right now where I could easily get a hit or two of whatever I wanted. Plus, your mom would be with us, and after hanging around here and hearing all the stuff she says to you, I know she'd be watching us like a hawk." He glances up at me. "I'm just worried about talking to him about this. I don't want to push him further in and make things worse. Everything has to go right. Otherwise we're going to fail and he's going to run."

I sink down on the bed, thinking about the few episodes of *Intervention* I watched where people didn't get help and bailed out. "I get what you're saying, but how can we help him if we don't try?" My mood starts to sink as I think about how much I've tried and tried and how I just want it to work this time. I think he can see the hopeless feeling on my face, because he gets up from the chair and walks over to me. He sits down beside me and puts an arm around my shoulder.

"We'll try," he says. "Just don't put all your hope into it, okay? You know things don't always go how we plan."

"I know that." But honestly I *am* putting a lot of hope into this. Hope that forgiveness is what Quinton needs. Hope that he'll stay in the same place. Hope that nothing will happen to him before we get there.

August 22, day ninety-nine of summer break

Quinton

I think I can remember doing something stupid, but I'm not 100 percent sure. I swear to God I talked to Nova in the middle of the meltdown I've been having for the last few hours, but my memories are too hazy to be certain. Nancy bailed out on me a while ago. She's been gone for hours, maybe days. I haven't had a hit in a while, and I think the smack is cleaning its way out of my system. It feels like my skin is melting away like candle wax, and my mind feels like it's going to explode into pieces. I have no money and only two choices: try to steal some drugs off someone or just end it. Throw myself off the roof and say good-bye to all this. I'm sitting on the edge right now, rocking back and forth, silently telling myself to just give in. Fall. Just go. It's time. I'm alone. I have nothing. I've become nothing. I'm losing my mind. I'm no one. The person no one wants. The person who shouldn't be here.

No one.

"Quinton." The sound of her voice makes me wonder if I've fallen off the roof and haven't realized it yet, if I'm dreaming, dead, and this is what I want to see and hear. Still, I turn around, pulling my legs to my chest, blinking several times, and realize that yes, I must be dead. I finally went through with it.

But no matter how many times I blink, Nova continues to walk across the roof toward me, taking cautious steps, like she's afraid of me. My eyes are locked on hers, and all I want to do is reach out and touch her, but I can't. She's untouchable. Unreal. Not really here.

"Nova, be careful. The roof feels like it's going to collapse." Tristan walks out from the doorway, and he doesn't look real either. He looks healthy and stronger than the last time I saw him. He looks better.

"It's fine," Nova insists, her eyes still fixed on mine. She puts her hand out as she stops just short of me, and I'm not sure what she wants me to do. Take her hand? "We're here to help you," she says, reaching out to me. I catch her assessing my body, and she swallows hard and her fingers start to shake. I figure she's afraid of me, but when she looks at me, her eyes are full of warmth, just like I remember them. "Quinton, come with me...We're going to get you help."

And then, as if things weren't bad enough, I see someone I haven't seen in a very long time step out onto the roof. A man who has the same brown eyes and hair as me, but who's older and less burdened with death.

My dad looks really out of place up here, glancing around at the large signs around the rooftop, and then his eyes widen when they land on me. "Son," he says in an unsteady voice. "We're to help you."

That snaps me out of my trance and wakes me right back up. "Shut up! All of you! You can't help me." I get down off the ledge, hurrying toward the other side of the roof, putting distance back between us. But even when I get as far as I can, it's still not far enough, Nova's heat and words and kindness smothering me from all the way over here.

Her arm falls to the side as her gaze sweeps around the roof. Then she turns to Tristan, and he looks at her with his brows furrowed. Nova whispers something to him and my dad says something to him as well. Then Tristan warily nods before he cautiously steps up beside Nova and they both start inching toward me. Together. I hate that they're together.

"What the hell's going on?" I ask, backing toward the edge, wishing they'd stop taking away my space. "Why the hell are you all here?"

Nova stops before Tristan does. My dad barely takes a few steps, and then stops beside a smaller sign, looking like he's struggling to breathe at the sight of me. They've all stopped moving toward me, though, and I start to breathe freely again, but then Tristan starts walking toward me again, step by step, inch by inch. It's driving me crazy, him being here, healthy, looking at me like he wants to fucking help me, too, when he was in my place once.

"Why the hell are you here?" I shout again with my hands balled at my sides. I don't know what to do. Knock him down. Knock Nova down. Knock them all down and flee to the door or just back away and jump off the roof.

Tristan flinches at the loudness of my voice but keeps on walking until he stops right in front of me. "I came here to tell you something." His voice shakes like he's nervous, which I don't understand. He's never nervous around me. I'm the one who is because of what I did to him—what I took from him. He raises his hand in front of him, and for a second I think he's going to shove me off the roof. But instead he rubs his arm across his forehead and wipes some sweat from his brow. "I came here to say thank you for saving my life that day. For not letting me OD on the side of the road. For giving me CPR and calling the ambulance. For trying to help me with that whole Trace mess, when I caused it in the first place."

His words are like a strike to the chest, hot, painful, sharp, like my scar is torn open and I don't have anything to numb the pain. "I didn't fucking do anything...and you were only there because of me! Because I killed your sister!"

"That's not why I was there, man," he says, taking a cautious step toward me. "Nothing about my life is your fault, just like Ryder's death isn't your fault. Or Lexi's."

I stumble back. "Stop saying that, you fucking asshole."

"Why? It's true," he says. "What happened...the accident...It was just that—an accident."

"Yes, it was." My voice is sharp. I know he doesn't mean it.

He can't. It's impossible. No one can ever forgive me. "It was my fault and you know it, just like your parents know it."

"My parents are messed up and need to blame someone," he says, stepping toward me, his voice and steps growing steadier. "But the truth is, if they really looked at it, they know that accidents happen. That you were all just in the wrong place at the wrong time."

"Stop saying that . . . It is my fault. Everything is my fault!" I step back and my foot clips the edge of the roof. My weak legs wobble a little and Nova must think I'm going to fall because she starts to rush toward me, but Tristan sticks out his arm, stopping her.

"No, it wasn't. None of this was your fault. Not Ryder. Not what happened to me. If it wasn't for you, I'd be dead," he says, and this time his voice is firm, full of meaning, full of the truth.

And then my dad steps up. His voice is not so firm, but he says something I've been wanting to hear from him for a very long time. "Come home, son," he says, moving away from the signs and getting closer to me. "I want to get you help—want to get my son back."

"You never had one!" I shout. "You've never liked me from the day I was born!"

He looks stunned. "What are you talking about? Of course I do."

"No, you don't," I say, but my voice is starting to fade, my willpower fading along with it. "You blame me for Mom's death, just like you blame me for Lexi's and Ryder's."

His skin goes white, and he starts to walk quickly toward me. "That's not true. Quinton, I—"

I stick out my hand, standing as close to the edge as I can. "Don't come any closer or I swear to fucking God, I'll jump."

As soon as I say it, Nova starts to cry. No, not just cry, but sob hysterically. At first I can't figure out what I've done, but then through my stupid strung-out brain, I remember. Her story. Her pain. And the fact that I'm about to make her relive it.

"Please just stop this," she says, wiping the tears from her eyes even though more spill out. She continues to cry, and Tristan looks like he's considering comforting her but is a little unsure. Finally, she stops trying to wipe the tears away and lets them pour out as her hands fall to her sides. "If you love me at all, then you'll get off the damn edge of that roof!" she shouts, her sudden spurt of anger alarming me. "Because I can't take this anymore..." Her shoulders heave as she cries. "I swear to God, if I lose one more person I love, it's going to kill me." More sobs. More tears. "Please, just get down off the roof and get help."

Her words and tears slam me in the chest hard. I'm not sure what it is, Tristan's words, my dad's, Nova's tears, anger, begging, or the fact that she said "love," that make me step away from the edge. Perhaps it's a combination of all those things. Or perhaps I'm just so fucking tired and strung out that I can't find the energy to do anything else. As soon as I take a step forward, my legs give out, buckle. I collapse to my knees, not knowing what to do, what to say, what to think or feel. How to react to all of this. Part of me thinks this isn't real. That I'm dead. Or drugged out. That none of this is happening.

I wrap my arms around my head, trying to curl up in a ball and disappear. I can't breathe. Can't think. I can only feel. Everything. It's too much. I'm drowning in emotion. Regret. Sorrow. Guilt. Pain. Anger. Fear. I'm so afraid. Of what lies ahead for me. The unseen future I just chose by stepping away from the edge.

No matter how much I fight it, I start to cry, soundless tears, my entire body trembling. I'm not even sure where the hell they're coming from. Years and years of piling up maybe and finally they've burst out.

Seconds later I feel arms wrap around me. As soon as the scent and warmth of her reaches me, I know that it's Nova. My initial reaction is to jerk away, but I'm too tired, so I lean in to her and cry and she holds me as I collapse.

Nova

I've been holding on to him like nothing else in the world matters, refusing to let him go, even when we leave the roof and get into my car. I hold him in the backseat, stroking his back as he keeps his face buried in the crook of my neck, his hands grasping my shirt, while my mom drives us to the hotel. He's stopped crying by the time we get there, and I can tell he's about to pass out from exhaustion. Tristan tells me he's crashing and that he'll probably fall asleep until we head to the airport later tonight, which might make it a little bit easier for his dad to get him on a plane and to the rehab center in Seattle. If not, then Tristan says it's going to be a pain in the ass and that we might have to give him something to keep him sedated; otherwise he might flip out.

It's a lot to take in as we make our way up to the hotel room. Tristan and his dad help Quinton make it there by each taking one of Quinton's arms and draping it over his shoulders so they're walking on either side of him. I'm not sure how long it's been since he's eaten or drunk anything, but he's in pretty bad shape, dehydrated, dry skin and lips. Sores on his body.

After my mom gets the room unlocked, they get him in, and I lie down on the bed with him, front to front. I think he's out of it, but then he scoots closer to me and entangles his legs with mine. Then he presses his head against my chest, breathing in and out as I wrap my arms around his head.

"I'm going to go get the bags," Mom says, gathering the key and her purse. "Do you want to run down to the food place I saw downstairs and get some food and water?" she asks Quinton's dad, who seems a little awkward with the parenting thing, unlike my mother. She nods at Quinton. "He looks like he needs some food and water."

Quinton's dad nods and heads for the door. "But are they going to be okay up here by themselves?"

My mom glances at me. "Are you guys going to be okay for a minute?"

I nod; then she hesitantly leaves the room and Quinton's

dad follows her. She looks more worried than I've ever seen her. I don't blame her. Quinton looks really bad. Like he's reached the point where he should be dead. He's filthy, he's lost a ton of weight, he has no shoes or shirt on, and his eyes are sunken in. But the good thing is he's here and still breathing and we're going to get him help.

"I'm going out to smoke," Tristan tells me, heading toward the sliding glass doors that go out to the balcony. He looks worn-out, and I don't think he slept on the way down to Vegas. Plus, I'm sure what happened back on the roof had to be hard for him. To see Quinton like that. Be in this environment. Feel the emotion in the moment. I know it was hard for me. Painful. Raw.

"Are you okay?" I ask him, resting my chin on top of Quinton's head and pulling him closer.

He nods, taking a cigarette from the pack, and opens the sliding glass door. "Yeah, it's just a little intense being back here...too many memories..." He pops the cigarette into his mouth as he starts to step outside. "I'm just glad we're going back tomorrow." He pauses, retrieving a lighter from his pocket. "And that we got him this far."

I draw a line up and down Quinton's bare back. "The marks on his arms...What does that mean? I mean, I know what it means, but...how much harder does that make it for him to quit?"

He gives me a sad look as he lights the cigarette. "Honestly?" he asks, and I nod. "He has a fucking hell of a struggle in front of him, especially coming down. Maybe even one of the hardest things he's had to do . . . He's going to feel like he's losing his mind. Plus, his body is going to freak out from withdrawals. But it's not impossible to overcome." He gestures at himself and then starts to shut the door as smoke enters the room.

"Tristan," I call out.

He pauses with the door cracked. "Yeah."

"Thank you." I say it softly.

"For what?"

"For coming down here and helping him," I say. "I'm sure it wasn't the easiest thing for you."

He stares at me quizzically, holding his cigarette between his fingers, and then his expression relaxes. "Thanks." He shuts the door all the way and goes up to the railing to smoke and look out at the casinos glowing around us.

I lie with Quinton on the bed, afraid to move, to breathe, to do anything that will break apart this moment. I just want to hold on to it—hold on to him and never let him go. I want to know that he'll be okay. And I want to cry, because he's here, because Landon's not here. Because this time I did something instead of standing by. No matter how hard I fight them, though, the tears escape. I try to keep quiet, but eventually it becomes too much and I start to sob. I'm not sure if he's awake or he's just moving around in his sleep, but his hold on me tightens.

I let the tears flow, feeling the slightest bit freer, feeling like I can breathe again.

Epilogue

August 21, day ninety-eight of summer break

Quinton

I feel like I'm dying. Like I'm being buried alive under the dirt, yet for some damn reason my heart's beating and my lungs are breathing. My dad keeps saying shit to me about going to get help, but I'm not so sure that's possible. It felt like maybe it was when Nova held me in her arms, but now everything feels so impossible. I feel so empty. My body is too drained of smack and I can feel everything, from the sting of the sun to the pinpricks of the wind. And it all hurts, like my body is slowly being torn apart and I'm on the verge of throwing up, shivering even though I feel like I'm burning.

"We're going to get you better, son," my dad says as he drives us down a road bordered by trees. I know I'm in Seattle. That I flew here with him, but the last twenty-four hours are all blurry and I barely remember anything, even saying good-bye to Nova. I think they might have given me something to keep me sedated, but it's wearing off now and I just want to go back to my smack. I want to taste it again. Feel something other than what I'm feeling now. This gnawing ache deep inside my chest, below my scar.

After what seems like hours, my dad finally stops the car in front of a building with few windows and only one door. There are trees enclosing the small fenced yard and a blue sky above.

"Where are we?" I ask groggily as I raise my head from the window, and vomit burns in the back of my throat.

He turns off the engine, takes the keys out, and gets out of the car without saying anything. Then he winds around the front of the car and opens my door. Just in time, too. I hurry and lean forward, barfing all over the ground. My stomach aches with each heave and it feels like it's never going to end. Eventually it does, but I don't feel better at all.

"Get out of the car, son," my dad says, holding the door open for me. "We're going to get you help."

"How?" I nearly growl, wiping my chin with my hand. I don't understand anything other than the fact that it feels like my veins are on fire and I'm melting into something else. "What's going on?"

He doesn't answer me, stepping back and motioning at me to get out. "Just get out of the car."

I figure he's dumping me, so I climb out, stumbling a little as the cold air hits me. I've been so used to the sweltering heat, but now I just feel cold all the time.

"Where are we?" I ask, wrapping my arms around myself. I have a jacket on, but it's still so cold.

He looks at me with pity as he shuts the door. "I already told you, we're getting you help."

I don't know why he keeps saying this, but then I look over at the sign on the building and I understand. "I'm not going to rehab," I say, reaching back for the door handle. "Now, take me out of here."

He shakes his head and puts his hand on the door. "No, I won't."

"Why the fuck not?" I ask, jerking the door open, my body starting to shiver uncontrollably.

He pushes on it and slams it shut. "Because I'm not going to let you ruin your life anymore."

I almost laugh at him. "Anymore? Why the change of heart? After all these years?"

"Because it's what your mother would have wanted," he says in an unsteady voice, but it looks like he's holding back, not telling me the entire reason. "And I should have realized that a long time ago."

He's barely spoken about my mom in the twenty-one years I've known him and now all of a sudden he is. More emotion piles over me and I'm not high so I feel it. It's been a very long time since I've been this sober, and I feel so lost and disoriented. Sick to my stomach. Overwhelmed. Maybe it's because of this that I go inside. Or maybe it's the simple fact that when I look down the road that will take me out of here, it looks so far and I feel so goddamned tired and beaten down. But I walk into that building with zero expectations, because I can't even think that far ahead yet. I'm moving forward by a half step at a time and sometimes it feels like I'm moving backward. But I manage to get checked in. They take everything of mine away, which is pretty much nothing. Then they give me something that will supposedly help me deal with the withdrawal, but I know it won't help because it's not a shot of heroin and that's the only thing that would make this whole process less painful.

I go into a small room with a bed and a dresser, and then sink down on the bed, feeling too much of this moment. It's excruciating, the fire in my veins burning hotter and hotter. I feel like ripping my skin off, banging my head on the wall, anything to get the fire—the emotion—out of me. I start desperately begging, to the door, to the ceiling, hoping someone will hear me and help me, but all I have are the four walls surrounding me. No one is going to help me out of this. No one is going to hurt me like I want to hurt myself.

So all I can do is take the next breath and then another.

Quinton Carter aches for Nova Reed, the girl who helped him see the world with clear eyes. After shocking news, Nova will need Quinton like he once needed her. Can he take the final leap out of his broken past... and into her heart?

See the next page for a preview of

Nova and Quinton:

No Regrets

Chapter One

Two months ago...

October 30, day one in the real world

Quinton

I write until my hand hurts. Until my head is numb. It's the only outlet I have at the moment. My attempt at a replacement for the drugs I've done for years. But most days it can't fill even a small part of the void I feel inside me since I stopped pumping my body with poison, slowly killing myself. But there are a few times when it briefly instills a small amount of silence inside me, makes taking one breath, one step, one heartbeat, just a bit more bearable. And so I write, just to feel those few and far-between moments of peace.

Sometimes I feel like I've been reborn. Not in a religious way. But in the sense that it feels like part of me has died and I'm learning once again to live with the new, remaining parts of me. Some of which I don't like, parts that are ugly, broken, misshapen, and don't seem to quite fit right inside me. But my therapist and drug counselor are both trying to build me back up to a person that the pieces can fit into again.

I still don't know if it's possible. If I can live with a clear head, feel the sting of every emotion, the weight of my guilt, the heaviness of each breath, the way my heart beats steadily inside my chest. I'm trying, though, and I guess that's a start. I just hope the start can turn into more, but I'm not so sure yet.

"Quinton, are you ready?" Davis Mason, the supervisor of the Bellevue Rehab Facility, enters my room, rapping on the doorframe.

I glance up from my notebook and nod, release a nervous breath trapped inside my chest. Today is the day that I'm going back into the real world, to live with my dad, no walls around me, no restrictions. It scares the shit out of me, to be out there, free to do whatever I want, without anyone watching me, guiding me. I'll be making decisions myself, and I'm not sure if I'm ready for that.

"As ready as I'll ever be, I guess," I say, shutting my notebook and tossing it into my packed bag on the floor beside my feet. I aim to appear collected on the outside, but on the inside my heart is hammering about a million miles a minute, along with my thoughts. *I can't believe this is happening. I can't believe*

I'm going out into the real world. Shit, I don't think I can do this. I can't. I want to stay here.

"You're going to do awesome," Davis assures me. "And you know if you need anyone to talk to, I'm totally here, and we've got you set up with that sobriety support group and your dad got you a really good therapist to replace Charles."

When I first met Davis, I thought he was a patient at the drug facility, with his laid-back attitude and the casual plaid shirts and jeans he always wears, but it turned out he was the counselor that I'd be spending two months with during my recovery here. He's a pretty cool and oddly enough was once an addict, too, so he gets some of my struggles. Not all of them, though.

I get to my feet and pick up my bag. "I hope you're right."

"I'm always right about these things," he jokes, giving me an encouraging pat on the back as I head past him and out the door. "I can always tell the ones who are going to make it." He places two fingers to his temple. "I have a sixth sense for it."

I don't understand his optimism. I'd think he was this way with everyone, but he's not. I overheard him once talking to one of the nurses, saying he was worried about one of the guys leaving. But he seems sure I'm going to be okay and keeps telling everyone that. I'm not, though. I'm going to fall. I know it. Can feel it. See it. I'm terrified. I have no idea what's going to happen to me. In the next minute. The next step. The next moment. I'm feeling so many things it's hard to even think straight.

I swing the handle of my duffel bag over my shoulder and walk down the hall with Davis following behind. I say good-bye to a few people I met while I was here and actually developed friendships with. There's not a whole lot—it's hard to make friends when you have to focus so much on yourself.

After the brief farewells, I head to Charles's office, which is right beside the front section of the facility. Every time I'm in this part of the building, I get a peek at the outside world, the cars on the highway, the pine trees, the grass, the sky, the clouds. It always makes me want to lock the door and stay behind it for the rest of my life, because behind that door I feel safe. Protected from myself and all the scary things out there. Like the last two months. And now I'm about to go into the wild.

"Quinton, come on in." Charles waves me in when he notices me lingering in the doorway, staring at the exit door just to my right.

I tear my attention away from it and step into his office, a narrow room with a couple of wooden chairs, a desk, and scenic paintings on the walls. It's plain, with minimal distractions, which might be on purpose to force whoever is in here to focus on nothing but himself. I've had a few meltdowns in this room, a lot of them stemming from when Charles urged me to pour my heart and soul out about the accident and express how I felt about the deaths of Lexi and Ryder. I haven't talked about everything yet, but I'm sure I'll get there. One day. But for now I'm taking things one step at a time. Day by day.

"So today's the big day," he says, standing up from the chair behind his desk. He's a short man with a bad comb-over and he wears a lot of suits with elbow patches. But he's nice and gets things in a way most people don't. I'm not sure if it's because of his PhD hanging on the wall or because maybe he's been through some rough shit. If he has, he never shared it with me. "This is about you," he always said whenever I tried to turn the conversation around on him. "And what you've been through." I hated him for it. Still do a little bit, because he opened a lot of fucking doors I thought I'd bolted shut. Stuff poured out of me and is still continuing to stream out of me, like a leaky faucet, one I can't get to turn off, but now I'm not sure I want to.

"Yeah, I guess so." I move to the center of the room and stand behind one of the chairs, gripping the back to hold myself up because my legs feel like two wet noodles.

He offers me a smile. "I know you're a little worried about how things are going to be out there, but I assure you that as long as you stick to everything we talked about, you're going to be okay. Just keep going to meetings and keep writing." He strolls around the desk and stops in front of me. "And keep working on talking to your father."

"I'll try to," I say with apprehension. "But it's a two-way street, so…" My father has visited a few times, and Charles mediated for us. "Rocky" would be one of the words to describe the time we spent talking. That and "awkward" and "uneasy". But it helped break the ice enough that it's not completely and utterly terrible to know that I'm going to be living under the same roof with him again. Just terrible, maybe.

Charles puts a hand on my shoulder and looks me straight in the eye. "Don't try. Do." He always says this whenever someone shows doubt. *Do. Do. Do.*

"Okay, I'll talk to him," I say, but just because I will doesn't mean my father is going to reciprocate. I barely know him anymore. No, scratch *anymore*. I've never known him, really, and it feels like I'm moving in with a stranger. *But I can get through this. I am strong.* I tell myself this over and over again.

"Good." Charles gives my shoulder a squeeze and then releases me. "And remember, I'm always here if you need someone to talk to." He takes a step back toward his desk. "You have my card with my number, right?"

I pat my pocket. "Yeah."

"Good. Call me if you ever need anything from me." He smiles. "And take care, Quinton."

"Thanks. You too." I turn for the door, my chest squeezing tighter with every step I take. By the time I exit into the hallway, I'm on the verge of hyperventilating. But I keep moving. Breathing. Walking. Until I get into the lounge area near the doorway, where my father's waiting for me in one of the chairs in a corner of the room. He has his head tipped down and his glasses on as he reads the newspaper that's on his lap. He's wearing slacks and a nice shirt, probably the same clothes he wears to the office every day. He must have had to leave early to pick me up, and I wonder how he feels about that, whether he's irritated like he always used to be with me or glad that I'm finally getting out. I guess that could be something we talk about in the car.

I don't say anything as I cross the room toward him. Sensing my presence, he glances up right as I stop in front of him.

He blinks a few times like I've surprised him with my appearance. "Oh, I didn't even see you walk out," he says, setting the newspaper aside on the table beside the chair. He glances at the clock on the wall as he rises to his feet. "Are you ready to go?"

I nod with my thumb hitched though the handle of my duffel bag. "Yeah, I think so."

"Okay then." He pats the sides of his legs awkwardly, glancing around the room like he thinks someone's going to come out and take me off his hands. Realizing that nothing is going to happen, that it's just him and me, he gives me a small smile, but it's forced. Then he heads for the door and I reluctantly follow. Ten steps later, I'm free. Just like that. It feels like it happens so fast. Faster than I can handle. One minute I'm saying good-bye and the next I'm walking out the door into the outside world and fresh air. There are no more walls to protect me, no people around me who get what I'm going through.

I just exist.

The first thing I notice is how bright it is. Not hot, but bright. The grass has also browned, along with the leaves on the trees. It's managed to turn from summer to fall during my two-month stay here and somehow I didn't even notice.

I've been outside and everything, but not outside with freedom. It makes things feel different. Me feel different. Nervous. Unsteady. Like I'm about to fall down.

"Quinton, are you okay?" my father asks, assessing me as he removes his glasses, like that'll help him see what's going on inside my head or something. "You look like you're going to be sick."

"I'm fine." I squint at the general brightness of being outdoors. "It just feels a little weird being outside."

He offers me another tight smile, then looks away and starts toward the parking lot at the side of the building. I trail behind him, grasping the handle of my bag slung over my shoulder, the wind grazing my cheeks, and I note how unnatural it feels. Just like the cars driving up and down the highway that seem way too loud. Everything seems extremely intense, even the fresh air that fills my lungs.

Finally, after what feels like an eternity, I make it to the car and get my seat belt secured over my shoulder. It grows quiet as my father turns on the ignition and the engine rumbles to life. Then we're driving up the gravel path toward the highway, leaving the rehab center behind in the distance, the place that for the last couple of months protected me from the world and the pain linked to it.

I stay quiet for most of the drive home, and my dad seems pretty at ease with that at first, but then abruptly he starts slamming me with simple questions like if the heat is up enough or too much, and am I hungry, because he can stop and get me something to eat if I need him to.

I shake my head, picking at a hole in the knee of my jeans. "Dad, I promise I'm okay. You don't need to keep checking on me."

"Yeah, but..." He struggles for what to say as he grips the steering wheel, his knuckles whitening. "But you always said you were okay in the past, but then after talking to you with Charles...it just seems like you needed to talk to me but you didn't."

He's probably thinking about how I told him, during one of our sessions, that I felt sort of responsible for my mother's death because he never seemed to want to have anything to do with me. He was shocked by my revelation, and I was equally shocked that he didn't seem to have realized that's how I felt— at how differently we saw things.

"But I promise I'm okay right now." I ball my hands more tightly into fists the closer we get to the house. Deep breaths. Deep breaths. *I can do this. The scary part is over, right? I'm sober now.* "I just ate before we left and I'm warm, not hot or cold. Everything's good. I'm good." Which I am, for the most part.

He nods, satisfied, as he concentrates on the road. "Well, let me know if you need anything."

"Okay, I will." I direct my attention to the side window and watch the landscape blur by, gradually changing from trees to a field, then ultimately to houses as we pass through the outskirts of the city. Before I know it, we're entering my old neighborhood, made up of cul-de-sacs and modest homes. It's where everything started, where everything changed, where I grew up and where I decided I was going to slowly kill myself with drugs. Each house I've passed a thousand times on foot, on bike, in the car, yet the surroundings feel so foreign to me and I feel so off-balance. The feeling only intensifies when we pass one of the houses I used to buy drugs from. I start wondering if they still deal or if that's changed. What if they do? What if I have drugs right on hand? Right there? Just blocks away from where I'm living? Can I handle it? I'm not sure. I'm not sure of anything at the moment, because I can't see five minutes into the future.

My adrenaline starts pumping relentlessly, and no matter how hard I try to get my heart to settle down, I can't. It only beats faster when we pull into the driveway of my two-story home with blue shutters and white siding. I've been in this house more times than anywhere else in the world, yet it feels like I've never been here before. I'm not even sure that it ever really was my home, though, more simply a roof over my head. I'm not sure about anything anymore. Where I belong. What I should feel. Who I am.

Reborn.

But what am I going to be reborn into?

"Welcome home," my dad says, again with a taut smile. He parks the car in front of the shut garage and silences the engine.

"Thanks." I return his forced smile, hoping we're not

going to pretend that everything is okay to each other all the time because it's going to drive me crazy.

He takes the keys out of the ignition while I get my bag out of the backseat; then we get out of the car and walk up the path to the front door, where he unlocks it and we step into the foyer. It hits me like a bag of bricks, slamming against my chest and knocking the wind out of me. This is bad. So bad. I needed more preparation for this. The memories, swirling in torturous circles inside my head. The good ones. The bad ones. The ones connected to my childhood. Lexi. It's too much, and I want to run out the door and track down one of my old pothead friends, see if they're still into drugs and if I can get something—anything—to take away the emotions swirling around inside me.

Need.

Want.

Need.

Now.

I suck in a sharp breath and then turn for the stairs, telling myself to be stronger than this. "I'm going to go unpack," I say as I head up the stairs.

"Okay." My dad drops the keys down on the table by the front door, below a picture hanging on the wall of my mother and him on their wedding day. He looks happy in it, an emotion I've rarely seen from him. "Do you want anything in particular for dinner?"

"Anything sounds good." I remember how many days I

could go without eating dinner when I was fueling my body with crystal and smack. Getting healthy was actually part of my recovery over the last two months. Exercising. Eating. Thinking healthy. I actually chose to get some tests done just to see how bad my health was, if I'd done any permanent damage to my body with the use of needles. Like HIV or hepatitis. Everything came up negative and I guess I'm grateful for it now, but at the time I felt upset because disease seemed like the easy ticket out of the hellhole coming off of heroin and meth created. I'd hoped that maybe I'd have something deadly and it'd kill me. Then I wouldn't have to face the world and my future. My guilt. The decision between going back to a world full of drugs and living.

When I reach the top of the stairs, I veer down the hallway, walking to the end of it to my room. I enter gradually, knowing that when I get in there a lot of stuff I've been running from is going to emerge. I thought about asking my dad to clean everything out for me: the photos, my drawings, anything related to the past. But my therapist said it might be good for me to do it because it could be the start of giving myself closure. I hope he's right. I hope he's right about a lot of things, otherwise I'm going to break apart.

I hold on to the doorknob for probably about ten minutes before I get the courage to turn it and open the door. As I enter and step over the threshold, I want to run away. I'd forgotten how many pictures I had of Lexi on the walls. Not just ones I drew. Actual photos of her laughing, smiling, hugging me.

The ones I'm in with her, I look so happy, so different, so free. So unfamiliar. Less scarred. I don't even know who that person is anymore or if I'll ever be him again.

There's also a few pictures of my mother, ones my grandmother gave me before she passed away. Some of them were taken when my dad and mom first married, and I even have one from when she was pregnant with me, her last few months alive before she'd pass away bringing me into this world. The only pictures of her and me together. She looks a lot like me: brown hair and the same brown eyes. I was told a lot by my grandmother that we shared the same smile, but I haven't smiled for real in ages, so I'm not sure if it still looks like hers.

I manage to get a smile on my mouth as I look at a photo of her giving an exaggerated grin to the camera. It makes me feel kind of happy, which makes me sad that I'm supposed to take them down. It's what I've been taught over the last few months: let go of the past. But I need just a few more minutes with them.

After I take each one in, breathing through the immense amount of emotional pain crushing me, I drop my bag onto the floor and wander over to a stack of sketches on my dresser. I lost my most recent drawings when the apartment burned down, and this is pretty much all that's left. I'm not sure if that's good or bad. One thing's for sure, I'm glad I don't have any of my self-portraits. In fact, I hope I never have to see myself look the way I did two months ago. I remember when I first looked in the mirror right after I got to rehab. Skeletal. The walking dead. That's what I looked like.

There's a mirror on the wall to the side of me and I step up to it. I look so different now, my skin has more color to it; my brown eyes aren't bloodshot or dazed. My cheeks are filled out instead of sunken in, my arms are lean, and my whole body is more in shape. My brown hair is cropped short and my face is shaven. I look alive instead of like a ghost. I look like someone I used to know and am afraid to be again. I look like Quinton.

I swallow hard and turn away from my reflection and back toward my sketches. I fan through a few of the top ones, which turn out to be of Lexi. I remember how much I used to draw her, even after she died. But during the last few months of tumbling toward rock bottom, I started drawing someone else. A person I haven't seen in two months or talked to. Nova Reed. I haven't talked to her since I got on a plane to go to rehab. I wrote her a few times, but then never sent the letters, too afraid to tell her everything I have to say, too terrified to express emotions I'm pretty sure I'm not ready to deal with just yet. She tried to call me a few times at the facility, but I couldn't bring myself to talk to her. A month ago she wrote me a letter and it's in the back of my notebook, waiting to be opened. I'm not sure I'll ever be able to do it. Face her. Be forced to let her go if that's what she wants. I wouldn't blame her if she did. After everything that I put her through—having to visit me in that shithole I called home, my mood swings, the drug dealers threatening her.

Blowing out a heavy sigh, I get my notebook and a pencil out of my bag, then flop down on the bed. I open the notebook up to a clean sheet of paper and decide which I want to do more—write or draw. They're both therapeutic, although I'm way better at drawing. After some debating, I put the pencil to the paper and start drawing. I know where it's headed the moment I form the first line. I lost all my drawings of Nova when the apartment burned down. Not a single one remains. It's like the memory of her is gone. But I don't want it to be gone—I don't want *her* to be gone. I want to remember her. How good she was to me. How she made me feel alive, even when I fought it. How I'm pretty sure I love her, but I'm still trying to figure that out for sure, just like I'm trying to figure out everything else, like where I belong in this world and if I belong in this world. Everyone keeps telling me yes—that I belong here. That what happened in the accident wasn't my fault. That yes, I was driving too fast, but the other car was, too, and took the turn too wide. And that Lexi shouldn't have been hanging out the window. And I want to believe that's true, that perhaps it wasn't my fault entirely. That's the difference between now and a couple of months ago, but it's hard to let go of something I've been clutching for the last two years— my guilt. I need to find a reason to let it go and to make life worth living in such a way that I don't have to dope my body up just to make it through the day.

I need something to live for, but at the moment I'm not sure what the hell that is or if it even exists.

About the Author

The *New York Times* and *USA Today* bestselling author Jessica Sorensen lives with her husband and three kids. When she's not writing, she spends her time reading and hanging out with her family.

Learn more at:

jessicasorensensblog.blogspot.com

@jessFallenStar

Facebook.com